CW00864445

Helter Skelter

Stuart Pereira

Cover design and Artwork by Robin Pereira
blueqube.org.uk

i

ISBN-10: 1508900469
ISBN-13: 978-1508900467

DEDICATION

This book is dedicated to the remarkable men I was privileged to serve alongside so many years ago. They know who they are. Each of them far more capable than I at doing an extraordinary job under challenging conditions. I am honoured to have been a tiny cog in such a wheel.

This story is a work of fiction. Any similarity between any of the characters and any persons living or dead is purely coincidental

Many of the locations described within are real, the actions as described within or around them are, however the product of a fertile imagination.

CONTENTS

ACKNOWLEDGMENTS

My thanks to:
Alison Taft for reviewing my manuscript and for her
professional guidance.

David Newton for having the patience to read the
manuscript and giving me useful feedback.

Cate Anderson, Howard Benn, Di Spence, Myrna Moore
and other members of my creative writing groups for their
invaluable feedback.

Special thanks to John Kerbotson and Mick Brennan for
allowing me to tap into their memories.

Robin Pereira for his professional skills and advice.

GLOSSARY

CO	Commanding officer	
Brigadier	General; CO of a Brigade	5000 men
Colonel	CO of a Regiment.	700 men
OC	Officer commanding	
Major	OC of a Squadron.	C.100 men
2 IC	Second in Command	
SAS	Special Air Service Regiment	
Comms	Radio Communication	
Basha	Shelter made from ground sheet	
RV	Rendezvous, A rallying point, meeting place.	
ERV	Emergency RV – used if patrol separated	
SA80	Assault Rifle (standard British issue)	
M16	US Assault Rifle used by British Special Forces	
Colt Commando	US Assault Rifle used by British Special Forces	
AK47	Russian Assault Rifle	
GPMG /Jimpy	General Purpose Machine Gun. Belt fed	
50 Cal	Heavy Machine Gun. Belt fed	
LUP	Lying up position. Patrol hide during daylight	
SOP	Standard operating procedure	
OP	Observation post.	
Cuds	The countryside	
Rupert	An officer (Derogatory)	
Combats	Camouflage trousers	
TAB	Walk (Tactical Advance to Battle)	
DZ	Drop zone (for parachuting)	
LZ	Landing zone (Helicopter)	
Rubber Dick	False information, rumour, a con	
Head Shed	Headquarters	
Stag	Period on watch	
LURRP	Long Range Reconnaissance Patrols	
CQB	Close Quarter Battle (Unarmed combat)	
TQ	Interrogation (Tactical Questioning)	
RTI	Resistance to Interrogation (training course)	
RSM	Regimental Sergeant Major (God)	
Nine Milli	Pistol and or 9 millimetre ammunition	

1

Tuesday 16th June 1998
Hereford, England

Skelter awoke in a pool of sweat gasping for breath. The same dream as, the darkness – his face buried in the pillow; suffocating, a great weight on his back; screams stifled; his arms pinioned. Then came the pain, sharp stabbing pain so real it forced his eyes open, his heart racing like an express train. Always the same but he could make no sense of it. The psychiatrist believed that it probably resulted from his experiences on operations but Skelter could make no connection. He was convinced the dream had nothing to do with the job. It was something else. Something he couldn't put his finger on.

Rising quickly he went downstairs to the kitchen switched on the kettle and devoured a bowl of muesli almost before the water had boiled. He swallowed a pill made a mug of tea and took it upstairs to the bathroom. There he slowly began to relax under the shower, spending more time than usual taking particular care shaving and grooming. He had not been on a date for eighteen years. Lucy was the first woman he had looked at even half way serious since Jane's death.

The tea was cold by the time he remembered but he

drank it anyway. The difficult bit was choosing what to wear. Skelter was well out of his comfort zone getting ready for lunch with a woman ten years his junior, who he had met only three days ago. He would rather face a band of armed terrorists. Taking the middle route he decided on grey needle-cord Levis and a lemon linen shirt. She had seen him in T-shirt and jeans at Diane's Barbecue.

Just before he left the house Skelter went into the front room, walked over to the bookcase and touched the spine of an old volume of Arthur Mee's Children's Encyclopedia, for luck. The ten well thumbed volumes were the only link he had to his grandfather. The well of information, which inspired his thirst for learning. Ever since he could read he had been sucking up information from their pages like a hungry tench scavenging the bottom of a pond; memorising shapes and colours of exotic insects, sea shells and flags of the world. One volume, the one whose spine he had touched so reverently, was worn more than the rest. Volume seven; the one with the double page spread of dragonflies in full colour.

Lucy Ryder walked into the beer garden wearing a sleeveless navy blue dress nipped at the waist by a matching narrow belt. The wedge heeled mules made the most of her legs. Over her shoulder hung a handbag not much bigger than Skelter's wallet.

'You came,' he said. 'I wasn't sure…'

'Why wouldn't I? It was lovely of you to ask me, Mark.'

Hearing his name took him by surprise. No one had called him that since Jane. He was 'H' to the lads. He was surprised to find he liked it.

'What can I get you to drink?' he said.

'A glass of dry cider would be lovely thank you,' she said. 'I like the shirt, the colour suits you.'

'Oh God I'm sorry. I was supposed to say that

2

wasn't I? Out of practice you see...'

'Relax, Mark, I'm not going to bite you.'

'Sorry, and you do... look nice I mean, er, lovely, really.'

'Thank you,' she said with a broad smile.

'I'll get the drinks.' Skelter headed inside to the bar to regroup. 'Pint of Guinness and half of dry cider please, Eddie, and give me a large Grouse. I'll have the Grouse first.'

'You'll be wanting the cider in a lady's glass,' Eddie said, handing him the Scotch.

'Please,' he replied, necking the Scotch in one.

Eddie gave him a knowing look. 'It wasn't a question H.'

Skelter picked up the glasses and headed outside. She was looking across the river towards Hereford cathedral. He noticed for the first time how tiny her waist was. *Be yourself, act natural,* said the voice in his head as he placed the drinks on the table. Handing Lucy a menu he sat down opposite her.

'I love the river,' said Lucy, 'she's so peaceful.'

'She?'

'I like to think of her that way, she's so alive don't you think?'

Skelter gave her a puzzled look.

'Oh don't mind me everyone who knows me thinks I'm mad.'

'And are you?'

'Not really, just a bit off the wall. Too much time alone at my easel.'

'You a painter?'

'Botanical illustrator, but I paint birds and animals too. Whichever pays the bills.'

'Oh, I never met an artist before.'

'We can be a bit odd but we're harmless, honest.'

'So what does the artist fancy to eat then?' said Skelter.

'I'm torn between the chicken and the ham, what about you?'

'I'm going with the steak pie and chips.'

'Okay, then I'll have the ham salad please.'

Skelter got up. 'I'll go and order. Back in a jiffy.' He made his way inside and up to the bar. It was relatively quiet. 'Eddie can I order some food please? I'll have another Scotch too while I'm here.'

This brought a wry smile from the landlord as he took the food order and placed the Scotch in front of Skelter. 'I'll put it on the tab with the food shall I?' said Eddie, watching Skelter drain the glass.

'Please.'

'Maria will fetch your order when it's ready.'

'Cheers,' said Skelter as he turned towards the door and made his way outside. 'So where's home then, Lucy?' Skelter asked, as he resumed his seat at the table.

'A little cottage in Bodenham. What about you, do you live on the camp?'

Skelter felt the hairs on the back of his neck bristle. This was way too early to be discussing his work, not that he would or could even, given the sensitive nature of it.

'Who says I'm in the army?'

Laughing, she tossed her head her auburn hair reflecting the rays of the sun. 'Let me see. Mid forties not an ounce of fat, fit, short back and sides and a pager on your belt. Have I missed anything? Daddy served with The Regiment when I was little. You see, I even know to refer to it as The Regiment and not,' she silently mouthed the letters 'S. A. S.'

'Are you mocking me?'

'Only a teeny bit.'

'When did he serve, your father?' Skelter asked steering the conversation away.

'Seventies, in Oman. He never talks about it except to mention the flies. He hates flies with a vengeance, even now. Besides, Diane told me at the barbecue.'

'How do you know my sister in law?'

'I don't. I bought a ticket like everyone else. My best friend from school had breast cancer.'

'Sorry to hear that.'

'She's free of it now, thank God.'

'So which school was that?'

'Norton Park in Cheltenham.'

'Bit of a trek from Bodenham.'

'I lived in Ross then, in a big old empty house.'

Skelter waved a wasp away from his glass and gave her a quizzical look. 'Still a fair way. An empty house you say?'

'That's what it felt like at the time. Daddy was always away playing soldiers.' She took a sip of cider. 'It was a boarding school.'

'I see,' said Skelter, wondering whether to ask about her mother. He thought better of it. What did she see in a squaddie from a council estate? Posh Tottie's bit of rough? He was *not* going to get his hopes up.

'I think this might be ours,' she said as a young woman with enormous dark eyes approached with two plates and a fistful of cutlery.

'Lovely to see you again, H, it's been a while.'

'You too, Maria, how's your Mum?'

'A lot better now thanks. She'll be back behind the bar in couple of weeks. Enjoy your meal.'

'Thanks.'

'Thank you,' said Lucy with a smile before turning to her companion. 'Tell me, Mark Skelter, how come everyone calls you H?'

'Helter Skelter. That used to be my nickname, got shortened to Helter, Hell, and finally H. My friends are a lazy bunch.'

'Of course, obvious now you've said.'

Later that afternoon as they walked and talked in the warm

sunshine beside the river they discovered a common interest in wildlife and fishing, as well as a shared passion for blues music. Later Skelter shared the taxi with Lucy as far as Saint Martin's church.

'I suppose you're on duty on Friday, Mark?'

'No, I'm off until Monday.'

'Wonderful, will you come to Daddy's with me? It's his birthday and I should be so bored listening to his old cronies spinning the same tall stories I've heard every year since I don't know when. Please say yes.'

Skelter wanted to say yes, even as the voice in his head questioned the speed at which things were moving.

'They have a Clay Pigeon shoot in the afternoon. It'll be fun. I promise.'

'I'm not sure they'll let me sign a shotgun out of the armoury,' said Skelter, his face deadpan.

'Don't worry about that Daddy has a cabinet full.'

Lucy was easy company and despite his misgivings about their different backgrounds Skelter could feel his defences weakening under her velvet onslaught. He had not felt so at ease with a woman for a long time. 'This do on Friday, what's the dress code?'

'Daddy is the high priest of informality. You'll love him, everybody does. He had enough of formality in the officer's mess. These days he spends most of his time in old rags. He's been mistaken for the gardener more than once. It will be fun I promise you. Stay until Sunday, you're not on duty.'

'Are you sure your father…'

'Daddy will be thrilled. Never happier than when he's with soldiers. It's civilians he's not keen on.'

'In that case how could I say no? Thank you.'

'My pleasure,' she said, looking into his eyes. 'I want a chance to get to know you.' Skelter felt his pulse quicken. 'Pick me up around ten o'clock.' She passed him a business card. *Lucy Ryder, Botanical and Wildlife Illustrator. Kestrel Cottage, Bodenham, Hereford.* The taxi pulled up outside the church. 'Thanks for a lovely time, Mark, I really enjoyed myself.'

'Me too,' he said, reaching awkwardly for her hand as he got out. Lucy leaned forward and just managed to kiss his cheek as he stepped back onto the pavement.

Skelter watched the taxi disappear before entering the graveyard. He stood in silence beside one of the graves in the stillness of the Regimental plot, absorbing the atmosphere and savouring the smell of freshly mown grass. He remained for some time, before walking towards the gate where he paused briefly, patted his pockets as if he had forgotten something and turned to check three hundred and sixty degrees. Satisfied he was alone and unobserved, he reached into a crevice in the stone wall and took out a small black plastic dog shit bag, which he replaced with an identical but empty one, from his pocket. He slipped the full bag into the pocket of his Levis and left the churchyard heading for town, as the chattering of an agitated blackbird broke the silence.

2

Friday 19th June
Herefordshire

The black and white half-timbered cottage was straight off the front of a Victorian greetings card, apart that is, from the red Audi parked on the gravel at the side. As he opened the gate Lucy walked through the door and planted a kiss on his cheek catching him off guard. She smelled fresh with the slightest whiff of perfume. 'I'm ready,' she said, holding up a small sports bag.

'Is that it?' said Skelter.

'Don't look so surprised, I travel light. I have more of my things at Daddy's than I do here. He has so much more space.'

Skelter took the bag and put it in the back of the Range Rover. 'Where are we heading?'

'Ross on Wye please.'

The journey was full of easy flowing small talk and passed in the blink of an eye. Lucy directed Skelter along a road hugging the side of a steep wooded valley above the river. 'Turn in here please,' she said, indicating a pair of imposing gate-less stone pillars. Skelter followed the long, sweeping, gravel track through a stand of mature beeches. At the end of the drive stood an impressive nineteen-thirties detached house complete with tennis court.

Must be worth a bomb, Skelter thought, slowing to a crawl to admire the breathtaking views over the river deep below in the gorge. 'Beautiful place, Lucy.'

'Yes, isn't it.'

Skelter gazed out past the stable block towards the Wye taking in the paddocks, gardens and woods. He pulled up at the front and walked around to open the door for Lucy.

'Come and meet Daddy.'

'I'll get my kit.'

'Leave that, Mark, Wilkins will fetch it later and take it up to your room.'

The front door opened as they crunched across the gravel. Framed in the entrance a smiling figure in corduroy slacks and a lovat-green sweater stood feet apart with his hands in his pockets. Not quite the military bearing Skelter had been expecting. Lucy ran forward and threw her arms around the man, stretching on tiptoes to kiss his cheek.

'Daddy, this is Mark.'

'Pleased to meet you, sir,' said Skelter.

'Rollo,' he said, warmly gripping Skelter's outstretched hand. 'We're not on parade. You must be pretty special for my daughter to bring you out here.'

'Daddy!'

'When did you last bring a man to see me? You can't count that wet rag from the tennis club, must be eight or nine years ago. What was his name?'

'You know perfectly well it was Robert, Daddy.'
Rollo grinned.

'Would you care for a drink, Mark? Or should I call you H? I usually have a G and T on the terrace around eleven-thirty.'

'Thank you, sir, I will er…'

'Rollo please, H. You're down at Stirling Lines, I gather. B. Squadron. My spies in the camp tell me H is your preferred tag. I still have friends in The Regiment,' he explained. 'Don't worry – no one tells me anything they shouldn't.' He led the way through an oak-panelled hall into the large square kitchen. 'What's your poison?'

'Beer if you have it,' said Skelter, 'You are well informed.'

Rollo opened the fridge and offered Skelter a Bishop's Finger and a bottle opener. 'Old habits I'm afraid. I used to be part of the contradiction we know as Military Intelligence.' He passed him a glass and walked out onto the terrace. 'Have a seat, young man,' said Rollo, indicating a small glass topped table and a pair of well-worn wicker armchairs.

As Lucy had predicted, her father's relaxed open and friendly manner meant Skelter could not help but like the man. Lucy joined them on the terrace for a ploughman's lunch, after which she showed Skelter to the guest room overlooking the river in the gorge below. 'Daddy's cronies will be here at half three.'

'And they are?'

'Colonel Catastrophe and Major Disaster.'

'And your father, do you have a pet name for him?'

'Brigadier Blunder of course.'

Skelter jerked to attention. 'Your father's a brigadier? I thought he might be a major, or a half-colonel even – but a brigadier.' In his day job Skelter was rarely taken by surprise. Mixing with generals was a long way from the sergeant's mess and a lot further still from the council estate where he grew up. Despite this he felt comfortable, which was completely at odds with his expectations. 'Your mother, Lucy, will she be joining us?'

'Mummy lives abroad. She got fed up of waiting for Daddy to come home from whatever foreign field he was campaigning in. They haven't seen each other in years.' Lucy pushed open the door to the en suite. 'The Shower is through here. I'll leave you to settle in. See you on the terrace. If you could be there by two-thirty we can get you kitted out with a gun and skeet vest. You will join us for the shoot won't you? Daddy hasn't beaten them in the pairs for three years.'

'Pairs?'

'I want you take my place with Daddy.'

'She paints, she's beautiful and she shoots.'

'Not very well though.'

'Don't believe a word, sir, she used to shoot for the county.'

'Wilkins! How long have you been there?' Lucy asked, her cheeks flushed.

Ignoring her question, Wilkins entered the room and placed a tray beside the bed. 'I thought Sergeant Skelter might like a coffee Miss Lucy.'

Making a swift exit Lucy ushered Wilkins through the door before her, before Skelter had time to say thank you.

'Shot for the county now did she?' Skelter muttered aloud to himself, 'and she will know the layout like the back of her hand.' *No pressure then,* he thought, reaching into his pocket for a Valium and swallowing it with the coffee before making for the shower.

At fourteen twenty-eight precisely Skelter walked out onto the terrace to find Lucy idly twirling a bunch of keys around her slender fingers. 'This way,' she said, heading inside. The room was obviously Rollo's office. A large old oak desk had pride of place in front of the tall window. Upon its well-worn, green leather surface an old imperial typewriter sat incongruously next to a beige computer. The walls were lined with bookshelves, floor to high ceiling. Lucy pressed the spine of a large old volume. The false front swung open with a click, to reveal a glass-fronted cabinet. Skelter counted eight shotguns, and a bolt-action deer rifle with a telescopic sight. Selecting a couple keys from the bunch, Lucy unlocked and opened the doors. 'Whichever takes your fancy except the Berretta on the right; that's Daddy's.' Skelter tried the rest for balance and fit and settled on a Browning over and under. He broke the gun, checked the breech and snapped it shut again before settling the butt plate of the twelve bore in the crook of his elbow. Stretching his hand towards the trigger he found he could reach it with ease. A fraction too much ease. It would shoot high. He needed a longer stock. 'Try this,' said Lucy, offering him a recoil pad sleeve extension.

He slipped the butt into the sleeve. His finger still reached the trigger but closer to the tip this time. 'That should do it.' He looked into the ends of the barrels. The chokes fitted were quarter and half, okay for novices but too wide a pattern for serious shooters. 'Any tighter chokes?'

'Here' she handed him a box the size of a cigarette packet.

'Thanks.'

'Be an angel and pick up that box of cartridges would you, Mark?' Skelter lifted the heavy cardboard container while Lucy found him a skeet vest, locked the cabinet and clicked the false front into place. 'You don't mind me press ganging you, do you?'

'Course not. I just hope your faith in me is justified.'

The shooting ground was beside a small lake surrounded by trees. Skelter scanned the middle and far distance sweeping his gaze to the shoreline across the water.

'Behind the trees,' said Lucy, 'and in trenches in front of them. Automatic traps,' she explained, waving what looked like a pair of TV remote controls.

'I'm impressed.'

'We can trigger singles or pairs up to four at a time. Wilkins has the other controls, he's just doing a final check on the traps.'

Skelter really was impressed. 'How many...?'

'Don't worry you wont run out of targets. One hundred and fifty clays in each trap.'

Skelter smiled. *Four multiple auto traps, remotes, clays, four grand's worth at least. Some set up.* He inserted the key into the Browning's barrel and began unscrewing the wide chokes and replacing them with three quarter in the bottom barrel and full in the top, to tighten the shot pattern. He was just tightening the last one when two men in green moleskin trousers and skeet vests approached. One wore a tweed flat cap, which failed to conceal the fact that he was bald. They looked as if they had stepped off the cover of shooting times. Both had expensive acoustic ear defenders around their necks. Skelter had brought his own from home.

'Morning, Rollo.'

'Good morning, gentlemen,'

'Rather formal aren't we, Rollo? Trying to impress Lucy's young man?' The shorter of the two stepped forward and offered his hand, pumping Skelter's in a bone-crushing grasp that almost made him wince.

'I'm Peter,' said the major, 'Delighted to meet you,'

'H.' Said Skelter, responding. 'Good to meet you too sir.'

'Betwix'd, between, be-bolloxed to that sir, nonsense, Peter, please. No rank nor class here, Lad.'
West Yorkshire, thought Skelter, *Leeds or Bradford maybe*. He had encountered many accents during his years of service and enjoyed testing himself. He took an educated guess.

'Leeds?'

'Spot on lad. As you will have guessed, my esteemed colleague here is Paul, not Colonel Catastrophe as young Lucy would have you believe. Great sense of humour that girl, eh? You might find Paul more of a challenge to place. Talks with a mouth full of plums, not that he talks much.'

'Can't get a word in edgeways that's why.' Tall and rangy, Paul offered his hand with a nod of his head, extending his hand to take Skelter's in a positive but unenthusiastic grip.

'H.'

'Paul,' Skelter acknowledged.

'I say, Rollo, how many bullets do we get?'

'Stop taking the piss, Peter. It's a two man flush. Same as every year. As many *cartridges* as you can shoot before the target's gone.'

'Just checking.'

Rollo turned to Skelter. 'Four clays in any combination, no limit on cartridges, fire as fast as you can reload. Say when ready and they will come at us in batches. No warning from which direction or whether high or low. Two hundred clays each pair. Each pair will shoot alternate stands of twenty. Toss of a coin for first up. All clear?'

Skelter nodded. *Two-man flush, perfect.* Quick reaction shooting relying on instinct – the centre of Skelter's comfort zone.

Introductions over they made their way to the stand. Lucy and Wilkins back from checking the traps had adopted positions on the left and right, each holding two radio remote controls for their respective pairs traps. They all had a ten bird warm up, which allowed Skelter to get acquainted with the Browning. It was shooting straight but still a fraction high. He adjusted aim accordingly. He turned the dial on his ear defenders to allow him to hear the ambient sounds while cutting out the frequencies of the gunshots.

Major Peter and Colonel Paul took the stand first and shot a creditable nineteen out of the first twenty. Rollo and Skelter stepped up to the firing point next, ears alert for the distant twang of the trap spring. The first four came together left right and right to left low and fast, crossing in front at thirty yards. They disintegrated under a hail of lead shot, leaving grey dust hanging in the air. Rollo and Skelter smoked eighteen targets and then Rollo missed a pair. Just when topping one hundred and sixty made victory look certain, Skelter missed a single and then another. The air was thick with the smell of burnt powder. Nip and tuck until with twenty clays to go each, Rollo and Skelter trailed one behind. The last twenty were the trickiest but the colonel and the major excelled themselves until with the very last flush of four to come they had not missed once. If they kept it up victory would be theirs. Three came at once low, left, and away, difficult to pick up against the trees. Four shots punctuated the air with only one hit. The pair broke their guns in unison, ejected cartridges arcing in the sunlight. Next came a single high climber towards the shooters. The last clay. It was almost overhead when the major managed to close his gun after reloading and took a brilliant sweeping, vertical double snapshot breaking the clay with the first and vapourising the pieces with the second. That put the pressure right on Skelter and Rollo, leaving them just two in front. They had to score a perfect last round. The pair held their nerve and with two clays to go they had shattered eighteen of the last twenty. They were tied and guaranteed a shoot off. The last two clays came from left and right, the former straight at the firing point, the latter high and away; a long shot at fifty yards. Skelter switched the trigger selector to the full choked top barrel, picked up the long shot and held until he saw Rollo smoke the incoming one. Only then did he fire. He missed. No matter. Victory was theirs. The losers graciously congratulated the victors and hip flasks were passed around. Skelter was enjoying himself.

The shooting party returned to the house and set up camp on the terrace. There was much good-humoured banter as guns were cleaned, oiled and racked, followed by liberal doses of alcohol. Skelter excused himself and went to his room, returning shortly afterwards with a bottle of Talisker twelve year old single malt. 'Happy birthday,' he said, handing the whisky to Rollo.

A wide smile lit up Rollo's face. 'Thank you, H, this is much appreciated.'

They christened the Talisker with enthusiasm.

'A fine choice of Malt, young man,' said the colonel savouring the aroma as he passed the glass beneath his nose.

'Aye,' his fellow officer agreed, passing the peaty

liquid under his nose. 'Where did you find this fellow, Rollo?'

'Not me, Lucy.'

'Yes of course, senior moment. Well, he seems to know his whisky as well as he knows his way around a sporting shoot. Good man, H.'

'Thank you,' said Skelter, raising his glass in acknowledgement.

'So how long have you been in the Army?' Peter asked.

'Twenty years.'

'Been with The Regiment long?' asked Paul.

'Twenty years,' repeated Skelter. He glanced at Rollo.

'Enough chaps,' said Rollo. 'Treat the man with a little respect.'

Peter smiled. 'I apologise, Sergeant Skelter. Force of habit.'

Paul nodded.

'Accepted,' said Skelter. 'Suppose you tell me what you know and I'll do my best to fill in some of the blanks.'

'That's very fair, H,' said Peter.

It turned out they knew everything from his joining the Royal Marines at twenty in 1976, but nothing before.

'Not missing too much are you?' Skelter said.

'Cards on the table, H,' said Peter, 'we have sensitive issues to consider, a business to protect. Can't say much more I'm afraid. You know how it is. The background check was necessary. Nothing personal you understand.'

'Fine,' said Skelter. 'How much of not much can you tell me?'

At this point Rollo stepped in to calm the rising waters. 'We all have the same background as I am sure you are aware, H. In the intelligence world no one ever really retires. We are still wired in to the system.'

'Still on the company payroll?' Skelter asked.

Rollo gave a non-committal shrug.

Skelter's shoulders dropped a fraction, the tension in his hands relaxed. He weighed up how much he should say about the missing years. Given enough time they would find out anyway he decided, but even so no need to volunteer all.

'I was born David Rees in Cwmbran, South Wales in nineteen fifty-four,' slight raising of eyebrows at the name change, 'went to sea at fourteen as a cabin boy. Left the sea eventually and came back to the UK. Joined the Marines. The rest you know about.'

'Your candour is appreciated,' said Peter. 'We have connections to parties who know people who are always on the lookout for experienced men like yourself for discreet work in the private sector.'

'The circuit you mean?' said Skelter, referring to the well-trodden path taken by ex members of *The Regiment* seeking work as bodyguards or training the soldiers of third world countries.

'We tend to work a little below the circuit's radar,' said Peter.

'I see,' said Skelter, not entirely sure that he did. What he did see was a possible opportunity for future lucrative employment when his time with The Regiment expired, which could be soon. Glasses were raised, more toasts made to the winners of the shoot and backs slapped in a virtual sense. The mood mellowed with the intake of alcohol and the anticipation of the meal to come as the aroma of roasting bird pervaded the atmosphere. By the time Wilkins announced dinner everyone was salivating and happiness reigned. The atmosphere continued all through an excellent meal of Goose cooked to refection with all the trimmings. Lucy made an entrance wearing a black cocktail dress topped with a single string of pearls and pearl earrings. Simple but effective, it had got Skelter's attention. He was getting it bad and it made him anxious.

During the dessert course, while Skelter and Lucy were engaged in conversation with Rollo, Paul and Peter spoke in a low tone to one another at the opposite side of the table. They were speaking in French. Lucy placed her hand over Skelter's, squeezed it and glared across the table at Peter. The two men reverted to English Later during cheese and crackers out on the terrace, he approached the two men.

'Messieurs,' Skelter began, 'Mes compliments pour votre excellente maîtrise de la grammaire française, l'accent a besoin d'un peu de travail, mais bien fait.'

They each looked as if they had been smacked in the face with a stoker's shovel.

'Mark,' said Lucy taking his hand, 'let me show you the summer house.' She led him away, across the lawn. Once there she sat down, patting the seat beside her. Skelter, nursing a full whisky glass complied like an obedient puppy. 'I must apologise for that display of rudeness, I can't believe they would do that. The fact they were saying nice things about you does not excuse them.'

'You understood?'

'Mais certainment, mon cherie,' she paused, 'My mother is half French.'

'Your family certainly get about.'

'Yes, we do have itchy feet. Mummy was born in Kenya. My grandfather was a pilot in the Rhodesian Air Force, my grandmother was born in Marseilles. She was a nurse.'

Skelter shuddered at the mention of the French city.

'Are you alright, Mark?'

'Yes, I think someone just walked over my grave, that's all. I'm fine. A nurse you say.'

'She was working in a hospital in Bulawyo when they met. We spoke French every day at home, when I was growing up. Where did you learn? In the Army?'

Skelter nodded.

'That was sweet of you today,' Lucy said.

'The whisky you mean?'

'Not that, although it was a lovely thought. No, I

mean you missing that last clay. You waited for Daddy to get his, you knew then that you'd won. You let him score higher than you.'

'No, really I missed...'

'Bollocks, Mark, I shot for the county remember? Actually, I was county champion three times and had a trial for the England Team. I may be a bit rusty now but I know a deliberate miss when I see one. So does Daddy.'

'Oh,' said Skelter, realising he had been rumbled.

She slipped her arm through his and put her head on his shoulder. 'Don't worry he'll be impressed. He likes you.'

'You think so?'

'I'm certain.'

'Does that matter to you?'

She did not answer. He looked into her eyes. She blinked.

'Yes Mark. It matters.'

When Skelter returned to the house Peter approached.

'Sergeant, might I have a word?'

'I need to powder my nose anyway,' said Lucy, making a tactical withdrawal.

'Sergeant Skelter, I wish to offer you my unreserved apology for our unforgivable behaviour earlier. We seriously underestimated you. I am truly sorry. It will not happen again.'

'May I add my apologies to my colleague's,' said Paul who had wandered over to join the conversation. 'We will not insult you further by asking where you acquired your excellent French.'

'Right answer,' said Skelter. 'If you had asked I wouldn't have told you, but since you didn't, I will, just as soon as I refill my glass.'

'Allow me,' said Peter picking a bottle up from the table.

Skelter waited until his glass was charged, took a slow sip and then spoke. 'When I was eighteen I missed my ship in Marseilles. Got drunk. I was young, trying to keep up with the old hands. Passed out at some point, don't remember the details, you know how it is. Anyway these two Legionnaires picked me up and looked after me. Changed my life. I joined up. I don't know if you know, but all recruits are required to take a new name when they join the Foreign Legion. After two years they can revert if they wish. I'd grown to like my new name by then, so I stuck with it. I was selected for Seconde Régiment Étranger de Parachutistes.'

'The second REP,' said Peter. 'They only take the cream from the top for the Paras.'

'Skip the bullshit gents, your apology is accepted. And it's H.'

'Thank you, H, you are most gracious, dear boy and we are suitably chastened,' said Peter. 'You will appreciate that language skills are a valuable asset in our business and attract good bonuses.'

'Fluent Spanish, workable Somali, Basic German and Arabic and for what it's worth schoolboy Welsh,' said Skelter, answering the implied but unasked question.

3

Saturday 20th June
Ross on Wye, Herefordshire

He was suffocating, clawing to reach the air, gasping as he finally managed to fill his bursting lungs. His eyes were open but it was black as pitch. There was a swooshing sound. Bright moonlight flooded the bedroom casting Lucy in silhouette as she hooked back the curtains.

'Jesus, give me a break,' Skelter hissed under his breath. The last thing he needed now was his demon throwing a spanner in the works with Lucy.

'You were having a nightmare,' she said, 'I heard you through the wall, came to see if you were all right.'

'I'm fine,' said Skelter, embarrassed.

She sat down on the edge of the bed, so close he could smell the woman in her. 'Daddy still has nightmares. Not so often now but he still gets them, awful sometimes. Mother never understood, said if he wanted to play soldiers then he should accept the consequences.' She placed her hand on his arm. 'Bunk up, Mark, it's chilly out here.' It was plainly an order, and not a request. He obeyed without hesitation.

'You're a strange woman, Lucy Ryder. I never met anyone like you. Look I'm not...'

'Me neither,' she interrupted, 'I'm not that kind of a girl, well actually... it's just, well, you need a hug and so do I.' She lightly kissed his cheek then snuggled close to his chest. He put his arm around her shoulder and stroked her upper arm through the brushed cotton of her pyjama top.

'Not very sexy are they?' Lucy said. 'If I had known

I'd be night visiting I would have worn something more alluring.'

'They'll do for me,' Skelter said, feeling strangely at ease lying beneath the sheets with a woman he had met only a few days ago. 'Here we are in bed together and I know hardly anything about you.'

'Perfect opportunity to find out though don't you think? What would you like to know?'

'Everything.'

'Well, I was born in this house on April the fifteenth nineteen sixty-six, the middle child of three. My baby brother Simon is a Lieutenant in the Household Cavalry. My big brother works in Whitehall. A bit hush-hush. You now how it is. We're a military family, most of my uncles have served at some time or other.'

Father a brigadier, brother a spook, what next? Skelter thought, absently stroking Lucy's hair.

'Ooh that's lovely, Mark. Don't stop,' Lucy whispered, snuggling even more tightly against his chest. 'I studied illustration at the Royal College of Art and I make a modest living from it. I've never been married and my longest relationship ended by mutual consent, five years ago after four and a half years. My hair and teeth are my own – but I do tint my hair, oh and I once wore false eyelashes to the Hunt Ball. Your Turn.'

'Chalk to your cheese. Youngest of four boys on a Cwmbran council estate. Dad was a steelworker and local hard-case. Left home at fourteen, signed on as a deckhand on a tramp steamer out of Cardiff. Joined up at twenty-one and been soldiering ever since.'

'What about your family, do you still see them?'

Skelter hesitated for a moment and then let out a long sigh. 'Not since Mam's funeral in nineteen seventy-nine.'

'I am sorry. Was it a long illness?'

'It was a long time ago.'

'Oh.' Lucy snuggled in.

After a while Skelter could feel the tension leaving him as slowly he sank further into the pillows.

'That's better,' said Lucy, surrendering a long sigh past her lips.

'What was that for?' Skelter asked.

'That, was for you,' she said. 'It's good to see you relaxed again.'

'Thanks to you.'

'All part of the service, sir,' she said. 'I suppose I ought to return to my room now that you don't need me anymore.'

Skelter caught her arm as she made to get up. She turned and kissed him, on the lips this time, but briefly. She tasted of spearmint and warm promise. Deep inside him he let the latch slip on a door that had slammed shut more than ten years ago. April the seventeenth, nineteen eighty-seven. The night that Jane died.

'I can't make you out Lucy.'

'I'm a woman. You're not supposed to. So long as you stick around and keep trying I don't care.' Lucy rose from the bed and passed through the door, closing it quietly behind her.

Skelter lay awake a long time trying to understand why a woman with her background would be interested in him. She did not seem at all bothered by his background. She was making all the running, something which would normally have sent him diving for cover and yet he felt reassuringly comfortable around her. He fell into a happy if somewhat confused sleep.

'I trust you slept okay?' Rollo asked Skelter as they tucked into fried eggs and dry cured best back bacon.

'Like a baby,' he lied, trying to avoid eye contact with Lucy as she raised an eyebrow in his direction.

'Good. Look I have some business in Leominster. I'll gone most of the day but Lucy will look after you. We'll meet up later for a drink perhaps?'

'I'd like that.'

'Excellent.'

The shallows were full of green waders, wax jackets and fishing flies, the banks studded with cow parsley and brown eyed Herefords contentedly grazing the lush green sward, tails swishing at the clouds of buzzing flies. Over lunch at the Old Ferry Inn, Skelter sank two pints of Guinness while Lucy demolished twice the equivalent in strong cider. They walked along the riverbank for a while exchanging snippets of their past lives, listing favourite films, music and childhood memories, until at Lucy's suggestion they sat down upon the grass at the water's edge in the shade of an of an ancient pollarded Willow. A pair of geese flew a circuit overhead before flaring for landing on the river, braking with webbed feet in a long rippling wave upon the green water. 'Branta canadensis,' said Lucy. 'Canada Geese.'

'Show off,' said Skelter.

'Sorry, force of habit. I have to know the scientific names for my illustration work. You must think me awfully rude.'

'Not specially, we all show off sometimes, part of being human. Besides I like to learn stuff.' A flash of iridescent green suddenly shimmered in the sunshine less than five feet from where they were sitting. 'What about that then?' said Skelter, admiring the airborne predator's balletic performance.

'How beautiful,' said Lucy.

'Yes, but what is it?' said Skelter.

'A Dragonfly silly.'

'Yes, but what kind?'

'No idea, sorry not good on insects, but I will look it up and let you know. Promise.' Her cheeks were flushed, she avoided eye contact the conversation stalled. They sat next to one another, occupying the same space, yet not together for what seemed ages.

A group of youths approached along the path swearing at the tops of their voices, swigging cans of strong cider. As they drew level one of them threw an empty can into the river.

'Cut that out,' shouted Lucy, leaping to her feet. The culprit stopped, stared at Lucy and gave her the finger.

Oh bollocks, thought Skelter, *there goes a quiet afternoon. What is it with women?* He would have to get involved now. Lucy walked across to remonstrate with the young man. His response was predictably abusive. The others formed a semi circle around her and joined in. Skelter's mind went into overdrive. He needed to take the heat out of the situation and fast. If he got involved in a brawl and it got back to *The Regiment* he would be in deep shit.

'Take it easy, boys,' said Skelter.

'Fuck you,' said the can chucker, tall, tattooed, late teens.

'Does your mother know you use language like that?' said Lucy, 'Make you feel big does it?'

Skelter now stood face to face with the loud-mouthed yob. 'Get on your way boys, and calm it down okay?'

'Listen to granddad,' the youth said, turning to his mates.

One glance confirmed to Skelter, which way this was going. They were well tanked and itching for trouble. He could almost taste the testosterone. Clutching Lucy's arm tight enough to get her attention, he jerked his head towards the rear. 'Go and sit under the tree.' He squeezed her arm tighter, 'Now.'

'Mark?'

'Do it.'

Lucy moved away.

'Oooo look at macho man,' the gobby one mouthed off.

'Okay, boys, you've had your fun, now be on your way.'

Gobby stepped forward, hands by his sides, fists hard clenched, purple faced, head straining at the neck, spittle on his lips, right in Skelter's face. Tipping point. Gobby's back thudded into the ground as Skelter's head butt smashed the bridge of his nose. The youth to his left hardly had time to register surprise, before Skelter's balled fist slammed into his throat and he collapsed, coughing and gasping for air. Stepping forward, Skelter kicked a third hard in the side of his knee, following with an elbow to the back of the neck as the youth lost balance, taking him down. He turned to face the remaining two, standing still, legs wide, balanced on the balls of his feet.

'Now fuck off,' he said.

They needed no more encouragement. Gobby was still on the ground, his face a bloody mess, nose broken and probably a black eye in embryo. Any appetite the other two may have had for a fight had evaporated.

'Lets go,' Skelter said, taking Lucy's arm and heading off along the riverbank away from the scene of the confrontation.

She stumbled to her feet looking dazed. and complied mechanically. Skelter set a cracking pace. They had covered almost a mile before he eased up and looked for a place to sit. There was a stile leading an offshoot of the path into a meadow. He climbed over and sat in the long grass, his back against the bole of a stunted oak. Lucy climbed over, almost overbalancing before flopping down a couple of feet from him. The cider was kicking in. She was trembling slightly.

'Are you cross with me, Mark?'

'You don't understand much about men do you? Macho culture? Those boys were never going to listen to a woman. The minute you got involved, you got me involved. I could loose my stripes if this gets back to the Regiment. All for the sake of one drunken idiot throwing litter.'

'But Mark...'

'Three kids with smashed faces, macho pride destroyed, humiliated in front of their mates. Have you any idea how angry that's going to make them? Who do you think they'll vent that on? Some poor innocent who isn't able to stand up to them, that's who.' Skelter exhaled hard through clenched teeth.

Lucy took a tissue from her shoulder bag, blew her nose, wiped and sniffed twice.

'Are you okay?' He asked.

'It's seeing all that blood. That boy's face.'

'There were five of them and they weren't up for negotiation. What did you expect me to do, wait for him to hit me first? What if he'd had a weapon, a knife maybe?'

Lucy fell silent looking lost and confused.

Skelter's anger slowly dissipated. 'It's done now. Best we move on.' He moved closer to her and put his hand on hers.

'Will you really get into trouble?' Lucy asked.

'Only if they find out. Don't worry I'm sure they wont.'

'I'm sorry, I didn't think.'

'No worries,' he said.

They lay back amongst the scabious and vetch enjoying the heady scent from the mass of wildflowers. Small blue butterflies danced among the daisies while red admirals fluttered from campion to cornflower. They fell silent, remaining that way for some time just enjoying the sun. It was too lovely a day to spoil.

'So what made you chose the Army?' asked Lucy, breaking the silence.

'Didn't fancy the Steelworks. The thought of going down the pit didn't exactly fill me with joy either. The only other option was to move away. Best thing I ever did. God only knows where I'd be now if I hadn't joined up – jail most like.'

'So which regiment did you join?'

'The one I'm in of course.'

'Oh no you don't,' said Lucy, '*The Regiment* doesn't take civilians. You have to have served or be serving in the Army. You are forgetting I was brought up with this.'

Skelter grinned at her and lay back against the oak's rough bark.

'Or another branch of Her Majesty's armed forces, like the RAF for instance?'

'You were in the air force?'

'Did I say that?'

'Stop teasing, Mark,' she said playfully slapping his hand. He caught and held it, marvelling at how cool and slender her fingers were.

'Lucy, last night ...'

'Don't worry, Mark, my lips are tight shut. Look.' She screwed her mouth in an exaggerated grimace, her face inches from his, then relaxing her facial muscles she continued, 'unless of course you would like to...' she left the sentence unfinished.

'You don't have any shame at all do you woman?'

'None whatsoever,' she said, her voice slurred with cider. Moving closer she put her hand on his chest, her fingers toying with the top button on his shirt. Skelter placed his free hand on hers.

She looked hurt. 'What's the matter don't you find me attractive? I know you're a bit old fashioned and you probably think I'm rushing things, but I've had my eye on you for ages.'

'How's that?'

'I've seen you in the Grapes with your mates.' Skelter felt his anxiety level rise. He couldn't remember if he had taken his Valium that morning. 'Diane told me I was wasting my time,' Lucy continued, 'that you had no interest in women, not since...oh now I *have* said too much.'

Skelter gently removed her hand and stood up.

28

'You're right,' he said, 'she is beautiful, the River Wye.'
'Sorry, Mark, too much cider.'
'No sweat, girl, time we were heading back.'

4

Saturday 20th June
Ross on Wye, Herefordshire

Sitting on the terrace watching the crimson sun slowly sink below the trees, Skelter swapped stories with Rollo over a glass of fine single Malt. He was at ease again, the awkwardness of the afternoon pushed to the back of his mind. Lucy's father was charming company. Skelter felt comfortably at home.

'You've got a beautiful house, Rollo,' said Skelter as the whisky hit the spot, 'and a beautiful daughter too.'

'Glad you think so. My father had the house built here in 1937, the land's been in the family for generations. As for my daughter, she can be a bit overwhelming at times as you will discover, if you haven't already that is.'

'She's certainly different,' said Skelter.

'Try not to let it put you off my boy; she's a good girl underneath. She doesn't follow protocol. Her mother was exactly the same, if she saw something she wanted she went all out until she got it. I never stood a bloody chance.' Rollo reached for the bottle and leaned in close to Skelter, topping up his glass. In the quiet tone of a confidant he continued. 'My daughter has a good heart, but like most women, she just doesn't understand that nothing scares us chaps more than a forward woman. They see guys in The Regiment as men of action afraid of nothing, but we know different don't we?'

'Exactly right.' Skelter replied. 'I've never been much good with women. To be honest, they all scare me a bit.'

Rollo raised his glass in a toast. 'Women, God bless 'em. Can't live with them, can't live without them.'

They clinked glasses just as Lucy walked onto the terrace.

'What are you two up to? You look like a couple of guilty schoolboys.'

The two men exchanged glances in silence.

Dinner was a spicy, aromatic Lamb curry with poppadums, pilau rice and chapatis; a good old fashioned army favourite. Skelter felt well stuffed when he finally made it to the brandy on the terrace. 'Your man Wilkins is a genius, where did you find him, Rollo?'

'He was with me in Oman, joined The Regiment at the same time. Secret is, his parent unit was the Catering Corps. Fully qualified chef. Good isn't he?'

'Good? That Curry was fabulous.'

Later Skelter accepted Lucy's offer of a stroll around the garden by moonlight. He was getting to like her more and more, but still the little voice in his head warned him to tread softly. After so long alone he was in no hurry. They walked back to the house and as they reached the terrace Skelter took Lucy's hand, held it, stopped and looked into her eyes. Lucy stood perfectly still, half closing her eyes as he drew her so close he could feel her breath on his cheek. His lips parted. 'Anax imperator,' he whispered.

'Pardon?'

'Anax imperator, the emperor dragonfly.'

'Bastard,' she said. 'How did you find... You knew all along.'

Skelter shrugged, his eyes twinkling.

She shook her head. 'Serve me right for showing off.'

5

Saturday 20th June
Indian Ocean 6 miles East off Kenyan Coast

As the molten candle wax struck the man's nipple, a smirk of satisfaction stole across Bell's face. Despite the soundproof two-way mirror he heard the stifled cry as the man bit deep into the scarlet rubber gag. The new headphones had been a sound investment Bell mused, oblivious to the unintended pun. Watching the girl dripping wax onto the man's milk white skin, Bell sighed with contentment. She was clearly enjoying her work.

'What are we going to do with this worm, Sister Two? He is so unworthy.'

'He is,' Sister One. You are an unworthy slave, aren't you?'

'Yes, mistress,' the man mumbled through the gag.

The second girl ran the tails of the cat across the soft flesh of his abdomen. The man's loins stirred. Bell studied her face, he had chosen well.

'We cannot hear you, slave,' said Sister Two. 'Louder you pathetic worm.'

'Yes, mistress.'

'Good girl,' murmured Bell, 'keep the pathetic little shit happy.'

Sister Two began flicking the leather tails, teasing with skilled precision that belied her youth. The leather thongs holding the gag dug into the man's cheeks, as the ropes creased the skin at his wrists and ankles. Apart from the gimp mask the man was naked. The crucifix to which he was strapped, like the rest of the bespoke furnishings, was worthy of the finest of cabinetmakers. The cabin was austere, but reeked of solid quality workmanship, reminiscent of nineteen forties utility furniture.

Bell removed the headphones and slid the blackout panel across the back of the mirror before opening the door and stepping out from the closet into his stateroom. He left the video camera running. Clicking shut the fine rosewood veneered panel to blend invisibly into the bulkhead; he left the cabin and headed topside.

Ten feet above the dungeon, Richard Bell settled his Armani shorts into a teak steamer recliner and surveyed the surroundings through his Ray Bans. At one hundred and twenty feet *The Golden Slot* rode her anchor like a well-behaved, tethered thoroughbred. *Not bad for the son of a drunken, illiterate, fairground showman* he reflected, gazing across the water as the burnished copper sun dipped slowly towards the horizon. Picking up a small brass namesake from the mahogany deck beside him, he rang once. Almost immediately a young Indian boy in a white tunic and white trousers, appeared at Bell's side. 'Margarita,' said Bell. 'Chop chop.'

'Yes, Sah. Margarita.' The Lascar hurried away.

Despite obvious signs of self-indulgence, Bell's body retained traces of a former, fitter, lifestyle. Fast approaching his forty-ninth birthday, Richard was as happy as his millions could make him. Glancing at his Rolex, he noted the position of the minute hand. Before it had covered three segments the boy returned with the cocktail. Taking the glass Bell delicately sipped from the salt frosted rim with an air of cultured sophistication, at odds with the calloused skin of a hand forged in hard graft.

The calming motion of the Indian Ocean brought a relaxing smile to Bell's face as he watched the waves lapping the palm-fringed, coral sand of the island – his island. *What would the old man have made of this,* he wondered with a tinge of regret? He was worth ten of his old man – even on a bad day. Bell nursed a yearning to have him back one last time to show the bastard how wrong he had been, before giving him a good kicking and throwing him to the sharks.

Peace reigned for another ninety-seconds; the time it took for the battered Skiff to round the headland and declare its intentions. The wooden craft was heading directly for the yacht at what must have been near its outboard's maximum speed. Before Bell's crew had time to react a burst of gunfire from the bow of the vessel threw up fountains of foaming ocean within yards of the yacht.

Bell's head of security stuck his head out of the forward hatch before racing below; returning less than a minute later clutching a Colt Commando assault rifle. Chuck Riner had come highly recommended. The yet untested, ex US Navy Seal's swift reaction, impressed and reassured Bell. The Skiff was now fifty yards away. Riner lined his sights on the machine gunner in the bow, thumbed the fire select lever to fully automatic and squeezed the trigger.
Click... Misfire.

Richard Bell stared in horror and disbelief as Riner struggled with the rifle's mechanism. 'Do something for Christ's sake.'

Frantically tugging the bolt Bell's security guard's debut performance was signally unimpressive. Jammed solid in the breech, the round refused to budge. The yacht juddered as something struck the hull somewhere aft. A scrambling sound like rats running came from the stern betraying the presence of a second pirate boat, confirmed when a trio of tattered tee shirts appeared behind the menacing black muzzles of three AK47s. Riner's Colt clattered to the deck as he let go of the weapon and raised his hands.

'You useless bastard,' said Bell. His lawyer had recommended Riner as one of the best. *God help that sorry piece of shit when I get hold of him,* he thought.

The smallest gunman motioned Riner to the rail at

the side of the yacht. The youth wore a grubby Red T-shirt emblazoned with the Coca Cola logo over his skinny frame and looked no more than fifteen. He reeked of stale fish and marijuana. Transfixed on the AK, Bell wondered if the dirty rust-coated weapon was capable of firing. As if telepathic, the youth answered his unspoken question with a five round burst to Riner's chest catapulting him over the side into the ocean. Bell watched in stunned silence as the water turned crimson around the twitching body of his former bodyguard. Staring in disbelief at the still smoking gun, Bell's mind went into overdrive, looking for a way out. Clearly high on some form of narcotic, the gunmen were unlikely to be open to reason. *Negotiate.* It was what he knew. He had done deals with Sheiks and shysters; in all currencies. It was what he was good at. *They'll understand hard cash.*

Somewhere below deck a woman began screaming. She stopped abruptly. Bell felt a sudden blow between his shoulder blades pitching him forward onto the deck. Despite protestations he was trussed up and dragged towards the rail. He caught a brief glimpse of Charles Parish, stark naked, still wearing the scarlet gag being bundled onto the deck at gunpoint, before a second blow to his head sent Bell spiralling into darkness.

Reaching up to touch his wound Bell was gripped by panic. He could not see his hand, the blow to his head had left him blind. A shuffling sound close by made him freeze. 'Who's there?'

'Richard?'

'Charles? Is that you?'

'Richard, are you okay? I can't see, so dark...'

'Thank God. I thought I'd gone blind. Can you move, Charles?'

'Not easily, the floor's covered in chains and rope and rubbish, be careful. I think we might be in a ship.'

'Could be,' said Bell, 'stinks of fish and diesel, and Christ knows what else.'

'What about the others?' said Parish. 'Do you think...?'

'Who gives a shit, dead for all I know, the crew's worth nothing to them. They'll pass the girls around 'til they get tired of them.' He shook his head and blinked repeatedly but it made no difference, the darkness remained total. 'It's me they want. They smell money. It's just a matter of negotiating the price. Did you see that Coca Cola kid? He shot Riner. In cold blood. Had his hands in the air He is seriously fucked up. He got off on wasting Riner.'

'Jesus, Is he dead?'

'Shark bait. Better pray they don't do anything stupid before I can get us out of here.'

'And how do you know it isn't me they want? It could be some kind of...'

'...terrorist plot? This bunch of morons? Get real, Charles, fucking amateurs. Money, Charles, that's what this is all about. I'll get us out of here. Relax, I've enough to buy what ever Somali shit-hole these little bastards come from without my accountant noticing.'

Charles Parish had managed to crawl across to Bell and the two of them sat upon coils of greasy rope and coarse netting reeking of rotten fish.

'What makes you think they're Somali?'

'I don't think, Charles, I know.'

Bell's eyes had begun to adjust to the darkness and he could now make out the vague outline of his fellow prisoner but little else. His head was throbbing, the side of his face caked in blood, but he was alive and confident he could buy his freedom once their captors put in an appearance.

Right on cue a scraping, rasping sound above them was followed by a thin shaft of sunlight stabbing their darkness. Something struck Parish's shoulder and bounced from his naked knees onto Bell's lap. The basket contained a goatskin flask, four overripe bananas and a bundle of cloth, which upon closer inspection turned out to be a smelly, well-worn boiler suit. The inrush of fresh air served only highlight the foetid atmosphere inside the hull. The hatch closed again.

'At least they've given you something to cover your embarrassment, Charles,' Bell remarked, groping towards the vague outline of his fellow prisoner. 'Here.' He pushed the boiler suit into his hands. Bell sniffed at the contents of the flask before taking a tentative sip. The water was warm, but welcome, despite being also stale with a hint of oily fish. Bell passed the flask to Parish. He took a swig, but declined the bananas.

'So what happened, Charles, after I went out?'

'Put a blindfold on me and a sack over my head. Made me lie in the bottom of the Skiff. Threw you on top of me. I think the others went in the second Skiff. I can't be sure. We were going for ages then we bumped alongside a bigger vessel.'

'This one you mean?'

'No, it was a wooden one. Anyway after an hour or two I fell asleep. I was exhausted. Next thing I know I'm being dragged off the boat up some earth bank so I know we must have made land. Then there was a plank, narrow and wobbly and I was dumped in a heap. The next bit was scary, untied my hands, stuck a gun, at least I think it was a gun, in my ribs and I was swept up in the air. In a cargo net I guess and dropped here. I got the blindfold off as they were closing the hatch.'

'How long...'

'You came round just after it slammed shut.'

'Well, they don't intend to kill us, at least not yet, or they wouldn't have bothered bringing us here. They've given us food and water, and your boiler suit. The next move is theirs. All we can do for now is wait.'

Sitting in the dark, still, silence, time dragged.

Neither man had a watch; stolen no doubt by their captors and in any case reading the time in almost total darkness would have proved a significant problem. Not that it mattered. Only one thing mattered. Getting out alive.

On the positive side it was warm if a little oppressive and they were not badly hurt. Bell's head had a hell of lump and still throbbed, but he did not feel sick or dizzy and his thinking seemed to be unimpaired.

'We should try to sleep,' suggested Parish, 'conserve our energy. It will help pass the time quicker.'

'Not my style, Charles, I've had enough of waiting,' Bell replied, feeling around the floor with both hands. It took a couple of minutes to find what he was searching for, not that he knew what it was, not exactly that is. He knew enough to be confident it would suit his purpose and that was enough for now. It was cold enough and heavy enough for steel, long as a cricket bat and round in section. A length of old scaffold pole? Whatever, it fitted his hand perfectly, might even make a useful weapon if things got desperate, but right now Richard Bell had other plans for it. Sitting back and allowing his captors to retain the initiative was not his way to do business and Bell knew all about business. He was very successful. It had made him so rich he was not sure how much he was worth but he knew that it was more than enough. Not that that stopped him making more. He wouldn't know how to stop if he'd wanted to and he certainly didn't want to. To Bell, making money was a bigger hit than a line of coke stretching around the equator. 'You might want to cover your ears, Charles, it's going to get noisy in a minute.'

'Come again?'

'Just do it man, cover your ears.' Bell began beating the steel hull rapidly and repeatedly, steel ringing against steel, echoing and reverberating inside the dark void. The noise was deafening, like being in a belfry in the middle of a long peal. It didn't take long to get a response. There was a sudden shaft of sunlight as the hatch was drawn back and a ring of skinny black faces glared down into the gloom. The inrush of warm air was a welcome foil to the fish-foul air in their dungeon. Red T-shirt yelled something. Bell ceased banging.

'English. Any of you black bastards speak English?'

'For Christ sake, Richard, don't'…Charles Parish was cut short from above.

'No more noise, white Boy. Cut off hands. Hear I? No more.'

'How much you want?' Bell shouted back. 'Money. How much?'

At this the faces disappeared but raised voices began arguing numbers in Somali. Richard Bell caught the gist. It had been some years since he had heard the Somali tongue and it stirred memories of hard graft, humble beginnings and his early days at sea. Escaping from home was all he ever dreamed of as a young teenager. He was a great disappointment to his father, who simply assumed that he would step into his showman's shoes when the old man retired. That was not on Richard's agenda. He had ambition. Richard wanted respect, the kind that comes from social standing, which, if you are not born to it can be bought. Everything has its price.

The faces appeared again. 'You quiet, or hands cut, hear I. Tomorrow. Talk money tomorrow. No noise.'

'What about some decent food?' Parish asked.

'Tomorrow.' The hatch closed and again they were plunged into darkness that cloaked their shoulders like medieval chain mail.

Bell felt around for the goatskin bag and pulled the cork. The water might have been warm and stale but somehow it wasn't so bad as he'd remembered. He was adapting. 'Drink, Charles?' He offered the goatskin, which was eagerly taken, before being just as eagerly rejected. 'Progress, Charles, tomorrow we get Lucky.'

'I don't follow you, dear boy,' Parish's puzzled public school tone breathed back at him from the darkness.

Bell laughed. 'Of course you don't, how could you. Ever wondered where all my money came from. Hard graft my friend, hard graft. Not everyone is born with silver spoon in his mouth. Some of us have to work for it.'

'No need to take offence, Richard,' said Parish.

Bell drew his knees up to his chest and rested his chin upon them in an attempt to get comfortable. 'Cawaale, Charles, they said they were waiting for someone called Cawaale. It means Lucky in Somali. He is the one with authority to make decisions. I think these boys have taken us on a whim and they're not sure what to do. A crime of opportunity.' His eyes adjusting to the darkness, Bell could now again make out the vague form of his fellow prisoner, imagining the confused expression he knew must be starring hard at him from a couple of feet away even though he could not make it out. 'Like I said I made my own money. I worked my bollocks off seven days a week as a deckhand aboard ship. I saved every penny I could lay my hands on...'

Charles was grinning from ear to ear in the darkness. He knew more about Bell than he was letting on. 'So how come ...'

'Speaking Somali? That's what I'm telling you. Britain was built on commercial shipping, but apart from the officers, most of the crews aboard merchant ships are foreigners, Lascars from India, Chinese, Arabs and lots of Somalis. I spent years living and working with them. We had a donkey-man aboard a tug I crewed out of East India Dock. His name was Cawaale. Tomorrow, we talk to Lucky. Correction, I talk to Lucky. I can strike a deal to get us out of here. No offence, Charles, but his kind of negotiation is my territory.'

'Fine by me if you can pull it off, dear boy, now can we get please some sleep? I am exhausted.'

Sunday 21st June
Ross on Wye Herefordshire

Sunday morning was overcast, but warm and dry. After breakfast Lucy took Skelter for a walk around the estate, which was bathed in sunshine. She led him through a belt of alder and birch trees to an open glade with a hardwood bench which overlooked a large pond.

'My favourite spot,' she said, 'I come here to be inspired.'

'And are you?'

'I'm thinking flag iris,' she answered, looking at the tall graceful yellow flowers rising from the shallows. 'I never tire of painting these.'

'They are beautiful. Did your father plant them?'

'Good heavens no. Yellow flag is a native species. The pond has been here for more than a hundred years as far as we know. It's fed by a spring and the outflow trickles down the gorge into the river.'

Skelter got to his feet and walked to the pond. He knelt down and examined the mud at the water's edge. 'Deer tracks, Roe by the look of it.'

'Muntjac,' said Lucy. 'Too small for Roe, although we do get both species look,' she said pointing to scattering of fresh droppings. 'They were here earlier this morning. Come with me tracker man.' She led him around the pond pointing out signs of other visitors. A water vole feeding station and burrow, rabbit droppings and old signs where bark had been ripped from the alders by deer stripping the velvet from their antlers.

'How did you learn all this stuff?'

'When I came home from school in the summer holidays. We had an old gardener, John Slaughter. He taught me. He knew everything about the countryside. Lovely man. I still miss him.'

'Maybe I should get you to teach the lads up at the camp. We are always looking for expertise for survival training.'

'Very funny.'

'I'm serious. Know anything about foraging for food?'

'I know what mushrooms taste good and which ones will make you sick or kill you. Slaughter was from gypsy stock.'

'Would you consider teaching a lesson or two?'

'You really are serious aren't you?'

'Deadly.'

'All right I'll think about it, but no promises.'

Relaxed and refreshed from the walk, they sat on the terrace with coffee and chocolate digestives. Lucy gently pried into his history.

'Please don't take offence, Mark, but for someone who left school at fourteen you don't come across as lacking in education. Yesterday by the river you were waxing lyrical about the history of the blues and there was that dragonfly. How...?'

'When I was a kid I used to sneak into Mam and Dad's bedroom and borrow books, well one book really, Arthur Mee's Children's Encyclopedia. It was in ten volumes, I used to sneak one out at a time. I knew Dad would never notice. Only thing he ever read was the Daily Mirror. It had been my granddad's. Old dark red covers, with fancy embossed gold lettering. It felt like treasure to me. Early nineteen-thirties by the look of the photographs of aircraft and cars, but the insects and animals were what I liked. Full page illustrations in colour. I learned loads from that book. Still have it, all ten volumes. Sentimental, but I do thumb through now and again, especially if I am having a bad day, it makes me feel good.'

'I can see it made a big impression on you. I sometimes wonder if all the money my parents spent on my education was worth it. I'm sure they expected me to be a doctor or a barrister.'

'You went with your talent, girl. Never regret that.'

'The army education corps has an excellent reputation I understand.'

'I got mine through the Navy.'

'You were a sailor?'

'No, well yes and no.'

Lucy looked confused. 'Mark...'

'I was a merchant seaman for a while when I was a kid. Galley boy. Anyway later I joined the Royal Marines. Three and a half years. I was in Four Five Commando when I did selection for The Regiment. They gave me a good schooling and supported me all the way, with equipment grants for books and such. The Marines really know how to build your confidence. Not just physically mind, all round. Emotional and intellectual, I got so I could hold my own anywhere; away on ops or in a room full of Ruperts.'

'Ruperts? Officers you mean, like my father?'

'Officers yes, but not like your father. He's a one off. Never met anyone like him before.' Skelter stretched his arms above his head interlocked fingers and flexed his back muscles. 'Enough of me spouting rubbish, I don't know about you but I could do a bit more exercise. Fancy getting for a bit, on the river maybe, rent a boat or a canoe?'

'Sounds good. Let's.'

They spent a couple of hours paddling and drifting, watching brown speckled trout snapping at flies while moorhens juddered and jerked amongst the marginal vegetation. High above the wide and winsome Wye soaring buzzards rode thermals generated by the steep rocky gorge, cut by the river over centuries. Surrounded by thick and ancient woodland, patrolled by herds of fallow and roe deer; a magical place. Hunger finally drove them to shore and into a local hostelry for sustenance. The home made steak and ale pie proved the perfect complement to Skelter's Guinness while Lucy lingered over linguine and red pesto with pine nuts. This she washed down with a large glass of Australian Merlot.

Walking to the Range Rover after lunch, they held hands. Skelter could not remember who instigated it. It just happened and he was comfortable with it. He held the door open for Lucy. As she climbed in she hooked her hand around the back of his neck and kissed him upon the lips – slowly, softly, deliberately. He made no attempt to resist but did not reciprocate.

'Thank you for a lovely time on the river,' Lucy said, a look of disappointment clouding her face as she turned away to get into her seat, a manoeuvre she was unable to complete, owing to Skelter's restraining arm. She turned again to him.

'Sorry about that,' he said. 'Caught me off guard you did. Could you do that again? Please?'

'Sorry, you need to grab the opportunity when it's there.' She turned away. It was Skelter's face that registered disappointment this time.

'How was your day out, daughter?' Rollo asked when they returned. Lucy gave him a summary of their canoeing, recited the lunch menu, passed comment on the culinary skills of the chef and then excused herself, citing the need for a shower leaving the men to continue with the male bonding exercise. The two men retired to the terrace to chew the fat about life love and other nonsense over coffee.

Lucy reappeared an hour or so later, wearing jeans and tee shirt. Lucy was settling into the conversation when Skelter's pager started bleeping. He read the message.

'Use the phone in my office.' Rollo said.

'Thanks.'

Skelter reappeared after a couple of minutes. 'I have to go back to camp.'

'Off course,' said Rollo.

'Sorry, Lucy,' Skelter said.

'Do you have to go now?'

'Afraid so.' He turned to Rollo. 'Thank you for your hospitality. I've enjoyed myself.'

Rollo held out his hand. 'Me too, come back soon, please.'

Lucy looked at the whisky glass in Skelter's hand. 'I could get Wilkins to drive you if...'

'I'll be fine. I have to go. Sorry.'

7

Sunday 21st June
Somalia

Bell and Parish were stirred from their fitful sleep by the sound of the hatch sliding open. Staring up into the daylight they gorged themselves on the warm, fresh air. The rotten atmosphere inside the hold had invaded their oral and olfactory orifices causing them both to retch repeatedly. The near vertical aspect of the sun through the hatch told Bell it was around noon.

Three gaunt, black faces appeared, the kind you see on BBC News or when someone is making an appeal for the latest African famine victims. Animated figures, pointing down at them as if viewing animals in a zoo, jabbering away in Somali. A fourth face appeared, a new one. Hardly fat, but fuller than the others, better fed and if his headgear was anything to go by better clothed too. He said nothing. He just looked. A rope was thrown down. A rope with a loop tied at the bottom. A loop too small to fit over a man's head but large enough to accommodate a foot. Richard Bell grasped the rough hemp firmly with both hands and placed his right foot into the loop. Minutes later both he and Parish were sitting upon the deck hands clasped behind their necks under the muzzles of their captors' Kalashnikovs.

Despite their predicament this was a major improvement in the comfort stakes. Fresh air, sunshine and an opportunity to see where they were; some kind of barge, grounded on a sandbank at the edge of a wide, sluggish, dirty brown river. As far as the eye could see the landscape was stunted scrubland, arid and empty with no geographical features other than the river. They were in the middle of nowhere.

Fuller Face spoke in English, fluent but with a trace of the transatlantic. 'I must apologise for the accommodation. Not what you are used to I am sure. However, with your cooperation the matter can soon be resolved and you can return to your former lifestyle and get on with your business, whatever it may be.'

'How much?' Bell asked.

'I see you are a businessman,' said Fuller Face, 'I like your directness. I am sure we can solve this little matter swiftly.'

'How much?' Bell repeated.

'Five hundred thousand dollars. American dollars,' stressed the well-fed man in the sweeping Persil-white robe and turban, his mouth widening to a grin, revealing extensive and expensive gold capped dental engineering.

'Two hundred and fifty-thousand,' said Bell deadpan. He had expected the demand to be at least double.

'A businessman with a sense of humour, I like that. Most amusing. There is too much gloom in this world today. We need more people like you. It would be a shame if you were...' His voice trailed away, the sentence unfinished, though the implication was clear.

'Two hundred and fifty-thousand,' said Bell.

'For Christ's sake, Richard,' Parish squealed, 'It's only money. You said you had...'

'Shut the fuck up,' said Bell glaring at his companion. 'I know what...'

'Your friend is right,' interrupted fuller face. 'It is only money and you are in no position to bargain with me, when it is I as you say, that holds all the cards.'

'Yes, and you'll be playing Solitaire for peanuts if anything happens to us,' Bell replied. 'We are worth nothing to you dead.' He knew there was a deal to be done. Haggling was in these people's blood. They expected it, respected those who entered into the spirit of the negotiations. Bell was in his element. He lived to do deals, the higher the stakes the better he liked it. These were the highest stakes he had ever seen on the table and the adrenalin rush topped every sensation he had ever experienced. Richard Bell was skydiving on acid, with no idea if his parachute would open.

Fuller Face turned to the skinny kid in the red Coke T-shirt. He spoke to him in Somali. A couple of short, sharp sentences. Red T-shirt nodded. Careful not to give any indication of comprehension, Bell translated the gist of the one-way conversation in his head. He swallowed hard as he gasped the gist. Fuller Face gestured towards the hatch. The rope was produced again and the prisoners were dragged to their feet.

'Tell you what,' said Bell, 'you were right about the accommodation. It is not up to the standard we are used to. Now I can see local resources are limited, but I must say the air up here on deck is much more agreeable, not to mention the view. If you could see your way clear to an upgrade? Shall we say twenty-five thousand?'

'Fifty thousand.'

Bell nodded..

A broad smile swept across Fuller's face. 'Each,' he demanded, a twinkle in his eye. Fuller Face, or Cawaale, AKA Lucky, for that was surely who he must be, was now clearly enjoying the game.

'Naturally,' agreed Bell, smiling inwardly at his small but significant victory. Escape was out of the question. Where would they go? Without water in that barren landscape they wouldn't last five minutes and their captors knew it. To ensure a supply of water they would have to stick to the river making re capture inevitable. No they couldn't escape, but at least they could be relatively more comfortable and Bell was not done yet. 'How about some shade up here?' he enquired. 'Sheet or a Tarp we could use? We Europeans have delicate skin you know. And some water?'

The man laughed aloud. 'You are a funny man, I like you.' He spoke to one of the Somali gunmen who nodded and disappeared towards the wheelhouse. There will be a cost you understand?'

'Let me guess,' said Bell, now smiling also. 'Fifty-thousand?'

'You are very perceptive. Fifty thousand each, makes another one hundred...'

'That makes four hundred and fifty-thousand,' said Bell.

'You are forgetting the fees and disbursements, my friend.'

Bell almost laughed out loud. *Lawyers. Thieving bastards.* 'Let me take a wild guess. Fifty-thousand?'

'Such insight. Remarkable, truly remarkable. It is a pleasure to be doing business with you my friend.' Cawaale walked away towards the wheelhouse and spoke to one of the Somalis.

The gunman went inside and came out again with not one, but two cheap, woven plastic tarpaulins and a dirty grey blanket. He also had a handful of odds and sods of lengths of twine and the ubiquitous goatskin bag of tepid water. They were moved to the stern, where in less than ten minutes they had a low roofed shelter nine feet by nine secured to the rusty guard rail and the back of the wheel house. It was high enough to sit upright under in relative comfort and the slight breeze blowing over the water helped to cool the space beneath. Besides the obvious benefits of remaining on deck there was the possibility of overhearing conversations between their captors and any information Bell could harvest might prove useful later on. They seemed happy to talk openly, assuming not unnaturally, that their prisoners would be unable to understand. Bell had never been fluent in the language but in years of working and living alongside

Somali sailors in the close confines of small ships he had picked up more than enough to get by.

Charles Parish said. 'What about the others? What's happened to them?'

'Your little playmates you mean? What do you think? God you are naive. How the hell did you get a job in…'

'For fuck's sake, Richard, keep your voice down.'

'Relax. Just worry about yourself. There's nothing we can do about the others.'

Cawaale returned to the prisoners. 'You will write a letter,' he said, 'to your business associates, bankers or whoever, asking for the money – in cash of course. Twenty-dollar bills and smaller. I will tell you what to write.' He handed Bell the paper and a pencil and began dictating. It was short and to the point. Addressee details and a few crisp sentences. *Too short* Bell thought.

'How are we going to deliver the money?' he asked his jailer.

'You do not need to concern yourself with the details, not for the moment.'

'Your English is excellent,' Bell remarked, hoping to appeal to the man's vanity. 'Where did you learn?'

The man puffed out his chest, 'UCLA, California,' he said, before he could stop himself. 'I studied law.'

How ironic, thought Bell. The man had more in common with his prisoners, if indeed they were his prisoners, than he had with the jailers.

'We can do no more today,' said Cawaale. 'Tomorrow we take a little trip, but until then I shall bid you farewell.' He gestured to the freaky one in the Coke T-shirt and after a brief exchange he walked over the wobbly, makeshift gangplank and disappeared into the scrub on the bank.

Coke T-shirt shouted at the other jailers who produced two sets of leg irons. These were obviously originally black, but mostly now they were red rusty, battered but still serviceable. Probably genuine relics from the slave trade thought Parish as he resigned himself to his fate. Not too far away in the bush a diesel engine coughed into life followed by the sound of gears meshing and hard rubber grabbing gravel and dirt.

'I was wondering how he got here,' said Bell, as the manacles clicked shut around his ankles. 'Well, Charles, at least we have fresh air and shade.'

'Thanks to you, my boy, I shouldn't have doubted you.'

'That's right you shouldn't. I know my job and I am damn good at it.'

Charles simply sighed 'I just want to go home.'

Ignoring his fellow prisoner's moan Bell continued. 'This guy's been brought in to negotiate after the fact. He's no mastermind behind a plot. This is a crime of opportunity, spur of the moment piracy. They didn't think it through.'

'You think so?'

'Sure of it. These dick-heads saw a way to make a load of money fast and went for it. The problem with kidnapping, Charles, is getting the ransom money delivered without getting caught. Now that is real tricky, even for a well-educated clever lawyer. A gang of ill educated, dirt-poor, fishermen cum-would-be-pirates? Forget it. This lot couldn't organise an orgy in a brothel.' Bell was back to his old confident self again. 'Piece of cake dealing with these fucking peasants. Lucky was a pushover. Thinks too much of himself, that one. Don't you worry, Charles, I promised I'd get us out of here and I will. You can count on it.'

8

Monday 22nd June
Somalia

Sleeping on deck was not the improvement that Bell had hoped for and he was not sure if he had made a wise move. The leg irons were heavy and cumbersome, uncomfortable and a damned nuisance, but they weren't the main problem. The problem was lighter than a feather, so light that you would need highly specialised laboratory equipment to determine its weight. Anopheles arabiensis, common throughout Somalia, was one of around four hundred and sixty insects of the Anopheles Genus, of which only around thirty to forty commonly transmit Malaria to humans. Anopheles arabiensis was one of these. Parish and Bell did not have the luxury of Mosquito nets to protect them, nor did they have access to Mepacrine, Quinine or any other anti Malarial drugs. Their night was a restless round of relentless, irritating, blood sucking and by the morning they were covered in swollen red bites, dog tired, ill tempered and feeling lower than a viper's belly. Rotten fish was on the breakfast menu. Both declined, settling for stale tepid water from the goatskin. They had hardly woken up from what little sleep they had managed to snatch when an engine could be heard, growing louder until it sounded like a bag of bolts in a spin dryer.

Ten minutes later they were bouncing around on the load bed of an old pick up, still in leg irons, but now also wearing blindfolds. Hessian grain sacks for hoods completed the ensemble. Their hands were bound behind their backs with coarse twine that creased and cut into the skin. Bell couldn't help but wonder if Charles Parish was getting a hard on. 'Fucking hell,' he said as the truck hit a rut, slamming the hard metal deck against his back, making his eyes water. Bashed, battered and bruised by every bone jarring bounce, Bell was begging for it to end a good half an hour before it did. When the pick up finally stopped he was angry. As he lay gasping for breath, sucking in air through the coarse fibrous sacking over his parched cracked lips, he swore that what ever it took, however long, no matter the cost, these men would suffer.

Hands, bony fingers, nails digging into the mozzie-bitten skin of his upper arms, dragging him from the back of the truck over the tailgate and onto the ground. Choking dust burning his throat, stinging his eyes. No words. Total silence; except for the distant sounds of bleating animals, which Bell could only guess to be goats. Manhandled over the dry dirt he was dragged through a wooden doorway. He knew it was wooden from the sound and feel of his elbow scraping across the rough splintered surface as they bundled him inside and dumped him upon what felt like a pile of sacks. The place smelled of livestock. Off came the bag, blindfold and bindings. He blinked and rubbed at his wrists to try to restore circulation. Sitting upon a stool four feet away was Fuller Face. His spotless robes looked out of place against the dirty mud walls of the hovel. Other than the chair there was no furniture at all, in fact the room contained little other than a hoe, spade and broken pieces of what once might have been a primitive plough; that and a stack of grain sacks upon which Bell found himself. A military style field telephone, was sitting in the middle of the dirt floor.

'Water,' he said.

'On the floor beside you,' Fuller Face said, 'We are not uncivilised, despite what your western prejudices may have you believe.'

Bell looked down at the pitcher. A metal ladle hung from its rim. He drank greedily.

'Your friend also is drinking. You do not ask of him? You do not ask of your crew or your other guests. You are not I think, a man who cares much for other than himself.'

'Spare me the moral lecture; what you think is of no concern to me. You want me to make a phone call right? So let's get on with it.'

'Write the name and number on this piece of paper,' Fuller Face said passing a pencil and a crumpled sheet of paper torn from a note book.' Bell complied, eager to move the process on towards a conclusion. The man took the sheet back then cranked a handle on the side of the canvas cased device. He lifted the receiver and spoke. There was no dial, no push buttons. He spouted Somali down the line to some operator in some exchange in some city somewhere, probably hundreds of miles away. After an agonising wait the man began nodding his head and then reached into his robe and pulled out another sheet of paper. He passed it to Richard Bell. It was the letter he had dictated the day before.

'Read only what is on the paper. Say anything else and you will regret it. Understand?'

Cawaalle squatted next to the telephone and picked up the receiver. After a short wait he spoke into it to some operator as far as bell could make out. There was a long wait and finally he spoke again. 'Mister Harmon, good day to you. I am representing the interests of your client, Mr. Richard Bell, who speaks highly of you. You are his Mister Fixit I understand. Now time is of the essence so I need you to concentrate.' Fuller Face held the receiver away from his ear as a torrent of audible abuse poured into the atmosphere.

Fuller Face barked a command. The door opened. A skinny face with an AK walked in and pointed the rifle at Bell's head. Fuller held the receiver out to Bell. 'Tell him to be quiet and listen to me.'

'Nigel…'

'Richard, where the hell are you? We've been worried….'

'For Christ's sake, Nigel, shut up and listen to the man. I've got a gun in my face. Yes, dammit; a gun. He'll use it too – these boys aren't kidding. Look they just want money okay? You need to get a fix on this understand?'

Cawaale removed the receiver from Bell's face. The rest of the conversation was strictly one way and Harmon was the passive partner. Cawaale moved the receiver back to Bell.

'Nigel, just listen. I need you to concentrate. I want you to get $500,000, in the next seventy-two hours. No police, tell no one, repeat no one. Have you got that?' The line was a little crackly but he was pretty sure he'd got through. Just to make certain, He asked Nigel Harmon to repeat it all slowly.

Bell pictured the smart Soho offices of Harmon and Goldstein, Nigel Harmon taking a call on his private direct line, the one that by-passed his super efficient secretary. The one that rang rarely and then only when trouble was brewing. He wouldn't need to ask who was calling. Only one person had access to the number, the man who paid for its installation, line rental and calls. The same man who paid Nigel Harmon to manage all his financial affairs; paid him handsomely on the understanding that he would weave his money magic at a moment's notice and not ask any unnecessary questions. *Now earn your money,* thought Bell.

He passed the receiver to Cawaale. 'Remember Mister Harmon no fancy tricks, tracking devices, exploding dyes or such. Do exactly as you are told and your people will be returned unharmed. I will call you in two days. You will wait for the call. Remember lives depend upon your discretion.' He replaced the receiver.

Bell had enough time for a quick drink of water from the pitcher before the blindfold and hood were pulled back on and he was bound and dragged out to the truck for another two hours of torture, banging around on the load bed.

'That you, Richard?' Parish called out as a body was dumped on his legs.

'Who were you expecting, Kylie Minogue?'

Parish ignored the question. 'What's going on? What's happening? Did you get any water? They gave me water. Hood off but kept the blindfold on. I was damn thirsty. This bloody heat. How do people live here? How ...?'

'Calm down, Charles, who gives a shit? I've been booking us a flight out of this hell hole.' Bell filled his companion in with the details before mercifully, against all odds they both fell asleep from sheer exhaustion. They woke frequently as the suspension fought with the worst ruts but they soon succumbed again.

9

Skelter sat in the briefing room with the rest of the troop as he had on numerous previous occasions. He was not expecting much. Most potential operations started out like this only to be cancelled at some point along the line, often without any reason being given. The squadron commander entered and addressed the men.

'Good morning, gentlemen. We have a developing situation in the Indian Ocean, off the coast of Kenya. As of now Boat Troop is on forty-eight hours standby until further notice. Captain Thompson will fill you in on what scant details we have.'

A bespectacled intelligence officer that Skelter did not recognise stepped up to the lectern. He pressed a button on the remote and the first image filled the screen. It showed a large luxury yacht moored at a jetty with palm trees in the background.

'Five days ago this vessel left the Seychelles for Mombasa in Kenya with a crew of eight and it is believed, four passengers, including the owner. Radio contact was lost on the second day out. Forty-eight hours ago the boat was located drifting and abandoned, by an RAF Nimrod. A boarding party from a Royal Navy Frigate has searched the vessel and subsequently confirmed that there was no one aboard.' The projector whirred and the image was replaced by one of a man in a suit with a bundle of papers under his arm.

'Charles Parish, MI6, special advisor to the Cabinet on counter Terrorism; one of the passengers.' The next image appeared. 'Richard Bell, the yacht's owner; multimillionaire entrepreneur and a major financial supporter of the government.' A murmur of understanding spilled from Skelter's lips as the sensitive nature of the situation began to unfold. 'The other two passengers are believed to be young women employed by Mister Bell as…' There was a slight pause, 'cocktail waitresses, in his London nightclub.' This caused a ripple of mirth from the troop. 'Blood was found on the starboard rail and three cartridge cases have been recovered from the deck. Seven point six two by thirty-nine, Chinese manufacture, almost certainly from an AK47. We have no intelligence at this time as to the whereabouts or condition of the missing passengers and crew. We have to assume they have been abducted by persons unknown. The yacht's rigid inflatable is missing. The motive is most likely political, possibly to negotiate a prisoner exchange for terrorists we have in our jails. However we are keeping an open mind. The most likely source of our problem is Somalia. There is an operational file here for you with all the information we currently have. It will be updated as a priority one as and when information becomes available. Any questions?'

'What information do we have about the crew?' asked Lieutenant Glass, the new twenty-four year old troop commander.

'There are profiles of all crew members and passengers, in the file. Everything we know, including photographs where we have them. There are a few gaps I am afraid, but we *are* working on them.'

There were no other questions.

'Thank you, Captain,' said the squadron commander, once more taking centre stage. 'Gentlemen, as of now we do not know when, how or even if, you will be deployed but I know you will give this little problem your full attention. We may have an opportunity to win friends in Downing Street, which can only do us good. We should have an update later this afternoon after the COBRA meeting. Nothing you have heard leaves this room, gentlemen. Nothing is to be discussed with anyone not directly involved in this operation. Nothing, is that clear?'

A ripple of 'Sirs' fluttered back in reply.

'One more thing. Lieutenant Glass, Sergeant Skelter, report to my office after the briefing.'

'Sir,' Skelter and Glass replied in unison.

'Tenner says we don't go,' said Biscuit, troop pessimist.

'Biscuit, you little twat, what's with the negativity all the time?'

'Listen, Tash, I'm a realist. We never go do we? I mean when was the last time we went? We train 'til we can do the business in our sleep. We get put on stand by, we train some more, we train harder, get wound up tighter than a clock-spring and then what? We get stood down. That's what. The gig gets cancelled. That's the way it is.'

'We've got to go sometime mate – law of averages.'

'Don't hold your breath,' muttered Biscuit under his.

'Right lads, listen in,' said Lieutenant Glass. 'I know we still have to get to know one another, but a live operation could be the perfect opportunity. I am new to Special Forces so I will be looking to you senior NCOs for guidance. I am not new to soldiering. I have been in the infantry for five years.'

'Hark at young Fragile,' said Biscuit under his breath,'

'We don't have much to go on,' continued Glass, 'but we can make a start by checking all equipment and drawing up a list of kit we might need.'

'Talk about University of the pissing obvious,' Biscuit mumbled.

'Give it a rest you whinging ginger Jock,' hissed

lance corporal Tash Tasker.

'I'm only saying...'

'We heard you,' said Tasker.

Even sat down, the Lancastrian lance corporal towered above the squat Scot.

'Speak up, Corporal McVitie,' said Lieutenant. Glass, 'feel free to share your constructive ideas with the rest of the Troop.'

Despite the offer Biscuit declined to expand.

Skelter stood at ease beside Lieutenant Peter Glass in front of the squadron commander's desk. Major Collingwood looked a little uptight. 'I've just had the PM's office on the blower. Cobra meeting at four o'clock this afternoon. I want you both to attend with me. This is a serious crisis for our lords and masters and the PM has accepted my suggestion that it would save a lot of time if you could sit in as observers and get everything straight from the horse's mouth as it were. Helicopter from the parade ground in one hour. Any questions?'

'Sir? Dress, sir?' said Glass.

'As you are, man, the rumour mill can do without the lads seeing you in number twos flying off in the middle of an op.'

Collingwood looked at Skelter, who remained tight lipped. 'One hour. Dismissed.'

10

4 pm Monday 22nd June
10 Downing Street, London

Dominating the room was a massive table surrounded by plush, green leather swivel chairs. Seated down one side were representatives from the Ministry of Defence, Foreign and Home Offices, Joint Terrorist Analysis Centre and Special Branch. Facing them across the polished hardwood were spooks from MI5, MI6, the Joint Intelligence Group and GCHQ; a full turnout reflecting the gravity of the situation. Beneath the fine grained English oak a maze of wires ran the full length of the table connecting individual monitors in front of each member, carrying live feeds to his or her office support teams. Looking down upon the gathering the wall from TV screens at the end of the table were members of various agencies in overseas stations, the only clue to where being the tropical palm trees visible next to the Mosque in the background of one of them. Skelter and Glass sat on either side of Major Collingwood. It was a new experience for both of them.

A deep frown creased the prime minister's brow as he settled somewhat uncomfortably into his seat. COBRA meetings, not exactly a daily occurrence, are by their nature cause for concern. The rumour mill was grinding slow on this occasion and no one seemed to have a clue what was up. Seated at the right hand of the prime minister, slowly twirling a pencil through his fingers, a serious looking fifty something suit chewed his bottom lip, while on his left a senior Foreign Office civil servant chaired the meeting. The pencil twirler's aquiline nose supported lightweight half frame spectacles, from behind which, pinpoint pupils switched from TV to delegates, to monitor and back with the speed and focus of an owl searching for prey.

The hum of voices and the shuffling of papers as the committee members slid into their respective seats while exchanging snippets of news, evaporated like brandy on a crêpe suzette the minute the prime minister entered the room.

'To business,' he announced without pre amble. 'What news? Clockwise from me if you please.'

There was precious little until it came to the last quadrant, which included the Secret Intelligence Service and GCHQ. What they had between them was not much.

'There is one small glimmer of hope,' said a spokesman for Parish's section, 'Charles has a portable Magellan GPS and we know he took it with him on holiday. The good news is that despite a targeted thorough search, no trace of it had been found aboard the yacht. The bad news is that no signal had been traced, which probably means that the instrument is switched off. Charles would have activated it if he was able, but if he still has it then it is possible he might yet find a way of activating it.'

'For God's sake is that the best you can come up with?' said the PM 'That's not just thin it's transparent. It could be at the bottom of the ocean for all we know. Even if he still has it until it's switched on it's as much use as an ashtray on a motorcycle. The abductors may well have found it and wrecked it.' The PM shook his head from side to side, his face a mask of displeasure. 'What about agents in the area?' he asked. 'What assets do we have?'

Skelter watched as a pencil twirling, grey haired, grey suit rose to his feet and looking over the top of his half frame spectacles pointed a laser towards the bank of monitors. 'We have a man in Mombasa who has contacts in southern Somalia, Prime Minister, but since we can only guess the whereabouts of our missing people it does not help much. Our best guess as to their location, based on time and distance from the Yacht's final position and the assumption that the kidnappers will have made for the nearest landfall, is here.' The large screen-wall flickered into life showing a map of East Africa. The red dot danced along the coast as the image zoomed in to the border region between Kenya and Somalia and then gradually morphed into a full satellite image. 'The area we are interested in covers one hundred miles of coastline from the Kenyan border north up to and including the city of Kismayo. The port of Kismayo is three hundred and twenty-eight miles south of Mogadishu, on the mouth of the Jubba River, population one hundred and eighty thousand. As you will no doubt be aware the region is in a state of civil war with a number of factions using armed force to pursue their own personal agenda. The main player is the SPM – Somali Patriotic Movement, who control the whole of the south of the country. However the SDM and SDF cannot be entirely ruled out.' The map changed to a simple outline, which divided the country into no fewer than ten different coloured areas. 'Their territories border the Northwest. As you can see the country is littered with tribal factions. Our worst-case scenario is that our people are somewhere in the middle of this urban sprawl. If they are, even if we locate them, getting them out will present a considerable challenge.'

The aerial view tracked south down the coast towards Kenya revealing mile after mile of arid scrubland with little sign of habitation save for the odd collection of half to a dozen huts, sparsely populating a few of the numerous small islands that ran like a broken necklace close to the sandy shoreline. There were only three other significant features.

'Notice the three rivers. These are the other favourites as hiding places for our suspects. They are the only sources of fresh water in the region which is dry for most of the year. Having said that more than half the annual rain falls between the beginning of May and the end of June. We are in the rainy season, but this year has been exceptional and they have not had much at all as yet.'

'Thank you,' said the PM 'What about our military assets Colonel Greaves? Is there anything we can do now?'

Greaves remained seated stroking his moustache with an air of deep concentration upon his craggy face. 'I have spoken to Colonel Baines at SAS HQ in Hereford this morning. They have put B Squadron on standby.' He nodded to Collingwood, 'My colleague Major Collingwood will be happy to answer any questions regarding B Squadron's involvement. They are being fed all the intelligence as we gather it. Might I suggest we send an advance party to the area to get acclimatised and put eyes on the ground? We have access to a Kenyan army training facility close to the border, which the SAS have used before. It is discreetly located and well equipped. There is an airstrip nearby which can take light aircraft up to the size of a Skyvan.'

'See to it will you, Geoffrey?' The colonel nodded. 'Better make sure you have a Skyvan in place,' added the PM as an afterthought.

Geoffrey Greaves, put his hand over the mic, *'Teach me my fucking job why don't you,'* he said, half under his breath, just loud enough for Skelter to catch while at the same time nodding compliance, before punctuating with *'Cretin.'*

The PM spoke, oblivious to the colonel's mutterings. 'Unless anyone has anything else I shall declare the meeting closed. Timed at five thirty-seven. Gentlemen and Ladies, we will reconvene at eight o'clock tomorrow morning, unless anything develops in the meantime. Thank you for your attention.

11

7.30 pm Monday 22nd June
SAS HQ Stirling Lines, Hereford

The Gazelle landed on the parade ground at half past seven. 'I hope that was useful,' said Collingwood as soon as they had de-bussed and were far enough away to be heard above the engine noise.

'Most illuminating,' said Glass. Skelter nodded.

'Good, I have a couple of phone calls to make. Drop by my office in say, twenty minutes will you, Sergeant?'

'Yes sir.' *Drop by my office? What's that all about?* thought Skelter, *bit informal.* 'If you will excuse me sir, I must check on the lads.'

Collingwood nodded.

Skelter doubled away across the parade ground. He needn't have worried Biscuit had everything organised. They had drawn up kit lists, sorted most of the normal admin crap and were discussing what extras each would take in their rations so they could raid the shelves at Sainsburys.

Skelter stood outside the Squadron commander's office, adjusted his beret and checked his boots for shine. Balancing on each leg in turn he wiped the dust from the toecaps on the backs of his combats, then, satisfied he could do no more, he rapped on the door. 'Enter,' said a voice from within. Skelter turned the knob and stepped through the entrance, marched the three paces to Major Collingwood's desk, stamped to attention and threw up a sharp salute. The major ran a hand over his chin as if deciding whether he was in need of a shave. He had an air of vagueness about him, a carefully cultivated air designed to camouflage a keen sense of awareness and acute observational skills, honed over many years of close surveillance work in Northern Ireland and other trouble spots around the globe. 'Sit down, Sergeant, relax. Informal chat, off the radar. Okay?'

'Yes, Sir.'

'Informal,' the major repeated.

'Okay, Boss,' Skelter replied.

'Lieutenant Glass, what do you think to him? On paper he is excellent, but he's fresh out of the wrapping. I know you haven't had much time to get to know him, but first impressions?'

'His record over selection was exemplary according to the guys on training wing and he certainly is focused. His manner seems fine, still feeling his way a bit, establishing his authority, but he doesn't put up with any nonsense. Firm but fair I'd say. I think he'll probably do okay Boss. More than okay.'

'But?'

'Boss?'

'There is always a but, H. I have known you too long, so come on, what's his Achilles heel?'

'The obvious one – never been under fire; never been across the water. Seems to have spent most of his career in Catterick. Not his fault I'm sure, but this job that's come up...'

'Yes. The job is something else I need to talk to you about. I want you to lead an advance party out to Kenya, to Camp Winston. We need eyes on the ground close to Somalia. The intelligence guys are convinced that is where the targets will be.'

Skelter knew that sending an advance party when no

one knew what was going on was more political than practical. The cabinet office would be screaming for the army to do something, anything. Yes, it had some merit – getting eyes on in the area was not a bad thing, even if the main purpose was to show the suits in Whitehall that things were happening and acclimatisation is always useful. The use of the word targets, rather than hostages, set a small alarm bell tinkling at the back of Skelter's brain.

'You understand,' Collingwood continued, 'how delicate this is, I'm sure. Charles Parish has a great deal of highly sensitive knowledge locked up inside his head. Knowledge that potentially can threaten the lives of many of our intelligence sources around the world. If that knowledge was to fall into the wrong hands?' Major Collingwood leaned forward across the desk interlocking the fingers of both hands as his brow took on the appearance of a ploughed field. 'Be in no doubt, Sergeant, we will find them, all the stops are out. The PM is driving this himself. Effecting a rescue however, may well prove challenging.'

Skelter now knew where this was going, but kept schtum.

'Whatever happens,' Collingwood continued, 'Charles Parish's knowledge must not fall into the wrong hands. I am clear on this one?'

'Crystal, Boss. Can I have your permission to poach Lofty Larcombe from D Squadron? I know he's out in Iraq but...'

A smile of recognition smoothed the ploughman's furrows from the major's brow. 'Perfect choice, H, Larcombe's father was head Ghyllie on our estate on Skye, a legend in the Highlands. He taught his son well. Nobody better in The Regiment for this job. I will see to it.'

'Thanks Boss.'

'You fly out tomorrow from Lyneham. Corporal Larcombe will be at Winston to welcome you. With full kit, you have my word.'

The major rose from his chair and walked around to the front of the desk. He held out his hand as Skelter got to his feet. 'Good luck.' Skelter grasped the hand and shook it firmly, 'I know I can depend on you and your team.' A deliberate pause, a barely perceptible nod. 'This conversation never took place, Sergeant.'

'Sir, Lieutenant Glass?'

'Don't worry about your troop commander; I will see that he doesn't interfere. You are free to get on with your job, Sergeant. Any problems, refer him directly to me.'

'Sir.'

Turning smartly on his heels Skelter exited the office and headed briskly for the pay phone in the accommodation block. He thought about using his mobile but the cost put him off. He was not happy at the way Lucy and he had parted. He wanted to explain his clumsiness. Not responding to her kiss. It was just embarrassment. He was new to the dating thing There was no answer from Lucy's number. He called Rollo's house. Wilkins answered, but Lucy was not there either. He left a message, which Wilkins promised to pass on at the earliest opportunity. He thanked him, replaced the receiver and went to find Tash and Biscuit and give them the good news.

The boys were in the training room, studying the contents of the folders with the rest of the guys from the troop. The room was hardly crowded but it wasn't oozing space either. There were twelve men in the troop excluding the commander. Skelter caught the attention of Tasker and McVitie and discretely told them to meet him in his billet, before leaving the room.

Skelter's quarters were hardly palatial but at least he had a space he could call his own, a bed, desk – complete with ancient angle-poise lamp, a double wardrobe and bedside locker. He had a kettle, tap to fill it and a sink in which to wash the mug, his face, hands and any other part of his anatomy he cared to and to clean his teeth over. There were two chairs. One was an old dark bentwood with a round seat, the other a more modern, light, beech-wood framed piece, lifted from someone's kitchen. Biscuit bagged the beech while Tasker perched his lanky frame on the bed. The bentwood was already occupied. 'Push the door to, Biscuit, you can smoke if you want to,' said Skelter, opening a notebook and scanning through the most recent entries.

McVitie complied without rising from the chair, while at the same time taking cigarette packet from his cargo pocket.

'Okay lads,' Skelter continued as Biscuit lit up, 'this is the latest. We will be out of here, when I say we; I mean us three, in less than twenty-four hours. Destination Camp Winston, Kenya. We've been before so you know the drill. If you want to make any calls to family you will be away for around a month, usual story, training course, you know the score. As you know Taff is still on crutches recovering from his operation. His replacement, or should I say replacements, will join us at Winston.'

'Any idea who that will be, H?' Tasker asked.

'Lofty Larcombe and he'll have Turbo Thompson with him.'

'Turbo. That's brilliant,' said Biscuit, who in the words of Tash Tasker "was long on attitude and short on altitude." He would now have someone he could look down upon, in the physical sense at least. On the doorframe of the quartermaster's stores a series of lines were marked in black felt tip, starting at the top with one marked six feet six inches and followed downward at two inch intervals until it reaches one at five feet six inches then three inches below that there is another mark simply labelled TURBO. Talking to Tasker was giving Biscuit a permanent crick in his neck and Lofty was even taller, but

Turbo; Turbo was the opposite end of the spectrum.

'I understand Lofty has a bit of a rep as a sniper?' said Tash.

'Bit of a rep? He a fucking legend,' said Biscuit. 'When he went down to Lympstone on the Royal Marines sniper course they couldn't teach him anything. He out stalked all the instructors, out shot them too.'

'How'd he manage that?'

'Ghyllie's son, raised in the Highlands, on one of the biggest estates in Scotland. Shadowed his father up and down the glens since he was a bairn. Soon as he could walk. Big ugly bugger he is, six feet four, and yet he can make himself invisible. Lofty is magic with camouflage. When it comes to taking a shot if he touches the trigger the target's toast.'

Skelter was happy with the mix, all three men had worked together a number of times, on live operations where on at least two occasions the proverbial had hit the fan. They were rock steady and reliable. 'We've got little idea what we're up against,' Skelter confessed, 'and speculation at this point is pointless. All we can do is prepare for all eventualities. We have a bright green light on kit. You can draw anything you feel you might need. This comes all the way from the head shed in Whitehall, I am reliably informed.'

Tash gave a low whistle. 'That big?'

'That big,' Skelter confirmed. 'Questions?' There were one or two, which Skelter answered to the satisfaction of both men. Five minutes later they dispersed to prepare for the move.

The next few hours were spent drawing kit. Emergency rations; radios; batteries; binos and listening devices; camera kit and cam cream, mepacrine; medic packs; and mozzie repellant. There were personal weapons to be issued, night vision goggles and heavier stuff, all to be listed, checked, manifested, signed for and palleted, ready for transportation to RAF Lyneham. There were civvy bags to be packed too. R and R (Rest and Recreation) was always remote possibility after the job was complete, but more likely they might need civvies to operate covertly. If they needed to blend inx rather than play tourist then no doubt 'fancy dress costumes' would be available in theatre. Skelter went across to the intelligence boys to see if any update was available. There was nothing, disappointing but not unexpected. If there had been anything they would have found him. He knew that, but he couldn't resist checking. Next stop the armoury. Whatever the lads decided for themselves, Skelter wanted to add a little local colour to the mix. They needed to be as anonymous as possible so using Brit kit was not on, they must blend in. Somalia was a lawless tribal country where carrying weapons was not so much commonplace as compulsory, the weapon of choice being the AK47 assault rifle.

Mikail Timofeevitch Kalashnikov's brainchild, the most copied firearm in the world, with around one hundred million examples in circulation around the globe has just eight moving parts. Engineered to wide manufacturing tolerances meant it could be abused, misused and neglected, yet still kill at up to four hundred metres – even after total immersion in water. Simple to use, strip and clean, it took less than an hour to train a peasant to use one. The camp armoury had several examples available for issue, both Russian originals and Chinese and Pakistani copies. Skelter only needed five. Camp Winston had ammunition in abundance for these firearms. They had AKs too but Skelter did not want to leave anything to chance. He needed well-serviced weapons he could rely on.

It was two forty-five when Skelter finally crashed out, but he didn't get to sleep right away. He lay on his back staring at the blistered paint on the ceiling, running through everything he had done in the past few hours, checking and re-checking, mentally ticking boxes. He was also worried whether his supply of Valium would last. He always kept a good two-week supply as backup, plus the three weeks he picked up from the wall in the churchyard so he should be okay. He was always anxious however, as to how he might cope if he ran out. As if that was not enough he ran an endless loop video through his head, rehearsing possible near future scenarios, calculating options and outcomes until finally his brain gave up and allowed him to slip away.

12

Tuesday 23rd June

The PM looked tired and he was not the only one. It had been a long fruitless night. The Security Services had been working around the clock, checking in with overseas stations, desperate for any scrap of information that might help narrow the search for the hostages. In Cheltenham, GCHQ computers monitoring telephone calls were being reprogrammed to look for new combinations of trigger keywords. Yacht, Parish, Bell and so forth being added to the mix.

The Security Services had nothing. No group had claimed responsibility for the kidnapping, no demands received, no anything.

'So what you are telling me,' said the PM, 'is that we can be reasonably certain that the hostages are somewhere in southern Somalia. Beyond that you haven't got a clue?'

The grey haired, grey suit looked over the top of his half frame spectacles and nodded. 'This assumes that they have not been transported by air, which although highly unlikely, cannot be ruled out. If the terrorists had access to a light aircraft or helicopter, then we are looking at a much larger search area.'

A nine-minute cab ride away from the Cobra meeting, at the offices of Harmon and Goldstein, Nigel Harmon loosened his tie and undid the top button on his hand tailored shirt. It wasn't hot. He was on his direct line, making urgent final arrangements to have half a million dollars in cash made available for collection from The Chase Bank in Mombasa. He had already booked a flight from Heathrow to Mombasa, in the name of Caroline Warren, Richard Bell's Personal Assistant; his longest serving and most trusted employee. Harmon would have preferred to oversee the delivery himself but he had to remain to take instructions from the kidnappers. Caroline was the obvious choice. She had too much emotional investment in Richard Bell to let him down. What she saw in creep like Bell was a complete mystery to Harmon. Smart, savvy, sexy and single, she could have her pick. What was it about some women that attracted them to men like Bell?

It was raining steadily in Hereford as the convoy passed through the main gate at Stirling Lines and slinging it down by the time the first white van turned left onto Bath Street for the half mile stretch of the A438 before the roundabout, where they would take the exit for the A49. There were four vehicles; the second white van was low on its springs. The pallets in the back sat on floor, the each one over a manual pump truck pallet lifter. Their combined weight of two and a half tons was near the maximum payload for the Transit. The second white van was empty. Belt and braces; backup in case of mechanical failure. There was a plane to catch. At the wheel of an anonymous Range Rover in an unremarkable shade of grey as drab as the weather, Skelter spearheaded the convoy. Bringing up the rear was a blue Volvo V70 estate – an unmarked police escort in case some traffic officer wanted to stop the vehicles for spot checks or a speeding violation. There were two officers in the car. Both men were in plain clothes. Both carried Glock pistols. As if they were not sufficient, there were enough firearms distributed amongst the other vehicles to start a medium sized war.

Thankfully the journey passed without incident and no weapons were needed during the one hour and forty minutes it took to reach to RAF Lyneham. The police escort and the backup Transit peeled off at the gates, while the remaining two vehicles stopped for security. They were told where to report by a corporal with a clipboard and were on their way in ninety-seconds. The rain had stopped by the time they drove into the hanger, which was situated as far away from the main buildings as it was possible to get without getting too close to the boundary. The entrance was guarded by an RAF policeman with a sidearm and a big German Shepherd. Two members of the RAF Regiment, carrying SA80 assault rifles patrolled the perimeter.

Nigel Harmon was a man of many talents, at the centre of a spider's web of connections that reached right around the globe, which was why Richard Bell paid him so handsomely. He was Mr Fixit, with a capital F. He had an exemplary record in the field. The current crisis however, was a little off piste. Nonetheless, Nigel was up for the challenge. He made another call to Kenya, to a contact he had used twice before. The man had proved both discreet and reliable on each of those occasions. A short conversation followed, during which, Harmon related the bare bones of what he required. The voice at the other end asked two questions.

'Where is the drop to be made?' was the first.

'I only know approximately, they will give me a set of co-ordinates when they call next on Thursday. It will be somewhere around three miles off the Somali coast south of Kismayo.'

'When?'

'That I don't know, but I would guess Thursday.'

'Okay, leave it with me, I'll get back to you in an hour.'

Harmon put the phone down and buzzed through to his secretary. 'Could I have some coffee, Margaret, please? A pot would be nice. I could do with a dose of caffeine.'

At eleven thirty-two the call from Kenya came in. Less than an hour – Harmon was impressed. The fee was agreed, payment on delivery in US Dollars. All was in hand. The details were faxed to him within minutes of the call ending. Everything was running like snake-oiled clockwork.

It was Caroline Warren's habit to always let the phone ring at least four times before answering it. To appear available at such short notice was not good professional practice. Often she would answer, ask the caller to hold as she had a call on the other line and make them wait. She would then apologise and charm the hell out of whoever had actually called. Not this time; this time she snatched the receiver from its cradle.

'Nigel, any news?'

The only news concerned a plane ticket, a hotel and the Mombasa branch of the Chase bank.

'Caroline, did Richard have any guests staying with him on the Yacht?'

'You know I cannot comment on my employer's private arrangements, Mister Harmon. It would be unprofessional.'

'Look, Caroline, lives are at stake here and I could be sticking my neck out a long way. We both know the circles Mr. Bell moves in and the kind of people he entertains. There could be a sensitive issue here and I'm working blind.'

'I am so sorry, Mr. Harmon, but that is privileged information. I could lose my job. Speaking of which, reminds me, I have an urgent phone call to make. I must call Charles Parish's secretary. You know Charles, I believe. Didn't you meet last year at the do at the Dorchester? He is away on holiday at the moment. Somewhere warm and sunny I believe.' She could sense the frustration at the other end of the line from Nigel Harmon's loud sigh. 'I don't know what I have done with her number, I had it on a post-it somewhere, ah here we are. I get worse as I get older, Nigel,' she said. 'I have difficulty making out my own writing, now is that a five or a six. It's a six I think. Seven seven six four five eight, or is it seven seven five, no, seven seven six, that's it 776 458, Sorry, Nigel, nerves you know. You will let me know the minute you have any news?'

'Of course. I'm sending your plane ticket and hotel details around by courier now,' said Harmon, scribbling the number on the palm of his hand while cradling the receiver between his neck and shoulder.

High above a remote pass in the Kurdish region of northern Iraq a tall, lean man with eyes like an eagle lay motionless on a sun scorched, windswept rocky outcrop. He was wearing desert pattern combat fatigues and smock. In his hands he held a pair of Bausch and Lomb twelve by twenty-four rangefinder binoculars. His spotter, corporal Turbo Thompson would normally be holding them, but he was busy decoding a priority message that had come over the radio minutes before.

Alongside the tall man, resting on its butt and bipod was an Accuracy International Sniper Rifle. Chambered for the .338 Lapua Magnum round, which gave the bolt action weapon an effective range of a shade under one mile. It had a magazine capacity of five rounds. This superb piece of British engineering was topped with a German Schmidt and Bender telescopic sight. The perfect mixed marriage.

'Good news, Lofty,' said the small man on the radio,

'we're leaving. We have precisely two hours and twenty-six minutes to get to the emergency RV for extraction by air.'

'Where are we off?'

'Fuck knows, but anything beats this,' replied Thompson.

'Aye right enough, we've been here how long, ten days? Seems more like weeks.'

'Yeah and we've seen what?'

'Four-fifths of five-eighths of precisely fuck all, that's what. C'mon let's get out of here.'

The two men began gathering up and stowing their gear, carefully avoiding exposing themselves to the area of observation, in case by some miracle someone did decide to show up at the last minute. When both men had packed their bergans they moved them three yards beyond the area they had been occupying for the last nine days, before painstakingly sanitising the area, removing every last trace of their occupancy, including the triple bagged former contents of their respective colons. They were a landlord's dream, always leaving each place exactly as they found it, right down to the direction in which the grass was bent; only on this occasion there was no grass. No vegetation of any kind, nothing but unforgiving, hard, dry, rock.

In a little under an hour the gear was loaded, Skelter, Tash and Biscuit, strapped into their seats and the C130 Hercules transport was taxiing out to the runway. Skelter checked his watch. Flight time to Kenya twenty-six hours. Another four hours to transfer to the camp. Allowing for the time difference, ETA at Winston was twelve thirty pm local time tomorrow, in time for lunch. Ideally they would have discussed tactics and gone through the intelligence files together in detail, but anyone who has ever flown in the cargo hold of a C130 knows that is not only impractical, but also almost impossible. The cargo space is cavernous, large enough to hold twenty tons of palletised freight, three light armoured vehicles or a couple of large lorries. At the front of the load area next to the bulkhead that divided it from the flight deck, sat the loadmaster. This was his man-cave. You could be a general, or an air vice marshall it made no difference. In here his word was law. Any shift in weight distribution had the potential to affect the flying characteristics of the aircraft. It was the loadmaster's job to ensure that did not happen. He wore bulbous head phones and a throat mic through which he communicated with the cockpit crew sitting feet away up on the flight-deck. Sound insulation in the back of a C130 would have been an unnecessary luxury. The empty space now reverberated with the noise of the four big turboprops as they wound up to take off pitch, each Allison engine thrusting out four thousand two hundred shaft horse power, the airframe vibrating to their tune as the Hercules gathered speed along runway until at ninety-eight knots it left the ground, climbing steeply into the grey overcast. The passengers all wore ear defenders, but they didn't completely eliminate the noise inside what was effectively a giant echo chamber separated from the engines by a few millimetres of aluminium.

A long whine announced the retraction of the landing gear, punctuated by a dull thump as the undercarriage doors closed. Noise levels eased a fraction as the pilot climbed to twenty-two thousand feet before levelling off and throttling back to cruising speed. They would be wearing the ear defenders until they reached the refueling stop in Cyprus. If they were lucky, they might get an hour's respite there. The biggest enemy for the next twenty-six hours was boredom. Tash's coping strategy was to sleep a lot, Skelter liked to listen to blues music on his Sony Walkman. The wires disappearing under the cushioning around the edges of Biscuit's ear defenders told Skelter he was not alone, but McVitie was more into Tammy Wynette than T-Bone Walker. They say it takes all sorts. All three had brought paperbacks.

13

Tuesday 23rd June

Lofty Larcombe shouldered his bergan, picked up his six point nine kilogram killing machine and followed Turbo Thompson along the goat track that wound westward down the mountain in the general direction of Baghdad. Trudging along with an all up load of thirty-five kilos, Lofty picked his way between the rocks. Because he had the radio kit, Turbo was carrying a similar load – more than a stone for each foot of his diminutive frame. Lofty, at six feet four, with almost twice the stride of his comrade, never ceased to be amazed at Turbo's prowess as a pack mule.

Plodding towards the emergency RV, sweeping left, right, front and rear for signs of potential danger, the pair moved in silence five metres apart. The views from their elevated position were spectacular and would have been worth the hike even if they were not under orders. Descending was in some ways harder than the climb had been. Turbo felt every step on the hard rocky trail as it jarred his joints, his knees in particular. Each step was purgatory. The load was at the limit of his capacity, but he gritted his teeth and kept going, still finding time to appreciate the scenery, which he was seeing for the first time. The ascent had been made in the dark and anyway, carrying a bergan uphill you are bent so far forward with the weight, all you can see is your boots. They were both looking forward to letting the helicopter take the strain and spare their aching legs. It would be a treat to ride to the next assignment the army had waiting for them. Whatever it was, it would be hard to beat the one they had left, in the boredom stakes.

At the same time as the C130 crossed the South coast, between Bexhill and Hastings, down on the ground one hundred and fifty miles to the Northwest, a telephone rang. Rollo took the call in his study where he was catching up with his mail, both electronic and paper.

'Henry, to what do I owe the pleasure?' Rollo's expression slowly changed from cheerful cycling through thoughtful; puzzled; concerned; perplexed; finally bottoming out at anxious. 'How reliable is your source?' Rollo asked. 'I see. You're sure?' There was an extended pause and then: 'Thank you, Henry, I am most grateful to you. No, of course not. Not a word, but keep me informed please, will you?'

The receiver clicked off as he replaced the handset. Rollo reached into the deepest desk drawer and took out a Waterford crystal tumbler and a bottle of Glen Livet.

Skelter dozed fitfully in the webbing and scaffold pole instrument of torture that the aircraft manufacturer described as a seat. Unable to get comfortable, he finally gave up. Biscuit was snoring his head off cocooned in his sleeping bag laid upon a rollout carry mat on the floor of the cargo hold. Skelter decided to follow Biscuit's example only he went one better, pulling a lightweight nylon mesh hammock from the side pocket of his bergan. Using karabiners he attached one end to the scaffold cross brace at the back of his seat the other end to the net sling at the top of the pallet. He looked across to the loadmaster who nodded and gave him the thumbs up. Unrolling his sleeping bag and laying it out in the hammock, Skelter climbed in and closed his eyes allowing himself the luxury of self-indulgence. He thought of Lucy. Wondering what she might be doing, wishing they had parted without a cloud hanging over them.

The water in the jam jar turned a darker shade of green as Lucy swirled the sable-hair and then rinsed the Winsor and Newton number two, watercolour brush in a jar of clean water. She studied the results of her labour with a critical eye, frowning at first then sliding into a smile. *Primula vulgaris*, the primrose, once a common sight alongside the backroads of Britain had all but disappeared, having been picked by generations of innocents until the banks and hedgerows where once it thrived had been purged. Lucy felt she had captured its essence. She only hoped the client would share her view, wondered what Mark would make of it. It had never occurred to her to show either of her previous boyfriends her work. For one thing they would not have been interested, but Mark seemed different – or was that wishful thinking? Whatever, his opinion mattered to her and that was something new. Boyfriend? Well, aside from the fact that at forty-four he was hardly a boy, she hardly knew him, and yet? Somehow she knew, or wished or felt she knew, that she wanted him in her life, despite the fact that she was still cross with him for his lacklustre response to her kiss. The look of hurt and disappointment on his face when she refused his plea for a second chance at it, went some way towards making up for it however. Maybe he was attracted to her, just nervous. She certainly hoped that was the case. The stomach churning, heart tumbling, tingling, induced by his proximity, she could feel even now in some small measure, just thinking about him, and that had never happened with any other man.

Rollo poured himself another Malt. The first had missed the sides on the way down. He was in a quandary. There was nothing he could do he knew that. Only wait for news, which was fine, he had faced this kind of thing many times before in the service of his country, but this was different. This was personal. The question was should he share the information? If he shared it with one he would have to share with the other. The answer was simple, first principal of security. They didn't need to know. Easy conclusion to reach when you are being professional and detached, not so easy when it is happening so close to home. What if it all went pear shaped and they found out afterwards that he'd known all along but hadn't told them? His life wouldn't be worth living. Oh he could make a solid enough case for keeping it to himself all right. Keeping quiet to avoid compromising the situation, making it worse, preserving what was precious. Playing God is how they would see it. Whichever way he looked at it, he was holding the shit end of the stick. He slowly sipped his whisky. No point in going anywhere. Better to stay by the phone and the computer.

Lofty and Turbo made the RV with twenty-eight minutes to spare. They settled down to wait, eyes wide alert, although there was little need. Turbo loosened the straps but sat with his bergan on as a backrest, his rifle across his knees. Lofty sat beside him but facing in the opposite direction so they covered three hundred and sixty degrees.

'What's next then, Loft?'

'Anyone's guess but it must be important to pull us off this job. Be great if it was somewhere more comfortable.'

'Armchair sniping you mean? In your dreams. Fiver says it's wet, cold and miserable.'

'Sorry, pal, but no takers. I hope I get a chance for a shower and some decent scoff before we're deployed, preferably off a proper china plate sitting at a table. I'm sick of eating of ration pack food tasting of aluminium, off my knees.'

'Shouldn't scrape the mess tin so hard with your spoon then should you, you big lummock?'

'Up yours, short-arse.'

'No need to get personal,' said Turbo, 'I'm only saying...'

'Save it. If I want to whinge I will. It's every soldier's right to whinge. It's historical.'

'Hysterical, more like. I'll settle for a couple of pints before we go back out in the field.'

'Couple? A skin full you mean.' Lofty shook his head. 'I don't know how you do it. Where the fuck do you put it all? If you had hollow legs they'd only hold half a pint a piece.'

Turbo let it sail over his head. 'Ever think what you might do when you pack the Army in?'

'I'm twenty-eight, knob head. You might be thinking about retirement, old man, but there's loads of life left in me yet.'

'Me too, thirty-seven isn't old it's just, well you know, this is a young man's game. It's like football and we're in the premier league. You can't carry on much past your thirties. I just think it pays to think ahead. Face it, pal, you may be the best sniper in The Regiment but there's not much call for your peculiar talent in civvy street. Anyway your lass'll want you to settle down eventually. She's a woman. They all do.' Turbo took a small green towel from the side pocket of his bergan and wiped the sweat from the back of his neck and his forehead, at the same time flexing his arms to unstick the shirt from his sweat-soaked back.

'So how come you never got married then?' said Lofty. 'Scared of the responsibility or what?'

'Had a shot at it once. Not marriage, living with a lass.'

'You never said.'

'You never asked.'

'I just assumed you liked playing the field. You spend enough time at it.'

'You're only jealous.'

'Not me, mate, Suzy's all the woman I need or ever will.'

'Pass the bleedin' sick bag,' said Turbo, miming projectile vomiting.

'Now who's jealous?'

Turbo seemed stuck for a riposte.

After several seconds silence Lofty asked. 'So what are you going to do when you're too old for The Regiment then?'

'Actually I have started seeing a lass,' said Turbo ignoring the question. 'Not too serious like but…'

'You dark horse. Do I know her?'

'She works behind the bar in The Barrels.'

'Not the blonde with buck teeth?'

'Cheeky twat. Janice, dark hair, real long, but she wears it up for work.'

'You're kidding. Little Janice? She's dead fit that one. Great legs. Well I'm buggered you little cradle snatcher. How long?'

'Couple o' months, give or take. Like I said, nowt serious like, not as yet anyway and she's thirty-two, if you must know.'

'No offence, she certainly doesn't look it. Sounds like you're keen. Good for you pal, about time you settled down, I hope it works out.'

'Cheers Loft.'

'So what will you do after the Army then?'

'Join the circuit I guess. Lot of money to be made on private security contracts, minding some rich B list Bimbo or guarding offshore oil rigs. Five years saving a shed load then buy a small bar on the Costa del Sol, I reckon.'

Lofty looked at his companion and slowly began shaking his head from side to side. 'You are kidding yourself. You know that don't you? Deep down. I mean you. A bar? You'd drink the place into the bankruptcy courts inside a year.'

'Your faith in me is touching,' Turbo said, brushing the insult aside as he squinted towards the eastern horizon. He raised the binoculars to his eyes, scrolling the wheel to focus on a speck in the cobalt distance. 'Taxi's here, Loft.'

The heli came in low and slow. It was a Russian built Mi8, drab dirty brown, no national markings, no airframe number, nothing to identify it beyond the type. The two men huddled together eyes and mouths shut, hands clamping hats to heads, backs to the dust cloud torn up by the rotors. A slick, sweet pick up. The pilot was good; the wheels hardly touched the ground. No words were exchanged between the two special forces' soldiers and the crew chief. Not for the whole hairy, winding, thirty minute flight, fast and low through the mountain pass and across the border into Turkey. Silence reigned all the way to the helipad at the northern end of the runway at Kavurma airport on the shores of Lake Van, where an RAF Learjet was waiting to take them the next seven hundred miles to Cyprus.

The two men looked at one another, at the jet and at one another again, both eyes wide. Lofty shrugged, Turbo rubbed his stubbly chin. *An executive jet? For the two of them?* This was getting more interesting by the minute. He reached into his bergan and pulled out a cylindrical aluminium flare tin. 'I'm having a cig before before I get on that plane,' he said, unscrewing the top and tipping out a lighter and a pack of Bensons. Fank fuck,' said Turbo, drawing hard on the coffin nail.

'When are you going to quit that filthy habit,' said Lofty. 'You know it can kill you?'

'Yeah? Just because the job doesn't come with a health warning, doesn't mean it's not dangerous. Think I should give that up?'

'Smart arse.'

Turbo finished his cigarette and stubbed it out on the lid of the tin, before putting the butt in his pocket. He shouldered his began and climbed aboard.

They had been hoping to get a shower and some hot scoff. What they got was a pack of wet wipes and a plain white cardboard box each containing ham and cheese sandwiches, an apple, banana and a bag of crisps. They did get comfortable reclining seats and hot coffee served by an RAF steward. A major improvement over their eagle's nest in the mountains and there was a flushing toilet. There were no complaints.

Lucy picked the two bags of groceries from the back seat of the Audi and nudged the car door shut with her hip. She plipped the lock and headed for the back door of the cottage. With some difficulty she managed to get the key in the lock without putting the bags down and made her way through to the kitchen. Once the kettle was filled and switched on, she set about putting the groceries away. Finally settled in the conservatory with a mug of coffee, Lucy watched a great tit acrobatically swinging from the bird feeder, stabbing at the peanuts through the mesh with its tiny pointed beak, while a pair of collared doves looked down from the branch above. Inevitably her thoughts strayed to Mark, wondering where and how he was. When she might see him again.

14

Tuesday 23rd June

Harmon decided that he could wait no longer and placed the call to Charles Parish's secretary. Handsomely paid though he was, it was not enough to cover leaving his arse exposed to the kind of trouble Parish's friends could cause him. The conversation was brief; Harmon hung up and poured himself a coffee while he waited for the shit to hit the fan. He buzzed his secretary.

'We may have unscheduled visitors visit in the next hour, Margaret. Show them straight in will you?'

The Somali sun was scorching, the air devoid of moisture. The rough deck timbers cracked and split under its radiation. Bell and Parish lay beneath the makeshift awning like beached dolphins, listless and sweating, struggling to breathe. The pirates were inside the wheelhouse, all except Coke T-shirt that is. He sat in the bow, seemingly unaffected by the heat. He had a threadbare canvas bag across his lap from which he produced a slab of pitta bread and some dates. When he had eaten he pulled something else from the bag. It looked like a cross between a portable telephone and a TV remote control. He had picked it up from the cabin on the yacht. He had picked up a few other trinkets too, including a gold Rolex. He seemed confused by it. He couldn't figure out what the object was or what it did. He banged it on the deck a couple of times and in the end threw it through the open hatch into the hold.

'Someone's not happy,' said Parish, stating the obvious.

'Fuck him,' replied his fellow prisoner through cracked lips, unaware of the importance of the pirate's action. The youth had unwittingly helped them more than they could imagine. The GPS had struck a heavy chain link as it landed in the hold, with enough force and at the right angle to knock the switch and turn it on.

There were two of them, one late forties, the other thirty-five, six. Saville Row from top to toe, they were armed with nothing more deadly than a rolled umbrella, but they scared Harmon more than a heavy with a sawn-off shotgun. His secretary showed them straight in.

'Tell us everything you know, Mister Harmon, and when you knew it. Every tiny detail.'

No niceties, no preamble, straight down to business. Harmon spoke without interruption for almost five minutes while the younger of the two men held a voice recorder in his face. When he had finished the elder of the two spoke.

'How many in this office, besides you and your secretary?'

'That's it.'

'Tell her you won't be needing her anymore today. Give her the rest of the day off, there's a good fellow.'

Nigel broke out in a sweat, squirming on his executive leather.

'Relax Mister Harmon,' said the younger one. 'You've been watching too many American television programs.' Harmon breathed out, buzzed Margaret and sent her on her way, assuring her everything was fine. The younger man picked up the telephone from the desk and dialled a number. When he got through he passed the phone to his colleague. There was a brief exchange and then, the man held the voice recorder to the mouthpiece and pressed play. Following this, there was another brief exchange and then the man put the phone down. 'I'm afraid I must dash, Mister Harmon,' said the older man. 'A delight meeting you. Thank you for your help. My colleague will be staying. Keep everything as you have planned, regarding your arrangements. This has not happened, yes?'

'Absolutely,' agreed a confused Nigel, his breathing beginning to slow down to normal.

The PM chaired the meeting himself; his face relaxed somewhat at the news. It was the breakthrough he had been praying for but it was the kind of thing that happened only in thrillers, never in real life. Not to him. Not until now. The meeting had been hastily convened and the room was bubbling with expectation as people found their way to their seats and settled in. First to speak was the PM

'We have some positive news, people, I will hand over to Bernard for a full update.'

Bernard the pencil twirler stood up and addressed the assembly in a measured monotone. 'We have identified a signal originating from Charles Parish's GPS and have pinpointed its location. It is on or close to this river, here.' He pointed to the map with his laser. 'The area is largely uninhabited scrubland, no buildings and no real roads, only dirt tracks. The only thing of note is an abandoned wreck of a barge of some kind, right on the coordinates. We have asked the Americans for help with satellite images to confirm our belief, but it looks promising. There is another development, which is active now and I hope to have fuller details before the end of this meeting. We received a call from Charles Parish's private secretary half an hour ago. It seems that a ransom demand has been received by a firm of accountants, from someone claiming to represent Richard Bell. The man dealing with this is being interviewed as I speak. When we have established what is going on I will let you all know.'

The PM was beaming. 'Thank you, Bernard. Geoffrey what is the status of our military assets?'

Colonel Greaves stood up as the pencil twirler resumed his seat. 'The advance party are in the air and should arrive at Akrotiri for refuelling around midnight. Estimated time of arrival at Camp Winston, fourteen hundred hours local that's eleven hundred GMT. B Squadron, 22 SAS is on two hour standby.'

'Then "Cry havoc," Geoffrey, "Cry havoc."' The PM was bobbing like a cork in millrace, drawing worried looks from around the table.

A green light began blinking next to the monitor in front of pencil twirler. He pressed a button and lifted a telephone receiver.

'Wait one,' he said into the mouthpiece, as he stood up and raised his hand to the PM

The PM nodded and the room fell silent.

'Live intelligence, people. On speaker now,' he pressed another button and replaced the receiver.

Nigel Harmon's words filled the room. No one spoke. Everyone focused on the stream of words, trying to understand the significance of the content and how it fitted with what they already knew. There was little observable reaction, apart from the odd raised eyebrow. When it finished, Bernard said. 'Thank you. Maintain the status quo until you hear from me.' He pressed the button to end the call.

The room was hushed for several seconds as the information seeped into the delegates' consciousness. It was the PM who broke the silence.

'Initial analysis, if you please.'

Bernard sucked in his breath. 'Best guess; an opportunistic criminal act, purely for financial gain. I doubt these people have any idea who Charles Parish is. They see an expensive yacht and decide to rob it. They realise that they can make a lot more money if they hold the owner to ransom.'

There followed an open discussion where everyone had a chance to throw into the pot. When each had had their say the Prime Minister called for order.

'Well, Bernard, what do you think?' he said.

'I suggest that we allow the ransom delivery to go ahead. We want to avoid making the kidnappers nervous. The rescue plan should go ahead as planned with the rider that the surveillance team stand off and observe without intervention until the ransom is delivered. If the hostages are freed at this point we will have achieved our objective. We can then retrieve our military assets and know one will know we have been in the country.'

'And if they are not freed?' asked the PM

'My colleague, Colonel Greaves is best placed to answer that question. Geoffrey?'

The colonel got to his feet. 'The assault team should be dispatched to Camp Winston to be kept on standby. They will be ready to intervene as soon as authorised. The surveillance team will have limited independent assault capability if we need to act immediately. The main assault force is thirty minutes flying time from the target.'

The PM frowned. 'What are the chances of success, Geoffrey?'

The colonel hated the anticipated question, the way a doctor dreads the recently diagnosed cancer patient asking: *'How long have I got?'* He didn't have a crystal ball, nor did he have sufficient reliable intelligence to do much more than guess, which is precisely what he did.

'Eighty, eighty-five percent, Prime Minister. Casualties zero to ten percent of troops engaged. The hostages will be the most vulnerable. If it is the kidnappers' intention to kill them then the minute the money is handed over their chances drop like a stone. Normally I would take the view that if money is all these people want, I doubt they would be willing to bring the wrath of the British government and the international community upon them. However, we are likely to be dealing with unsophisticated, ill-educated peasants and life is very cheap in Somalia.'

'Are you saying we should send the troops in before the ransom is delivered?'

'That would be my advice, yes.'

The PM ran a tense hand through his hair and stared down at the table. He said nothing for several minutes. People began shifting in their seats, shuffling papers and coughing nervously. Finally he lifted his head. 'I will take Colonel Greaves' advice. We will allow the ransom delivery to go ahead but initiate the rescue mission before the exchange. Thank you all for attending. This meeting is now closed.'

Rollo took another call in his study at three PM He thanked his source for the update, went straight to the bookcase and took a large atlas from the bottom shelf. Opening the book on his desk Rollo thumbed through it until he reached the page that showed the horn of Africa. He quickly identified the area he was interested in, poured another large Malt and silently said a prayer. That was when Lucy walked in. She had always been Daddy's girl, closer to her Father than ever she was with her mother.

'Daddy?'

'Hello, sweetheart, I wasn't expecting you.'
The slur in his voice was slight, imperceptible to anyone except her, and Wilkins possibly.

'What is it?' she asked, frowning.

'What?'

'Daddy, this is me. You don't give the Scotch a

caning like this unless something's up, so tell me. A trouble shared and all that.'

'I'm sorry, Lucy, I can't. Not just now.'

Lucy looked at the Atlas. Rollo closed the cover, but not before she had seen the map. 'It's not Mark. Tell me it's not. Daddy ple...'

'He fine, I'm sure, sweetheart. I promise you. This is nothing to do with him.' Even as he was finishing the sentence a small blip pinged on his radar. He believed that what he had told his daughter was the absolute truth, but suddenly realised that it was remotely, but entirely possible, that he was wrong. Skelter's sudden recall to camp could be for any number of reasons. It happened all the time in The Regiment. Mostly it turned out to be nothing.

'Whatever it is this is not going to help,' said Lucy, picking up the bottle and walking through the door. 'It's coffee you need,' she called over her shoulder, on the way to the kitchen.

15

Tuesday 23rd June

About the time that Lucy was medicating her father with loving care and coffee, the Learjet carrying Lofty and Turbo began circling over southern Cyprus, waiting for a landing slot. Both men had two things on their mind. Shower and hot scoff. The standard of catering on RAF bases was unrivalled and no one ever monitored how much you put on your plate. A drink would be good too but that would have to be NAAFI tea. Whatever the reason for the recall it was not for R and R. There was a job in the offing, one important enough to warrant a ride in a Learjet; something serious.

Once on the ground the two men were whisked away with their kit to a Portakabin, in a quiet spot at the eastern end the airfield. Inside was basic but there was a good shower, four bunks, a sofa and a couple of chairs. There was even a TV set with an old VHS video and a shelf full of tapes, mostly feature films. There were fresh towels, bathrobes and even pairs of flip-flops in shrink-wrap plastic.

'Beats the fuck out of lying on the ground does this,' observed Turbo blowing smoke rings as he tested one of the bunks. 'Wonder if there's anything on telly. Bet you can't get countdown out here. I could do with a dose of Carol.'

'Aye gawpin' at her on the box is as close as you'll

ever get. She wouldn't want you giving her a dose. Carol Voerderman's got taste. She's way out of your league.' Lofty took off his boots. 'I'm away for a dump. Is there anything to read in here?'

Turbo chucked him a dog-eared copy of RAF News. Lofty withdrew to the inner sanctum to await evacuation. When he reappeared twenty minutes later Turbo was piling up the zeds so he grabbed the vacant shower. Fifteen scrubbing, soaking minutes later he emerged, clean and fresh, feeling like a new man, wondering if he would be able to ring Mandy later. He shook Turbo by the shoulder to waken him.

'C'mon, laddie, get showered, it must be nearly time for scoff.'

'What did you wake me for, you bastard? Carol was about to...'

'In your dreams.'

'Exactly my point.'

'Get ready you pocket size Para or I'll not wait for ye.'

'Bastard,' repeated Thompson under his breath, as he stomped towards the shower.

Two and a half thousand miles to the south of Lofty and Turbo's temporary home two men in even more need of a shower and modern toilet facilities, lay swatting mozzies on the deck of the barge.

'I thought this was supposed to be the rainy season in East Africa,' moaned Charles Parish. 'Dry as a bloody bone. Not so much as a drop.' He took a swig from the goatskin. 'Ugh dis...gusting.'

Richard Bell was not listening. He needed some sleep. He had got used to fine Egyptian cotton sheets and a bespoke mattress. Three days of roughing it was three days too long. Both men were feeling the strain from inedible food, heat and lack of sleep. Parish had filled the bucket twice, shitting through the eye of the proverbial needle.

'I'm staying the night, Daddy,' Lucy announced. 'No buts. Whatever it is that's bothering you, you shouldn't be alone.'

'I'm not alone. Wilkins...'

'Not the same. You should eat. Let's see what's in the fridge.'

'Don't fuss, Lucy,...' She was gone, rummaging through the kitchen cupboards and searching the fridge and freezer. Meatballs and spaghetti in tomato sauce followed by tinned rice pudding was what she came up with. Rollo knew better than to resist. He fought to appear calm while inside he was in turmoil. When the phone rang he nearly jumped out of his skin. It was a cold caller conducting some kind of marketing survey. He hung up.

'Who was that?' asked Lucy.

'Some stupid sod selling something,' replied Rollo. 'No honestly, it was.' She did not look convinced, but let it pass. He looked at his daughter with a feeling of guilt, as concern for the fate of his son, Charles, festered away inside. He hated keeping her brother's situation from her, but he had no choice. Not that it made it any easier.

'Food's on the kitchen table. Come on, Daddy, before it gets cold.'

The chefs at RAF Akrotiri were magicians, the aroma of the canteen stirring the senses, the menu such that both men struggled to make a decision at first. Lofty finally settled on chicken pie with suet crust pastry, peas and a shedload of chips, all drowned in a sea of rich onion gravy. Turbo plumped for pork chops, roast and new potatoes, veg and Yorkshire pudding. He was less liberal with the gravy. They ate like condemned men in complete silence, and then went back for sponge pudding, custard and coffee. Half way down his second cup Turbo finally broke the silence. 'Ever get the feeling you joined the wrong service, Lofty? We never get grub like this. They're spoilt rotten these blokes.'

'Aye and that's a fact. I wonder if we could get a transfer?'

'I'd be like a house side in a couple of months,' declared Turbo. 'Seriously I would. My mother'd be 'appy, though. She's always trying to fatten me up when I go visit.'

'You've got a mother?' mocked Lofty. 'I thought you were cloned, like Dolly the sheep.'

'Cheeky twat,' Turbo replied, 'I'll have you know I not only have a mother but a father and a sister.'

'Well I hope she's better looking than you ye ugly bastard.' Lofty screwed his face up as he looked at his companion. 'Don't have much going for you do ye?'

An RAF corporal approached the table. 'Excuse me sirs, did you come in on the Learjet earlier?'

'We might 'ave,' said Turbo, eyeing the young lad up and down. The lad was not as green as he looked and not the least bit intimidated by Turbo's tone.

'You have orders to report to the Movements Officer at twenty-three forty. A vehicle will collect you and your kit from your accommodation at Twenty-three twenty five.'

'Cheers, laddie,' said Lofty. 'Twenty-three twenty five. Okay.'

The corporal turned smartly on his heel and marched away.

16

Wednesday 24th June

Caroline Warren's Boeing touched down at Mombasa at nine thirty-two local time after an overnight flight from Heathrow. She was comfortable enough in business class, but it had been a long flight and she was eager to get to the hotel. Eight hours in the air was a lifetime for Caroline. She was looking forward to the ransom delivery with less enthusiasm than a condemned murderer facing the gallows, her fear and anxiety about flying being inversely proportional to the size of the aeroplane. Wondering if Richard Bell would ever fully appreciate what she was doing for him, she fantasised about what form his gratitude might take, hoping it might be more physical than financial. Caroline was at the top of the tree in her chosen profession. At forty-two it was time for her to settle down, and Richard wasn't getting any younger.

The Grand Hotel was an opulent throwback to British Colonial Rule. Ornate Victoriana, plush and over fussy; not at all to Caroline's taste. The room was however, spacious, the bed soft, which suited her and there was a generous balcony and a modern mini bar sitting incongruously amongst the period features. She ordered coffee from room service. The drink would have to wait. She needed a clear head – and a shower, but first, coffee. Thirty-five minutes later she stepped out of the bathroom and stood in front of the full length ornately framed mirror. Letting the towel slide to the floor she ran a critical eye over her naked body. Her ample breasts had had just the right balance of firmness and softness, un-ravaged by children. Stomach still flat – the aerobics and Yoga classes took care of that. Her bottom, probably her best asset was pure peach.

'You have no idea what you're missing, Richard,' she said aloud, addressing the mirror.

Skelter slept for a couple of hours then tried to read but he found it impossible to concentrate so he lay swaying in the hammock, eyes closed, remembering the river, the canoe and Lucy Ryder. She was getting under his skin, but in a pleasant way. A warm glow of contentment of a kind he had not experienced for many years enveloped him. He was enjoying this escape from monotony when his dreaming was rudely disturbed by the loadmaster shaking his arm. The man was tapping his watch then holding out both hands, palms spread, fingers wide. Ten minutes to landing. Skelter stowed the hammock, secured his bergan and strapped himself into his seat, nodding to Tash and Biscuit. He checked his own watch, coming up to midnight, the bright Cyprus moon streaming silver through the starboard windows as the Hercules turned onto the final approach to RAF Akrotiri.

Turbo answered the rap on the Portakabin's door. He and Lofty were primed and ready, kit packed. The Land Rover drove around the perimeter of the airfield and delivered them to a small door in the side of a large hangar. They de bused and humped their kit inside. The floodlit hanger housed a variety of small aircraft, including a couple of gazelle helicopters, all undergoing maintenance. Engine covers were off while Erks with spanners and screwdrivers burrowed their way into their guts, checking, tightening loose connections and replacing bent and broken bits. There was another Portakabin in the hanger, which housed the Movements Office. The Movements Officer was a female flight lieutenant brimming with no nonsense efficiency. Inside ten minutes she had sorted the paperwork, manifest, kit log etc. and explained the procedure.

'Your aircraft is due to land in four minutes, refuel and checks; forty minutes. I have scheduled seventy, to allow your mates to get a meal.'

'Do you have numbers on these mates?' asked Lofty. 'We're knee deep in mushroom compost. You know how it is.'

'Keeping you in the dark are they?'

'And feeding us bullshit,' Turbo interjected.

'I am familiar with the concept. I have three personnel listed. Skelter, Tasker and McVitie. Mean anything?'

'Some,' said Turbo, recognising Skelter's name.

Flight lieutenant efficiency pointed out that they would see their mates soon and suggested they might join them for something to eat or at least a coffee if they were not hungry.

'Your kit will be safe in here,' she said. 'I'm on duty for another four hours. Shall I call a cab?'

'That would be good,' said Turbo.

Lofty unzipped the dry bag and took out his beloved rifle. He removed the bolt and put into the cargo pocket of his combats, before zipping the bag up again.

'Transport's on its way,' said the flight lieutenant, replacing the receiver.

The C130 touched down seven minutes late at zero thirteen GMT Wednesday. It taxied to the apron and by the time the boots of the B Squadron trio had kissed the concrete, Turbo and Lofty were on their way over in a

Land Rover.

'I did a job in Colombia with a McVitie, from Glasgow. Goes by the name o' Biscuit.'

'Aye, Loft, Skelter's name rings a bell too. Biscuit's troop sergeant, his name were Skelter. Everyone called him H. No idea why.'

'I've worked with him once. He's sound.'

'Top bloke, so I've heard. No idea about the other guy.'

The Land Rover pulled up on the apron under the wing of the C130, next to the B Squadron boys. Skelter stepped up to the front passenger window.

'Lofty, I wasn't expecting you until we got to Winston. Good to see you again.'

'You too H. Winston, who's Winston? What's the Craic? They told us fuck all.'

Skelter grinned, 'I'll fill you in while we eat if we can find a quiet enough corner. It was me who requested you for this job.' Lofty 's eyes widened.

The rest of the men clambered over the tailgate and the vehicle set off for the canteen. Filing past the vast array of food on offer, the men felt spoilt. Having already eaten Lofty settled for coffee, but Turbo couldn't pass up another sponge pudding and custard. Sitting together around a table, thoughtfully provided in an area screened off from main body of the mess hall, Skelter brought Lofty and Turbo up to speed with the details of the job, in between forkfulls of shepherd's pie. The men swopped tit bits of their histories and explored common acquaintances, while weighing each other up and making a start at getting to know one another or rekindling old friendships. By one twenty-two they were back on board the aircraft, kit checked, strapped in and ready to roll.

At home in Herefordshire, Rollo lay awake, the mug of hot chocolate his daughter had insisted making for him, cold and untouched upon the bedside chest. He longed for sleep to come, to release him from the thoughts ravaging his brain. He needed some respite, if only for an hour or two.

On the other side of the wall Lucy lay awake also, re-running her time with Mark in an endless loop in her head, smiling at the images while at the same time butterflies danced inside her stomach as she worried about what was eating her father. The moon was visible, bright and clear through open curtains, the stars like diamonds on black velvet. Why would anyone want to shut out such a lovely view? The house was overlooked only by the occasional owl prowling for prey, or else roosting in the great copper beech that spread its grey bark branches over the soft green lawn. No point in settling down, she would fall asleep when she was ready.

The long drawn out, engine-droning journey was nearing its end as the late afternoon African sun lit the wings of the Hercules, with its golden glow. Like the rest of the men Skelter had slept as much as he could, partly to alleviate the boredom, mostly because he knew from experience that once they were deployed they would rarely get the chance to do more than snatch at sleep, it would become the most elusive of luxuries. He was not looking forward to hours on end of lying on hard ground, unable to raise himself any higher than his elbows, with no hot food, drink, no talking above a whisper. He looked at his dozing comrades with a sense of pride. They were the best in the world at their job and they were his men. They would stay alert watching a fixed point for hours, waiting to react to something, which almost certainly would not happen. Surveillance work, like most of the tasks The Regiment undertakes, was very tedious. He was reassured by the presence of men like these.

The wheels hit the runway at fourteen forty-six local time, eleven forty-six GMT. The Hercules rolled past the passenger terminal and turned left onto a taxiway running on for some way before finally coming to a halt alongside an isolated hangar, outside of which were parked two Kenyan Army four ton trucks. The hydraulics whined as the loadmaster lowered the ramp. Warm air spilled into the cargo bay. A forklift appeared from somewhere and got stuck into the pallets. They were loaded onto the trucks almost before the guys had finished stretching.

'What is going on, H?' asked Biscuit. 'The whole operation's running like clockwork, has been since it started and now this. It's incredible. What ever happened to the army we all know and love?'

'The ginger whinger's right, H. This is surreal.'

Skelter smiled, slowly nodding his head. 'It all depends whose balls are in the vice boys. When it's one of their own it's amazing how the army can get its act together, especially with Number 10 shoving a missile up the MOD's arse.'

Toilet facilities were available inside a low building beside the hanger and on a small trolley inside the hangar itself a steaming, shiny, stainless steel tea urn sat on an old metal trolley.

'It keeps getting better,' Tash said, grabbing a bag from the stack on the table next to the urn and pulling up a white plastic garden armchair. He delved into the bag as Biscuit took a pew beside him, his fat fist holding a mug brimming with tea.

'What you got, Tash?'

'Chicken I think. You?'

'Chicken. There's fruit and cheese and biscuits. Good brew too,' he remarked narrowly avoiding slopping the overfilled mug down the front of his crumpled combats.

Inside it was marginally cooler and away from

prying eyes. The rest of the lads sank into the chairs like they were the chesterfields in the sergeant's mess. After the steel and webbing torture rack in the hold of the Herc they certainly felt like them.

'Right, lads, listen in,' said Skelter, when their bellies were full. Moving in five. We are operational so get switched on and apply your SOPs. (standard operating procedures). Don't forget your malaria tabs, and fill your water bottles. That's it. Five minutes, okay.' It sounded like a question but clearly it was an order. From here on in things would be serious.

The journey was dry and dusty. Skelter travelled in the cab of the lead truck, which was marginally more comfortable than the back. The Kenyan Army driver was not the talkative type or else he had been well briefed. Skelter looked though the windscreen at the road ahead, a ribbon of grey tarmac, which gave way to a gravel and dirt road through the bush for the last six miles or so, until at long last the lapboard and wriggly tin huts of Camp Winston loomed out of the bush. After checking in with the guardroom the trucks drew up on the MT park and the men climbed wearily down from the vehicles, clutching bergans, belt-kit and weapons. A guard was placed on the trucks courtesy of the Kenyan hosts and a pair of Land Rovers was summoned to take the men to their quarters. They went off to their beds with Skelter's passing words ringing in their ears...

'Parade outside our accommodation, oh five thirty, boys. Now get some rest.' *Better to let the lads rest now and get them up early, fresh and alert,* Skelter thought.

Once they got their bed spaces allocated the four men started to strip and clean their personal weapons, magazines, sort their kit and square it away. Then it was time to get showered and such. By the time that was accomplished and they had got a brew there was not much daylight left. There was not a lot to do at Winston. The camp's main function was training and as a forward base for anti ivory poaching operations. Besides a dirt and gravel football pitch there were no recreational facilities other than a rudimentary canteen come shop where it was possible to buy essentials like toothpaste and boot polish, cigarettes and chocolate. It did have on old TV set and a video player, but that was it. Skelter swallowed a Valium and went to find the Adjutant to see what news, if any awaited him. Gratefully accepting the offer of coffee he lowered himself into a chair across the desk from the Kenyan Captain.

The brown envelope contained an encrypted signal from the Head Shed in Hereford. Skelter downed his coffee, almost scalding his tongue in the process, then excused himself. Ten minutes later back in the room which he had been allocated at the end of the hut he poured over the numbers with a pencil and one time pad and de-cyphered and then decoded the message. It confirmed the location of the hostages.

The lads were settling in. Walking outside as the sun was setting, Skelter watched the huge, blood red fireball, sliding behind the thorn scrub, bathing the heavens in orange light. He checked the time by his watch, fifteen thirty-seven, he was still on GMT. Of course at home it would be just turned half four given British Summer Time. He altered his watch while walking across to the Adjutant's office. There he used the telephone, calling Hereford to acknowledge receipt of the signal deciding not to share it with the team until the morning. The lads had had a long day. The more rest they could put in the bank, the more efficient they would be in the field. He burnt the papers in a mess tin and took off his boots. He'd had a long day too.

17

Thursday 25th June

No one was late for parade. The four men stood in a single rank as Skelter addressed them in the dark. The sun would not rise for another hour. 'We have all been here before, some of us more than once so no need to go over admin points. We are all adults; with the exception of corporal McVite, of course.'

Biscuit feigned shock and hurt. 'That is unkind, H.'

'As unkind as it is accurate,' H replied. 'To business. We have two hours before breakfast. I want the pallets off the trucks, unloaded and stowed in hut six, which is the one behind me next to our accommodation. We will be deployed tonight during the hours of darkness, delivered to a point five K from the target by helicopter, courtesy of the Kenyan Air Force. Our job is to set up a hide as close as practical to the target and observe. All the kit on this list,' Skelter waved a sheet of paper torn from a signals pad, 'we will need. Once the kit is unloaded and you have separated out the gear, priority one is comms. Tash, you will sort the radios. Priority two. Lofty, check all the AKs and draw ammo for them from the armoury. See the adjutant for authorisation. Issue each man with five magazines plus two bandoliers. That includes you as well, in addition to your rifle. We will be on our own in no position to call in a quick resupply and we have no intel on enemy strength or weapons. I hope to get an update before we deploy. As soon as we have achieved our immediate goals here, we will go to the firing range and test weapons. Don't forget, breakfast at zero seven thirty. Check your watches, gents. Time is now zero five forty-three....four, check. Two men to remain with the kit at all times. Biscuit, sort the rota.'

Breakfast was much the same as you would get in a greasy spoon transport cafe on the A46. Bacon, sausage, oily mushrooms and beans, topped with a couple of snotty eggs and fried bread, a throwback to years of colonial rule. The tea was a good strong local grown, Kenyan brew, full of flavour. Tash and Turbo had drawn the short straw for second sitting. They both stared at the food. The standard of catering was barely adequate. They had been spoilt rotten by the RAF. The Kenyan cooks couldn't come close. They filled their stomachs out of need rather than desire.

The next three hours was a period of concentrated activity. Tash tested the radio sets, worked out the frequencies, antennae lengths and configurations, established a local net between himself, the camp radio hut and Turbo and Lofty's set and filed a signals plan. Turbo stripped, checked, cleaned and test fired the AK47s on the range at the back of the camp and Lofty signed for two thousand rounds of ammunition from the armoury. Fifteen hundred for the operation and five hundred for familiarisation, test firing and zeroing. Bergans were packed, belt kit crammed with whatever might be needed for emergencies. Belt kit was personal. Each man shoehorned in whatever he felt he felt appropriate; emergency rations, Tommy cookers and hexamine solid fuel tablets, fishing lines, waterproof matches, lighters, sterilising tablets – whatever felt right for each individual. Skelter's contained all the afore mentioned, plus a generous supply of Valium.

A Kenyan soldier presented Skelter with a signal. 'Keep at it lads,' he said, before leaving for the accommodation to decode it. The message was short...*B Squadron ETA Winston 21.00. Opposition likely criminal not terrorist - repeat not terrorist. Ransom demand received. R. Bell intended kidnap target. Motive - money. Deploy to observe. Gather Intel. Transmit to Assault Team....* Skelter read and re read the decrypted message carefully to ensure he fully understood and then went outside to rejoin the team.

Two hundred and twenty miles North East of Camp Winston, as the Vulture flies, a small wiry Somali man with bad teeth and an untidy grey beard, was shinning up a telegraph pole with a knapsack slung around his shoulders. In bare feet using only a loop of rope in the same manner that Polynesians climb coconut palms, he was up in less time than it takes to tell. He was not looking for coconuts. From his knapsack he produced two wires with crocodile clips at the ends, which he attached to the telephone wires. This achieved he scuttled back to earth trailing the wires behind him and passed the knapsack from which the wires emanated through the window of a mud hut to a waiting pair of hands. These were the hands of Cawaale, or Fuller Face, as Richard Bell had christened him. The wiry man with the untidy beard entered the room through the door and connected the wires to an old black telephone receiver.

Nigel Harmon felt as if he had just gone ten rounds with Mike Tyson. The camp bed and sleeping bag provided by MI5 or 6 or whoever they were, was not what he was accustomed to. He should have been tucked up in his own bed, with a Scotch-laced Latte and a copy of the financial times. He was far from happy. His mouth tasted like the bottom of a compost bin and he desperately needed a change of clothes. His minder from the day before had arrived to take over the day shift from his nighttime colleague.

When the telephone rang, the minder said, 'Calm and natural, Nigel, remember we are not here.'

He was referring to the man with the headphones and laptop computer that was connected to the electronic box of tricks that was rigged to the telephone. Nigel Harmon took the call and wrote down the instructions that the caller gave him. Not that it mattered if he forgot any of the details. The man with the earphones was recording every sigh and whisper. The line went dead.

'You did fine, Nigel,' said his minder.

'Where the hell is Margaret,' Nigel moaned, 'I need my coffee.' His secretary would not be coming into the office until further notice. A quiet word had been had. If Nigel wanted coffee he would have to make it himself.

Caroline Warren let out a huge sigh when she got the call from Harmon. The waiting was fraying her nerves. Her night had been restless. The bed was comfortable and although the air conditioning worked fine, every time she closed her eyes, visions of her beloved Richard being abused by faceless kidnappers filled her head, causing anxiety resulting in panic attacks. She was used to making things happen. It was what she did. Sitting around twiddling her thumbs in hotel rooms, no matter how luxurious, was torture.

'Nigel, thank God. What news? No; fire away, my pen is poised.' She wrote rapidly in a small red notebook and then read back to Harmon what she had. 'Right got it. Anything else? Good. I'll be in touch.' Caroline Warren replaced the receiver and checked her gold Cartier. Bang on noon. She rang reception, ordered a taxi, went to the wardrobe and took out a small clamshell flight-case, then after pausing briefly to check her appearance in the mirror, she left her room locking the door behind her. Her taxi was waiting by the time she got down to the lobby. The bank was less than ten minutes away. She told the driver to wait, hinting at a generous tip if he obliged. Chase Mombasa was ultra modern by comparison to the hotel, bleached hardwood, European Ash, bizarrely, with Italian porcelain floor tiles in pale grey, stainless steel fixtures and acid etched ballistic glass. The manager himself showed her into a grand plush office and the cash was brought in through a separate door. Richard Clark had a great deal of influence in the Chase banking corporation. He owned shares in it. A lot of shares.

In less than twenty minutes Caroline was on her way back to the hotel, the clamshell somewhat heavier than it had been on the way out.

In Camp Winston, Skelter's team had almost finished sorting the operational kit. Five orderly stacks of equipment stood at the feet of five beds. Skelter had his at the bottom of a spare bed in the main billet with the rest of the men. The bergans were almost bursting at the seams and yet there was still a fair bit of kit to pack. There were two five-gallon Jerry cans of water, a Russian RPG-7 rocket propelled grenade launcher with five rockets, extra rations, additional camouflage netting and a roll of chicken wire. Wire snips were already packed in Skelter's bergan.

Biscuit stood looking at the pile of kit and shook his head slowly from side to side. 'How far did you say we have to TAB (march – Tactical Advance to Battle) with all this kit, H? Seven K?'

'Pretty much, the heli can't risk any nearer or they'll hear us. It'll be a bit less. The target will be seven K but we'll lay up about half a K short, so you're looking at four miles in old money.'

'Piece of piss then,' said Turbo, laughing.

'No one said this would be easy. We have zero intelligence on the enemy strength and capability. We need to be prepared for anything. It wont be as hard as it looks.

For one thing the ground is firm and flat.' There was a pregnant pause. 'So I am told. Maps are on the way from Nairobi and should be here by four o'clock. Sunset is at eighteen thirty-seven. We take off from the parade ground at nineteen hundred. Right lads, time for grub, Lofty and I will stay with the kit while the rest of you go for your scoff. Come and relieve us soon as you're done, okay?'

'Wilco, boss,' Tash replied, rubbing his belly and making a swift exit, closely followed by Biscuit and Turbo. When they had gone Lofty walked along the line of kit carefully scrutinising everything but saying nothing.

'I know,' said Skelter. 'I said it won't be easy. We'll have to leap-frog with half the kit then go back for the rest, every five hundred metres and we will need to have at least one man with the kit at all times. Three leap-frogging. It's going to take time but that's something we should have plenty of. We have the GPS to locate the target, so knowing when to stop and lay up should be no problem.'

'Tricky bit'll be camming up quietly in the dark,' said Lofty, 'It's awful close to the target and if the ground is as open and bare arsed as you say it is....'

'I know, but we've got no choice. We'll have to suck it and see, the sound of the river might help a bit,' Skelter answered, grim faced.

Caroline Warren picked up the telephone and called the pilot who was to fly the ransom money to the drop off. She had no idea where that was so couldn't answer his obvious question, not yet. All she knew was the course that he was to fly, which to her was a just jumble of numbers, which described a triangular point to point flight with an endurance of three hours. Nigel would let her know in plenty of time, or so he said, the precise point of the drop. He would pick her up at nine in the morning outside the hotel. Used to the well-oiled machine with her hand on the button, having to rely on others whom she did not rate highly and worse still were strangers, made Caroline decidedly nervous. She had never been this far out of her comfort zone before.

'Damn you Richard.' The words slipped out as frustration gripped her. She thought of the following day's flight in a small aircraft piloted by a man she had never seen, whose competence she was not qualified to judge. The hell with it – the mini bar it was. Three large G and Ts later she began to relax, if only a little. All she could do now was wait and waiting was always the hardest. She poured another drink.

'Scof time, H,' said Tasker, as he and Biscuit, their bellies full, entered the hut. 'Not too bad, better than the fry up we had this morning at any rate. Chicken curry, and chapatis, there's rice pud too.'

'Where's Turbo?' said Lofty.

'Said he had something to look into. Acting all mysterious he was,' Tash glanced at Biscuit, who nodded.

'Aye right enough Tash, but he'll no be long I'm sure.'

Skelter and Lofty set off in search of curried chicken and rice pudding.

Tash sat on the bed and took his latest toy from his combats cargo pocket, flipped the lid and began to type onto the tiny keyboard.

'What's that you've got there?' Biscuit asked, 'I've not seen that before. Latest sigs kit is it?'

'Kind of,' said Tasker. It's a Nokia nine thousand, Communicator.'

'What's it do?'

'It communicates, dummy. It's the latest in mobile phone technology. Besides being a phone it's got a keyboard and a full screen built in. Makes it easier to send SMS messages. Here look.' Tash demonstrated the machine, which was the size of a large TV remote control when shut. 'See? Type on the mini keyboard and you can read the text on the screen. Vast improvement over my Nokia twenty-one sixty bit heavier, bigger too but worth it.'

'Not issue kit then?'

'No, civvy, my own personal.'

'Must have cost an arm and a leg.'

'Got it on monthly contract.'

'Over my head pal, I don't have a mobile phone. Don't trust them. Anybody could be listening in and the microwaves fry your brain cells.' Biscuit grinned. 'Still, that won't affect you will it? Enjoy your toy, gadget man, I'm going for some Egyptian PT.'

'Go have your kip ye bloody dinosaur. You wait. Ten years from now everyone's going to have one of these beauties.'

When Skelter and Lofty returned from lunch, a smug looking Turbo, grinning like a Cheshire housewife's Moggy, greeted them enthusiastically. The other two looked cheerful too. At the foot of Turbo Thompson's bed was a tubular steel and canvas contraption with two wheels the size of large dinner plates. A relic from the Second World War, it belonged in a museum, being well past its prime. It was however, in working order.

'Where did you nick that?' asked Lofty. 'From some poor bastard's allotment?'

'This fine example of British military ingenuity,' Turbo declared, 'was designed in the nineteen forties for use by our intrepid airborne super-soldiers and deployed to great effect at the battle for the bridge over the Rhine at Arnhem. Gentlemen, I give you the folding, collapsible airborne wheelbarrow.'

'Didn't we lose the battle of Arnhem?' said Biscuit.

'Moving on,' said Turbo, unfazed. 'This beauty can carry a shed load of kit. I reckon it will handle all our additional stuff, water included. The ground is flat, one on each handle and we've cracked it. No need for leapfrogging.'

Skelter examined the two-wheeled trolley. 'Where the hell did you get it?'

'Last time I was here, two years ago I think it was, we did some anti ivory poaching patrols with the local boys and they had it on the truck. Used it for hauling the tusks. I guessed it would be still around somewhere and sure enough, it was in the stores.'

'Well done, Turbo. You signed for it I hope?'

'Naturally, in your name of course, H.

'Cheers.'

18

Thursday 25th June

Lofty Larcombe was not only a first class sniper but also a fully qualified and highly experienced armourer. He knew almost as much about firearms as the men who designed them, which is why, despite their experience, Skelter insisted on the team listening to Lofty's foreign weapons lecture. He included himself in the class.

'You all know what this is,' said Lofty. 'The AK47 assault rifle. You have all used AKs before but only occasionally and not for some time so pay attention. This might keep you, or more importantly me, from getting shot. Kalashnikov's brainchild might be the most reliable automatic rifle ever made, but nothing is foolproof. Rounds can fail to go off for any number of reasons. Faulty ammunition or a damaged firing pin, cartridge case stuck in the breech, I could go on. In the heat of a firefight it is essential that each man can clear the problem and get the weapon working again in short order. It has to be practiced until it becomes instinctive and automatic.' Lofty scanned the men's faces to see that they were paying attention. 'The most common reason for a weapon to stop firing is what? Somebody enlighten me.'

'Round jammed in the breech,' said Biscuit with an air of boredom.

'Well? Is he right?'

Turbo and Skelter remained non committal, sensing

a trap. Tash spoke. 'My squat Scottish friend is incorrect as usual,' said the lanky lance-jack.

'Would you care to expand, Lance Corporal Tasker?'

'Empty magazine,' said Tash.

'Correct,' said Lofty, holding up an empty magazine. No bullets. The most common reason for a weapon to stop firing is no bullets. It has run out of ammunition. Hollywood heroes like Bruce Willis can keep firing until the cows come home. You gentlemen, are not Bruce Willis. In the real world most assault rifles including this one, have a magazine capacity of thirty rounds, enough for three-seconds continuous firing on fully automatic. Three-seconds, gentlemen. The length of time it takes corporal McVitie to make love to a woman.'

There was a ripple of laughter, at Biscuit's expense.

'Changing a magazine,' Lofty continued, 'can never be practiced too much; it could be the difference between life and death. It may seem blindingly obvious to you sat here on the firing range, but in the heat of a firefight I promise you – you will forget.'

Lofty put everyone through their paces stripping and assembling, clearing stoppages and changing magazines before finally shooting at targets. When he was satisfied, they broke for a brew and a whinge, before reconvening for the second half of the lesson.

'Each of you has also been issued with a back up weapon, either a CZ 75 or 85 pistol and three magazines. These are similar to our standard issue Browning, stripping and assembly is the same. They are familiar but untraceable, you will notice the serial numbers have been ground off.'

'What about our AKs? They still have serial numbers,' said Biscuit.

'Good question. They are all weapons recovered from terrorist groups and as such traceable only to them and not The Regiment. These are in common use around the globe by just about every terrorist faction going. Any more questions?' There were none. 'Okay then, last but by no means least, please welcome to the stage my glamorous assistant, Miss Turbo Thompson, who will demonstrate the features and capabilities of the RPG-7 rocket propelled grenade launcher.'

Turbo minced forward camping it up, much to the amusement of all.

'Do not be fooled by appearances guys,' said Turbo holding up what looked like a three foot length of drainpipe, with a wooden bit wrapped around the middle and a trigger mechanism underneath. 'She might not be pretty but this little baby is a very effective weapon. She is the most widely used anti tank weapon in the world – by a mile. One man operation is simple. Load the grenade at the front, acquire your target using the sights and cock the mechanism with your thumb.' Turbo held the weapon up and pointed to the cocking lever behind the pistol grip. 'Squeeze the trigger. It's that simple. If you only remember one rule in regard to this highly efficient tank killer, let it be this. Look behind you. I say again, look behind you. The clue is in the name rocket propelled. What makes the grenade fly forward is the blast of the rocket blowing out of its arse. Anything or anyone directly behind the weapon when it is fired is toast. Burnt toast. Remember also that any solid object like a wall or side of a vehicle for example will deflect the blast back onto the man firing the weapon. He too will be toast.' He paused to let the words sink in. 'The Rocket Propelled Grenade has an explosive warhead containing a shaped charge designed to penetrate the armour plate of a tank before exploding inside for maximum effect. Any questions so far?'

'What's the range?' asked Tash.

'Effective range two hundred metres, maximum, nine hundred and twenty, at which point it will self detonate. Velocity two hundred and ninety-four metres per second. It will penetrate between thirty and sixty centimetres of armour, depending on the type of ammunition used. Sixty in our case, which will be more than enough. 'For the benefit of the older members of the class,' said Turbo looking at Skelter, that is almost two feet.'

Turbo handed the RPG to Tash, who passed it around the others. Turbo then took them through dry firing drills until he was happy they were competent. The main thing was the key message had been sent about safety when firing. A couple of terrorists unfamiliar with the weapon once tried to ambush a British patrol with an RPG-7 from inside the back of a transit van. They fired, missed, cremated themselves and set fire to the van all in a couple of seconds.

'Thank you miss Thompson for that most illuminating lesson,' said Lofty. 'One more thing gents before we wrap up. We are likely to face opposition from guys with AKs. By all means pick up any spare mags from them if you get the chance, but be very wary. Their housekeeping will be shit, so don't be tempted to use them unless you have emptied and cleaned them or have no choice. We don't want any embarrassing stoppages. Clear?

A murmur of confirmation.

'Good job, Lofty, Turbo,' said Skelter, when the lessons had finished. 'Thanks for that. I'd forgotten how rusty I was.'

'Any time, H,' they chorused.

The kit had been packed and repacked, packed again and tweaked. Nothing had been left to chance. Two hours left before take off. Time for Skelter to check for any updates with the radio operator and the Adjutant before the final briefing. There were no updates, but the maps had arrived, not that they showed much, just thousands of acres of arid bush with thin green strips clinging to the river banks. The chronic lack of rainfall this year, was causing much hardship among the rural communities in Somalia. Many farmers, dirt poor at the best of times, faced losing their meagre source of income. It was no wonder some of the people were desperate enough to turn to piracy.

The briefing took place around Lofty's bed, mainly because it was in the middle. 'Right boys,' Skelter began. 'Ground: Mostly flat scrubland, dry, no water except for the river. The weather,' he said adopting a serious tone. 'The Met boys reckon that the drought may be about to end. Good news for the poor peasants trying to scratch a living out of this barren landscape, but not for us. Be prepared for heavy sustained rainfall in the next seventy-two hours. Apart from the impact upon our personal comfort it could present us with problems from reduced visibility, which is the last thing we need on this operation.'

This news was greeted with a collective murmur.

Skelter continued. 'Situation: Enemy Forces: They are a group located aboard a derelict river barge. Strength unknown. Weapons unknown but expect AK's and possibly RPGs at minimum, capability unknown. Intel suggests the enemy is not an organised terrorist group.' Skelter paused to allow the words to sink slowly in.

'The word is, and I am assured this is straight from Whitehall…'

'Bound to be bollocks then,' Biscuit interrupted.

'Zip it,' said Skelter. 'The word is, a ransom demand has been received in the offices of the yacht owner. It seems that we may have a simple act of piracy for financial gain. Now get this, I do not intend to take this intel at face value. We've been rubber dicked before.' Skelter scanned their faces for reaction. There was none. He continued.

'Friendly Forces: None. Assume all others to be hostile.'

Nothing new there, thought Turbo.

'Mission: to establish an OP from which to gather intel on enemy movements and report back to HQ. Clear so far?' Nods all round.

'Execution: We will be inserted tonight at approximately twenty-two hundred hours by Kenyan Air Force helicopter. The pilot and crew have been fully briefed on their part of the mission, which is to get us where we need to be without waking up the neighbours. Beyond that they know nothing. Make sure it stays that way. We've worked with these guys before and we know they do a good job. As far as the situation on the ground is concerned we will assume worst-case scenario. I have no wish to haul this load of kit for the fun of it, but we will be isolated and we must be able to react to any threat we might reasonably expect to meet. I do not propose going through the kit list, we all know what we are taking and why.'

Biscuit threw a quizzical glance at Tash, who responded with a barely perceptible shrug.

'We have orders not to intervene, just observe,' Skelter went on, 'but we all know that plans have a habit of going pear shaped the minute you hit the battleground. Stay flexible. Adapt, improvise, overcome. It's what they pay us for and don't forget we are the world's best in our chosen profession.'

Skelter continued with the briefing giving the grid references of the barge as well as where they would be dropped off and the area proposed for the OP. At that point he stopped to take a long swig from his water bottle. 'Finally command and signals. Tash is on the radio, he has a full list of frequencies, codes etc. He will give the signals brief after I've done. We all have personal radios. These little Sony walkie talkies are not what we are used to but we cannot risk taking signature kit into the area in case we have to shoot and scoot. This is a deniable operation. The sets are reliable and at the sort of ranges we'll be working at we shouldn't have a problem. Passwords. Challenge is Galahad, answer Excaliber. This will remain for the duration of the operation unless circumstances dictate otherwise, in which case I will issue new ones. That's it.

Any questions?'

After dealing with what were mostly points of detail, Skelter's final words before he handed over to Tash Tasker for the signals briefing, were:

'Be sure you are all sterile before you leave here. Go through your pockets and make sure that anything that can identify you is left here in the camp. Most important, this is the last chance to fill out your will forms. Don't forget.'

'Ever cheerful,' said Turbo smiling.

Tasker's signals briefing was short and sweet. They only had one radio and the only other one on the net was the camp. The most important man beside Tasker was Turbo who was a first class advanced signaller, although every man had completed the basic course. Tash was ex Royal Signals and could operate in his sleep – if the equipment worked. It was not unusual for it to fail.

In Ross on Wye, Rollo was energetically digging in his vegetable garden; anything to keep himself occupied. There had been no news from his contact and although Lucy had said nothing, it was clear that she was becoming increasingly anxious. She appeared in the corner of his vision carrying two large, steaming, china mugs and a packet of hobnobs. He didn't want to stop but he knew he had no option. Ramming the fork into the soil he straightened up, taking off his gloves.

'Bless you, sweetheart. I could do with this.'

'Liar. You wanted to keep out of my way. Don't fret. I know better than to ask. You'll tell me when you are ready, and able I guess. You never actually retired from the Army, did you?'

He smiled at the innocent accuracy of her remark, but did not comment, preferring to take the mug and taste the coffee. Rollo was drawing on all his years of military discipline to hold in the hurt that not confiding in his daughter was causing him.

The Kenyan sun dipped towards the horizon as the slapping sound of the Puma's rotor blades reached the ears of the SAS men waiting on the parade ground with their small mountain of equipment. A big aircraft, designed by the French company Aerospatiale in the nineteen sixties, the reliable workhorse could carry sixteen troops or two and a half tons of kit. As it made its final approach the men knelt down in a huddle around the kit hands clamping bush hats to heads, face veils across mouths, eyes tight shut as the rotor induced dust storm swirled about them.

The big chopper settled on its wheels and the pilot cut the engines. Gradually the dust storm eased as the resistance of the air slowed the unpowered blades. The large side door slid back and a big black face with the whitest teeth Skelter had ever seen, waved them forward. As soon as they could see to operate the men dragged the kit to the helicopter and began heaving it into the cabin. Once everything was aboard and strapped down the men climbed in and found somewhere to sit on the floor. Pearly white nodded as Skelter gave the thumbs up and spoke into his throat mic. The engines cranked up and whined into life again, as the door was firmly closed ready for takeoff. The noise inside the aircraft rose to a crescendo as the Puma lifted off and peeled away to the Northeast, slap slap slapping across the darkening sky towards the Somali border.

The men sat quietly cradling their weapons, lost in their own thoughts as they headed through the deepening darkness towards the unknown. Skelter rummaged in his pocket for the reassuring feel of his secret little talisman. A soapstone statue of Buddha the size of a pullet's egg. Lofty fiddled with a set of Tibetan worry beads, while Turbo ran his hand along the paracord attached to his belt to make sure his lucky bottle opener was still attached to the end in his pocket. Tash thought of his wife and young son, wondering if he would be back in time for Charlie's sixth birthday in ten days time. He desperately hoped so. He had missed the last two.

On the balcony of her hotel room in Mombasa, Caroline Warren sat cradled in cushions in a comfortable cane chair, staring out at the lights reflected from the yachts riding at anchor. She was clutching a large gin and tonic like it was a lifejacket, wondering about the morning. *The bastard better show his appreciation for this when he gets back,* she thought, then it hit her, *if he gets back. What if he didn't make it? Who knows what these criminals are capable of?* She needed another drink, another large one. Rising unsteadily to her feet Caroline made her way to the mini bar. There was no gin left. Sod it, rum then, rum and coke. At least there was plenty of ice in the cooler. It was going to be a long night.

The Puma whupped its way through the African night at low level, the pilot juggling the controls to achieve the optimum balance between power for lift and keeping the noise levels as low as possible without stalling. He was doing a good job. The man with the pearly-white teeth held up two fingers to indicate two minutes to drop off. He slid back the door and the desert air rushed in mixing with the smell of damp canvas, hot kerosene and warm lubricating oil. The men cocked their weapons applied safety catches and began unhooking the straps securing the kit. By the time that was done the aircraft had almost ceased all forward motion and was down to twenty feet. Pearly-white was laying face down, head and shoulders out of the aircraft relaying instructions to the pilot through his headset. They jinked left, back, then twice right and they were down, soft as landing on marshmallow. The boy was good.

Skelter and Lofty jumped out and did a quick three sixty. No sign of anyone or anything. They gave the thumbs up and everyone pitched in with the offload, except Lofty who maintained watch. Five minutes later the Puma pattered away, fading into to the distance, lost first to sight and then to sound. They were alone in a vast empty wilderness. The scrub was sparse and did not appear to grow much above a couple of metres in height. The ground was firm, gritty and strewn with small rocks.

The Airborne wheelbarrow proved effective, even though it was loaded beyond its specified capacity. Tash and Lofty took first haul with Biscuit behind left, Skelter forward right and Lofty as lead scout with NVGs and an AK. His precious rifle was on the barrow. Skelter navigated using the stars, which were amazing, there being no light pollution whatsoever. At regular intervals he cross-referenced with the GPS to be sure but he needn't have bothered. He'd been doing fine for years without any electronic wizardry and he would sooner trust his experience.

19

Thursday 25th June

Progress through the bush was slow but more than adequate. It was slow for tactical reasons. Stealth was the watchword. Unless they could get into position and cammed up completely undetected before first light, they might as well have stayed at home. Lofty kept the NVGs slung around his neck relying on hearing as his primary warning system, stopping to use the goggles every two hundred paces or so. Biscuit was covering the left flank and rear arc, Skelter the right and rear overlapping with biscuit. At one point there was a hairy moment when they disturbed some creature prowling the bush, but whatever it was it was probably more scared than they were and it made off. The barrow haulers were concentrating on the donkeywork. After thirty minutes Tash and Turbo changed with Lofty and Biscuit and by two forty-five they had less than one thousand metres to go. Skelter called a halt and they closed in around the wheelbarrow.

'We will advance another seven-hundred metres and then go to ground,' he whispered. 'Lofty and I will go forward from there and look for a good spot for the OP. One of us will come back and guide you in. Okay?' Nods of agreement all round. The patrol pushed on cautiously for another forty minutes until, having calculated that they had covered the seven hundred metres, Skelter again called a halt. He and Lofty dropped their bergans and slipped forward into the moonlit, star spangled desert. Without the crippling weight of the bergan, Skelter felt like an astronaut marching on moon dust. The night was cooler than he expected now that his body was not converting so much energy into heat. They moved easily together in almost total silence, save for the odd brush with thorn scrub or the scrunch of boot on gravel. Soon they could see the silver ribbon of the river cutting across their vision. Lofty adjusted the NVGs and after a long sweeping scan jerked his head back to the right and settled. Taking his cue, Skelter took out the binos and turned the knurled focus wheel. Bingo! The barge was bigger than he expected, aground, judging from the angle of the vessel, which was in their favour, giving them a view over the sloping deck. When daylight came they should have a good chance of seeing anyone topside. At least they would if they could stand up, which of course would not be possible. The low scrub was sparse but given the distance and the number of overlapping patches, they would not be able to see a thing. Skelter pointed two fingers at his eyes, made a motion like a snake with his right hand tapped his shoulder and then Lofty's. Lofty nodded, his dusty face grey as the moon.

The two men crept forward slowly, watching every footfall, weaving around bushes like a pair of matadors with an invisible bull. Gradually they closed to one hundred metres from the river, which was a fraction over three hundred from the barge on the opposite bank. Here the scrub petered out until at fifty metres from the water's edge it reduced to a bush here and there and not one above half a metre in height. Skelter decided they would have to establish a forward OP at that point with two men and a blind laying up position with the radio a couple of hundred metres back in the scrub. They spent twenty minutes scouting for a place to set up the forward OP but the ground was so uniform it made little difference.

There were no lights, no sign of movement, and no noise coming from the barge. A tarpaulin obscured part of the deck. Skelter could only assume that all were asleep. He handed the Binos to Lofty. Finding the rest of his patrol was not easy in the terrain but Skelter had counted his paces out to the first stop where the bush thinned out and by counting back and referencing the stars he made it without any drama. He was not met with a password as it would have been pointless. To keep it quiet enough not to risk the sound carrying on the still air and over the water would have meant him being close enough to be recognised anyway. The lads were alert and eager for news. Skelter appraised them of the situation and picked up his bergan. Eager hands helped him get it on his back and when that was done he heaved Lofty's up to balance precariously on the wheelbarrow. It seemed wrong to think of it in those terms as it was twice as wide as a builder's barrow and much longer with two wheels. The tubular steel scaffold frame sagged a little in protest but they got it going and once moving it was easier to keep up the momentum. There was no escaping the fact, however, that it was damned heavy. Nonetheless in a little over thirty minutes they had reached the objective.

'Right you three, get sorted out here. Get cammed up, set up the radio and establish comms. with base. Test your walkie talkies now. Channel 3. Use the pressel switch. No talking unless absolutely necessary. Biscuit, you are in charge here. I'm going up with Lofty. I'll send him back for his gear. Are we all clear?' Nods all round.

Leaving the three men to get cammed up Skelter opened his bergan, took out sleeping bag, poncho, carry mat, two spare water bottles, one with the large letter P on it made from gaffer tape, added some extra rations, then dropped the lot into a heavy duty plastic garden refuse bag. He took the wire cutters and snipped the roll of chicken wire into six two metre lengths which he rolled together and tied with a bungee. He put the snips and a bundle of tent pegs into his pocket grabbed the wire and refuse sack and went forward to find Lofty, or rather to allow Lofty to find him. Once Lofty went to ground with his camouflage trickery he would only be found if he wanted to be. And so it was. Skelter got pretty much to where he figured he had left him and stopped to listen. A low whisper real close called 'H... H...' and Skelter felt something poke him in the back of his leg. It was a harmless stick, on the other end of which was Lofty.

Skelter pulled a small reel of tripwire from his cargo pocket. He then took a long steel tent peg and skewered the spool securely to the ground through the centre of the reel, at the base of a thorn bush, and handed the loose end to Lofty. 'Sigs line,' he whispered. Lofty nodded. Skelter set the bearing to the patrol on Lofty's compass, indicated one hundred and fifty paces, that he was staying put and that first light was zero six hundred.

Lofty had an hour and a half. He made his way back to the others, trailing the wire behind him and found them with no problem. He handed the wire to Biscuit along with a fresh spool. They fashioned loops at the ends of the two wires with Lofty's Leatherman multitool, before joining these with a short length of nylon paracord. They now had a way of passing radio signals received to the forward OP. Tie a bag with the decoded signal page to the paracord, tug the cord and let H reel it in. Any answer, write on the back and reverse the reeling. Low tech to perfection. The wire would also make it easier to find the way when the camouflage was fully fledged. It was strong gunmetal grey and being tripwire, so thin as to be almost invisible.

Skelter had made good use of the time scraping a shallow depression in the ground alongside Lofty's using his gloved hands to avoid noise, carefully removing as many sharp stones as he could find by feel. He then laid out his carry mat and topped it with the sleeping bag. The chicken wire was bent to fashion three curved covers like cloches, which he secured with the tent pegs forming a tunnel over his depression. This he topped with his poncho, then taking his personal cam net he suspended it to float above using green nylon cord attached to the scrub and fibreglass rods pushed into holes in the ground made with a tent peg, before finally decorating it with pieces of thorn scrub.

Forty-five minutes later, just as Skelter had finished, Lofty appeared beside him, clutching his bag of kit and his Accuracy International. *I'm glad he is on my side,* thought Skelter. By the time the sky was showing the first grey streaks of the false dawn Lofty had completed his little hide next to Skelter's and both men had settled in. They would work two hours on, two off. Sleeping when possible to conserve energy and stave off boredom.

In the LUP Tash had set up the radio, draping the aerials over the thorn bushes. Hardly ideal but it was all he could do. Tash was not getting through. He kept trying while Turbo and Biscuit hung the cam nets from the bushes and the handles of the barrow, which now stood on end. They were invisible to anyone further away than a few metres. The aerials, which were the only give away were woven though the bushes to minimize their visual impact. Happy they had done all they could working by moonlight, they settled in. Biscuit took out his Sony walkie talkie and squeezed the pressel switch once; *'click.'* He got a reply almost immediately, *'click, click.'* He looked about. Tash having finally got through on the radio, stopped for a second and acknowledged receipt with two squeezes on his Sony closely followed by Turbo who was on watch. Turbo, being an advanced signaller, would spell Tash later. Biscuit had stood himself down for the next two hours. If his main specialist skills were not needed for the operation, it would please everyone. Biscuit was the patrol Medic.

20

Friday 26th June

Richard Bell watched the sunrise from his bed-space beneath the tarpaulin, drawing his weary, aching knees up to his chin and tucking his espadrilles under the dirty blanket. Charles Parish was still fast asleep. Today the hand of fate was hovered over him; Bell guessed that this was the day the ransom would be delivered; the day that he would be released, if all went according to plan. The pirates were sleeping forward of the wheelhouse or inside it. They were not bothered about security, after all their prisoners couldn't go anywhere. Even if they were not wearing leg irons, they had no idea where they were or where the nearest civilization was. They could guess the obvious that it would be near the river, and downstream towards the coast would be the only logical direction. All that meant was that any escape following that line would end in recapture within hours. Deviate away from the river – die of thirst. Simple. No, the only way was to play along, pay up and hope. Their captors had nothing to gain by killing them, but then again Coke T-shirt had shot Chuck Riner without blinking. Bell concluded that he was quite probably a psychopath. He had been high as a kite, but then apart from Cawaale they all were most of the time. Bell knew from his early years aboard ship the Somali drug of choice was khat. The leaves of the slow growing shrub, contained cathinone, an amphetamine like stimulant, which caused excitement, and euphoria. Common throughout the Horn of Africa, one of its side effects, a loss of appetite, proved useful in a region suffering from frequent famine. Right now Bell was thinking that he could do with some. Any kind of escape, even virtual would be a blessing.

Although he believed that the money would buy him his freedom Bell knew there was no guarantee. People had double-crossed him before, in his business deals, in the early days. It had not happened for years. He had learned fast and it was widely known now that crossing Richard Bell carried consequences. Out here in the wilds of Somalia, however, his reputation was unknown and even if they were it seemed unlikely that they would be intimidated by it.

Charles Parish stirred, stretched and blinked at the daylight. 'Any water left?' he asked. Bell tossed the goatskin across.

'Well, we should get a result soon, Charles. My guess is they'll arrange the drop today. Sooner the better for them.'

'What if the ransom deal doesn't work? They might kill us anyway? What are we to them? Nothing once they get paid; nothing.'

'Take it easy, Charles, you need to keep cool. They won't want to antagonise the British Government. It would only cause them more trouble than it's worth.'

'That's bollocks and you know it. They don't give a shit for anything outside of their little world.'

'Look, Charles, this is the best deal we have. Face it it's the only deal we have, the chances of your precious British Government launching some kind of rescue mission are as likely as the Pope giving birth to triplets, so have faith and stay focused.' Grinding and gnashing his teeth Bell turned his back on his fellow prisoner.

From his position on the opposite side of the river, Skelter studied the barge through the binoculars. Poking out from behind the stern he could see an outboard motor attached to the stern of a narrow Skiff nestled between the barge and the bank. He could see clearly in great detail the rusting hull, the decaying, sun-bleached deck timbers and the wheelhouse. He could see the blue tarpaulin stretched low across the foredeck. What he could not see was if there was anyone beneath it. He had been watching for over an hour, since before it was light enough to make out any details. Disappointed, but not disheartened, years of this type of work had taught Skelter patience. Beside him Lofty rolled slowly over and rubbed his eyes, took a packet of Polo mints from his smock pocket, popped one in his mouth and offered one to Skelter, who took it, savouring the freshness it brought to his mouth.

A flight of pelicans swooped low over the river as if about to land and then at the last minute apparently changed their minds and flew around in a circuit before repeating the process. After a third approach they settled on the water with a flurry of foam and flapping wings. It was a welcoming and entertaining distraction from the monotony of the job.

Lofty removed the lens covers from the Bender and Schmidt and tucking the rifle's stock into his shoulder sighted on the wheelhouse. He calculated the range using a combination of information he had memorised from the map and his years of experience. Carefully he turned the dials the required number of clicks. The range was short, an insult to his skill almost, but a job is a job. Anyone taking a round at this distance wouldn't know anything about it. They would be dead before the sound of the shot reached them. Skelter's walkie talkie clicked once. Biscuit with a radio check. Skelter answered, squeezing twice. Lofty followed suit. At least someone was awake in the LUP.

Someone was awake in the Grand Hotel, someone nursing a Queen-size hangover and the floor of a hamster's cage for a tongue. Caroline Warren rang room service and ordered coffee and Alka Seltzer for breakfast. It was eight-thirty and the sun was blinding. *Did it ever do anything else but shine in this part of the world?* She doubted it. It had been streaming in through the window since before the pain behind her eyes drove her to close the curtains. While waiting for the hangover cure she opened the clamshell case and checked that the tightly wrapped bundles of greenbacks were still snug in their waterproof sleeves. Satisfied, she clicked the case closed and put it in the bottom of the wardrobe. She rang room service to find out what had happened to the Alka Seltzer, but there was a knock on the door before she got connected. Caroline cradled the receiver without speaking and called softly for the boy to come in. She took the tray, dropped the tablets into the glass of mineral water and stirred with the long handled silver teaspoon provided. While the Seltzer fizzed she tipped the boy and sent him on his way. She was expecting a call from Nigel with the final details in half an hour. The pilot was picking her up in an hour. If only she hadn't drunk so much last night.

Nigel Harmon brushed his teeth in the washbasin in the cloakroom next door to his office, wishing he had gone ahead with the plans to put in a shower five years ago. He rejected them as extravagant, a typical accountant's response. He was not short of money and from where he was now standing it seemed great value. The minder stood watching him.

'Where the hell would I go, for God's sake? You don't have to keep breathing down my bloody neck,' said Nigel, running the Remington cordless over his stubble.

'Just doing my job, sir,' said the young man.

'Just doing my, job sir,' mimicked Harmon, shocked

at the disheveled image facing him in the mirror. His nose began to twitch as a pleasant aroma found its way into his nostrils. The young man had made coffee for them both. Something he supposed, but Harmon longed for normality to return. He was a creature of habit. He liked routine. Routine was never boring, it was comforting, like the blanket who's corner he had chewed to shreds as child, lying awake at night waiting for sleep to save him. There were chocolate digestives for breakfast and a bunch of bananas had appeared somehow. The minder, Harmon guessed, who else? He was half way through peeling one when the call came in. The minder snapped his fingers and the man with the headphones, who until that moment had completely escaped Nigel's notice, clicked into action. Nigel lifted the receiver, grabbed the pen and pad and began writing. There was no preamble, straight in. He read the notes back, said 'okay' and the line went dead.

Caroline's head was still pounding when Nigel called. It took a huge effort of will on her part to concentrate on what he was saying.

'Slow down, Nigel, for Christ's sake, give me a chance to take this down.' She wrote in longhand for fear of her making a crucial mistake in translation from her undeniably excellent shorthand. No sense in taking chances. 'Okay, I've got that now let me read it back to you.' She related her notes, got the okay From Nigel and then for good measure repeated them. She felt nauseous and had difficulty focusing her eyes, relieved when he ended the call and she could go to the bathroom. Sitting on the toilet with her head lolling on the side of the washbasin, holding a wet face cloth to her forehead, she waited for the inevitable, remaining like that for what seemed an age. Finally her stomach heaved and surrendered its contents to the cool white porcelain. Not long after she began to feel marginally better, still lousy but not so bad as she was earlier. Caroline crawled into the shower, sluiced herself, mindful of time and somehow managed to towel herself dry. By the time her lift arrived she had cleaned up and changed into a comfortable cream chiffon blouse and grey Ali Baba pants, sandals on her feet. Her hair was the problem. It was not quite dry, but she managed to roll and pin it up in a passable style and cover it with a silk headscarf a la Audrey Hepburn. Quick lick with the mascara brush, smear of lipstick and that would have to do. She was waiting outside the hotel clutching the clamshell for dear life when the battered BMW pulled up. The driver leaned across and opened the passenger door.

'Caroline Warren?' he enquired.

'Yes,' she replied, climbing in next to the man.

A big, fat fingered, freckled hand pushed the lever to select drive and a flip-flopped foot depressed the accelerator. The automatic gearbox performed its technical wizardry and the three litre vee-six slid smoothly forward and out into the chaotic Mombasa traffic. Caroline looked across, scrutinising the man from behind her overpriced designer sunglasses. What she had been expecting she was not sure, only that what ever it was, he was not it. He looked in his mid sixties, but she guessed that might be due more to lifestyle than longevity and he might be considerably younger. There was a dark smudge across his not so white XXXL T-shirt where the steering wheel rubbed across his beer belly. His eyes were sunken and lost looking, above the beetroot beacon of his nose. Too much sun? Too much Tequila more like. He smelt like a distillery. Caroline took a small bottle of Chanel from her Louis Vuitton handbag and gave herself a fifty-dollar burst. Judging by the freckled face his white hair had probably once been ginger.

'Got the cash?' he said, nodding to the clamshell clamped between her knees.

'Of course,' replied Caroline Warren, 'and your

instructions. Do you have the plane and the pilot?'

'Yes, to both, lady,' he said, suppressing a laugh, as he switched lanes without warning, ignoring the barrage of honking and abuse from other drivers. Caroline felt sick. Surely not, he was winding her up. He couldn't be. His sunken eyes said he was. She felt bile rising in her throat. The thought of getting in a small aircraft with a stranger had been bad enough, but this man?

Richard Bell called out to the dozing guard slumped against the wheelhouse, indicating that he needed to relieve himself. The man shuffled over and released the leg irons from their fastenings at the rail. Bell crawled from beneath the tarpaulin and stretched his aching limbs before hobbling to the side and urinating into the river. Parish needing to perform the same function joined him moments later. No sooner had he finished than Charles began heaving over the side, brown bile spilling into the swirling current. Bell stepped back to avoid getting splattered. The Somali waved them back to their bed spaces with the muzzle of his AK, but Parish was in no fit state to go anywhere.

Three hundred metres away on the far side of the river, Skelter logged the first sighting of the hostages in his notebook. Positive I.D. eyes on R. Bell; C. Parish. One hostile; grey T-shirt; AK 47. No spare mags. Result! These were the main priority. Maybe the other passengers and crew were aboard also. Not enough room under the Tarp, unless that is it covered a hatchway to below deck. Skelter breathed out long and slow, feeling his shoulder muscles relax a little. *So far so good.* He leaned across through the cam net and tapped Lofty.

The sniper slipped off the lens caps and squinted down the riflescope. Perfect, clear as day. Used to shooting at a thousand metres plus the detail at this range was breathtaking. He could see the individual hairs on the back of Parish's neck.

If the drive to the airstrip was any measure of the man's flying skill then Caroline Warren was convinced she had seen her last sunrise. Perhaps she should have made a will before she left? No time and anyway no point. Who would she leave it to? Her mother was the only family she had, since her father finally succumbed to cirrhosis of the liver last year and as next of kin she'd get it anyway.

Caroline had a sense of foreboding, she did not want to go with this man, but how else was she to know he hadn't just kept the money? The hangover seemed to be getting worse and death was becoming a less unattractive option as the clock ticked on. She stumbled out of the car into the wall of heat and followed the man into the hangar. The smell of kerosene and rubber was overpowering, causing her to gyp. The aircraft looked like a toy compared to even the smallest city hopper she had flown in. It definitely had seen better days, with dents and dinks, scratched, scuffed and scraped paintwork and well-worn tyres she would not have entertained on her Lexus. The bad feeling she had, had just got worse.

Caroline watched as the man walked around the aircraft poking the tyres and manipulating the flappy bits on the wings and tail with his mole like hands. He lifted the engine cover, peered inside, poked about a bit and checked the oil, wiping the dipstick on the bottom of his T-shirt. Apparently satisfied he opened the cockpit door and leaned in to fiddle with something behind the seat. Next he put an oily finger and thumb into the corners of his mouth and produced a piercing whistle which sent shock waves through Caroline Warren's delicate head.

Two Africans wearing faded blue boiler suits appeared from the back of the hangar, one wiping his hands with an oily rag, which he thrust into his pocket. The three of them then pushed the plane outside and onto the hard standing.

'Right, give me those final instructions then get your gear aboard, lady, and climb in.'

She took a deep breath, swallowed hard and handed over the envelope. Then with a churning stomach and liquid legs, she climbed into the aircraft and strapped herself into the front seat beside the pilot's. Despite being not at all religious she was not surprised to find herself praying, for the first time since Sunday school. The man was talking to himself.

'Doors closed and locked, parking brake set, flight controls free.' He kept this up for what seemed ages. Something about a rudder? Had she misheard? Boats have rudders, not aeroplanes. The engine whined into life, the smell and sound adding to Caroline's misery. He muttered something about the runway as they turned onto the strip. Caroline jammed her eyes tight shut. Everything started vibrating, the noise increased along with it and she was convinced the plane would shake itself apart. The kerosene smell of aviation fuel made her retch.

'You can open your eyes now, lady,' said the voice of a forty a day man. 'We're airborne.'

The PM's brow resembled a freshly ploughed field. The news from his press secretary was a potential bombshell. He addressed the Cobra meeting. 'Gentlemen, and Ladies, there has been a development in the Somali situation. Sky News has reported, quote: *"A senior civil servant, believed to be a Government advisor on terrorism has been kidnapped by an unknown African terrorist group."* Not entirely accurate but I do not have to tell you how potentially damaging this is. Get the leak plugged immediately and find the person responsible. I want his head on a plate.' The PM took a deep breath, and then exhaled slowly before continuing. 'I will hand you over to Bernard for analysis.' Looking immaculate in his Saville Row, the signature pencil poised between his fingers, Bernard appeared uncharacteristically stern. Charles Parish was a close friend and his situation had gone from bad to potentially dire. The PM speculated privately as to when Bernard would progress from twirling his pencil, to chewing it. Bernard stopped twirling, cleared his throat and began speaking.

'If the kidnappers get wind of this then the stakes will be considerably raised. At the moment we have an act of criminal extortion. If these people have access to this news then they will at best demand more money. More likely they will attempt to hand Charles Parish over to one of the terrorist groups,' he paused for effect, pushing his right index finger up the aquiline nose to arrest the slide of his half frames. 'This would be an enormous propaganda coup. There is a strong probability that Al Qaeda could become involved. We cannot allow Charles Parish to fall into terrorist hands.' The eagle eyes flashed and danced around the room gauging the impact of his words. 'This situation is serious and we must address the problem immediately.'

'Thank you, Bernard,' said the PM as Bernard Morgan resumed his seat. Next to speak was Geoffrey Greaves. The colonel was blunt and single minded.

'We have a five man patrol in situ with eyes on the target. They have positively identified Parish and Bell. A sixteen man SAS assault group arrived at our base camp in Kenya during the early hours this morning. They will be ready to deploy at last light. We have no firm intelligence on the kidnappers. We can only guess at their strength and capabilities. Our best estimate is less than a dozen, most likely carrying small arms, probably AK47s. I do not anticipate any difficulty in conducting a successful operation, however I cannot predict the behaviour of an unknown adversary.'

The PM intervened. 'What you are saying is the hostages could be killed, is that correct?'

The colonel nodded, 'Exactly that Prime Minister.'

'How likely is that in your opinion Colonel Greaves?'

'Fifteen percent chance of them becoming casualties.'

The PM ran a hand through his hair and stared at the desktop. 'Thank you, Geoffrey. Can we hear from Geraldine Collins please?' he asked, looking at the prompt on his monitor.

A rather serious looking woman in a lamb's wool sweater a couple of sizes too large for her small frame addressed the committee. She launched straight into a prepared speech.

'Forensic analysis of the blood samples found on the deck and in stateroom has revealed they are from two different groups. The stateroom sample is A Positive, common, but this is Charles Parish's group. The deck sample, which I understand was significantly greater, is B. Negative. This is only found in one percent of the British population. Our American cousins have confirmed from their records that Bell's bodyguard, an ex US Navy Seal, rejoicing in the name of Charlton Riner, shares this blood group. Riner is a U.S. citizen. I have no information on what percentage of the American population has this group but it is likely to be very low. I believe it reasonable to assume that the blood is his. There is no information on the other nine missing people.' She sat down the moment she had finished.

Next to speak was another woman, forty something, smartly dressed in a navy blue suit and white cotton blouse. 'Good morning, I represent the Meteorological Office. As you may know Somalia has been suffering from drought conditions for many months, despite this being the middle of the rainy season. This year rainfall in the area has been almost non-existent. That is about to change dramatically in the next twelve to twenty-four hours. A Tropical storm in the Indian Ocean is pushing its way towards the coast. We expect it to make landfall in the next couple of hours. This will mean monsoon conditions for at least forty-eight hours, probably longer.'

The PM caught Geoffrey Greaves eye across the table. It was hard to say which of them looked the most worried. 'Deploy the assault team immediately,' the Prime Minister told the colonel, 'before the weather closes in.'

The meeting concluded after the committee had shown their support to the PM's decision to give the go ahead for the SAS Assault. Geoffrey Greaves and Martin Sixsmith, the Head of MI6, stayed behind for at téte a téte, their faces stony. What they discussed was for their ears only.

21

Friday 26th June

Turbo had taken over from Tash when the flash message came in over the radio at seven thirty three. He had never received a flash message before. They were normally only sent in the most serious of circumstances, such as a declaration of war. He passed it to Tash to decode. A few minutes later the plain language transcript was snaking through the scrub on the trip wire express.

Back at the LUP Turbo received another message. It was short and quick to decode. Short and unambiguous. Short, sharp and shocking. After reeling back the carrier he put the transcript into the bag and jerked the wire.

Skelter read the second signal, blinked twice and read it again.

News leaked to press. Assume enemy knows C.P. is valuable asset and may contact Al Qaeda. C.P. must not...repeat must not be taken. Tropical storm imminent your location.

Reading the message in the hide was not easy. The sky darkening rapidly Skelter noticed. The wind was getting up too.

Two minutes later Skelter was trying to get his head around it. It was plain enough. Turbo had written clearly in block capitals. GREEN LIGHT PARISH. To be extra clear he had written it in full again beneath. Skelter passed the message to Lofty. His eyebrows arched as he read it but that was all. He had not been in this position before, but nothing surprised him, he had been in the job far too long. Half an hour passed with no activity on the barge when a figure emerged from under the tarpaulin. It was Parish who unsteadily made his way to the side of the boat and hung over the rail. Lofty moved the rifle a couple of degrees and put his right eye to the scope. He could clearly see that Parish was being sick over the side. He looked across at Skelter, gave a thumbs up and settled back to the scope. He had a clear shot.

Rollo replaced the telephone receiver and went out to the terrace where he knew Lucy would be. 'Daddy what is it? You look awful.' He grasped both her hands in his.

'Sit down darling, I have some bad news.'

The bad news for Caroline Warren kept piling up. First the hangover, then the pilot, the plane and now the weather. Visibility was deteriorating and the turbulence had caused her to fill two sick bags already. There were only two left. The pilot, whose name she didn't know was struggling to follow the course as it was taking them into the path of the storm. Then the lightning started. She began shaking, desperately trying to maintain her dignity and position. She was praying again, even harder than before.

Lucy Ryder was praying too, her head on her father's shoulder, tears soaking into his shirt. Rollo was relieved to have unburdened himself, while at the same time hurting to see the anguish his daughter was suffering.

'Does Mummy know?' she asked.

'Not from me, I only got the call myself a few

minutes ago.'

'We must ring her. If she sees it on the news...?'

'Of course,' said Rollo getting up.

'I'll do it, Daddy,' said Lucy, her composure returning.

'If you're...'

'Positive. Do you want to speak to her as well?'

He nodded. He had not spoken to his ex-wife for some years, not that there was any real animosity, just a wide gulf of opinion and a long distance as the crow flies. Four thousand five hundred miles, give or take. Lucy made the call. Her mother was old school unflappable. Brought up on a Kenyan tea plantation, Natalie Ryder had lived through the years of the Mau Mau terrorist emergency in the nineteen fifties. She had been a schoolgirl then and vividly remembered her mother carrying a rifle everywhere she went. Her father had given her a revolver and taught her how to use it, shooting at tin cans at the back of the bungalow. It was a bad time with many white farmers being butchered with machetes, sometimes by their own servants. They were a tough breed, the old colonials.

When Rollo took over the call he did his best to reassure her that absolutely everything was being done to bring the situation to a safe and satisfactory conclusion. She seemed gentler and more receptive than he remembered, but then much water had passed beneath many bridges since they had shared a life together. Family is family and even though Charles was born two years before Rollo had met Natalie, he had always thought of him as his own. He handed the phone back to Lucy so she could say her goodbyes and wandered into the kitchen to put the kettle on. Wilkins was emptying the rubbish. It was bin day tomorrow.

'Any more news, Sir?' he asked.

'Yes, Wilkins, I'm rather afraid it isn't good.' Rollo brought him up to speed as the kettle boiled.

'Here let me do that for you, Sir. It will all turn out

all right, you see if it don't.'

'Your glass is always half full, isn't it Wilkins?'

'Always best to look on the bright side, I find. Will miss Lucy be having coffee?'

'I expect so. What would I do without you, Wilkins?'

'Oh I expect you'd manage, Sir.'

Charles Parish was still hanging over the side of the barge his empty stomach retching, his neck nestled in the crosshairs of Lofty's telescopic sight. Skelter's brain was working overtime computing his options. The window of opportunity to kill Parish was shrinking. Soon he would be back beneath the tarpaulin, hidden from view. The leaden swirling sky said heavy rain soon, with reduced visibility. This might be the only chance to prevent his possible capture by Al Qaeda. There was however, no evidence the kidnappers knew of Parish's importance, or even if there was more than the one kidnapper they had so far seen on the barge. Skelter's humanity revolted against the orders while professional training pleaded the case for the bigger picture and the lives that could be put at risk. Devil and the deep blue. Sergeant Skelter had a decision to make. And fast.

Flying parallel to the Somali coast, four miles out at two thousand feet, Caroline's pilot was talking to himself again, only this time the language was much more colourful. He was cursing and swearing a lot. The little Cessna 182 was being buffeted and battered by the rainstorm and he had sensibly taken the decision to abort the flight and return to the airstrip.

Caroline was almost past caring. She had thrown up all over the clamshell case still clamped to her stomach, her chin sliding against the vomit covering its smooth aluminium finish. The pilot's breathing was rapid and ragged, his voice had gone up an octave and the language had descended beneath the gutter and into the sewer. She caught something about 'the coast' and 'beach.' It all seemed to be going horribly wrong. She looked up but could see nothing but the rain lashing the windscreen. The pilot was frantically flipping switches and wrestling with the controls. 'Mayday, Mayday, this is Cessna flight two zero three, position forty-two fifty-one east one thirty-nine south, losing power, Mayday May...Brace yourself. Brace yourself.' His voice was off the soprano scale now. Caroline closed her eyes and flooded her Janet Reger. 'We're going down. We're going down. Brace bra....'

22

Friday 26th June

Skelter heard the first drops of rain striking the camouflage-covered groundsheet above him as humanity wrestled with duty in the dark recesses of his mind. The sky light up with a brilliant flash of lightening and the heavens opened. Game over. No shot. Visibility vanished. He was off the hook. Both men breathed a sigh of relief. Divine intervention? Who knows? The storm brought with it a whole new set of problems. Keeping dry was not one of them. Keeping dry under the present conditions was impossible. One advantage the rain did give them was the ability to use the Sonys for voice communication. No one would hear them above the downpour. The noise level was incredible. They might even have a problem hearing each other.

Skelter squeezed the pressel several times before he got an acknowledgement. 'We need dry bags for the weapons. Get a couple up here now.'

'Roger.' It was Turbo. The same Turbo who came sloshing through the bush shortly after, looking like the proverbial drowned rat. He dropped the bags and looked at Skelter.

'Cheers, nothing to report apart from one hostage puking over the side into the river. I guess the food's not so good on their cruise ship.' Smiling, Turbo turned about and squelched into the bush. Lofty, so far relatively dry

148

beneath his poncho roof, stripped the rifle, wiped it dry and rubbed it over with a rag soaked in WD 40, before stowing it in the dry bag. Skelter followed suit with his AK, they both had their pistols for close defence but it was most unlikely that they would need them.

In Camp Winston the B squadron assault force was grounded. There was no way they could fly in such a fierce storm even if the Kenyan Air Force had been prepared to bend the rules and risk it. The plan was unravelling like a roll of razor wire. Lieutenant Glass poured over the maps in the makeshift operations room. On paper insertion by vehicle looked feasible. His Kenyan advisor however, shook his head. 'The roads here cease to exist once you get close to the border. There are barely discernible tracks, which are okay for four-wheel drive most of the time in the dry, but now? This is a late rainy season, but when it comes, everything on wheels stops in the bush; everything.'

Glass was caught in a vice. The pressure from the top brass to get the job done whatever the cost, winding in from one direction, verses the pressure from his commanding officer for him to make a mature judgement call and demonstrate his suitability for a Special Forces career on the other. If he did nothing, at best he risked a charge of indecision, at worst one of cowardice. If he risked the overland operation and got stranded by the conditions he risked being found in Somalia without a legitimate reason, possibly sparking an international incident. He could also lay himself open to a charge of recklessly endangering the lives of the men under his command. The press would have a field day embarrassing the British government and his career would be over. Glass might be new to special forces operations, but he knew they were not like Hollywood makes them out to be. They are about carefully calculated risks delivered with dash and daring and commitment. They are not about being reckless, His soldiers were the most highly trained specialist troops in the world. Training which takes years and costs a large chunk of British taxpayer's money. Precious few, too few to risk losing them through recklessness.

It could be argued that Caroline Warren had been reckless to fly without a lifejacket, but she had not realised they would be flying over the ocean and anyway she was never given the option. It was too late now anyway. She knew did not have long to live. They must be close now. The engine was screaming, the airframe shaking itself senseless while the pilot, poured a stream of high-pitched venomous invective upon the machine as he hauled back on the stick trying to get the nose up. He had to hit the water tail first to have any chance at all. Despite appearances he was a skilled and experienced bush pilot. Caroline could see the water now, coming up fast. All composure had gone. 'We're going to die, sweet Jesus, Jesus Jes...'

The world was green and swirling, a weak white light was beckoning to her as Caroline's fear dissolved at the soothing sound of her grandmother's voice. The light got brighter and brighter and her grandmother told her to take a deep breath. She had never disobeyed her grandmother and she was not about to do so now. Caroline Warren opened her mouth wide; a nanosecond after her face broke the surface of the rain swept sea. She had her arms tightly wrapped around the clamshell case her right hand gripping the carrying handle and her left clutching the extended towing grip. The ransom money had just gone up in value. The case was watertight and keeping her afloat. There was no sign of the plane or the pilot. She was alone in a rain lashed, storm tossed sea.

Skelter took a pencil and pad and began to compose a message, but soon abandoned the idea as the rain found its way through the gaps in his flimsy hide. The depression in which he was lying had been collecting water for a while now and he was beginning to feel like a mudskipper. Lofty had his Gore-Tex sniper suit to keep him snug but that too would soon succumb to the force of nature. Skelter squeezed the pressel and called for a radio check. Having raised Biscuit he asked for Tash.

'I need you to send a message, Tash. Take this down. Visibility one hundred metres. Target invisible. No shot. Advise on progress of back up.' Tash read the message back to Skelter.

'Wilco, H. Let you know soon as.'

'H out.'

It was over an hour before Skelter got the call. An hour of rain running off the brim of his bush hat and down the back of his neck. How could it be so cold this close to the Equator? The news was not good. The news was no news, no anything. Tash had failed to make contact.

'What's the problem?' Skelter asked

'The storm? Atmospherics? Take your pick, we have no comms. Not a peep. I'll keep trying but don't hold your breath.'

'Okay, H out.' Skelter wiped his wet face with a face veil and clenched his fists, grinding his teeth. 'Well, that leaves us then I guess,' he muttered under his breath. 'Oh joy.'

Lofty turned towards his companion. 'What's up, H?'

'Nothing, mate, just talking to myself.' He lay in the puddle that the hide had become and rattled the options through his brain at double time. He must assume they were not going to re establish communications with the head shed until the storm abated and that was not expected to be for at least another forty-eight hours. He could not afford to do nothing for that long. The assault team would not be able to fly in the present conditions. As to the ransom delivery he must assume that too had been cancelled. If he was in the kidnapper's shoes he would be pretty pissed off by now and might well feel like taking it out on the hostages, assuming that is, that they had not got a transistor radio to tell them the news that the value of their stock had gone through the roof. 'Lofty, it's time for plan B.'

'It better be good?' said the saturated sniper, 'I'm swear I'm growing gills.'

'Sorry, mate, but plan B needs you to stay put and watch the gear. If the weather eases and visibility improves you can cover us from this side. I intend to take the others across to do a CTR (Close Target Reconnaissance) then go in and lift the hostages. The back up's not going to happen. The river's rising fast, we must go now.'

'I'll move down to the water, cut the distance. I might get eyes on from there.'

'Good.' Skelter took out the Sony, Squeezed the pressel and told Biscuit he was coming in, then climbed out from under the camouflage and squelched away through the deluge into the scrub.

RAF Weapons Systems Operator Susan Shaw was sitting at her station, glued to her computer screen, surrounded by banks of electronic wizardry, which would make the average geek wet himself with wonder. Hers was not your average open plan office; in fact, space for her and her fellow NCOs was at a premium. The fuselage of an RAF Nimrod is narrow enough when empty, let alone after it has been stuffed full to bursting with advanced avionics.

Cruising in the clear blue skies way above the storm, Sergeant Shaw had been monitoring the electronic signal from a tracking beacon; a beacon that had been placed inside one of the bundles of US Dollars by British intelligence at the Chase Bank in Mombasa. Shaw had reported to her supervising officer that the beacon was static, cross-referenced the radar plot of the Cessna 128, which had ceased. She correctly deduced that the aircraft had gone down into the ocean. The Royal Navy Frigate, which had been shadowing the Cessna's course, was making for the beacon at full speed.

Twenty-eight thousand feet below the Nimrod, Caroline Warren was grimly hanging on to the world's most expensive lifejacket. She was cold, weak and struggling to keep her head above the waves, but she refused to die.

23

Friday 26th June

Skelter's plan B was a bit off the cuff but adaptability was the name of the game. The British soldier was the world's master of make do and mend, at playing by ear. In any event there was no time to go into detail. A quick huddle around the map under the ponchos forming the roof of the LUP and they all agreed that the best place to attempt a crossing would be around two miles upstream where the river doubled in width at a large sweeping S bend. It might be further to cross to the far bank, but it had to be a lot shallower and they might be able to wade across.

'We'll take two bergans,' said Skelter. 'Fill the spare refuse sacks with air, gaffer tape 'em and put them inside. One flotation bergan between two. Don't forget to tie your wepons to your belts or wrists. Spare mags in the bergan side pockets. Walkie talkies in dry bags. Change batteries for new ones first. Any questions? No? Right let's get to it.'

The patrol was on the move in less than fifteen minutes, Skelter setting a cracking pace. There was no need to move tactically. The monsoon rain would have drowned the sound of a heard of elephants and it cut visibility down to less than fifty metres. Even at the river's narrowest they could not see the far bank. Navigation was a breeze, just follow the river upstream. They had the wind behind them driving the rain against their backs, which was helpful, but they all knew they would pay for it once they crossed to the other bank. Then they would be heading into the teeth of the gale and be almost blind. Skelter checked his watch, wiping at it with his fingers. Four o'clock. It would be dark in two and a half hours, well, darker to be precise for it was pretty much like dusk already with the clouds and the rain. Four sodden soldiers sloshed across the soggy landscape, soaked through to the skin, gouged and torn by thorns, but relieved to be doing something positive at last. It's always the hanging around that brings a man down. Sitting, listening, watching, wondering and waiting. Hurry up and wait. That was the army way. Now at last they were doing what they were trained for, what they did best, better than anyone in any army anywhere in the world.

The storm was moving inland dissipating some of its energy as it met the warmer air. It was this that saved Caroline Warren's life. As she began to lose her grip the waves subsided and the wind dropped as the ocean flattened its waters under the eye of the storm. The strange calm in the centre of chaos. High above, her guardian angel, Susan Shaw, guided HMS Monmouth in what was now good visibility towards the pulsing beacon silently signalling from the clamshell suitcase. It was the last hour of daylight. According to Sergeant Shaw's calculations at its present course and speed the ship should be close enough to make visual contact in twelve minutes.

The bank sloped gently down to the bend in the river and the flow was less fierce at this point. Skelter and Turbo went down first closely followed by Tash and Biscuit. Each pair tied themselves to their shared bergan with a metre length of Para cord. Skelter had the impression that the wind had eased, or was it wishful thinking?

'Okay boys, ready to roll?' He looked into the eyes of his men, their faces streaming, uniforms pasted to their bodies by the rain. They nodded. 'If we get separated the emergency RV is exactly opposite here on the far bank, the start of the S okay?' Again they nodded. 'Let's go,' he said, gripping one strap of the bergan as Turbo grabbed the other.

'Hey, short-arse, you forgot your snorkel,' said Biscuit, tapping Turbo on the shoulder.

'Kiss mine, ginger twat,' he replied, wading into the water. The current was fierce, the riverbed stony and uneven, however they made it half way without too much trouble, the water coming no higher than knee level, or in Turbo's case, wedding tackle level. The river was shallower near the middle, where a sandbank, which before the rain had been fully exposed, stretched for twenty metres or so down stream. It was about six metres wide. Skelter could no longer feel his lower limbs. He looked around to the other pair who were a couple of metres away and held up his thumb. They reciprocated, Turbo nodded and stepped forward across the sand bank up to his calves. Then it got deeper. The good news was he could see the far bank. Gripping the bergan tightly Skelter tested the depth using his AK47 as a gauge. He moved forward. It was now up to his knees and the current pushed against him like a water cannon. He struggled to keep his footing. Turbo was on his downstream side, not that that would make much difference, but every little helped. Skelter hoped it might just be enough. Another step then another, the freezing torrent hammering his numbed thigh muscles, doing its best to sweep him away. Another step as again his boot fought to wedge itself between the stones of the riverbed striving for purchase. Ten metres to go, ten metres, they must make it now.

'Fuckin....'

Skelter didn't hear the rest, partly because Turbo didn't get to finish it, partly because of the shock, and partly because he was underwater. Swept rapidly downstream towards the lower curve of the S, both men hung on to the bergan kicking like mules for the bank, tantalisingly close but with no inclination to get any closer it seemed. They were making no progress in their uneven battle against nature. The current pulled them around the bend fast as they fought to keep their heads above water but as they came out of the curve Skelter felt his boots hitting the bottom. He tried to dig in and gradually managed a small kick here, a shove there and then suddenly they were caught in an eddy. Turbo found his feet, coughing, spluttering and spewing. He was thigh deep in relatively calm water three metres from the bank. Hauling hard on the Para cord tied to his wrist he managed to reel in his rifle. Miraculously Skelter still had his by the pistol grip, but he had lost the magazine and it's thirty precious rounds of ammunition. Not exactly a brilliant start. The two men staggered ashore and lay panting by the water's edge cradling the bergan. The rain continued to hammer down, but the wind had definitely eased. Skelter took a fresh full magazine from the side pouch of the bergan, put it on his weapon, and applied the safety catch.

'You okay, H?' spluttered Turbo, still fighting for breath.

'Think so. I won't need a drink for a while, that's for sure. You?'

'Yeah, let's get going to the RV before we drown to fucking death.'

The others were waiting at the RV having made it across by the narrowest margin.

'We thought we'd lost you,' Biscuit said, 'I wanted to run downstream to search but Tash wouldn't have it. Stick to the plan, he said.'

'Thank fuck someone can follow orders,' said Skelter as he took a Sony from the dry bag and tried to raise Lofty. It was a forlorn hope, but worth a try. No luck. They would need to get closer. *At least we're all across,* he thought.

24

Friday 26th June

It was an hour before dusk when Turbo led them off in single file, into driving rain stinging skin like steel needles. *This must be how Gulliver felt under the onslaught of a shower of Lilliputian arrows* Skelter thought, back bent, head down, arse up as they bullied their way into the storm. His jockey shorts were sandpapering his crotch and his belt had raised a weal around his waist. Hunger gnawed at his insides and someone had cleaned his teeth with turpentine. He was surprised he didn't need a piss. Maybe he had already had one. They plodded on, in the appalling conditions, outwardly miserable but inwardly totally focused on the job ahead. In theory, the opposition should present no problem. Skelter guessed that they were probably facing a ragbag collection of undisciplined druggies with rusty AKs. Against disciplined highly trained special forces soldiers: No contest.

Skelter knew however, never to underestimate the enemy. Rusty AKs still work; a boy with a loaded gun and narcotics in his veins is a formidable foe. Druggies have no fear and kids no conscience when they are high. They will kill you in a heartbeat. On his first visit to the country many years ago, when he was a young paratrooper in the French Foreign Legion, he had been confronted by a young Somali with a rusty AK47. The youth had the wild eyes of a young man so high on narcotics he was on another planet, hollow eyes devoid of hope, eyes of a man wanting to kill and with no fear of dying. It took eleven bullets to stop the skinny little youth's demonic charge. All of them from Legionnaire Skelter's assault rifle, travelling at twice the speed of sound. In four-seconds he had emptied a thirty round magazine at less than thirty feet. The other nineteen bullets missed. He was nineteen. He had never killed anyone before.

Lofty crawled forward towards the river through the gritty mud until he was a couple of metres from the rushing torrent. He scanned what little he could see of the barge through the riflescope. He could vaguely make out movement. Several figures were busying themselves about the deck but visibility was too poor to make sense of what was happening.

Bell and Parish were nervous. The activity was sudden and the kidnappers seemed agitated and excited.

'What's going on, Richard?' said Parish, 'Can you tell what they're saying.'

'Quiet, man.'

'Sorry.'

'Hush.'

The pirates were in a huddle just within earshot. They appeared to be arguing about something. After a couple of minutes the men dispersed, two crossing the plank and disappearing into the bush, while three others went over the side where the boats were moored.

'I think they're going to move us,' Bell said, 'I don't like it. Something's happened. Something bad.'

'What?'

'I don't know, Charles, but I've got a bad feeling. They were talking about taking us up river in the boats. The pickup won't start. I guess the two that went over the plank have gone to take a look.'

Sounds of shouting and praying, banging and hammering were coming from the three men in the Skiff, followed by the noise of metal scraping against wood.

'I hope that's not what I think it is,' said Bell.

'What's that?'

'Oh shit, the stupid peasants.'

'What?'

'They're swapping engines. They're taking the big outboard off my inflatable and trying to fit it on the Skiff, the stupid bastards. It'll rip the stern off. It's much too big. Too powerful.'

Lofty was watching intently through the scope trying to tie together the fleeting glimpses he got through the lashing rain to make some kind of sense of it. It was clear something was afoot and with the activity revolving around the boats, it was odds on they were preparing to move. He depressed the pressel switch on the Sony. No response. He kept trying. It was useless. They were out of range. There was nothing he could do other than wait and watch.

Parish and Bell were released from the manacles and dragged over the side into the Skiff where they were made to lie in the bottom near the bows. It was as Bell had feared. The thirty horse power outboard had been replaced by the one hundred and fifteen HP beast from the inflatable. The stern was low in the water under its weight and three Somalis sat in the bows with their feet on Bell and Parish to compensate. A fourth pirate sat in the stern operating the engine. Almost immediately they were in trouble. The boat rounded the stern of the barge, when, as the full force of the current hit them the man on the tiller opened the throttle and the engine surged, pushing the

Skiff forward and forcing the stern down. They started taking on water fast and the torque from the engine, being too much for the mounting, tore the outboard free. The helmsman screamed and leapt forward away from the danger as the engine disappeared beneath the surface throwing the Skiff into a three hundred and sixty degree turn sending it crashing into the bank.

Parish and Bell were thrown into the water along with their captors. Bell's feet struck the bottom and after a brief struggle he managed to stand. The water was less than waist high. He made it to the bank without too much trouble. Parish meanwhile was swept downstream for several metres before he too came ashore. Luckily the water was shallow so close to the bank and all emerged soaked, shocked and spluttering, but otherwise all right.

The helmsman, despite his ordeal, had somehow managed to grab the stern line of the now engineless craft and was digging his heels into the bank. He was lucky not to have been sliced by the prop as the engine broke free. The others came to his assistance as Parish and Bell lay gasping on the bank, half in, half out of the water. Cawaale, who had been in act of boarding the second Skiff in the lee of the barge, was going ballistic. When he had calmed down he ordered the hostages into his boat with two of the crew from the disaster. He told the others to fix their boat and follow in it or else in the pick up. The Skiff's screaming outboard struggled to make headway against the flow. Cawaale continued berating the unfortunate pirates as the boat began butting against the current, battering its way upstream with the wind behind it.

Lofty could only watch and pray for the hostages. *How much more drama?*

Things seemed to be deteriorating. He could see enough to understand what had happened but was not able to identify the hostages. He had no idea if they had become casualties and no means of communicating the developments to the patrol.

Skelter wiped the rain from his face in a pointless gesture. The river was rushing seawards yards to his right, the sound of the swirling torrent covering their approach to the target. From his mental log of the paces he had counted since they left the RV Skelter calculated that they were no more than five hundred metres away. The night was kettle black; perfect conditions for the attackers. The kidnappers would be huddled in the dry in the confined space of the wheelhouse with any luck. If the prisoners were still isolated on deck it would be simple. Grenade in the wheelhouse, shoot anyone coming out of the door. If the kidnappers were below decks, white phosphorous grenades down the hole, seal and booby-trap the hatches. No point in risking casualties going in after them. Grab the hostages and use the Skiffs to cross the river. Job done. Call for a heli back to Winston. Except the bloody radio isn't working. Well, one thing at a time, cross that bridge later. *Why the hell wasn't it planned that way from the start?* Skelter wondered.

Turbo stopped, dropped to one knee and place his hand palm down upon his head, the signal for Skelter to come to him. The others turned to watch the rear and flanks, as Skelter moved forward. The wind was now much less fierce and the volume of water falling from the sky had about halved, but it was still pissing down as far as Skelter was concerned. From Turbo's position Skelter could just make out the silhouette of the barge, its solid mass and angular lines at odds with the softer, surrounding, natural landscape. There was no sign of a light anywhere, but that was not unusual. The kidnapper's would not want to advertise their presence, then again they could be lying in wait, however unlikely that seemed. Skelter moved back to the others taking Turbo with him.

First he tried to establish contact with Lofty across the river. He squeezed the pressel. No response. Again. No response. Third time lucky? Not in this case. He turned to the patrol to brief them.

'We move away from the river, tab to a hundred metres downstream of the barge and sweep around into extended line facing the barge quarter beam on and advance to the river. That will clear the approach and should sweep up anyone waiting in ambush. It will put the wind at our backs and in their faces, give us the edge in visibility.'

There were nods of agreement. As they set off in single file away from the bank and into the bush, Skelter thought he heard the noise of an engine coming from somewhere near the barge, but dismissed it as paranoia. There was such a lot of amplified audio from the storm it was easy to imagine all sorts. After only a couple of minutes they came across a ribbon of mud that passed for a dirt track road. They crossed this and moved further into the bush until they were in position below the barge one hundred and fifty metres from the river. Here they got into extended line, with Turbo upstream on Skelter's right, Biscuit on his left and Tash left of Biscuit, nearest the water.

The men were wired and ready. Turbo pushed the invading images of pints of Theakston's Black Sheep Bitter to the back of his mind and psyched himself for the fight. Biscuit was impatient and itching to get on with it. Tash saw his wife pushing five-year-old Charlie on the garden swing in the sunshine as he steeled himself to the task ahead.

25

Friday 26th June

Skelter pushed the long safety lever all the way down with his right forefinger, selecting semi automatic. Full auto in an unfamiliar environment it would be asking to get the wrong people killed. The muzzle flashes of four AKs at night would blind the men making accurate shooting impossible. It would be chaotic, even without return fire from the enemy. It would also burn up precious ammunition.

Skelter gave the signal to advance. The four men moved forward slowly, keeping station three metres apart. Using peripheral vision they kept the line straight, adjusting pace as needed. They stopped dead as one, the second they saw it. A battered old Toyota pick up truck. Weapons sighted and ready the men advanced. Skelter's heart was hammering like a lead-workers leather maul, muffled but heavy. Adrenalin raced through his veins like a sled on the Cresta Run.

Turbo went in low, cast a quick look into the load bed, signalled clear and approached the cab from the rear. He edged forward inch by inch, the rain playing a wild, heavy-metal drum solo on the steel roof and bonnet. The only senses available to Turbo were sight and touch. Skelter stood upright ready to take out anyone who appeared, but

164

only as a last resort. Turbo leaned his AK against the truck and reached down for his boot knife. Four inches of double-edged, stainless, Sheffield steel. Despite the rain his mouth was bone dry. He gripped the knife tighter. Slow, steady and silent he placed his left hand on the door handle.

The Skiff had reached the wide sweeping S bend. It was now making better progress. Parish felt sick as a dog, fearful of another capsize as water cascaded onto him. He had been fearful of water ever since his father pushed him in the deep end of the tea planter's club pool in Nairobi when he was a child, in an attempt to teach him to swim.

A Somali pulled him up by the hair and thrust a small plastic bowl at him. He thrust one at Bell also. Parish held his beneath his chin as best he could, retching hard as the vessel veered violently from side to side.

Bell slapped Parish. 'Dickhead,' he said, as he began bailing with his own bowl like a man possessed.
Parish sheepishly followed Richard's example.

Caroline Warren was dead, at least that was the conclusion she had come to. Her last memory was of a flat calm sea after the heaving waves of the storm, then being overwhelmed by a sense of inner peace as her body was lifted out of the ocean and up into the heavens. She didn't remember the splash of the swimmer entering the water close by nor his gentle words as he slid the strop over her fuzzy head. She had no recollection of the whirring rotor blades or the winch man's iron grip as he hauled her aboard the helicopter

She lay staring at the white expanse above her as her eyes slowly adjusted focus. A woman's face appeared, so close she would have felt her breath had she not been wearing a surgical mask. It was then that she began to wonder, as she slid back into unconsciousness.

Sitting by the bedroom window Lucy Ryder stared out across the moonlit garden towards the River Wye, a scene so serenely peaceful it jarred with her innermost feelings, like the emergency brake on a runaway train. She had always been close to her big brother. She looked up to him the way younger sisters sometimes do. Lucy had never regarded him as anything other than a full blood sibling even though she always knew he was not. She feared for his safety. The possibility she might not see him again brought an ache to her heart. Allowing herself the luxury of letting go in the privacy of her room she sat hugging her sides, rocking backwards and forwards in silence, as the tears coursed down her cheeks. She wished Mark was with her to hold her and comfort her. *Why did you have to go away? Why now, now when I need you so much?* She wondered where he might be and if he was thinking of her.

Skelter's immediate focus was on the Toyota's cab. He no time to think of anything else. So focused he had ceased to notice the rain. His finger hovered over the AK's trigger.

Turbo, knife at the ready, took a deep breath and wrenched the door open. The exhalation of his lungs at the sight of an empty cab was akin to a Zeppelin bursting a gasbag. *At least the kidnappers are still here*, thought Skelter, *they wouldn't have left without transport*. Turbo nodded to Skelter, sheathed the knife and picked up his Kalashnikov.

Skelter made eye contact with the others, nodded towards the river and the line reformed. The men edged forward like cat burglars in a affluent suburb. The bush thinned out and the rush of the river told Skelter they were close. Suddenly there she was, big and black and foreboding. The gangplank, well plank, for that is all it was, had not been hauled in. Getting aboard would be simple – for anyone with a death wish.

Skelter clicked the pressel switch on the Sony and whispered Lofty's name. Seconds later he heard the click.

'Have eyes on barge. What is your position?' Lofty asked.

'Forty-metres. Moving in three. Stand by stand by.'

'*Click*, Roger, H.' Lofty settled his sights on the wheelhouse and waited. Visibility was poor but just enough to distinguish friend from foe – fingers crossed.

Biscuit and Tash took up covering positions focused on the Wheelhouse. From this side Skelter could see under the tarpaulin and the deck looked empty. No one at home. He assumed they had been taken below. He and Turbo moved forward down to the riverbank and stepped onto the Skiff. Next to it was a rigid inflatable with a big outboard mounting plate but no engine. Skelter laid the AK in the Skiff, put his back to the hull and interlocked his fingers to form a stirrup. Turbo slung the AK across his back and drew his pistol, cursing under his breath the cold rain running down his back. He pulled the slide back on the weapon and eased it forward so as not to make a noise. Right foot in stirrup, push off with left, Skelter heaving. Turbo somersaulted onto the deck like Olga Korbett in her prime. He rolled right and swept the deck with the barrel of the nine milli. No reaction. Skelter made it to the plank, AK at the ready. Turbo came forward, eyes on the wheelhouse. Skelter's turn with the door this time. He crossed the plank like a cheetah on speed, dropped to one knee on the deck and covered the wheelhouse. The only sound the rush of the river and the rain on the deck. Turbo holstered the pistol and lined up his AK on the wheelhouse door. Skelter crept forward, inching his way forward crouching below the window. He put his ear to the timbers but all he could hear was the dull monotonous drumming of the rain and the sound of his own heartbeat.

He glanced ashore. Tash and Biscuit were out there he knew, unseen against the dark of the sodden Somali bush. He laid the AK down and unholstered his pistol. Eyes wide, blood pounding in his ears he pulled the slide back and with his other hand reached up for the door handle. Crunch time. One, heart thumping, two, blood pumping, three... Empty. Just like the truck. *Where the fuck are they? Below decks? Must be.* 'Shit, that's all we need,' Skelter breathed.

It made sense of course to all get out of the weather. He'd have done the same in their shoes, but did it mean hostages and crew together? They couldn't seal and booby-trap the hatches. They were going to have to do it the hard way. This was where all the tens of thousands of rounds expended practicing in the killing house at Hereford were going to pay off. They would use pistols only. The AK was too powerful for a closed environment with friendlies in the firing line. Too much risk of ricochet and anyway the weapon was too long and unwieldy for the task. Tash and Biscuit appeared out of the dark. They understood the situation right away and slung their AKs.

After a quick, quiet tour of the deck, which turned up nothing, they made for the forward hatch Skelter in the lead. He took the Mini Maglite from his pocket, slid it into the holder beneath the barrel of the pistol, and switched it on, smothering the lens with his left hand. Turbo carefully opened the hatch doors, covered by Biscuit and Tash. No lights on below, no sound they could hear above the ever present hammering rain. Skelter steadied his breathing, swallowed hard, licking rain from above his top lip to lubricate his mouth and removed his left hand from the Maglite lens. The torch beam stabbed the gloom. No reaction. An empty staircase. Shit or bust time. Jackhammer heart, jelly knees, check the safety is off for the umpteenth time – deep breath, down the steps. At least it would be out of the bloody rain.

26

Friday 26th June

Inside the Hull it was black as pitch, save for the stark, blue-white, tungsten torch beam. There were only eight steps. The floor was littered with rubbish. The foul stench of faeces and rotten fish made Skelter gag. He hugged the left of the corridor to allow Turbo a shot on his right. Picking their way over the debris and detritus fouling the floor was difficult and dangerous. Dangerous because it would mean constantly looking down pointing the torch and thus the pistol to the floor and therefore away from any threat that might present itself. If not for the training and hours of practice that is.

Skelter kept his pistol trained at chest height, the beam stabbing into the dark where he might expect to find the centre body mass of adversary. All he had to do was throw a quick glance now and then at the floor below and in front, illuminated by Turbo's Maglite shining between his legs. It called for a great deal of trust, knowing that where that light shone it was backed by a dozen bullets waiting to take the same trajectory at the twitch of a finger. Skelter knew Turbo's finger would be extended forward along and outside of the trigger guard. His safety catch however, would be off.

The beam illuminated a closed door on the left. Skelter carefully stepped beyond followed by Turbo. Biscuit stood facing the door from the left, Skelter the

169

right. Turbo covered the corridor ahead, knowing Tash would secure the rear. Skelter tried the handle. No luck. Locked. He weighed up his options and knocked on the door. If anyone was at home they would hardly suspect anyone polite enough to knock of having evil intent now, would they? It gave the others a start. No response. He knocked again, harder this time. The air was thick with heavy breathing. It was like being in the middle of a convention for phone perverts, thought Skelter. Still no response. What next? Go noisy? Bust the door and announce themselves? Skelter tapped Tash on the shoulder, pointed to the door and along the corridor towards the stairs, gestured to the other two, tapped his own chest and pointed ahead.

Tash took up position covering the door and their escape route. The others moved forward. Turbo began sniffing the air. There was a distinct whiff of marijuana perceptible over the stink of fish and shit. Skelter caught it too. Sweat was running in rivulets searching for sanctuary in the most sacred parts of his body. Muscle and sinew were piano wire tight. Adrenalin hovered in the red zone. At the end of the corridor a doorless frame formed an entrance to a small cabin, empty apart from the coke cans, food wrappers, paper and other crap littering the floor. The next door was open. Skelter went right, Turbo left. They shone their beams obliquely across the large empty space that was the cargo hold. No reaction. Biscuit stepped smartly through and went left, past Turbo. There was a crash and a clatter. A curse and a gunshot, booming in the enclosed space. Skelter and Turbo instinctively ducked back.

'Biscuit.' Skelter yelled.

'I'm okay, okay. Fuck it, fuck it,' it was as if Biscuit had suddenly developed Tourettes, 'Clear, H. Clear. Fuckin fuckin fuck it.'

Skelter stepped inside followed by Turbo sweeping the scene with his bullet backed blue-white beam. It was apparent that the birds had flown.

Biscuit was sprawled on a pile of rusty old chains and rotting rope. He had sustained nothing worse than a twisted ankle, physically that at least. Far worse was the damage to his pride. A man with his years of experience, trained by the best to be the best. An N.D! He had never had a Negligent Discharge in all his career. He stared at his pistol in disbelief.

'Turbo, go tell Tash what's up.' Skelter ordered.

'On my way, H.'

Biscuit thumbed the safety catch on his still smoking pistol and kicked the side of the hull with his good leg.

'Forget it, Biscuit,' said Skelter, 'could have happened to anyone.'

McVitie was not to be consoled.

The smell of marijuana hung heavy in the hold. 'They can't have been gone long,' said Biscuit.

A faint scuffling sound could be heard coming from the far end of the hold. They dropped to their knees weapons towards the sound.

'Rats?' said Skelter, aloud this time.

He was answered by a blinding muzzle flash and a deafening burst of gunfire. Both he and Biscuit instinctively hit the deck and returned fire. The echoing cacophony was disorienting. There was another short burst, which stopped after Biscuit pumped the remains of his magazine at origin of the flash. Turbo at the door, Biscuit changing magazines, Skelter yelled, 'flash bang' and lobbed a stun grenade. The men shut their eyes, waiting for the blinding flash. The earsplitting bang in the confined space was nauseating. Turbo danced through the door and skipped over the rubbish towards the threat closely followed by the others. He fired four rounds from his pistol, two double taps at close range. They found two dead pirates, one still holding an AK47, and two spaced out live ones, cowering half hidden under an old rotting tarp. They recovered another three weapons. Two had not been fired.

Eyes stinging, ears ringing, everyone coughing. The two dazed live Somalis were searched and had their hands bound behind their backs with plastic cuffs, before Turbo trundled them along the corridor.

After double-checking the hold Skelter and Biscuit made their way back to Tash. They booted the locked door in. Turned out it was not locked after all but warped and wedged in the frame. The cabin was empty. The three men made their way to the bottom of the stairs to join Turbo and the prisoners. Climbing up far enough to stick his head outside, Skelter used the Sony to try to raise Lofty on the far side of the river. He was successful.

'Two enemy down, two prisoners. We'll try to get a boat across. Need you and the kit this side.' He could feel the relief in the sniper's reply.

'Roger the boat, H.'

'H, out.' Skelter turned to the prisoners. He began to interrogate them in Somali, but they were high as kites and too far gone to yield anything reliable enough to be useful.

'Tash, take these jokers back into the hold. Take Turbo with you. Separate them. Tie them up but leave them some water they can get at.'

A plan was forming in Skelter's brain. 'Biscuit, check out that Toyota. Find out why they left it. If it's broke, fix it. Check the fuel. Tash, while you're in the hull bring me as much rope as you can carry. Strong stuff. Start in the cargo hold. I'm going to check out the boats. Let's do it.'

The inflatable was new and in perfect condition, probably from the hostage's yacht judging by the quality. Shame there was no engine. The Skiff, little more than a dugout canoe, was also missing an engine and the mounting plate was damaged. An outboard lay on the deck of the barge, under the tarpaulin. It was certainly not big or powerful enough to get Lofty and all the kit across in one lift. The only good news was that the storm had eased and changed direction, rotating south across the border and deeper towards Kenya. The rain was still falling and it was only light, but enough to top up the water their clothes had already absorbed keeping them soaked through. Skelter's hands were white and shrivelled; the wind had died away to breeze. A quick examination of the Skiff turned up a small bag of tools. Skelter checked the damage on the mounting plate and concluded that it would take the outboard. He climbed back onto the barge as Tash and Turbo emerged from below decks, laden with rope.

'Turbo, I need a hand to fit this outboard. Tash, you stay on the rope run, okay?'

'Sure thing, H,' said Tasker dumping the rope on the wet deck. 'What about the bodies, H?'

'Leave them for now.'

'Okay.'

Tasker headed back towards the hatch to collect more rope.

'Amazing how you get used to the rain isn't it, H?' said Turbo.

'You think so?' said Skelter, rolling the outboard over to get a better grip. 'I can't say I care for it. It's like being back at Jungle warfare school.'

Turbo took the weight his side and together they lifted the engine and carried it up the sloping deck to the side above the Skiff.

'Look on the bright side,' Turbo said, 'at least there's no leeches.'

'Doesn't anything ever get you down?'

'Try not to let it, H. Don't always succeed.

Working in the dark up to their bollocks in river water was far from easy but they managed. When they finally climbed back aboard they lay with their backs against the wheelhouse. Skelter took along swig from his water bottle, then offered it to Turbo.

'Fanks, just the job.' After one good swallow he

climbed to his feet. 'I'll just go see how Biscuit's doing with the truck,' he said, 'he might need a hand.'

27

Friday 26th June

In Camp Winston the raging storm was nearing its height. It had swept across the Kenyan border, buffeting everything in its path. Lieutenant Glass was not reckless enough to attempt moving the assault force with all its kit at night. He had however, requisitioned the transport – four Bedford four-ton trucks and a Land Rover. They were loaded and ready to go, waiting for first light. The storm's increased intensity made him a worried man. Visions of his career as an SAS officer dissolving before it had got going, swam before his tired eyes. Problem was what to do about it and truth be told there was not a lot he could do. He would have to sweat it out until daylight and assess the situation then.

After several journeys Tash had accumulated a significant pile of rope on the deck. He went to look for Skelter and found him on the floor in the wheelhouse, eating his last melted, misshapen Mars bar, scanning the map by the light of the torch, now removed from his pistol.

'What's the rope for, H?'

'Later. Get in here and get a brew on. I'm going to check on the others.' Skelter had hardly made it past the end of the gangplank when Turbo and Biscuit squelched out of the darkness.

'The man's a genius, a friggin' genius, H,' said Turbo, slapping Biscuit on the back.

'It's running then,' said Skelter, not a trace of surprise in his tone.

'Aye, she's running fine,' said Biscuit.

'Where did you learn to do that?' said Turbo 'I know a bit about engines but...'

'REME, my son, six years in the Royal Electrical and Mechanical Engineers. Simple blocked air filter. Full of desert dust then down comes the rain, dust turns to mud and gunks up the works. Piece o' piss. Mind you it was good of the previous owner to leave the keys in the ignition.'

'Enough you two,' said Skelter. 'Get aboard. Tash is brewing up in the wheelhouse.'

'There is nothing more uplifting, morale boosting, or magic to a tired sodden soldier than a hot brew,' said Tasker, offering his steaming mug to the others. One man had to keep watch but Skelter deemed it safe to do so though the window. As briefings go it could not have been more casual. He talked as they passed round the brew while Tash filled another mess tin and put it on the yellow flames licking from the hexamine block burning in the tiny Tommy Cooker.

'We have no idea where the birds have flown to but Lofty has confirmed they've gone upstream. They wouldn't risk heading to the coast, too much habitation, too likely to be compromised. So upstream. In the big Skiff. They won't have gone too far fully loaded against that current,' he gestured towards the river, 'that's for sure. We have to assume that our back up isn't going to arrive any time soon, if at all, so it's up to us to carry on and get the job done. The only place I can find on the map in this God-forsaken wilderness is what looks like a farm of some kind. There are regular lines plotting what I assume are fields. It's pretty small, close to the river about ten K upstream. I intend to go and check it out. We have to assume there may be more of these guys at the farm. They could be local freedom fighters. Al Qaeda even. I'm open to suggestions.'

Everybody had his say and the ideas were tossed into the pot and debated.

'What about Lofty and all our kit?' Turbo asked.

'I have a cunning plan for that, lads. At first light two of us take the small Skiff across. Tash has found us a stack of rope. Fix one end to the barge – take it over. Secure it on far bank. Detach this end and re attach to the inflatable. Cast off and let the current pull the inflatable downstream to the end of the rope and into the far bank. Haul the inflatable up to Lofty's hide. Load the gear and bring the end of the rope back in the Skiff. Then repeat in reverse. Only essential gear mind we'll not have time for a second trip.' He paused for comment sipping at the Mug of hot sweet liquid.

'How much rope do we have, Tash?' asked Turbo.

'Tons mate, tons.'

'Enough to take two lengths across? We wont need to come back with the rope that way, just swop ends.'

'Good idea,' said Biscuit, 'it will save time and belt and braces is always good, if you don't want to be caught with your pants down.'

'What about our tactical situation, we'll be operating openly in daylight?'

'Good point, Tash, but we don't have a choice. It's shit or bust time. Those hostages are not going to last long if Al Qaeda gets hold of them. Remember we are in a remote area, the enemy has no air capability, the storm will have kept most people hunkered down, and as far as we know they have no idea we are even in the country.

There was little more discussion before all agreed to the plan. Skelter got on the Sony and relayed the good news to Lofty.

'Try to get some rest, lads. I'll take the first watch.'

They flopped exhausted, propped against the

wheelhouse walls, almost filling the floor space available. Skelter took his notebook out of its polythene zip bag and began to compile a list of kit he considered essential for the job. Top of the list was the RPG and all the grenades they had for it. He kept scanning through the window but there was only dark and drizzle to be seen. Behind him he heard the sound of steel sliding over steel as one of the lads began stripping and cleaning his AK. Kalashnikov's wonderful weapon might work fine when abused and neglected, but you can't stop years of training.

After two hours, Skelter woke Tash. It was one forty. 'Wake Biscuit in one hour, okay?'
Tash nodded. Skelter slid to the floor and fell instantly asleep. Tash stood, stretched and shivered with the damp, dreaming of a dry, cosy sofa; Linda and Charlie snuggled together with him watching cartoons on the TV and eating Maltesers. He checked his weapon and took up the watch.

Lieutenant Glass could have done with some sleep and he had nothing much else to do for the next five hours, except worry that is. A pointless and fruitless pastime, he knew, but nonetheless he indulged himself and by so doing kept himself awake, eroding his efficiency by a few degrees and decreasing chances of a successful outcome to the impending operation. Being a super soldier is hard when you're human.

28

Saturday 27th June

Parish and Bell were knackered, soaked, sitting on a dirt floor, backs against a mud wall, stiff and battered after the bruising journey in the bottom of the Skiff under the feet of their captors. They had travelled most of the night or so it seemed, not that they had travelled far, the Skiff's screaming outboard having struggled to make headway against the current. From what Bell had been able to glean from the arguments amongst their captors, the pick up wouldn't start. Everyone seemed to be blaming everyone else and Cawaale was losing patience with all of them. Bell and Parish knew where they were, locally that is. They had recognised the smell of goats, even with the hoods over their heads. These had now been removed, not that there was anything to see. Clearly they were at the same place where Bell had spoken on the telephone to Nigel Harmon to arrange the ransom. Ransom, which clearly was not now coming any time soon. Not until the storm passed at least. What they did not know was where on God's earth the goat herder's hovel was. It might as well be on Mars.

The door opened and two of the kidnappers walked in, grabbed Charles Parish by the arms, forcing a sack over his head before dragging him out, slamming and bolting the door behind them. He was roughly bundled along across the muddy ground and into a larger building, the hood being torn from his head before he was dumped upon the hard packed, dirt floor.

Cawaale emerged from behind a tattered grey blanket pegged to a line stretching across the room. Parish assumed it was to separate the sleeping quarters. To his right was a cooking fire and beside it were three small wooden stools.

Parish was forced to kneel in front of Cawaale, his eyes smarting from the dusty hood. A Somali stood on either side of him. Their AKs lay on the rough wooden table, exchanged for long sticks which the men intermittently swished through the air occasionally whacking into a pile of grain sacks. It didn't look good.

'What is your name?' Cawaale asked, holding up his hand for the guards to cease with the sticks.

'Charles,' answered Parish.

'Please forgive me, Charles,' said Cawaale, 'we have not been formally introduced. I am Cawaale. Tell me, Charles, what do you do? I assume you have a job?'

'I live off my investments,' Parish replied, thinking on his feet, or rather his knees. 'I have not worked in years.'

'You must be very rich,' Cawaale said, 'or a liar. You would not lie to me, would you?'

'No, why would I do that?'

'Because you are Charles Parish and you work for the British Government, yes?'

Parish looked up open mouthed. *How the hell? Did they find some I.D. on the yacht?* He had nothing on him when he was taken that's for sure but...

'You look surprised,' said Cawaale, 'let me enlighten you. You work for the British Government, as an intelligence officer.'

Parish stiffened as the Somali guards began swishing their sticks again.

'Relax, Charles, you are a valuable commodity, I do

not want you to suffer any damage. I have some friends who are looking forward to meeting you. I see by your expression that my information is correct.'

He nodded to the guards who grabbed his arms. As they dragged him away Parish caught a glimpse of two pairs of naked legs through the gap between the blanket and the floor. They were young legs. The legs of young boys, or women, possibly.

Turbo, stirred from his fitful sleep by the smell of coffee and hexamine from Tash's Tommy cooker, rubbed his eyes and reached out to touch his rifle. He had warmed up now that he was out of the rain.

Not yet light, but no longer completely dark the false dawn was minutes away.

Skelter rubbed his eyes also, then ran his tongue across the plaque coating his teeth. He unscrewed the cap of his water bottle and swilled his mouth. 'Don't forget your anti malaria tabs, lads,' he said popping one his in his mouth along with a Valium. He drained the bottle. Fill your water bottles too. He put his back in his belt kit making a mental note to replenish it and shoved a couple of Rennies onto his tongue. Taking a notebook from his pocket he ran through the kit list, in case he had missed anything. Water; RPG and grenades; spare ammo, radio, bergans.

'Quick brew and some scoff then to work, lads. Lots to do.' Skelter unfolded his cooker, lit a hexi block and half filled a mess tin from his second water bottle. He found a packet of American special forces instant porridge mix in his belt kit and pulled on the green nylon string attached to the buttonhole of his left breast pocket. At he end of the string was Skelter's second best friend. Every soldier's best friend is his rifle. His next best friend was his racing spoon. A dessert spoon. Always instantly available.

A little less waterlogged now, Skelter's weary warriors set to organising the ropes and the Skiff. Turbo and Biscuit were elected to make the crossing.

'River level looks to have dropped a bit, H,' said Turbo staring into the swirling muddy water.

'Not running so fast either, by the look of it,' Biscuit observed.

'We were overdue a dose of luck,' said Tash.

'Exactly right. Keep the positive attitude but don't get too cocky lads,' said Skelter. The outboard on that little skiff will have its work cut out riding against the current.

Turbo and Biscuit climbed into the narrow wooden craft in the lee of the barge. At the helm, Biscuit pulled the starter cord. It took four attempts before the engine caught and then he gunned it straight out into the torrent. The river had its way at first, pushing them down stream, but Biscuit cut across diagonally, working both with and against the current, the little outboard straining as Biscuit gradually began to stamp his authority on the river. Turbo had little to do but hang on and pay out the ropes. They were fifty metres downstream before they began to hold their own, Biscuit nursing as much as he could from the engine without wrecking it. It took a delicate touch, working it while being battered and buffeted by the rushing water. Biscuit had a way with engines like Casanova had a way with women. Gradually the Skiff made headway showing just enough hull to the flow to get them towards the far bank without exposing them to the risk of capsize. Biscuit was earning his government beer vouchers.

Despite the difficulties they made it across in twenty minutes, to a warm welcome from a bedraggled Lofty, looking like some sea monster from a nineteen fifties B movie in his wet, gauze-covered, Gore-Tex sniper suit.

'What kept you?' Lofty asked.

They completely ignored him, handing him the rope

ends.

'Get hauling, slack arse,' said Turbo to Lofty, who laughed aloud as he passed the rope around his back and gripped it in front, digging his heels in as anchor man ready to take up the slack. Turbo and Biscuit grabbed on the line too.

'Ready?' said Biscuit. 'Heave, heave, heave.' Boots fighting for grip in the red mud of the riverbank, the three sweating, cursing squaddies slowly got the inflatable moving. It took all their combined muscle power to haul the heavy craft free of the far bank. Suddenly it was out into the deep water.

'Fucking hell,' yelled Turbo as the current pulled the boat downstream, sweeping him off his feet and into the shallows.

'Hold her, hold her. Dig in.' Biscuit's cry was a waste of breath. They knew what had to be done. Cursing and bitching howling and straining inch by inch they fought for their ground but they still sliding towards the raging torrent

'Got you, you bastard,' yelled Turbo finding his feet again, this time up to his thighs in the river. They held. By sheer force of bloody minded will they held and the current took the inflatable out through the centre of the river and then the force of water edged it towards the bank.

'Haul in lads haul in,' said Biscuit, as Lofty leaned back hard forcing his screaming sinews to the limit, while Turbo kicked defiantly against the forces of nature stretching the rope to breaking point. Then just as he was sure he couldn't hold any longer, the rope slackened. The dingy had grounded.

'Well done, lads, that was fuckin' amazing,' Biscuit cried, almost weeping with relief. They all collapsed into the mud still gripping the rope as if their lives depended upon it, which they might well do soon. They lay inert for some time slowly recovering from the exertion until finally

Biscuit got them back on the job.

It took a further twenty minutes to haul the inflatable up to the hide position and beach it. At Biscuit's insistence, they then took a fifteen minute breather. He called Skelter on the Sony walkie talkie to update him.

'At least pulling it back across, should be easy,' said Lofty, 'even fully loaded, using the Toyota.'

'We've got to load her up yet, mate. My arms are killing me before we start.'

'Stop whinging Turbo,' said Biscuit, If you can't take a joke you shouldn't have signed up.'

Turbo held his forefinger upright and rigid. 'Swivel on that, you ginger Jock.'

'C'mon girls,' said Lofty, 'there's work to be done.'

With that they trudged downstream through the mud and secured the boat. Taking it in turns with two holding it on the rope and one loading they began filling the vessel with the stores vital to the operation.

Over on the other side Skelter and Tash had nothing much to do beyond bringing the Toyota closer to the barge. The four-wheel drive cut through the mud as if it wasn't there and both men sat in the cab watching the preparations on the opposite bank. In his head Skelter ran through options and alternatives in possible assault plans, for the farm. He was convinced that it was there where they would find the kidnappers. There simply wasn't anywhere else. If they were lucky the hostages would be being held in a separate room, building, or compound. This would be ideal for the assault giving more scope to hit the kidnappers with overwhelming firepower including the RPGs. They could also attack in daylight. If, however, they were all in the same room it would be tricky. They would have to go in covertly at night and get up close and personal. In that case the flash-bang grenades that were on the kit list to bring across the river, would be invaluable. Their noise and blinding magnesium light, would gain precious seconds to get in amongst and subdue the enemy, with deadly force if necessary, without causing permanent harm to the hostages.

29

Saturday 27th June

By nine-thirty the rain had stopped altogether, but one glance at the turbulent southern sky, dashed any hopes of the assault team coming any time soon. By ten o'clock the sun had come out, a great morale booster as it dried the uniforms on the men's backs while they toiled loading the inflatable. The downsides of this improvement in the weather were considerable; a real cause for concern. There would be nothing to mask the sound of their approach, the kidnappers were more likely to be moving around outside and in the now good visibility, they would also be more likely to see them coming.

'What about a brew, H?' Tash asked.

'Good idea.'

Tash got out of the cab and set about the task, while Skelter put his head back and allowed himself a brief escape. He fished the little soapstone Buddha out of his pocket and turned it over and over in his hands remembering the days with Jane in the Himalayan foothills on their last holiday together. His gut was churning. Then he thought of Lucy. Inside that part of his head was a ball of conflict, a bad place to be. He retreated to the pressures of the job in hand. So much for trying to relax.

The pressure was getting to lieutenant Glass studying the

latest weather reports in the radio room, while the rain hammered on the wriggly tin roof, which leaked in half a dozen places, dripping onto desk and floor. His face was ageing rapidly. He had a decision to make. To attempt the journey overland or to wait. The one grain of hope was that the storm was tracking south west, meaning that it would be clearing away from the target area first and towards his position in Kenya.

What Glass needed was a crystal ball. The overland journey was theoretically achievable in six hours in the dry season. Under the prevailing conditions, twenty hours minimum, if they had God on their side and a shipping container full of luck. On the plus side it would mean the men would be doing something active, which was good for morale and who knows they might pull it off. If they didn't, the danger was they could wind up getting stuck and need to be rescued themselves, a humiliating career setback. If he waited and the weather broke he could race to the rescue like the 7th cavalry and give his career a big leg up. If the storm continued for three or more days, as it might well do, then he could have the deaths of the hostages and maybe some of Skelter's men on his conscience. Nobody in The Regiment would want to work with him and his career would be down the toilet. Having consulted every available local expert's opinion he had all the information he needed. He still couldn't call it. He set himself a thirty-minute deadline and went to the small camp chapel to ask for guidance from the head of all head sheds.

The convoy of Bedford four-tonners, with half of Boat Troop aboard was making reasonable progress along the dirt and gravel road towards the Somali border. Lieutenant Glass had made his decision. The fourteen men in the other half waited at Winston, ready to go the minute the Helicopters were clear to fly. It was against all he had learned at Sandhurst, splitting his force in two with no idea of the enemy's strength or disposition. However, it beat brooding on top of a basket containing all his eggs, while doing nothing. At least this way he had doubled the chances of getting into the fight, even if it might be with only half his fighting men. The noise of the rain on the canvas was so loud that conversation in the back of the trucks was nigh on impossible. The Kenyan drivers were working by instinct, as the windscreen wipers were useless against the onslaught. Glass's frustration was growing by the hour, but he kept the lid on it. Slow progress was better than no progress.

Lucy looked at the bedside clock. Seven-fifteen on a fine morning in Ross on Wye. Sleep had been fitful. In the middle of the restless night she had got out of bed and gone into the next room, climbing into the one Mark had slept in. She silently cursed Wilkins for his efficiency in changing the sheets and removing any trace of his scent. Still she felt closer to him, being where they had lain together, and it comforted her. She hugged the pillow and savoured the longing she felt and the delicious tingling, turmoil tumbling deep inside of her.

She wondered if there would be any news today. Poor Charles had been missing for a week now. She prayed that he was coping.

Coping was something Caroline Warren did naturally, one of the skills that made her an excellent PA. Whatever her boss Richard Bell threw at her she dealt with without fuss. The abortive ransom delivery, was however, a little off the scale, yet here she was sitting up, swaddled in pillows, gradually warming through, chatting to a Royal Navy intelligence officer and a handsome one at that. Handsome he might be, but she couldn't make him smile, principally because she could not tell him anything he did not already know.

Whatever Nigel Harmon had learned from his short association with his security service minders he now knew nothing. Nothing at all. That had been made abundantly clear to him and to his secretary, reinforced by them each being reminded of parts of their past lives they had been sure were known only unto themselves. Private, potentially embarrassing things. They had already embraced the seeds of selective memory loss, relieved to return to their mundane everyday existence, without being followed everywhere by sinister suits from Whitehall.

Natalie Ryder paced around the kitchen sucking hard on a Gauloises while another lay burning away in an ashtray. In her left hand she held a mug of dark roasted Kenyan coffee.

'Please, you must eat something,' said Asha. The sweet faced, Kenyan servant girl held out a banana. 'You can't live on coffee and cigarettes. Cigarettes are bad for you. They will make you sick.' She prodded her with the fruit. 'It is only a banana. Bananas are good for energy. You need energy.'

Natalie said nothing, lighting a cigarette from the stub of the old one, which she then stubbed out in the ash tray. Asha began to cry. She made no sound but tears rolled down her smooth ebony cheeks. Even Asha's older brother had not been able to persuade Natalie to eat. For once she proved to be immune to the handsome, cheeky faced houseboy's natural charm.

Asha continued to follow Natalie around, prodding her with the banana, pestering and pulling at her until she finally turned on her. 'Asha, enough, I do not want a banana.'

Wiping away her tears with the back of her hand Asha said. 'Not want Ma, Natalie need. Must eat.'

With a loud sigh Natalie took the banana. Asha stayed with her until she peeled it and ate it, then took from her the skin, and put it in the trash can

30

Saturday 27th June

Skelter's Sony squeaked. He squeezed the pressel to acknowledge. The boys on the other bank were ready to come across, Biscuit and Turbo in the Skiff while Lofty took his chances on the unpowered inflatable. Skelter acknowledged and started up the Toyota, put her into gear and reversed the pickup into position close to the bank before climbing down and walking to the water's edge. Tash was on stag watching the approach from the Northeast where the farm was located, in case of trouble. The Skiff set off from the bank and headed upstream against the current before tacking slightly right to balance keeping pace with the current against crossing over without being swept down stream. Turbo watched out for the ropes as Biscuit handled the tiller. Skelter was treated to a fifteen-minute master class in small boat handling. The nearer he got to the bank the more difficult it became as they came closer to lengths of rope in the river. Catching the propeller on them could spell disaster. However, they made it safely across. The three men set to work, two hauling on the lines and acting as anchors until Skelter secured them to the rear of the Toyota. It was far from easy and at one point they almost lost one, but after ten tense minutes all was secure.

'Jesus I'm knackered,' Biscuit admitted to Turbo, who, fighting for breath nodded silently.

'Biscuit, get downstream and watch for where she comes ashore. Turbo, on the bank here.' Skelter stabbed the Sony's switch. 'Standby, Lofty, I'm going to take up the slack.'

'Roger, H.'

The big old diesel coughed into life. Skelter selected first gear and let in the clutch. Slowly the Toyota eased forward and clawed its way up the slope.

On the far bank, the inflatable, which had been partly beached by the bow was already at the point of fully floating from the pull of the current on the ropes as they were being towed across. Lofty sat on top of the pile of kit, the dry bag containing his rifle was already safely across, having gone in the skiff. The ropes went taut with a jerk, the heavily laden inflatable resisting momentarily, then sliding over the mud and into the water. The first part of the journey was fun, a bit like a theme park ride at Waterworld, but once the boat hit the centre of the river, the fun evaporated. Lofty clung to the cargo net lashing the kit to the deck and prayed.

Skelter kept easing the truck forward trying to keep as straight a line as possible, driving over all but the biggest thorn bushes, turning to look at the boat every few seconds, until he was too far from the bank and his view was obscured by scrub. He hauled on the brake. The heavy chassis creaked and groaned as the ropes strained against it. He hit the pressel switch.

'Turbo, get up here now.' There was an agonising wait, in reality only a few seconds, before the reply came, then another thirty-seconds before Turbo appeared at the window.

'Take the wheel and wait for the word,' Skelter ordered as he leapt down and sprinted for the bank. The inflatable was being buffeted hard and digging in against the current, too heavily loaded to be tossed about. It was asking a lot of the ropes, which were old and worn, but they were hanging on. Skelter hit the pressel.

'Take her forward, Turbo. Slow and steady.' Skelter knew that this was the critical phase, when the maximum strain would be exerted on the ropes. Once they were two-thirds of the way across the current would carry the boat to shore. Gradually as the truck pulled and the current pushed, they passed the critical point and the river did the rest. The inflatable made it to the bank about twenty metres downstream. One last surge from the Toyota and she grounded.

'Did Sir enjoy his white water rafting?' Biscuit asked as Lofty's boots hit the mud. 'Bring the wife and wee ones next time eh?' They were both grinning from ear to ear with relief. It wasn't just that everyone was safe, but the kit too. They had a job to do and without it their chances of success would have been in the bottom five percent. Moments later the Toyota arrived and the unloading began, carefully, with the kit nearest the river coming off first. Hand-balling everything over the kit packed in the bows was a pain but necessary. The bow was grounded on the bank. Doing it the easy way would lighten the load on the landward side until the boat simply floated off. This way the weight was kept on the correct end. When loading the pickup was complete, they dragged the empty inflatable back to the barge and secured it for possible use during the withdrawal phase.

Skelter gathered the men around him. 'It is thirteen forty-five, lads, we'll have a briefing in one hour. Get a brew and some scoff. I'm going to relieve Tash. Fetch me a brew out will you? Oh and by the way, well done all of you.' He picked up his AK and went off to find his sentry, mightily relieved the plan had worked and that the first phase was complete. His uniform, crumpled and thorn torn was now at least dry. He made a mental note to change his socks and underwear and get some foot powder into his crotch to ease the friction. His beard was itching and he contemplated shaving. It was a great morale booster in the field. Freshens a man up and makes him feel more human, more alert. *Should I order them all to shave?* He could imagine the response that would get. He binned the idea, took out his water bottle and washed down a Valium.

Cobra was wrapping up what had been a short update meeting. What news there was, was all bad. The PM seemed to have aged overnight. The weather, specifically the storm and its consequences, had been the main topic for discussion and a major cause for concern. It had brought the operation to a halt, severed communications with the SAS surveillance team and left the planners blind and deaf. All the planning in the world counts for nothing in the face of nature especially when she gets angry. Eisenhower learnt that on June the 5th 1944 when he had to postpone the greatest amphibious operation in the history of warfare, for twenty-four hours. Almost seven thousand vessels, from landing craft to battleships, loaded with over one-third of a million sailors and soldiers, stopped dead by a storm. Nothing new under the sun.

What was left of the body of Richard Bell's bodyguard had been washed up on a Kenyan beach, identified by his tattoos – the Indian Ocean sharks are voracious feeders

31

Saturday 27th June

Fed and watered, the men cleaned and oiled their weapons, loaded extra ammunition into their belt kit pouches and stuffed their pockets with chocolate, sweets and biscuits. Water bottles were filled from the Jerricans and the RPG and grenades were checked for damage. Each man loaded up with hand grenades; white phosphorous for smoke, stun grenades for rescue entry and blast bombs for killing. Skelter went through the manifest one last time. NVGs, Binos, Electronic listening devices, Sony walkie talkies, the list went on. Finally he seemed satisfied. He wished they had a machine gun, a little Minimi would do. A GPMG or even better still a big arsed Browning fifty calibre on the back of the pick up would have been brilliant spitting out eight hundred big bullets a minute. Bullets that could chew up a bungalow, brick by brick.

As it was they would have to rely on Lofty and his Accuracy International for fire support, at a more modest rate of five to six rounds per minute. What you got with Lofty was quality rather than quantity; a higher ratio of hits to shots fired. Lofty was value for money. The air was filled with the metallic sound of Kalashnikov cocking levers pulling working parts to the rear, followed by a chorus of clicking safety catches. Skelter programmed the farm's coordinates into the GPS, folded the map to show the area of operation and climbed into the cab.

Biscuit took the wheel with Skelter beside him and the others in the back. Turbo banged his fist on the roof to indicate they were ready. Biscuit fired up the engine. They did not have a great distance go and could only take the truck so far. Exactly how far was down to Skelter, but the wind had picked up again, which might mask the noise a little. However they were all expecting to walk the last couple of kilometres. Biscuit kept the revs as low as he could, creeping along the muddy track in third gear. The wind was definitely freshening, giving some small relief from the humidity, which was way up, making uniforms clammy, clinging and distractingly uncomfortable. It was worst for the two in the cab. Skelter's eyes were cycling from the map to the GPS to the track in a rapid succession as Biscuit nursed the pickup forward towards their destiny. Behind him standing on the load bed Lofty Larcombe watched the way ahead, his rifle resting on the cab roof, business end to the front. Covering the flanks and rear Tash and Turbo sat on their bergans quietly psyching themselves for the coming conflict. They had both been in firefights before. They all had, but it didn't make it any easier. The sky was darkening again, but no rain had yet fallen, when Skelter told Biscuit to pull off the track into the bush.

'Right lads, gather round,' said Skelter. He threw the keys to Tasker, saying, 'Tash, stash these under the passenger seat. I don't want to risk dropping them in the bush.' What he meant everyone knew, was whoever had the keys might not make it back. 'We've about two K to go to the farm. Tash, lead scout, Biscuit, you work with him on the right flank, Turbo, with me in the centre, Lofty, left. We have to recce the place, we need intel on the hostages. We must establish exactly where they are. Obvious choice for that job – Lofty.'

'Assuming they are there,' said Lofty.

'They're there alright, I can feel it.' Skelter paused to let the words sink in. 'Good, now get in close but don't get seen. We will cover you. If you can pull that off Lofty, work your way to the riverbank on the left flank and set up a base of fire to cover our assault, and cut them off from the boats. If it goes tits up, we'll wade in. You might want to take the spare AK as well as the rifle.' Lofty nodded agreement. 'One more thing, lads, Password. Challenge, "Kermit" counter, "Muppet." Got it? Don't forget. We'll be creeping about playing secret squirrel in poor visibility. I don't want any friendly fire fuck ups.' Skelter glanced at Biscuit, who winced.

'Right,' McVitie ordered. 'Get this vehicle cammed up, and let's get this show on the road.' Tash and Turbo set to with the net and bits of bush. Ten minutes and the big pick up had lost its shape, shine, shadow, silhouette, surface – the main principles of camouflage. It was effectively invisible from the track. Using an entrenching tool wrapped in chicken wire Lofty erased the tell tale tyre marks back to the track. By the middle of the afternoon they were ready. Tash lead off through the bush keeping the track just in sight moving parallel to it. The sky grew dark and the first drops of rain began to fall. Inwardly Skelter rejoiced. The worse the weather the better their chances of success. Tash stopped, dropped to one knee, held his left fist out to his side thumb down. Eyes on enemy. Skelter sighed with relief, his hunch had been right and now as the rain increased in intensity his anxiety eased slightly, although that might have something to do with the Valium he had slipped into his mouth while Biscuit was organising the truck camouflage. He moved up to join Tash.

Through the binos Skelter could make out the building through the squally rain. The thorn scrub provided adequate concealment in conjunction with the rain sweeping down from the North and washing across the river towards Kenya. The weather reduced visibility and would keep the opposition hunkered down, well, most of them at least. Under a rickety looking, rustic lean-to in the lee of the main building, a young Somali was sitting on a wooden stool cradling an AK47. He was wearing a Red T-shirt. He looked pissed off. The building was single story, mud brick built with a dense reed-thatched roof that appeared to be coping remarkably well with the wind. To the right of the building stood a separate smaller, round structure. There was no sign of an entrance, nor window. Skelter assumed there to be a door on the other side. A minimal rustic pole fence formed small corral next to this hut, stretching towards Skelter's soggy spying spot. He was immune to the rain, they all were. It had simply become a part of normal life now. Yes, it still ran down the back of his neck, soaked through his combats and made him thoroughly uncomfortable, but he now accepted that as the norm. He had adapted as he always did. That was all part of the job.

Skelter told Tash to keep watch, handing him the binoculars before retracing his steps to the others. 'We have eyes on one enemy, AK47, young male, Red T-shirt.' He went on to describe the layout of the farm and the cover available. 'The thorn scrub gives us good cover if we're careful down to two hundred metres. After that it gets patchy. You could use it, Lofty, but I wouldn't like to put money on any of the rest of us. Around fifty metres out it's pretty much bare arsed. I'm hoping the main building is one big space inside and the hostages are being held in the small round building. Red T-shirt seems to be watching it, so I'm hopeful. We need to recce the far side to see if it has a door and if it has any other guards. My guess is that Red T-shirt is supposed to guarding it but doesn't fancy getting wet. He should be able to see the other side of the hut from his position. He looks more concerned with keeping out of the rain than keeping on top of the job.'

Skelter looked at the faces of the three men gathered around him and was comforted by the presence of such a wealth of experience and accumulated skills in such a compact force. He almost felt sorry for the opposition. However many they were, they had eaten their last supper.

'Lofty, check in with Tash, then get yourself a spot between the river and the buildings. Stay covert and report anything you see. Do not initiate contact except to defend yourself, understood?' Lofty nodded, wiping a hand across the rain running down his stubbled face. 'When you are in position give me a radio check,' continued Skelter, 'and as soon as the shit hits the noisy fan feel free to join in with the weapon of your choice.'

Lofty nodded again, picked up the dry bag with the rifle and slung it over his shoulder. He took the pistol from its holster, removed the magazine, and pressed down on the top round three times to test the free movement of the spring before slotting it into the grip and pushing it home with a click. He pulled back the slide, cocking the hammer and then pushing his left thumb down between the hammer and the firing pin he squeezed the trigger allowing the hammer to fall under the control leaving the hammer resting on the firing pin with the weapon cocked. All he had to do to fire was thumb back the hammer and squeeze the trigger. Lofty holstered the pistol, picked up the spare AK and like a one-man arsenal staggered off towards Tash.

'Biscuit, get around the far side and see if there is a door to the hut.' Skelter made a wide sweeping motion with his right arm. It was totally unnecessary and he knew it, force of habit. Biscuit didn't need any telling. 'See if you can find any sign of the hostages then report back to me at Tash's position.'

Biscuit gave Skelter the thumbs up, checked the safety on the AK, high fived Turbo with a wink and squelched away to skirt through the bush. Turbo and Skelter checked, re-checked and checked their kit again. Weapons, walkie talkies, water bottles, watches, torches, bootlaces. Constantly they sought reassurance as all soldiers do when they are about to go into action. There was nothing wrong with their kit. They were well prepared and ready for action, which when it came would be a huge relief. Waiting was always the worst. The rain was steady now at forty-five degrees to the horizontal, with sudden squally gusts. Perfect conditions for the job. Skelter felt as if he had been blessed. The only thing that worried him was the exfiltration phase. There was enough room to squeeze on the truck, but where would they go? Tash and Turbo had tried the radio several times with no success. They would have to drive back to the barge and try again. If that failed the best option would be to head down river towards the coast. They were bound to establish comms at some point.

His driver informed Peter Glass that they had crossed into Somalia, not that he needed telling. The road had been bad enough to start with but now it had all but disappeared. The Land Rover forged on in low ratio, grinding through the mud and mush, sliding, slithering and bouncing through the rutted track in the hammering rain. It was not long before the first Bedford got stuck. They got it out in twenty-five minutes pushing with one truck and towing with another. Forty minutes and one mile further on they were stuck again. Men got out, unloaded what they could, cursed and heaved, sluiced in filth, while towropes strained and stretched until they conquered, but it was the law of diminishing returns. Soaked and sapped of strength, the seeds of doubt began to germinate.

Glass was new, eager to make his mark, but there was a growing consensus that he may have bitten off too much. To a man the guys wanted to get into action. That was not in question. Their mates were isolated in hostile territory, without support. Each man was able to put himself in the surveillance team's position, waiting for backup. Many had been there at one time or another, their lives on the line. Despite this it was clear by mid day that the convoy was going nowhere. Time for plan C. Glass called a council of war, which was held in the back of the middle truck as it had the most room. Shouting to be heard above the noise of the rain, he made his pitch. 'I don't have to tell you how important it is for us to get to the guys out there nor do I have to say how difficult that has become in the current conditions. It is clear to me that the four tonners are not going to make it, at least not in the timescale. I intend to press on in the Land Rover with an advance party of six including myself.'

There was an excited rumbling response as the soldiers volunteered to a man. Unswayed, Glass turned to a great bear of a man, squatting on the floor of the truck. 'Sergeant Sitiveni, you, Corporal Banks, Miller, Evans... and Reilly isn't it?' he said peering into the gloom.

'O'Reilly, Boss,' answered the big man at the back.

'O'Reilly, sorry. Double up on ammo and take a Jimpy. Make sure you have a spare barrel and as many belts as you can carry. Into the Rover, toot sweet.'

Glass assigned his Kenyan driver to the lead four-tonner. 'Laager up here for now, until the weather clears enough to continue. If that fails to happen in the next forty-eight hours return to Winston. I shall go on in the Land Rover. If we can get through we'll double the strength of our asset on the ground. Good luck,' said Glass to the man he had put in charge of the convoy. With that he climbed down and splashed through the downpour to the front of the vehicles and got into the Land Rover. Glass removed his bush hat and slicked back his hair with a wet hand. He slipped into gear and slowly eased forward through the ooze praying for luck as they set off through the blinding downpour. Rain leaked in from every split and seam in the canvas, every crease and crack in the aluminium body. Resigned to misery but resolved to the task the men prepared themselves for what was to come.

32

Saturday 27th June

Lofty checked in with Tash and lay with him for ten minutes, observing the buildings and committing the layout to memory. Using the rifle sight as a telescope he watched the youth in the Red T-shirt, chewing what Lofty assumed was Khat. The heavy sniper rifle lay safe inside the dry bag. It wasn't the rain that posed the problem but the mud. The Accuracy International is a robust weapon designed for the battlefield but even so any dirt or grit in the mud had the potential to cause the weapon to malfunction if it got inside the working parts.

Lofty turned his attention to the ground next, planning his route. He could use the scrub to reach the river and then use the bank as cover to get beyond the building unseen. After that he would have to rely on his stalking skills to close the gap between the river and the building. He needed to get within one hundred and fifty metres to be sure of good enough visibility. From that range the AK would be effective also. A nod to Tash, who tipped his bush hat in return and the Sniper began working his way down the left flank.

Away over on the right flank corporal McVitie was similarly engaged, at a cautious crouch through the bush. Biscuits, especially ginger ones are supposed to be hard and crunchy. He felt like a ginger biscuit that had been dunked in warm tea. He was that wet he was surprised he had not dissolved. Maybe Biscuit was an inappropriate nickname. Perhaps he should look for another. He reached a point where he calculated that he had put the hut between himself and Red T-shirt and advanced towards where he reasoned the hut should be. Three short crouched steps then stop, listen and look around, especially behind. He did not want to be surprised. Nothing but the incessant sound of pouring rain. He checked his watch. It would be dark in a couple of hours, not that it was that light now with the rain and all. Under normal conditions the best time to attack would be first light. He knew Skelter would not have them lying out for the twelve hours of darkness in the prevailing conditions. They would go in the next hour, hour and a half. He was sure of that. That didn't give him much time to complete his task. Moving forward Biscuit repeated the pattern of paces, stop, listen, look. And again. And again, until there the hut was right in front of him, forty metres away. He was blind side of Red T-shirt and could see no activity. The clock was ticking. Time to take a calculated risk. Creeping low through the thinning bush he halved the distance to the hut in double time. Ten metres out Biscuit dropped into the mud and leopard crawled towards its mud walls, cradling the AK in the crooks of his elbows like it was his first born son.

Lt. Glass was grinding onward through the mud, his stubborn refusal to give up, gradually elevating his status amongst the men. Glass was slowly getting them on board.

'Jesus, Banksy,' complained trooper O'Reilly, 'do you have to hog so much room?'

'He can't help having a fat arse, he takes after his mother.'

'You're asking for a slap, Evans.' he warned the ex

miner from Merthyr. Then in a quieter tone, 'Fragile couldn't have picked four bigger blokes to squeeze in here with all this kit and ammo if he tried.'

'We are not deaf here in front,' said Teo Sitiveni 'Good job you weren't picked for your brains, you bunch of muppets.' The Fijian sergeant shrugged his massive shoulders and clicked his tongue to his teeth.

Lance corporal Dusty Miller chipped in, 'don't you get it? We're the beefiest boys in the troop. Just what you need to push a Land Rover when it gets stuck in the mud, dick-brains.'

A murmur of understanding, barely audible above the rain on the roof filled the back of the vehicle. In the front Lieutenant Glass smiled to himself.

The Land Rover did get stuck and not just the once. The benchmark off-road four by four was very capable but it had its limits. Several times the brawn of his small group was called upon to use brute strength to unstick the vehicle. Glass had made a good call.

Biscuit made it to the wall of the hut. He carefully looked all around and satisfied it was safe to do so, he stood up slowly, grateful for the partial shelter of the overhanging thatch. The rain was still heavy but the wind had died down considerably. He gripped the AK and edged his way around the circular wall, peering around the edge until he could see the lean-to. Feeling ahead with his left hand, back to the wall, right hand gripping the weapon, finger resting lightly alongside the trigger, his left hand touched wood. *A doorframe?* He dropped quietly to the ground and crawled around until he got eyes on Red T-shirt, peeked left, saw the edge of the doorframe and froze. He could hear voices coming from inside. They were speaking in English.

Charles Parish looked a study in misery. He had puked down the front of his boiler suit and leaked liquid shit into the seat. Richard Bell had moved as far away from him as he could get, but the smell pervading the stale air in the hut was as inescapable as it was indescribable. 'For fuck's sake, Charles,' he kept saying, knowing there was nothing to be done.

'It's all right for you. You have a constitution like a horse. I'm not used to all this.'

'What makes you think I am,' said Bell, holding what had once been a white handkerchief of the finest Egyptian cotton, but now resembled a rag a mechanic might use to wipe a dipstick when checking the oil. Overhead the rain was thudding into the thatch like the arrows striking the battlefield at Agincourt.

'Richard, my boy I know all about you. It's my job. I work in intelligence. You were born in Cleethorpes on Christmas Day nineteen fifty. Your mother had a difficult labour. Your father was fairground showman and an alcoholic. You worked the amusement arcades and rides from the age of nine and later, as a deckhand. You served on dredgers and tugs, then tramp steamers between Grimsby, Lisbon and Amsterdam. You claim you worked your bollocks off to make your millions, but that isn't the whole story now is it? You have been economical with the truth have you not? Since when is smuggling such hard work?'

If there had been more light, in the windowless, mud walled, hut, Parish would have seen the look of surprise on his companion's face. He could only imagine it, but even that brought a warming glow of satisfaction to his wretched circumstance. 'Would you like to hear more?' Parish asked, taking a pull from the goatskin to wet his lips and lubricate his larynx.

'Surprise me, spymaster.'

'Decimalisation,' said Parish, 'nineteen seventy-one was a good year for you. You must have thought all your birthdays had come at once. Bought up every slot machine you could get your hands on, God knows where you got the money from.'

'My mother,' said Bell, spitting the words out like they were poison. 'My mother backed me with every penny she'd scrimped and saved and hid from her drunken bastard of a husband.'

'Don't upset yourself dear fellow. He's dead and gone.'

'Good riddance, evil bastard.' Bell said.

Parish went on. 'You rented a lock up, converted the machines to take the new currency and rented them out to pubs and clubs. Most men in your position would have sat back and watched the money roll in, but not you. No, you went back to sea smuggling pornography from Amsterdam, renting and selling from the lock up and the back of your old man's van. I could tell you the registration number if I had the file.'

'You bastard. Is nothing private any more?'

'Oh don't worry Richard, your secret is safe with me. My job can be somewhat stressful. I need the sanctuary and relaxation your little hideaways provide. I am not going to kill the goose with the golden eggs.'

Bell smiled, he was not in the least worried. He had videotapes of Charles and many others including members of Her Majesty's Government, enjoying the delights of his floating dungeon and other such venues at his private clubs. Judges, lawyers, senior police officers; it was some library.

Lofty did not have far to crawl, but he had to slide slower than a drugged slug. He was completely exposed for much of the way once he left the cover of the riverbank. Granted visibility was poor and no one was outside other than Red T-shirt, but the Somali youth had line of sight to Lofty's approach as well as to the hut in the opposite direction.

Lofty pulled up the hood to the sniper suit and smeared a little more mud on his face. Laying the AK aside, he opened the dry bag and assembled the rifle, attached the scope but left the lens caps on. He slid a hessian sleeve over the barrel to complete the camouflage. Slinging the AK across his back, he tucked the dry bag away and drew back the bolt on the rifle then pushed it forward and down, chambering a round in the breech. With an intake of breath he steadied himself and then letting it all out, slowly and silently he slithered over the bank like a migrating eel.

There wasn't much in the way of dead ground he could use, only the odd stunted thorn bush. The farmer had obviously cleared the patch for his own convenience. He would have to blend in. The artificial foliage and strands of hessian covering suit, trailed from him like khaki dreadlocks. His outline was further broken by bits of a thorn bush Skelter had attached to the centre of his back. As he inched forward cradling the precious rifle he could not help but think of the old western movies shown on TV. Wondering if anyone would point to him and say, 'Darn it, Zeke, it's injuns, I swear I saw that bush move!'

It was hard going crawling through the mud, carrying the equivalent of his girl friend in weight of weapons and ammunition. Keeping his eye on the lean-to and the main door to the building on the end elevation slowly, but surely, he advanced. A faint, flickering orange glow was visible through the window, possibly from a cooking fire. Every minute the building became clearer, like a camera lens focusing, until he could make out Red T-shirt slouched against the wall. Another couple of metres and there was a puddle indicating a depression in the ground. He was as wet as it was possible to get. This looked like home. He slid into the two inches of water like a salamander and slowly, smoothly, set up the rifle, extending the low bipod with absolute economy of movement. Gently off with the lens caps, eye to the sight, straight flat trajectory, no windage at such a short range. Dial up the next customer's details on the cross hairs. T-shirt was in the toaster. Now for the difficult bit. Lofty carefully reached into his pocket and with one eye on Red T-shirt inched out the walkie talkie, checked the volume was on minimum and squeezed the pressel twice.

Skelter breathed a long sigh as the call came through. Two clicks. Lofty was in position. He answered with one. Just Biscuit now. He must be close. Anyway, so far so good. It hadn't gone noisy. Turbo was sat upon the ground holding the loaded RPG, with three spare rockets in the stripped down pack on his back. The AK hung around his neck on a length of Para cord. He looked strangely happy sat in the mud, rain bouncing off his bush hat, like a small child playing at the bottom of the garden, while parents frantically searched the house for their missing offspring. Skelter felt like he needed another Valium. He felt something smooth and metallic on the back of his hand. It was like Turbo had read his mind, The hip flask was full, a testament to Turbo's willpower given they had been out for a week. Skelter took a good swig of the 101% proof Wild Turkey Bourbon and offered the flask back to Turbo who nodded in Tash's direction. Skelter passed it on and only when it had gone full circle did Turbo take a drink. The warm after taste settled Skelter, kidding him that he had had a bigger shot than he'd taken. The ritual of sharing had boosted his confidence.

The Sony squawked. Skelter nearly jumped out of his skin. It seemed loud. In reality the sound would not have carried more than twenty feet in the prevailing conditions, but it was in his breast pocket, not far from his ear. Three clicks. Biscuit. He answered with one. He got one back. Skelter looked out towards the building and listened to the rain. He clicked once and crawled away from the position into the bush for ten metres then squeezed and whispered into the mouthpiece. 'Is there a door?'

'*Click, click.*' – Yes

'Hostages in hut?'

'*Click, click.*' Biscuit's reply.

Another yes, Skelter's heart rate went up. 'Can you extract?'

'*Click, click, click, click.*' – Maybe.

'If we go noisy?'

'*Click, click.*' – Yes

'Do you want us to take out T-shirt?'

'*Click, click.*'

'Wait one,' said Skelter

33

Saturday 27th June

Skelter called Lofty next, knowing he would have listened over the net to his exchange with Biscuit. He would be expecting a call. '*Click*, zero one zero two.'

'*Click, click.*'

'Green light on Red T-shirt after minutes, five.'

'*Click, click.*'

That was Lofty and Biscuit in position and ready to go. Skelter squeezed and spoke. 'Stand by, stand by. All acknowledge, H, over.'

'*Click click click*,' Biscuit acknowledged. Four clicks next followed by five, Tash and Turbo.

Skelter gave the final order. 'Live after five. Stand by, stand by.'

Skelter checked his watch. It would be dark in less than an hour. He crawled back to Turbo and Tash, double-checked they had heard all the conversations and were up to date with Biscuit and Lofty's situations. He checked his watch again. Ninety-seconds to go. Turbo moved away from the others. He didn't want to fry them with the back-blast from the RPG and besides it had a prominent signature when fired. It was noisy and emitted a great cloud of smoke. Once he'd loosed one off he knew he would have to move and move quickly before the ground upon which he was standing became a bullet magnet for every weapon the enemy could bring to bear.

Twenty-seconds to go.

Lofty eased the stock into his cheek and slowed his breathing to a murmur. He had a clear sight of the target. He took up the slack on the trigger, concentrating on the shot, ignoring the water he was lying in, the rain hammering down upon him, and thoughts of home comforts, desperately tying to invade his thoughts.

Fifteen-seconds.

Biscuit crouched with his ear against the mud wall trying to hear what the men were saying. He could make out two separate male voices but he was unable to distinguish individual words above the noise of the rain. It was immaterial anyway, he could ask them later and as for the rain, well it was about to get a whole lot noisier. He tried in vain to see if he could spot Lofty in the gathering dusk knowing he had more chance of being struck by lightning twice in the same week. He knew he was there and he knew roughly where he ought to be. He could see zilch.

Ten-seconds.

Skelter slipped the safety catch off the AK and brought it up to his shoulder. The sights were set to two hundred metres. Dark in thirty minutes. *'Come on Lofty, take the shot.'*

A flash, more like a torch beam than a rifle muzzle, and not coming from where Lofty should be. Further away, much further away. No sound of a gunshot. Another flash and another, *'what the...?'*

Lofty was so committed he didn't register the approaching headlights. His master eye to the scope, left eye closed, he squeezed the trigger. Red T-shirt died instantly, unaware of the cause, his brain destroyed in a massive shock wave, a nano second before the sound of the gunshot bounced off the wall he had been catapulted into, the remains of his head matching the colour of his T-shirt. Lofty worked the bolt to chamber a fresh round from the magazine and switched his sights to the door.

At the sound of Lofty's rifle Biscuit stepped up to the door of the hut. It looked pretty flimsy. 'British soldiers,' he yelled at the top of his lungs, 'Stand clear of the door.' His size nine boot splintered the old timbers from their hinges. Stooping, he darted through and swept the interior with the under-barrel Maglite. The beam revealed the two hostages. No guards. 'Can ye walk?' he asked,

'Yes,' said one. The other simply stumbled out without a word.

'Stick to me like glue,' said Biscuit, bundling the dazed pair out into the bush.

Skelter was concerned. The approaching headlights could only mean trouble. There were at least two sets, possibly three and it was a safe bet they weren't delivering groceries from the local Tesco, not at this time.

The door to the building opened. An animated figure appeared waving an AK. He went down under a burst of fire from Tash's weapon before Lofty had time to squeeze one off. It went quiet. Only the sound of the rain now. Sensibly no one else tried to come through the door.

It was three sets of headlights and they were getting much nearer. 'Turbo,' Skelter called.

'I'm on it, H. Let em get closer.'

Skelter squinted through the binos trying to focus through the water droplets covering the lenses. Pick ups, three of them. Full of men, armed men. The first vehicle had a heavy machine gun mounted in the back. Looked like the tail end Charlie did too.

Lofty kept one eye on the approaching headlights but left the rifle trained on the door. The headlights turned away from the track, into the scrub before swinging back advancing in line abreast facing the SAS men. They were no more than one hundred and fifty metres from the building when they stopped again and switched off their headlights. *Should have done that before you stopped,* Skelter thought as through the binos he watched three men jump from the lead truck and begin to advance. They were well spaced out. *Straight out the school of infantry manual as translated for Al Qaeda training camps.* Skelter smiled. These boys aren't entirely stupid. The trucks were well within range but difficult to see through the rain.

Lofty swivelled the rifle on its bipod and switched his sights onto the truck on the far left, as Turbo delivered the good news to the one on the right with the RPG. Turbo's grenade struck the nearside headlight, bored through the engine compartment and exploded in the cab hurling bodies over the sides of the load bed as the vehicle bounced off its springs and crashed back to earth before bursting into flames. Seconds later the ground around Turbo's position was chewed to shreds with incoming fire from the big fifty calibre machine gun and a variety of small arms on the back of the other trucks. Not one bullet found the target. Like Elvis, Turbo had left the building, sprinting towards the river to find cover and to position himself to attack from the flank.

The walls of the building flickered in the gathering darkness, lit by the glow from the burning Toyota as the other two trucks wisely withdrew, bouncing and bobbing over the rough terrain until they were swallowed by the storm.

Skelter felt the hair stand up on the back of his neck as an extra charge of adrenalin surged through his system. He instinctively turned around, finger on the AK's trigger. He relaxed the finger as Biscuit's familiar frame emerged out of the dark, accompanied by the hostages.

Parish looked buggered and sick as a dog, the teeming rain incidental, washing his fouled boiler suit. It could not, however, cleanse his conscience.

'The girls; women; in the house.'

'What?' said Skelter.

'From the yacht. Two of them, we can't leave...'

'For fuck's sake, Charles,' said Bell, 'forget them, we need to get out of ...'

Skelter cut him short. 'How many guards?'

'Three at least, could be double,' said Parish.

'Biscuit, give me your flash bangs and get these two to the truck.'

Biscuit passed his stun grenades to Skelter and turned on his heel, pushing the hostages ahead into the rain swept bush.

Turbo couldn't see anything or anyone to shoot at. Lofty, likewise. The enemy had withdrawn behind the curtain of rain. The Sonys squawked and Skelter's voice came over the net. 'All stations cover main building. Tash, with me now. Friendlies in the farm. Acknowledge.'

'*Click*: I have the door,' Lofty replied, like he was a concierge outside Harrods.

'*Click*: On the windows and rear,' came back Turbo.

'Immediate,' Skelter said, keeping his cool as Tash appeared beside him. He nodded at the new arrival 'Two female friendlies, maybe six hostiles. You left – me right. Ready?' Tash nodded. Skelter was out of the blocks sprinting into the open, zig zagging in Lofty's general direction. Heart thumping in his chest, leaden legs straining every muscle, waiting for the bullet from nowhere, the one with H carved in its copper clad nose, he pounded the long, rain-lashed, weaving way across two hundred metres of killing ground. Tash galloped along on his left two metres behind.

Lofty set aside the rifle and covered the entrance with the AK, set to fully automatic. Anyone showing himself at the door would be hosed back through it at the end of a lethal stream of lead.

As Skelter and Tash closed to fifty yards, Turbo spotted them from the corner of his right eye. He lined up his sights and gave the windows a short burst each from the AK, waited a few seconds and sprayed them again.

Skelter made it to the wall right of the door, Tash crashing into it to the left a fraction of a second later. A burst of heavy machine gun fire from somewhere out in the bush lit up the raindrops with orange tracer. The fire was wild and ineffective, passing too high to harm. The bullet from nowhere never came.

Eyeballing each other from across the open doorway the two men switched on the Maglites, pulled the pins on their flash bangs and lobbed them inside. Flattening themselves against the wall they counted, 'One Al Qaeda, two Al Qaeda, three ...'

Tash made a swift sign of the cross. Even when you know it's coming, it still shocks. The earsplitting bangs, the magnesium flashes like an exploding silver sun and ...

Tash was through first, a nanosecond ahead of Skelter. There were no screams, no yelling, just smoking, choking, silence. Tash went left, low, crouching, sweeping the torch beam searching for targets. To the right Skelter was doing the same. He could see flames. The wall in front of him was ablaze. He swept the torch to the left and right. No target. He thought he heard Tash shout 'clear' above the ringing in his ears. The burning wall disintegrated and fell flaming to the ground. Beyond it, Tash's Maglite lit up two figures cowering in a corner, one holding a weapon. He died without firing it along with his companion. Skelter was firing now. A single gunman beginning to recover started to respond. Four rounds struck the youth in the chest. Lights out. Screaming now, mixed voices, male and female, all high pitched, from behind an upturned table. Skelter was screaming in Somali. One of the figures threw his hands up, reaching for the rafters, yelling at the top of his lungs. Tash caught the two girls in the Maglite's beam. Behind them a shadow, moving. 'Down. Get down,' Tash screamed in English.

The girls threw themselves to the dirt. Tash's AK stitched a row of red buttons across the man's chest. The one with his hands in the air doubled over as Skelter slammed the butt of the rifle into his gut, before bringing the barrel down hard onto the back of his neck.

Skelter and Tash dragged the girls towards the door but stopped short of the opening. The women were hysterical, carrying on alarming until Tash meted out some of their own medicine with the palm of his hand. 'British soldiers, you're safe now, safe. Shut up and do what I say.' It was down to a whimper. Skelter squeezed the pressel and spoke into the mouthpiece. We're coming out, coming out. Acknowledge.'

'*Click*: Turbo, Roger.'

'*Click*: Lofty, clear to move H.'

34

Saturday 27th June

The two rain and sweat soaked soldiers burst through the doorway, each hauling a woman. It was only then that anyone noticed the women were both naked. There was no time to go back for the sake of their modesty. Skelter hustled them into the bush closely followed by the other three. After they had covered one hundred and fifty metres he stopped. 'Look at me, look at me,' he ordered the two confused, frightened females. 'Do exactly as you are told. No questions. We will get you home.'

They stood shaking looking blank.

'Understand?'

They nodded furiously.

'Take 'em, Tash.'

'Stick close,' Tasker said, leading them into the storm lashed night.

'We'll give 'em five, then follow,' said Skelter. 'If they come at us it won't be down the track. Too obvious and they won't want another RPG up their exhaust. Lofty go right. Turbo left, stay in visual. On my signal close in for withdrawal.'

Skelter settled himself under a thorn bush, changed the AK's magazine for a full one and squinted into the darkness. He could just about make out the dying flames from the burning truck through the dark downpour, but that was all.

The fire in the truck's engine compartment might have died down but it was still playing ghostly games on the mud walls of the building. Inside the smoke had begun to disperse. The remains of the blanket partition lay smouldering, on a dirt floor hard packed by generations of Somali goat herders. The pungent smell of cordite and nitrate hung heavy in the air. The sound of coughing, strained and weak, came from behind the stack of feed bags. Cawaale eased himself to a semi-recumbent position, and tried to focus. He called out, but no one answered. As the smoke thinned and his stinging eyes recovered a little he began to see why. They were dead; all of them.

Five minutes was snailing by so slowly Skelter could feel himself ageing. He thought of Lucy and wondered if it was time to pack in the Army and take a job on the circuit body guarding some celebrity singer or sports personality for an obscene amount of money. He was shocked to realise he was considering settling down. *He had only just met the woman for God's sake what was he thinking of? How had she got under his skin so far, so fast?* He checked his watch. Close enough. He signalled the others to close in. The three men formed up in silence and headed off towards where they had left the Toyota.

Tash kept up a gruelling pace, ignoring the cries of the women as they splashed through the mud in their bare feet, thorns gouging the skin on their legs and arms. They stumbled, fell and were hauled to their feet, at least half a dozen times before they reached the Toyota.

Biscuit was lying in the bush, covering the approach, the hostages sheltering in the cab. 'Tash, ye old bastard. You remembered my birthday,' he said looking at the women.

'I remember, and it was months ago.'

Tash wrenched open the cab passenger door. 'Out,' he ordered the hostages. Parish obeyed like an automaton, Bell hesitated for a second. Tash's hand shot forward into the cab, then flew back out with Bell on the end of it. He landed face down in the mud. 'Get in,' Tash told the women, holding the door open. Reaching under the seat he retrieved the keys from where they had been concealed, pocketed them, shut the door and climbed into the back. 'You two up here.' Bell and Parish complied. Bell glared at Tash who completely ignored him, rummaging in his bergan. He grabbed a couple of items before closing it up tight and jumping down to the ground. He opened the cab door again.

'Here, best I can do for now,' he said, dumping a spare shirt and a T-shirt on the nearest lap. 'Sit tight okay? Don't worry, ladies, we'll get you home.' He closed the door and took up a firing position ten feet away under a bush in front of the vehicle, close enough so the women could see he had not abandoned them. Biscuit went to ground at the rear of the vehicle.

The rescue Land Rover containing Peter Glass and his detachment was stubbornly splashing its way through the dark wilderness. It was hard enough trying to drive through rain blurring vision so badly his eyes ached, but in the dark, it was a killer. Glass turned on the headlights in defiance of SOPs, all pretence of a tactical approach abandoned. He was worried that the men would think him gutless for not pressing on if he stopped for the night. Alternatively they might think him not smart enough to know it made sense to stop. He went with his gut. They still had miles to go. They might make it by first light if they kept going and given what intelligence he had about the situation on the ground he decided the headlights were worth the risk. *"Who dares Wins."*

Cawaale heard voices outside the farmhouse but he could not make out what they were saying for the ringing in his ears. The back of his head was caked in blood. He looked around in the flickering light of the cooking fire for something to defend himself with. He found an AK lying across the blood soaked chest of one of the boys. The sickly smell of death had joined that of cordite. He gripped the rifle and pointed it at the door. He felt sick and dizzy. He saw the three figures framed in the doorway. He pulled the trigger. Nothing happened. The safety catch. He had forgotten to release the safety catch.

'Cawaale?' a voice shouted through the smoky atmosphere. 'Is it you? It is I, Asad.'

Cawaale lowered the gun. He was a lawyer not a fighter. He knew about the AK, everyone in Somalia knew about the AK, but he had never fired one.

'What happened? Are you hurt?'

'My eyes hurt, I cannot see very well. The gas.' He burst into a fit of coughing and Asad took him by the arm.

'Come we must get you some air,' said Asad leading him through the door. Cawaale lifted his head to the sky letting the rainwater wash his eyes. 'They took our prisoners Asad, we must catch them.'

'Who were they?'

'Americans, British, who knows? The murdering devils will pay for this. We must get the prisoners back.'

'You should stay here and rest my friend,' said Asad. 'We will deal with the infidels.'

'I shall not. Allah has spared me for a reason. He has spared me so I may avenge these crimes. I must go with you, I must.'

'Very well, come take my arm.' Asad led the dazed white robed, figure to the vehicles and helped him into the cab of one of the pickups while others recovered weapons and ammunition from the bodies. Ten minutes later they moved off, the pickup without the Heavy machine gun in the lead, the one with, behind and between the lead vehicle and the river. They travelled at a fast walking pace without lights. Ahead of them on foot three runners trotted through the rain scouting for their quarry. These three men had a personal stake in the action. They each had relatives among the dead at the farm.

Lieutenant Peter Glass kicked the tyre of the Land Rover in frustration, a momentary lapse, soon shunted off into a siding. The men de-bussed, someone found the jack and the wheel brace and they began to jack the vehicle up. At least that is what they attempted to do. Instead of the Land Rover rising up, the jack sank – into the mud.

'Right lads, let's get unloading,' said the young officer.

The men set to with a vengeance, while Glass recovered the jack from the ouze. He grabbed a steel ammo box and worked it into the mud to use as a base for the jack and tried again. This time it worked. While he was so engaged another man unbolted the spare wheel from the bonnet and heaved it onto the ground with a splash, showering his commander in mud. Glass turned on him. The man braced himself for a bollocking. 'Bastard,' said Glass, bursting into laughter. He turned and removed the damaged wheel, stepping back with it to allow the disrespectful trooper to replace it with the spare. Twenty minutes later they were reloaded and on their way. They were closing the gap.

Skelter, Lofty and Turbo legged it through the bush, as finally the rain began to ease. The wind had dropped to a fresh breeze and the clouds were thinning. This was not necessarily good news. They might get through on the radio and arrange for evacuation by helicopter, but it also meant they were going to be easier to find by any pursuers. Skelter had one last ace to play – his SARBE emergency Search And Rescue Beacon. The small hand-held device was designed for pilots downed in hostile territory. When activated it emitted a homing signal which could be picked up by friendly aircraft who could pass on the position to enable search teams to affect a rescue. The three men made it to the Toyota without incident.

'Let's go, Tash. The barge,' said Skelter, jumping in the back with the others, while Tash climbed into the driver's seat. He slotted the ignition key in, turned it half way and waited for the plugs to warm. In the back it seemed like an eternity. Tash turned the key all the way. The engine struggled to turn over, wheezing like an old man with a bad cough. At the fourth attempt it cleared its throat and burst into life. Biscuit banged his fist on the side in exhilaration. Turbo exhaled like a burst balloon and Skelter stopped praying. Lofty, did nothing. Tash crunched it into first and they set off through the bush, weaving around the large bushes and over the small ones until they hit the track and then he went for it. No headlights, slip sliding and ploughing through the mud and waterlogged ruts, oblivious to the discomfort of the passengers in the back, who were hanging on for dear life.

Asad and Cawaale, were close enough to hear the Toyota's diesel engine kick into life. Asad told his driver to speed up. The scouts were so close that another ten-seconds and they would have had eyes on and a chance to open fire. Baying for blood the three Somalis jumped aboard as the pickups reached them.

Skelter thought it inconceivable that they would not be pursued, given the value of the hostages, particularly

Parish. Clearly the three truckloads were there to do business and not to buy goat's cheese. Heavy weapons on the load beds meant they were serious players. He was thinking on his feet or rather his backside as he bounced and banged about, crushed into the small space with five other men, five bergans and all the ancillary kit. Ideally they should cross the river but if they were being followed it would be suicide in an open boat. They'd be picked off like fairground ducks. They could keep going towards the coast, but then what? They would have nowhere else to go. They would have to stand and fight. The barge gave them the best, indeed the only defensible position with cover for the hostages. It was also the only ground they were familiar with.

'Biscuit, Biscuit.' Skelter yelled above the banging and rattling, the engine and the swishing of tyres. 'Get the hostages below soon as we get there, then get ashore. If they come they'll expect us to be aboard. Stick with Turbo and the RPG. Watch his back. Lofty, pick your spot.'

The Toyota slithered to a violent halt as the barge took Tasker by surprise. It took a few seconds for the sardines in the back to recover, by which time Tash had already de-bussed and was at the back, kneeling by the wheel arch watching the track covering the surrounding approaches, down the sights of the AK. Biscuit untangled himself, leapt over the side and wrenched the cab door open.

'Out, out, follow me. You too,' he said, addressing the back of the pick up.

'You heard the man,' Turbo said, helping Parish over the side. Bell followed swiftly. He'd got the message. Biscuit ushered them over the plank and towards the bows. He threw open the door and bundled them down the steps. 'Stay here and keep quiet until we come for you. Whatever happens stay put. Take this.' He held out his pistol to Parish, pulled back the slide and slipped the hammer. 'Safety on here see?' Parish nodded. 'Push the safety, pull the hammer back, shoot. Got it?' Parish nodded again. Turbo looked at the two women, at Bell and finally at Parish. 'You've four rounds. I'll leave the doors for some light but stay out of sight.' As an afterthought he added. 'Don't go further into the boat. It's not safe.'

'Give me a gun,' Bell said, 'I can fight.'

'Leave it to the professionals,' said Biscuit.

'But...'

'Don't argue,' Biscuit said jamming his face well into Bell's personal space. 'Do as you're fucking told.'

The sound of the pursuing pickup's engines could be clearly heard above the abating storm. They were almost upon them. Skelter fired a burst from his AK in their general direction. Lofty followed suit and then the two of them headed for the riverbank ten metres below the barge, while Tash, Turbo and Biscuit jumped into the Toyota and drove down river for two hundred metres before turning into the bush. Noting that the rain had almost stopped and the weather had calmed considerably Skelter activated the SARBE rescue beacon and checked his watch. Daylight was three and a half hours away. The tactical advantage lay with the defenders. They were dispersed on ground of their own choosing and the attackers, would be reluctant to use their heavy weapons until daylight at least, for fear of killing the geese that would lay them the golden eggs. Parish and Bell were first class tickets to every match in the world cup, in cash terms. In the world of Islamic extremism they were priceless in terms of kudos. Skelter could not be certain when the terrorists would make their play, only that they would. He guessed he would not have to wait long to find out.

35

Sunday 29th June

Almost two thousand nautical miles east of the African coast and just less than one thousand from the southern tip of India lies the island of Diego Garcia, a coral atoll in the Chagos Archipelago. Shaped like the outline of a footprint in the sand, the long narrow atoll varies between two and a half miles across at it widest point and a mere twenty-five metres at its narrowest. Only nine metres above sea level at its highest point it covers just ten square miles. The atoll is undeniably beautiful. Its location also makes it one of the most strategically significant and thus most valuable pieces of real estate on the planet. The British government snapped it up from Mauritius in 1965 for three million pounds – then promptly leased it to the USA. By 1971 all the inhabitants of Diego Garcia had been involuntarily relocated to other islands in the Chagos Archipelago, or to Mauritius, or the Seychelles, when the United States constructed a major base for air and sea operations.

A small RAF presence is maintained on the island, with the capacity to fly, among other aircraft, the Nimrod housing Flight Sergeant Shaw's airborne electronic warfare office suite. Susan was looking forward to indulging her favourite hobby when her shift was over. When off duty, RAF Weapons System Operator/Linguist Susan Shaw enjoyed snorkelling in the clear turquoise waters of the thirteen mile long lagoon. When she wasn't soaking up the sun on the palm fringed white sands that is. Flying over the Indian Ocean at eye level with the summit of Mount Everest, the temperature outside the thin aluminium fuselage was well below freezing, way too cold for beachwear.

The Nimrod's pilot had no time to admire the beautiful sunrise, he was focused on trying to thread a giant needle. Air to air refuelling is a delicate manoeuvre, requiring tremendous concentration and superb flying skill. The VC10 Tanker aircraft trailing out the hose towards the Nimrod was steady as a rock. The Nimrod Pilot lined up the probe sticking out above the cockpit, delicately balancing the controls as the aircraft jinked in the slipstream from the tanker. Just as the probe docked with the giant shuttlecock cone and the fuel began to flow, Susan Shaw picked up a SARBE signal and began tracking it, logging the location coordinates and checking it against all the listed known air and ground activity of friendly forces. In the time it took her to cross reference the information the Nimrod had taken on sufficient fuel to keep her in the air for another ten hours.

On the ground one thousand nine hundred miles west of the Nimrod, near the source of the SARBE's signal beacon the sun had yet to make it over the horizon. It was dark and damp, but no longer raining. Visibility had improved, not that that mattered to Lofty. His night vision sniper scope meant he could see his targets in total darkness, if there were no obstructions in the way that is.

The pickup trucks could be heard approaching but they had been smart enough to avoid using the track. The terrorists were too far back in the bush to see but when they killed the engines Turbo knew they had figured where the fight would be. He loaded a grenade into the RPG and went to ground. Waiting was always the worst – the time that played on the nerves. As soon as the action started he would be fine.

Lofty was used to waiting. Waiting for the sky to clear, waiting for visibility to improve, waiting for the wind to steady, waiting for the target to settle, to turn, to present a perfect angle to the bullet's trajectory. The relationship between the sniper and the target is a very intimate one, albeit one sided. Observing someone so closely for sometimes an extended, period brings a closeness, watching the target's expression changing from happy to sad, tense to relaxed. Noting his habits, the way he scratches the back of his head when puzzled, how he picks his teeth and how he blows his nose, knowing that the power to end it all rests in the crook of a well trained trigger finger. There is a strange closeness, much like that between a black widow spider and her mate.

Lofty could see no movement through the scope but he could see what he thought was a figure sitting motionless on the ground behind a thorn bush, no more than sixty metres away. Not sure enough or clear enough to take a shot, he referenced the direction of the position with three small pebbles, lining them up on the top of the river bank making a mental note of the distance. There was no way he was going to take a shot unless he could be sure of a kill. The instant he fired he would have to move; and fast. Skelter too. The muzzle flash was a dead give away in the dark. Daylight was the snipers friend, not the night time. He settled down to play the waiting game.

As the moon slipped out of the clouds lightening the sky, the figure sitting quietly beneath the bush stirred slightly. Lofty watched him put something into his mouth, observed the rhythmic movement of his jaw as he began to chew. It was getting really moonlit now, but there was no sign of the enemy pick ups. Too far back in the bush. The Somali continued to chew until the round from Lofty's rifle smashed through his sternum and exited his back, severing the spinal cortex on the way through before finally burying itself in the hip of another Somali several feet behind the intended target.

Skelter was taken by surprise by the muzzle blast and the deafening report. Silence reigned for seconds and then... First AKs blasting away wildly, knee-jerk, driven by shock and fear, then the measured dull drumming of the heavy machine gun tearing through the bush raking the rusting barge from stem to stern. The heavy rounds chewed chunks from the boat splintering wood, peppering and punching the metalwork. Skelter and Lofty kept their heads down, below the top of the riverbank as the gunner widened his scope searching for flesh and blood. Reconnaissance by fire the Americans call it. What he was also unwittingly doing was strimming the bush, stripping back the overlapping layers of thorn scrub hiding him from view. Skelter and Lofty moved ten metres further down river under the cover of the bank before going to ground.

When the firing stopped the cloud of smoke from the heavy machine gun's hot, heavy barrel acted as a signal beacon. Homing in on this beacon the lethal trio of Turbo, Tash and Biscuit were ablaze with adrenalin. The gun began hammering away again, slow and steady, dealing damage and destruction, demolishing the wheelhouse in a haze of flying splinters and explosive incendiary bullets. The remains of the wheelhouse was burning fiercely.

The AKs had stopped firing from the bush. They had settled down and established some fire discipline. No target to engage – no shoot. Skelter could hear them moving in the dark as they dismounted, but apart from what he guessed was an initial discussion about what they planned to do there was no talking. Taking advantage of the lull, Skelter got out his water bottle and took a swig.

'These jokers are no amateurs, Lofty, good noise discipline.'

'Ammo conservation too,' said the sniper. 'Wonder who trained them?'

'Us probably,' said Skelter. 'We train our friends and ten years later our friends are our enemies. That's politics.'

'Well trained, but not up to our standard, H.' The occasional sound of scuffing feet and metal against metal, gravel and rock bore testament to Lofty's evaluation. It was difficult to tell how many there were or how far away, but Skelter reckoned on around two in the cabs and between six and eight in the back max, so potentially twenty, more likely twelve to fourteen. They had one heavy truck-mounted machine gun and each man would have at least an AK, possibly a light machine gun or two as well. It went really quiet. Skelter strained his ears. The adrenalin was on slow flow, heightening his senses. Nothing. Not a click, clack or scuff. Either they had got their shit well together, or they had gone to ground. They maybe realised the danger of killing the valuable hostages. He looked across at Lofty, who was too engrossed in scoping the bush to notice him. Skelter swept the scrubland with his night vision goggles back and forth slow and steady, scrutinising the eerie radiation-green glowing landscape for any sign of the enemy. Nothing. 'What the hell were they waiting for? Daylight maybe?' That was the only thing that made sense, unless they were waiting for reinforcements. They were obviously well trained and it would be inconceivable that they were not in communication with other units. He checked his watch. 05.26. Sunrise in just over an hour.

Below the conflagration, Bell, Parish and the two women

huddled together in a heap, in the squalid filth of the barge, shaking, scared shitless, but relatively safe, oblivious to the fact that twenty feet away in the hold, two terrified, tied up Somali prisoners were cowering against the bulkhead in total darkness. Parish had vomited again.

'Jesus Charles keep it in can't you? And stop fucking whining,' he said to the women. 'Stop blubbering and pull yourselves together.' The crying subsided. Bell had lost patience with them, furious with himself for getting into the situation in the first place. More angry at his rescuers than grateful for their intervention, Bell was not used to being ordered about and he deeply resented it. That said he had faith in the ability of these soldiers to deliver him from his situation.

36

Sunday 28th June

With Biscuit and Tash covering his flanks, Turbo crawled forward towards the smoke from the big machine gun rising above the bush, gripping the RPG like it was the last bottle of beer on earth. He had a decision to make. When to stand up. He couldn't see anything from where he was, too low down. He ran through the action in his head; *stand up, visual sweep, locate truck, three seconds. Acquire target, arm, aim, fire, five seconds. Drop and leg it. How long would they take to react? What if he couldn't see the target when he stood? What if they were too close? Life's a lottery, fuck it. Get on with it.* One last nod to the flankers, pointing to the sky motioning upwards with the rocket launcher, the nod of understanding, legs shaking, arms on fire, lungs screaming, 'fuck you, fuckers.' AKs left and right pouring suppressing fire. Tash and Biscuit clearing the way. Upright now, weapon live, smoke seen, truck, target, trigger. Whoosh, drop, boom. Scuttling like rabbits dodging left and right, stumbling, tumbling, falling, flailing arms, piston pumping legs. Ragged firing, rounds cracking past hypersensitive ears, fizzing into the mud.

Thirty-seconds later lying in a shallow depression in the muddy ground, heart racing and gasping for breath, Turbo quickly ran his hands over his torso and legs.

'Everyone okay,' Biscuit asked.

'Check,' said Tash.

'Okay, I'm okay,' Turbo screeched. 'Did I hit it?'

'Fuck knows.'

'Me neither.'

'Did you hear that fucking bang? I must have hit something.'

Skelter and Lofty felt the blast from the RPG detonation.

'Turbo?' said Skelter.

Lofty shrugged. 'Hope so. Sounds like he may have taken out the machine gun, if he has it'll pull the their fangs a bit. Maybe they'll decide they've had enough and pack up and go home.'

'Fat chance,' said Skelter. If they don't, then it's time to go on the offensive. Attack is the best form of defence. We must crush their will to fight.' He laid the AK across his knees and put his head in his hands, lost momentarily in thought.

'Easier said than done,' said Lofty, 'these guys want to fight, they hate the West. They won't pass up a chance to take Parish, the propaganda's too valuable. They'll fight to the last man. We have to disengage or else kill them all.'

'Nowhere to disengage to,' replied Skelter.

'In that case you better pray we've got enough ammunition.'

'Amen to that,' said Skelter. He took out the Sony. 'Sitrep, sitrep,' there was a long silence. 'Talk to me, boys, I need a sitrep'.

'All okay, H,' was Biscuit's eventual reply on behalf of the bush babies.

'Received. H out.' Skelter eased himself up to get a view over the top of the bank. There was movement out there, but no clear target to shoot at. *Give me a little two-inch mortar to lob bombs high in the air and drop them right on their heads.* His dreaming was cut short by a burst of fire from the bush splashing the mud close to his right shoulder splattering his face with brick red flecks. He ducked below the bank, scampered past Lofty, and ran back up stream for five metres just as the sniper's rifle slammed, dipatching another round to send some Somali to meet his maker. Skelter sneaked a look, just in time to see figure flop out of the underside of a bush like a rag doll.

Lofty watched the man roll out as he worked the bolt to feed another round into the breech. He slid slowly down the bank and ran a hand over his chin, rubbing at the stubble. From his pocket he took a glacier mint, which he unwrapped with reverence before popping it in his mouth, screwing up the wrapper and stuffing it deep into his cargo pocket. Another burst of firing, ineffective this time. As both sides were using AKs it was impossible to tell who was shooting at whom, another unintended consequence of a strategic decision taken miles from the battlefield. Lofty took a swig of water. The bottle was nearly empty. He took a couple of steri-tabs from his belt kit and dropped them into the dregs then shook the bottle. After a minute he reached down to the water's edge inches upstream from his boots and filled up from the river.

A few metres away Skelter watched Lofty and gave his own bottle a shake. Okay for now he reckoned. More firing from the bush, then the dull percussive sound of a hand grenade, another, a fierce fusillade and then silence. Biscuit's bush babies were at work again. The heavy machine gun had not fired a round since the big bang so it looked like Turbo had killed it. It seemed like the battle was going well for team Skelter.

For Caroline Warren, things were also going well, her core body temperature had been expertly restored to something like normal and she was out of danger. Above the sick bay where she lay under the best care the Royal Navy could provide, the heli deck crew were beavering away with professional purpose, preparing HMS Monmouth's Sea Lynx helicopter for launching.

Five miles above Caroline's sick bed, Susan Shaw eased her backside out of the seat and massaged the dead tissue back to life, her eyes never leaving the screen. She was sending a continuous stream of signal traffic updating the communications centre aboard the frigate as to the SARBE's position, even though it had remained static since she first picked it up. According to all the information available to her there should be no NATO force in the immediate area. The signal code indicated it was a British Army device and not an RAF one as she would have expected. In any case there were no reports of missing aircraft of any kind other than the civilian Cessna, and that had been dealt with.

All this pointed to one thing – British special forces. A covert operation. One that was in trouble. Her supervisor was monitoring her work more closely than usual, something that had not escaped Flight Sergeant Shaw's notice. He clearly knew more than he was sharing. Need to know. That was the system and the system said she didn't. Did not need to, did not mean Susan did not know. She was highly experienced in airborne surveillance and had a shrewd idea what was going on. She had heard the news report claiming a senior spook from MI5 or MI6, had been abducted to Somalia and although this was the regular patrol area for the Nimrod, there had been an atmosphere of expectancy aboard the aircraft since the flight began. Normally she would be off duty now and heading for the beach, but the rendezvous with the VC10 Tanker had extended their airtime considerably and put her downtime passion on hold for the time being.

Looking across the river Skelter could see the angry storm a few miles away to the Southwest. No chance of the back up force coming anytime soon. The helicopters couldn't fly in that, but at least the storm was heading the right way. He calculated that the way it was moving there was a fighting chance Camp Winston could be clear for heliborne operations by mid afternoon. It might as well be next week. Lucky things were going their way. He looked out to the bush. Silent and still as a graveyard. He could see Lofty glued to his scope and that was it. Not another living soul in sight. It was quiet. The enemy had clearly taken casualties, but there was no moaning no yelling or screaming. That meant killed and or slightly wounded

37

Sunday 28th June

The air of expectancy in the room, fed by rumour, whispers and knowing glances as COBRA convened for the first time in twenty-four hours was almost tangible. The disc harrow had been working overnight on the PM's furrowed brow refining it to more modest allotment-like drills.

'Gentleman, and Ladies,' he began, 'I have some encouraging news. The RAF has picked up a signal from a search and rescue beacon near the hostage location. I will hand you over to Geoffrey for a full update.'

'Thank you, Prime Minister. The signal was picked up at four fifteen this morning GMT. We have identified the source as a special forces SARBE unit which leaves us in no doubt that our SAS surveillance unit is broadcasting. We can only assume that their radio is non operational. What we do not know is their current situation. Clearly they have asked for assistance. How much trouble they are in beyond requiring a lift home we have no idea. The follow up unit is still grounded by the weather but the good news is that the storm is moving away. The operational area in Somalia is currently storm free and we expect the same to apply in the Camp Winston area, in Kenya within thirty-six hours. I would like to pass you on to my colleague commander Frazer from the Royal Navy at this point.' Colonel Geoffrey Greaves resumed his seat, as a tall slim, baby faced Naval Intelligence officer stood up to address the meeting.

'Prime Minister, Gentlemen,...err and Ladies of course...'

'Get on with it, man,' said the PM's private secretary.

'Yes, sir, of course.' The young man took a deep breath. 'HMS Monmouth is preparing to dispatch a Royal Marines boarding party by Lynx helicopter, to offer assistance if required.'

'How many Marines make up the boarding party?' asked the PM

'Six, sir. The Lynx can only carry six, but they are highly trained, sir.'

'No doubt,' said the PM frowning. 'What if they cannot find a suitable landing ground?'

'Fast rope from hover, sir, on the ground in under a minute, the whole team. The Lynx has limited endurance but Monmouth is steaming full ahead for the coast to increase loiter time over the target.'

'What about offensive capability?' asked Geoffrey Greaves addressing the young officer.

'The mark 8 Lynx weapon systems are primarily anti subMarine, but she can be fitted with machine guns, sir.'

'Can be?'

'I am afraid I have no information on the specific configuration of the mark 8 in question, sir. I'm sorry.'

'Okay, thank you, commander, you may sit down.'

The meeting broke up after thirty-five minutes, having concluded that the assets assigned to the task should be sufficient for the job. In any case they were all that was available in the immediate area. The only way to add to them would be by going cap in hand to the Americans.

Aboard Monmouth the six man boarding party were

kitting up, checking weapons and ammunition while the pilot went through his preflight checks. The sea was relatively calm now that the storm had passed over, visibility was good and the target well within the Lynx's three hundred and twenty Nautical Mile range. The calculations predicted a loiter time over target at approximately forty-five minutes. The six Marines climbed aboard and settled themselves in as the Royal Marine door gunner checked his GPMG for freedom of traverse, elevation and depression. Minutes later the engines began to whine and the rotor blades started to rotate. The smell of avgas mixed with salt spray, sweat and testosterone, filled the cabin. The aircraft began vibrating rhythmically, the high-speed rotor blades cutting through the air as the pilot's eyes danced between the instruments and the bright orange gloves of the yellow-jacketed Flight Deck Officer. Wait for the signal. Clear for take off. Power up, transition lift, up and away, smooth as a bucket of frogs.

Skelter was ravenous. No shots had been fired for fifteen minutes at least. Biscuit had checked in over the net and all was well that end so he decided to take advantage of the lull and delved into his belt kit, pulling out a small tube of processed cheese with ham bits. Not army issue. Sainsbury's, Hereford. The biscuits he opened to accompany it were army issue and unpalatable without the cheese. He was tucking in to his second smearing when all hell broke loose. The air was filled with the crack of bullets breaking the sound barrier as they passed overhead, tore through the scrub and splashed into the ground throwing up fountains of mud and river water. He dropped the snack and hugged the bank. Lofty had unslung his AK ready for any frontal assault. Rounds began hitting the water close to the bank, no more than a metre from where he and Lofty were sheltering. *How the hell?* Skelter picked out the lower, slower drumming of a heavy machine gun in the midst of the higher frequency, rapid fire of the AKs. Had they fixed the gun? A second later reality hit him like a round from a rifle. Reinforcements! The fire hitting the water was coming from up stream close to the bank. It was a new heavy MG.

'Shit, where the fuck did that come from?'

Biscuit summed up the situation in trice, signalled Tash and Turbo to follow and went haring off away from the firing. After a hundred metres he stopped, turned and grabbed the others. 'We have to get round the flank, hit them from behind.' They nodded and followed Biscuit off into the bush. The firing sounded and looked like a bush fire, a fiercely crackling crescendo of noise and gun smoke.

What was worrying Skelter, was the uncomfortable accuracy. Lofty and he were exposed to incoming enfilade fire along the riverbank. It was time to move. No time for niceties, he grabbed Lofty by the belt and jerked, then, having got his attention yelled 'downstream,' above the noise of the one sided firefight. The two men legged it at a crouch, Lofty struggling to keep his long lean frame below the top of the bank, chest heaving and sinews stretching under the weight of weaponry. Bullets from the bush thudded into the bank above their heads and the newcomers poured streams of half-inch heavy machine gun bullets along the bank, spewing up fountains of muddy river water inches from the scrambling fugitives. Several hairy seconds later they found sanctuary in a natural cleft where the river had eroded the bank, scooping out a haven the size of a kids paddling pool. It provided cover from the boys in the bush whilst giving line of sight towards the advancing newcomers only from the edge of the cleft. They were relatively safe at the back. Lofty immediately set up office, while Skelter popped up like a meerkat, sprayed the bush with a burst from his AK and ducked below the bank.

Peter Glass stopped the Land Rover and opened the door, cocking his head towards the front. The rain had ceased and the going had improved marginally.

'That's a heavy machine gun,' said someone from the back, stating the obvious.

Glass slammed the door, put the Land Rover into gear and headed towards the sound. Less than ten minutes later they reached the river and turned downstream towards the noise. The sounds of the firefight were louder now and there was smoke on the other side of the river.

'Stand by, stand by,' said the young lieutenant, feeling the electric atmosphere of men chafing at the bit, pumped for action. Glass brought the Land Rover to a skidding halt and ordered everyone out. Across the river noise and clouds of smoke marked the firefight on the far bank a little down stream of their position. Peter Glass climbed onto the vehicle and stood on the bonnet. He began sweeping the scene through his binoculars. Dense smoke and thick thorn scrub made an in depth appreciation of the situation difficult, but he could see quite clearly two men hugging an indentation in the bank, close to the water's edge. They were pinned down by fire from a heavy machine gun mounted on the back of a pickup truck. They were clearly white and they were in serious trouble. 'Bring up the GPMG,' ordered Glass. The two-man gun group set up the machine gun on its bipod, slapped a belt on and cocked and locked. 'Gun group.' Glass delivered the order in calm measured tones. 'Target left of your arc, far riverbank. Range three five zero metres. Vehicle mounted machine gun; engage.'

The gunner set the rear sight, swung the barrel, lined up and opened fire, sending a stream of copper jacketed lead arcing across the water. Every fifth round a tracer glowing green like a supersonic firefly, marking its trajectory as it splashed into the bank behind the target.

The Somali gun crew on the back of the pick up were too engrossed in their grim task to notice that they had come under fire.

Neither Skelter nor Lofty, were aware that help was at hand on the opposite bank from them, one hundred and fifty metres upstream where Peter glass was quite literally calling the shots, in what had been until then a one sided firefight.

Glass observed the strikes from the GPMG through his binoculars. 'Adjust fire two metres right.'

The gunner complied, squeezing off steady five-round bursts, his number two feeding the belt of bullets into the breech as two others stood by, garlanded with fresh belts of ammunition, keeping it dry and away from the mud.

'On target, on target,' Glass's voice now up an octave, but still held steady.

The Somali manning the Russian made DShK heavy machine gun that was causing Skelter and Lofty so much trouble, found himself looking up at the sky, unable to raise his head from the mud in which he was lying. He was better off than the rest of his gun crew who were dead or dying in the back of the old Toyota truck, now so riddled it resembled a colander. A long burst from the GPMG across the river had sliced through the crew causing carnage, two rounds shattering the gunner's left shoulder and catapulting him clear of the pickup as tracer rounds struck a box of incendiary bullets setting it on fire.

'Cease fire, cease fire,' ordered Glass. The gunner released the trigger. Good job, well done. Well done, lads.

Peter Glass had been in his first firefight and had

made a positive contribution to the action. His decision to press on with such a small force had been the right one. The problem was, there were no more targets to shoot at and as their assault boats were back on the trucks they had no means of crossing the river to join in the battle. To attempt to wade across would be suicidal. He weighed up his options. Stand fast and hope for more targets, or move upstream out of range and search for a safe crossing. If he opted to move he could leave two men with the GPMG to cover from bank, but that would reduce his assault group to four, including himself, and all with light weapons. It would also increase the possibility of a friendly fire incident. This time he opted to stay, proceeding to scour the far bank for targets. He had lost sight of the two men by the riverbank. He offered a silent prayer for them and the rest of the team as he scrolled the focus wheel, probing the smoke and thicket. The other three men besides the gun team had adopted firing positions and were watching the action. There were no clear targets for their rifles and the last thing anyone wanted was to risk a blue on blue. The men across the river were their mates.

'H,' said Lofty, 'that MG. It's stopped.'

'I thought it was a bit quieter,' said Skelter. 'Changing belts?'

'Speak up I can't hear you,' said Lofty cupping a hand to his ear and grinning. 'There's a war on you know.'

'I said, they must be changing belts, you piss taker.'

'Too long for that, they have a problem,' said Lofty. 'Let's hope they can't fix it.'

'Amen,' said Lofty turning back to the job in hand.

A couple of Somalis ran to the peppered pickup truck. Asad climbed into the back and managed to kick the burning ammo box over the open tailgate. The other jumped into the cab and turned the key to start the engine. Amazingly it fired first time and the kid drove it downstream towards Skelter and Lofty. He pulled up behind a patch of scrub and jumped out and into the back to join Asad. They immediately set about clearing the bodies off the load bed and trying to get the gun back into action.

Glass's gun group opened fire, startling the young officer. 'Cease firing, cease fire,' Glass ordered. The gunner stopped. 'The target's too close to our guys. Engage with rifle fire, single shots and only if you have a clear target. Understood?'

The theory was fine but the dense smoke from the firefight made it a non starter. The new position of the truck now meant that any attempt to fire on it with the GPMG could endanger the SAS men of Skelter's men. Glass's team was powerless. All they could do for now was watch and pray.

Lofty settled down and got to work. His first target was a cocky youth running along the top of the bank waving a German G3 rifle and screaming at the top of his lungs. High on narcotics no doubt, thought Lofty as a round from the Accuracy stuck the youth in the chest. The man's forward momentum carried him another four strides, despite the massive shock wave, which destroyed his chest cavity. Before he hit the ground Lofty had worked the bolt, chambered a fresh round and acquired another target, a more cautious, older man, lying beneath a thorn bush. Head shot. Meet the ancestors. His third was more challenging, almost two hundred metres away, beyond the barge, advancing tactically. Skinny and sharp, scurrying from cover to cover, short dashes, swerving and swaying, down and rolling. The first round missed but not by much. It was a case of anticipating where the man was going to be before he squeezed the trigger. A burst from Skelter's

AK showered Lofty with hot brass, one of the smoking cartridge cases landing on his exposed neck, searing his skin causing him to wince as he squeezed, missing again. The man had a charmed life, but it was one with only twelve-seconds left to run. Momentum meant he kept running for fifteen, before skittering sideways into the mud, clutching his abdomen.

Down in the bowels of the barge, among the discarded detritus, the whimpering of the women was getting on Bell's nerves. 'For fuck's sake give it a rest.' He yelled, adding, 'fucking whores,' half under his breath.

Parish stared through the door along the narrow corridor towards the light coming through the hatch, gripping the pistol with both hands, knuckles white. The sounds of the battle raging outside seemed unreal. Like someone was watching a war film in the next cabin. He desperately wanted to wake up and find it had all been a dream. He knew it wasn't but clinging to hope was all he could do. That and praying of course. Everyone turned to prayer in such circumstances, well almost everyone. They say there are no atheists in slit trenches but God did not exist in Richard Bell's world. Had he faith in a higher being, it would have been Satan, but he didn't; Richard Bell's God was Richard Bell.

Lofty was now living on borrowed time and he knew it. Five shots taken from the same position, well concealed, but the odds were stacking up against him. Problem was there was no obvious place to move to. They were stuck. He reloaded the rifle, pondering what to do next when his bush hat was plucked from his head. He turned to Skelter.

'Stop fucking about, H.' Skelter stared at him holding the bush hat, wiggling his finger through the scorched edge of a hole in the crown.

Lofty exhaled. 'They're taking this a bit serious, don't you think?'

Skelter tossed the hat to him and fired a long burst into the bush. Ducking back he removed the now empty magazine and replaced it with a fresh one, jerking back the cocking handle.

Somewhere out in the bush another intense burst of firing broke out.

Turbo had stashed the RPG in his backpack and unslung the AK. The three men had got within thirty feet of the terrorists before, with bad luck and bad timing, they emerged at the rear of the burnt out truck at the same time as one of the Somalis decided to walk back to pick up water. He was young, sharp eyed and fast, ripping off a burst before Biscuit banjoed him with a headshot. Both he and Turbo emptied a magazine a piece towards the fleeting backs of a group in the bush swiftly followed up with phosphorus grenades before diving back into the unforgiving thorn scrub.

'Tash? Where's Tash?' Turbo looked about, frantic.

'Shit. C'mon,' Biscuit was already heading back into harm's way, changing magazines on the move. Turbo bounded after him. The terrorists had moved away from the contact point, no doubt confused at being attacked from the rear. With luck they may well think they were up against more than just three men. Two men. Tash had taken a round through the thigh severing his femoral artery.

Biscuit hurled himself at the wound using all his strength to try to stem the flow.

Turbo dove into Biscuit's cargo pocket for the medic pack, tore it open and pulled out the tourniquet. A jet of warm blood struck his chest as he struggled to get the tourniquet around Tash's thigh.

'Stay with me, Tash. Stay with me,' Biscuit pleaded.

Tash's face was ashen, draining colour as his heart pumped his lifeblood into the mud, baptizing his comrades in the process. Biscuit ripped the morphine syrette from around Tash's neck but his friend died before he had time to inject it.

Tash had fought his last fight.

Biscuit began mouth to mouth.

Turbo gripped Biscuit's arm. 'He's gone mate he's gone. Come on.'

'Fuck off,' said Biscuit slapping Turbo's hand away, his face drawn from the strain, wet with tears.

'Let's get the bastards. Let's get them for Tash. Come on mate.'

Biscuit let out a primeval roar, like a wounded elephant. He lowered Tash's body to the ground and brandishing his AK47, jumped to his feet. 'For Tash,' he cried.

'Tash,' echoed Turbo and the two men headed back into harm's way.

There would be more tears, but not now; they would have to wait until later. If there was anyone left to shed them, that is.

38

Sunday 28th June

Skelter and Lofty were taking heavy fire again from the machine gun on the back of the truck. The Somalis were getting bolder and had moved the pickup to within one hundred and fifty metres and were pouring rounds into riverbank above their heads. The pair were in no danger of being hit by the heavy half inch diameter bullets as long as they kept in defilade below the bank, as the mounting would not allow the gunner to depress the barrel any further. One round from the awesome weapon would tear a limb off and likely not be survivable. The gunner wasn't trying to kill them, just to keep them pinned down, hugging the bottom of the bank. Skelter and Lofty knew this. They also knew why – so others could approach under its cover to deliver the coup de gras. They braced themselves, backs to the bank, eyes on the edges of the small cut that they huddled in. If anyone appeared around the brick red mud they couldn't miss. Not at eight feet! Skelter's heart was banging like Keith Moon's bass drum, while at the same time aching for Lucy. He did not want to die, not here not now, now that he had seen a glimpse of a future. He tried to shrink into the bank, to make himself as small as possible. He was praying at light speed.

Something splashed into the mud at his feet. He looked to see what it was, but before he could focus Lofty scooped it up and lobbed it over and into the river, where it exploded, throwing up a geyser of water spraying both of them. A fraction of a second later Lofty's AK splattered a dark face that peered into their refuge. Skelter's whole body was electrified, like it was wired to the mains, adrenalin fires flashing through his veins – molten lava at mach one. His peripheral vision shut down, his entire world shrinking into the entrance to their sanctuary, just beyond touching distance. The AK went off, dancing in his hands, even before it seemed he had seen the next terrorist stick his neck out. The face disappeared again. He had no idea if he had hit him. Smoke curled up from the hot barrel, cordite stung his eyes. He felt like he was about to explode.

Turbo had retrieved the RPG and with Biscuit covering him, he made his way towards the sound of the other heavy machine gun, deep in the scrub, crawling on his belly towards the track, as the bushes began to thin out. He edged forward, aware of the concentration of incoming fire re-landscaping the riverbank ahead and to the left. He couldn't see exactly where the fire was coming from. He needed to get closer and quickly.

The Lynx was three minutes from target; the Marine door gunner lifted the feed tray cover and slapped a two hundred round belt of mixed ball and tracer ammunition onto the machine gun. He snapped the cover shut, pulled the cocking handle fully to the rear then pushed it all the way forward. He checked the gas regulator and opened it two clicks. The rest of the Marines, their cam-creamed, grim faces set for trouble, cocked and locked their weapons.

Aboard the barge the hostages could sense the battle was

coming to a climax by the sheer weight of fire that was ringing and pinging off the metalwork or thudding into the planking. Charles Parish was apprehensive, yet physically calm, in the way he used to be when waiting for exam results at Cambridge. It occurred to him that he had been given the pistol, not for defence, but to ensure none of them fell into the terrorist's hands. He wondered if he be up to the job if it came down to the wire. If it was he would have to shoot Bell first.

Another grenade landed next to Lofty's foot. He instinctively kicked it away but not far enough. Time froze. Both men stared into the shallows where it landed and waited to die. The swift current had enough force to carry it past the edge of the cut, protecting Skelter and Lofty from the bulk of the blast as it exploded with a loud bang. It left both of them deafened.

Three miles from the Battle, the Royal Navy Lynx pilot was listening to Susan Shaw's calm, velvet voice in his headset as she directed them to the target. She was watching over the action with cool professional detachment, following the battle on her second monitor live by satellite. Skelter's team didn't know it but they could not be in better hands. Susan's superiors had finally decided to let her into the loop and give her the details of what was occurring on the ground, confirming what she had already deduced from the information available to her. Three miles to a Lynx, the fastest helicopter in the world, is around forty-five seconds flying time.

Time however is relative. When you are fighting for your life, dodging bullets travelling at twice the speed of sound, forty-five seconds can seem like a lifetime, especially when you have no idea that help is on the way. Skelter was now resigned to death and determined to take as many with him as he could. He risked a quick glance at Lofty. They said their goodbyes with their eyes as a savage burst of fire from the heavy machine gun ripped the air above them and an RPG exploded on the top of the bank showering mud and shingle down upon the exhausted pair.

On the far side of the river, Peter Glass was watching the battle through his binoculars with increasing concern. There was a fog of gun-smoke obscuring the scene, but one thing was clear, The two men hugging the river bank under fire were in real trouble. Friendly fire risk or not he had to intervene.

'Gun Group. Three five zero metres, vehicle mounted machine gun, short bursts. Engage.'

Turbo stood up in the middle of the firefight, in sheer desperation, looking for the truck with the troublesome machine gun. He found it, dropped to the ground and crawled rapidly away from where he had exposed himself.

'You mad bastard,' cried Biscuit, 'you wanna die?'
Turbo answered the question by standing again, aiming the RPG at the truck and firing. He hit the dirt as a tremendous wind gusted, lifting him from the ground and slamming back down again, dented and deaf. Biscuit lay nearby shaking his head, coughing into the dirt.

Peter Glass's gunner squeezed the GPMG's trigger sending short controlled bursts at the pickup. He had fired less than twenty rounds when through the binoculars his commander saw the white smoke trail of Turbo's RPG melt into the target which blew apart in front of Peter Glass's astonished eyes. By the time he had recovered from the shock and ordered cease-fire, the gunner had already stopped, unaware that his last bullet had scored an own goal, slicing off a friendly earlobe within a centimetre of killing one of Skelter's men. That man was too pumped with adrenaline to realise he had been hit as yet.

Skelter and Lofty, protected by the riverbank watched in awe as bits of machine gun, parts of pickup and chunks of terrorist arced through the air, throwing up fountains of foam as they splashed into the river, and thudded into the mud all about. Asad the lion would roar no more.

Turbo couldn't understand what had happened. He could only assume he had hit a stash of RPG Grenades or other munitions. The silence was deafening after the mad cacophony of battle. The dramatic loss of their main support weapon might have been enough to persuade the terrorists to pack up and go home. For those in their ranks who were still undecided, the arrival of the Lynx clinched it. The remaining trucks pulled out, men running to scramble aboard, some dropping their weapons in the mad panic to get away.

Skelter and Lofty gazed skywards as the helicopter hovered above, Marines sliding down the ropes from both sides, while the door gunner encouraged the flight of the terrorists with bursts of seven point six two lead-lined copper. Like a deciding goal, in the dying seconds of extra time, it was all over. Nerve wrenchingly close, but a win for the away team. Skelter reached for the Sony and called for a sitrep.

'*Click, click.* We lost Tash.' Biscuit's voice was uncharacteristically sober.

'*Click.* Turbo?'

'*Click*. He's fine just a bit deaf like me.'

'*Click*. C'mon in. H, out.'

Skelter cautiously peered over the edge of the bank, his eyes level with a pair of parade ground polished boots. The young Royal Marine sergeant smiled and offered his hand. Skelter climbed up and shook it warmly.

'Steve Cox – Forty-five Commando at your service.'

'Skelter – Twenty-two SAS. Your timing's spot on. How?

'HMS Monmouth, Type 23 Frigate. We're about five miles off the coast. RAF picked up your SARBE and talked us in. They're up there somewhere watching over you. Give 'em a wave, why don't you.'

Skelter stared into the blue and raised a weary arm.

The smoke haze was too thick for Susan Shaw to see Skelter's gesture and anyway the zoom and resolution were not up to it. She had however received confirmation from the Lynx pilot via Monmouth that the Marines had been deployed. She breathed a sigh and massaged her neck waking up the blood vessels numb from inactivity. Susan Shaw had earned her pay today. Allowing herself the luxury of a smile before knuckling back down to the job, she offered up a silent prayer for the boys on the ground.

'Hostages,' said Skelter, as Lofty climbed the bank.

'Right oh, H.' He ambled off towards the barge, across a landscape littered with scorched earth; burnt bushes; brass cartridge cases; chunks of mangled metal flecked with blood and fleshy bits of badly burnt bodies. His eyes had receded into the back of his skull. He looked and felt like a dead man walking. He called down the hatch.

'You can come up. It's over.' Lofty repeated the words three times before he got a response. Gradually the hostages began to stir.

'Sure it's safe?' said a male voice.

'Watch the water. Don't look anywhere else okay?' They nodded. The one thing they could not escape, was the cloying smell of death, hanging heavy in the humid air. All around, the atmosphere was thick with the acrid smell of cordite, fresh blood and human entrails. It was a smell that would stay with them for a long time.

The Lynx had moved off to monitor the retreat of the terrorists. The co-pilot reported up to the airborne office and the ship. Susan Shaw logged the traffic and allowed herself to relax a smidgen. The pilot checked the fuel situation. They had used a lot, flying at maximum speed to reach the SAS men, but there was still enough to stooge around for thirty minutes. The pilot needed to land and with that aim in mind he circled around looking for a suitable spot. He eventually squeezed the aircraft into a bit of a clearing around six hundred metres downstream from the barge, the nearest suitable spot. He radioed the Marine team and after a brief discussion it was decided to take the hostages and three of the SAS men back to the ship, refuel and return for a second lift.

Lieutenant Glass exhaled loudly as he watched the Lynx circling. His shoulders relaxed for the first time since he left Winston. He ordered his signaller to set up and establish comms with the Camp. The weather being relatively calm now he figured it should be easy. It was. He made his report by voice, which the camp signaller would forward to Hereford, after encoding and encryption. Not that it mattered, Glass knew to be cryptic and give nothing away. His voice call was intercepted however, by at least one eavesdropper.

Susan Shaw gleaned enough from the signal to confirm her suspicions that Glass was part of another special forces group, probably from the same unit as the men involved in the firefight.

Turbo and Biscuit emerged from the bush sweating profusely, carrying Tash's ashen, limp, body between them. They laid him down at H's feet. The Marine sergeant took two paces back. Round and about the other Marines were scouring the scrub for stragglers and wounded. Skelter knelt beside his friend and said his goodbyes. Turbo walked off into the bush to retrieve the Toyota to transport the people to the helicopter. When it was done with they would wreck it to deny it to the enemy.

A Marine medic began treating three wounded terrorists. A fourth was made comfortable and given morphine. He had been shot in the abdomen and chest. He would not be around for long. The others were only slightly wounded; shrapnel from the exploding truck, legs and backs mostly. They would all live.

Susan Shaw reported to Monmouth. 'This is Angel two zero, Angel two zero, be advised unidentified friendly forces in position on the south bank of the river, opposite target location. Will advise further when identification verified over.' She threw a glance to a colleague at the next station. The airman shook his head.

'Thank you, Angel two zero. Sea Witch waiting out.' The signalman on HMS Monmouth, clicked off and relayed the message to the pilot of the Lynx, who passed it on to the sergeant in command of the Marine detachment.

'You got some of your blokes across the river?' Sergeant Steve Cox asked Skelter.

'No, just us five on this side. Four,' he stumbled over his correction. 'Us four,' he said.

'Eye in the sky says friendlies over there,' Cox gestured with his hand. Skelter looked across. At first he could see nothing and then he recognised the familiar outline of the Land Rover. He reached for his Binos and seconds later saw Peter Glass staring back at him through a similar pair. 'Fragile's made it, boys,' he shouted. 'He's over there, across the river. Look.'

The others followed the sweep of Skelter's arm.

'Hope he's brought a note from his mother,' said Biscuit. 'Turning up at this time. Useless muppet.'

Skelter and Biscuit elected to stay with the Marines and wait for the final lift. The hostages were shoehorned into the Lynx with as much of the kit as it could carry, then Lofty and Turbo climbed in. There was enough time to get three lifts in before dark, Monmouth having taken up station three miles from the coast. Skelter waved them off before getting into the driving seat and taking the pick up back to the barge.

'What do want to do with these guys?' asked Cox, nodding towards the walking wounded.

'Shoot the bastards,' said Biscuit, Tash's blood still sticky on his shirt.

'Easy mate,' said Skelter. 'Whatever you like, Steve, we've no use for them. As far as I'm concerned you can let 'em go. They can find their friends and get the dead buried. Oh and there are two more on the barge, tied up in the hold.'

'I'll talk to the ship, see if they want to interrogate them,' said Steve Cox. 'If not, then fair enough we can go with your idea.'

'Suits us fine,' said Skelter, noting Biscuit's hostile stare towards the sorry looking captives.

'Let's go and fetch the prisoners from the barge, Biscuit. Alive.' McVitie set off, chuntering under his breath, Skelter a couple of paces behind. The prisoners were intact, but terrified. Clearly they expected to be executed. They were made to carry the bodies of their fellow Somalis up onto the deck and across the plank and then lay them with the others on the riverbank. There were seven of them lined up in a neat row. There must have been at least three or four others when the truck was hit, but there were no bits of them left that were too big to fit in the cargo pocket of a pair of combats.

Skelter and Biscuit dragged the two traumatised and terrified pirates onto the deck at the stern, away from the hostages huddled near the wrecked wheelhouse.

Skelter began to interrogate the two youths, while Biscuit stood over them, adopting a menacing manner; not, for him, the most challenging of roles. The Somalis were shocked and surprised to be addressed so clearly in their native tongue, and were more than willing to cooperate. Skelter took down notes about the local terrorist group. Their area of operation, strength etcetera. Anything that could be useful. He was winding it down when a voice said, in English.

'I hope you're going shoot the little bastards.'

'You were told to stay by the wheelhouse Mr Bell,' said Skelter.

'Give me a gun and I'll do it,' said Bell. He repeated himself in fluent Somali. The prisoners winced.

It was Skelter's turn to be surprised. Not many Somali speakers in the white man's world.

'How about one each?' Biscuit said pushing the muzzle of his AK in the nearest one's face.

'Corporal McVitie, escort Mister Bell back to the others.'

Biscuit looked into Skelter's eyes. He got the message. He herded a protesting Bell back to the others.

'A word to the wise,' said Biscuit to Bell in a

whisper, 'H's bite is far worse than his bark. Easy going mostly but when he gets that look, you don't fuck with him.' Bell sat down with the others. 'We'll let you know when we're ready to move. Until then stay put.'

'Put them with the other prisoners for the Marines to sort out,' Skelter said to Biscuit when he returned. 'We need to think about what we do with our gear across the river.' It was said as much to distract, as it was to provoke debate. Skelter knew they had to find a way to take it with them or destroy it.

The sound of super fast rotor blades slicing the air heralded the return of the Lynx. The Marines had received orders to take the Somalis to the ship and bury their dead. Shovels had been sent in the helicopter. The task was impossible, given the waterlogged ground, and time available. The Marines sensibly ignored the order. The vultures would take care of it. The Lynx would have to squeeze in an extra trip

Skelter and Biscuit drove the Marines and the wounded to the helicopter in two trips. Skelter spoke to the pilot while the three wounded were put aboard. The seriously wounded youth had died and been laid alongside the rest. Parish and the two women climbed aboard, with the two Somalis from the barge somehow jammed in the cabin. Luckily together they weighed no more than the biggest of the Marines. The pilot agreed that on the final lift he would set down on the far bank to allow Skelter to consult with Glass, retrieve any vital kit from the cache and destroy the rest.

Bergans were loaded with the wounded. The Marines remained with Biscuit and Skelter, as did Bell. They climbed into the back of the pickup keeping watch in case the terrorists returned, unlikely though that was. Biscuit and Skelter laid Tash's body on his poncho and wrapped him with reverence, stringing the eyelets together with Para cord and wrapping it around with bungees. They placed him on the load bed of the Toyota. The two

257

youngest Marines looked at a loss, as if searching for something to say, but unable to find the right words. They shared chocolate and offered cigarettes. Skelter declined but Biscuit was delighted, having not had a fag for a week. He chained smoked three on the trot, as a result of which, he calmed down a lot, his mutterings about killing prisoners mellowing as the sun began sinking in the Western sky.

The Lynx came whirring in for the penultimate lift as the distant horizon began to clear. Tash was lifted aboard with the remaining kit and the pilot took to the air for the short hop across the river, where the he landed close to Lofty's original hide position. Skelter and Biscuit jumped down and the pilot wheeled away taking Bell with four Marines and the body of Tash Tasker to the ship.

Skelter linked up with Peter Glass for a quick catch up, while the two Marines pitched in with the recovery of the kit. Being fit and fresh, they soon hauled the wheelbarrow to the edge of the bush. Everything that could be salvaged was stacked ready to be loaded into the Lynx, water bottles were replenished from the jerrican. Skelter walked off to one side with his troop commander.

'Sorry for the late arrival, H,' said Lieutenant Glass. Poor excuse, the weather, I know. What's the situation with the hostages?'

'Unharmed and already aboard the Frigate,' said Skelter. 'To be honest we didn't expect you at all, Boss. Not in that storm. You come all the way in the Rover?'

'Got half way, with half the troop in the four-tonners. Got bogged down. We did manage to shoot up a pickup and take out a heavy MG. That was all though I'm afraid,' said Glass.

'That was you was it? We wondered why they

stopped firing. You probably saved my bacon — and Lofty's. Cheers for that. I owe you a drink.' Skelter was smiling through the gunsmoke grime coating his face.

'I'll hold you to that. I guess you'll be taken to the ship?'

'Yes, they'll want the doc to check us out. We lost Tash,' Skelter said.

'Oh bugger, I'm sorry, H. Any other casualties?' Glass was kicking himself for not asking for a casualty report first off. 'I should have ask...'

'Forget it' Skelter said, 'First time is always difficult. You'll get the hang of it.'

At that moment the sound of rotor blades announced the arrival of the Lynx. No sooner had the skids touched the ground than the two Marines began loading the kit.

'Outstanding job, Sergeant,' said Glass. 'It will be reflected in my report. Please pass my congratulations to the lads.'

'I will, Boss. You did a good enough job getting here yourself.'

'Thank you, Sergeant, coming from a man of your experience it means a lot.'

At that point Biscuit came over. 'Pilot's getting anxious, H.'

Skelter nodded, 'I'll have to...'

'Of course,' said Glass. 'Corporal McVitie.'

'Boss?'

'Well done.'

'Cheers, Boss.

The kit that could not be carried was left in the barrow. A couple of phosphorous grenades did the rest. With the barrow blazing fiercely, Skelter returned to the Lynx and the helicopter took to the air for the final time and set course for the ship. Skelter gazed back at the sparkling fire, watching the dense white smoke rising to meet the setting sun as the Lynx whirred across the bush towards the coast at full throttle.

'Right, lads, get aboard the bus, it's time we went home,' said Lieutenant Glass climbing into the Land Rover. He selected second gear and let in the clutch, feeling suddenly dog tired as he did so, praying silently for a smoother journey back than the outward one had been. Peter Glass was a happy man, he had been tested and he had passed, not exactly with flying colours, but not just by the skin of his teeth either. His men – he felt happy to call them that now, seemed closer to accepting him. He knew he still had a long way to go, both figuratively, and literally, but he had made a start. The good news was that the going was easier than on the outbound journey and without the rain visibility was now limited only by the vegetation.

They made excellent progress until they ran into the rest of the troop in the four tonners who were heading towards them, the men being disappointed to learn that they had missed the fun, but relieved that the rest of the troop were safe. The news that Tash had been killed shook them. The rest of the return journey was a sober and solemn affair.

39

Sunday 28th June

'Good news, gentlemen, good news.' The PM was beaming. 'The hostages have been successfully recovered to HMS Monmouth. The murmur of approval was muted amongst the smattering of female representatives around the table. The PM carried on unaware of his sin of omission. 'First reports indicate that they are in good health.' At this point the PM's voice lowered an octave as he his expression took on a grave countenance. 'It is with much regret that I have to inform the committee, that casualties have been sustained amongst the rescue force, including one fatality. I have no further details at this time. I am sure we would all wish to give our thanks to all those involved and offer our deepest sympathy to the family of the deceased.'

This was met with a chorus of 'here, here,' ringing around the room, from which no one abstained.

Next to speak was Bernard. His ever-twirling pencil, irritating to as many as to whom it was endearing, looked as if it had been gnawed by rats.

'Gentlemen, and,' he paused to emphasise the word, 'ladies, we have received unconfirmed reports that the crew of the yacht has been found unharmed, on a small island close to the Kenyan coast. The body of the American Charlton Riner, has been handed over to the US Embassy. As you might imagine they are not best pleased,

I'm afraid. However, that means everyone is now accounted for.' He tapped the end of his mangled pencil on the table and sat down.

'Thank you, Bernard. Before we conclude could I ask Geoffrey to stay, please. I'd like a brief word.'

What the hell does he want? Geoffrey wondered, as he nodded compliance. He was soon to find out. The room cleared as everyone headed off to go about their business. The PM and his private secretary remained.

'Geoffrey, I should like to do something for the men involved in the rescue. We cannot of course do anything official, you understand, I mean they all deserve medals of course but....'

'What do you have in mind Prime Minister?'

The PM frowned, 'I was rather hoping you might have a suggestion, Geoffrey.'

'Well, sir, a spot of R and R would be well received, I'm sure.'

'Look I have to leave, but you two put your heads together and come up with something,' he said, nodding to his private secretary, before turning and walking to the door.

'You don't like him much do you, Colonel?' said the PM's private secretary when the Prime Minister had left.

A grin painted itself across Geoffrey Greaves face. 'Whatever gave you that idea?'

'He's a good man,' the PPS said. 'Anyway how long shall we give our heroes?'

Greaves studied the speaker's face trying to determine if there was any sarcastic intent in the sentence. 'I suggest a couple of weeks,' he replied, deciding the word heroes had been sincere.

'Excellent, I will arrange an appropriate message from the PM. Will you clear it with their Commanding Officer?'

Geoffrey Greaves nodded and the men went their separate ways.

In Ross on Wye, Rollo had received a call from his contact. 'Lucy, Lucy,' again at the top of his lungs now, 'Looocyyyy'

She galloped down the stairs and into the study. 'What is it?'

'Charles is safe. The Navy has him.' He was shaking. His daughter threw herself at him and hugged him hugely. They both wept with relief.

'I need a drink,' said Rollo, 'a large one.'

'Here let me,' said Lucy, disengaging. She opened the cocktail cabinet, took out a bottle of Talisker and poured a generous measure. She handed it to her father and went into the kitchen clutching a tall glass with an inch and a half of Bombay Sapphire swilling around in the bottom. She half filled it with ice and topped with tonic from the fridge. Taking a small sharp knife from the beech wood block she sliced a generous piece from a lime and popped it in. Her Father was sat behind the desk when she returned, half the Talisker already trickling its way into his bloodstream.

'Can I ring Mummy?' Lucy asked.

'Of course, darling, I should have thought, the shock. Great news, great news.'

Lucy called Natalie and told her what she had been longing to hear. The line went quiet and Lucy could hear her mother crying. This was something she had never before experienced. It warmed her.

When Natalie had composed herself, Lucy passed the receiver to Rollo, who managed to keep the frog in his throat from croaking long enough to hold a brief conversation.

40

Monday 29th June

Skelter woke up in strange surroundings, struggling to make sense of what he could see at first. He had been in the middle of a vivid dream, not the nightmare, this time it was the river sweeping him away, and here he was in a comfortable bunk with clean fresh sheets. Now he remembered. The sick bay, the poking and probing; blood pressure monitor; light in the eyes; warm shower; lime scented soap; clean fatigues, T-shirt; soft pillow; lights out.

The sound of snoring came from the bunk above. Skelter did not need to investigate. Biscuit's nasal snorting was only too familiar. On the other side of the cabin Lofty was dead to the world, knees bent to accommodate his height, while below him Turbo's grinning face, cheerful as ever.

He winked at Skelter. 'I feel better for that, H. I was on me chinstrap.'

'Me too mate.'

'Think I'll go see what the crack on grub is and scrounge us a brew.'

'That'll be good,' said Skelter, rubbing his eyes and scratching his balls.

Turbo swung his legs onto the deck and without looking for something to put on his feet padded out to explore the ship, along the maze of dove grey corridors, looking for the galley.

'We are keeping you under observation,' the sickbay attendant told Richard Bell and Charles Parish. Mister Bell, you are pretty much okay, Mister Parish, we are treating you for a gastric infection. The good news is it is not thought to be serious and you should be fine in a few days. 'Is there anything I can get for you gentlemen?'

'I need to contact London urgently,' said Parish. 'Most urgently.'

'I will inform the duty officer right away, sir.'

Bell was too busy catching up with his PA, Caroline Warren to comment. Propped up on a pile of pillows with a wooly hat on and a saline drip in her arm, Caroline was milking her situation with all her accumulated skills, filling her pail. At last Richard might pay her the attention she longed for and felt she so richly deserved.

'How are you feeling, Caroline?'

'A little spaced out if you know what I mean, Richard. They pumped all sorts into me I think.' Her voice trailed away.

'You're in good hands, don't worry you'll be back at work in no time, me too.'

He doesn't seem at all bothered about the loss of the money Caroline thought, *even asking how I felt*, which was a first. *Could it be tiny cracks were appearing?* She inched her hand across the sheet towards his. Holding Richard's gaze for a few seconds, her hand crept closer, like a tarantula stalking its prey. Bell glanced down at the bed and withdrew his hand beyond her reach. She sighed, closed her eyes, and sank back into the pillow.

Turbo came across a young Marine standing guard outside a small cabin. He asked him where he could get a brew and as a parting shot said, 'What you got in there, the crown jewels?' At this point one of the two young nightclub hostesses stuck her head out to see what was going on. Turbo winked at the Marine, smiled and went on his way, wondering what bright spark had put an innocent eighteen year old to guard two tarts of their pedigree from the unwanted attention of sex starved sailors. They would eat him for breakfast. Talking of which...

By the time Turbo had returned to the cabin Lofty was awake. He passed a mug of tea to Skelter and shared his with Lofty. Skelter jabbed a finger into Biscuit's back in an effort to shut him up. He stopped snoring for no more than a few seconds.

'Noisy bastard,' said Turbo, 'bet they can hear 'im in Hereford.'

'So what's next, H?' Lofty asked. 'Will they be ferrying us to Winston or what?'

'No idea, but I'll try to find out what I can once I've drunk this,' he said, holding up the mug to Turbo in salute. 'Cheers for this mate, just the job. Say what's up with your ear, Turbo?'

'This you mean,' he said, touching the dressing covering his left lobe; or rather where his left lobe had once been.

'Yeah. Cut yourself shaving did you?' asked Lofty.

'The Doc called it a nice clean wound. Bullet, she reckons, took the lobe off sweet as a nut. Don't even remember it happening.'

'Painful is it?' said Lofty.

'Nah.'

'Shame,' said Lofty, looking at the site of the wound. *Lucky bastard! A centimetre and it would have hit the Artery.* 'Not exactly a hero's wound though is it? Nice little arm in a sling job to win the hearts of the female population.'

'Better than getting shot in the arse mind,' said Skelter, also noting just how close his friend had come to being tagged as killed in action.

There was knock on the side of the open door. 'Sorry to bother you gentlemen,' said the tall red haired nursing officer, 'I need to take a look at your injuries,' she said. 'It wont take long.'

'Injuries, what injuries?' Skelter asked. 'Turbo's the only...'

'You all have scratches from the thorns,' she said, 'I know you are big, bad, hairy-arsed tough guys, but you are as prone to infection as anyone else. Open wounds from thorn bushes that goats urinate and defecate on, can soon turn nasty enough to seriously compromise your operational ability. So, let me clean you up and give you some medication okay?'

'Yes, Sir!' said Turbo.

'My,' came back the reply in a husky voice that Mae West would have been proud of, 'you have been out in the field a long time.'

'Don't take any prisoners, do you?' said Turbo.

'None.'

Skelter began unbuttoning his shirt. 'Okay Doc, fill your boots,'

She put her bag on the table, took out a pack of surgical wipes and began gently swabbing the nasty gouges in Skelter's skin.

Turbo got to his feet, winked at Lofty. He took off his T-shirt, dropped his combats and with a flourish removed his jockey shorts. Nature has its way of compensating, like giving people with poor eyesight sharper hearing, or endowing those with poor academic aptitude, sporting prowess. In Turbo's case the trade off to his lack of height was a dick like a donkey's. The Nursing Officer looked Turbo up and down without a trace of reaction on her face. 'Thank you for your cooperation soldier, I will see you next.' She carried on cleaning Skelter's scratches, gave him some pills and five minutes later turned to Turbo, whose initial grin had by now faded. He fired up a fresh smile as she delved into her bag and fetched out – a large magnifying glass. 'Never as big as you hope they are going to be, are they?' she said, deadpan.

Lofty and Skelter exploded with laughter, joined by a now wide-awake Biscuit McVitie.

Charles Parish felt lousy. A bit shaky on his legs, he managed with an orderly to lean on, to make his way to the communications room. A hive of activity with technicians monitoring wall to wall, floor to ceiling, banks of electronic gizmos, it resembled a film set, ready for the climax of a Bond movie where double oh seven smashes the dials, screens and switches, destroying the villain's secret base.

Parish worked with a signaller who set up a satellite link, enabling him to speak directly to Martin Sixsmith, head of MI6. He made his report and duty done he hobbled back to the sick bay, where he found Bell at Caroline Warren's bedside. They were deep in conversation, like conspirators hatching a plot. The orderly helped Charles onto the bed and settled him into the mountain of pillows.

'We'll be serving breakfast shortly,' he announced. 'Are we all hungry? No veggies amongst us are there?' A chorus of no's came back at him and he was away.

'Richard.'

'Yes, Charles, what is it?'

'Do you have any plans for the next week?'

'Hardly, I had intended to carry on with the holiday but now that the boat's gone...'

'Good,' said Charles, grimacing as a sharp pain caught him in the gut. He took a deep breath and carried on. 'I've spoken to my boss and he's happy for me to stay away from the office for another fortnight. Thing is, my mother lives in Kilifi near Mombasa. She runs a holiday let business. Bungalows near the beach, that sort of thing, you know, basic but comfortable. She has recently refurbished half of the complex, so I'm pretty sure there will be plenty of accommodation if you fancy it. The invitation extends to you too, Caroline.'

She looked at Richard. A switch in her head flicked her into PA mode. 'I'm sure Mister Bell would welcome the opportunity to recuperate in such surroundings, thank you, Charles.'

'Not got anything planned, Charles, so why not,' said Bell slightly bemused at his PA's professional intervention, given their current circumstances.

'It might turn out to be a bit of a party,' said Charles. 'Although the way I feel right now I can't say it appeals. Still, a few days and I should be on the mend the Doc says.'

'Party?' said Bell.

'The PM is keen to reward the SAS chaps. Can't see them getting any medals, too sensitive, so he's told their CO to give them two weeks leave. I thought I would invite them along. What do you think Richard?'

'Great idea, I bet they like to party.'

Caroline Warren's face lit up. Two weeks with Richard in a tropical beach resort. If she couldn't work her magic on him in that time she wasn't worth her salary.

At that moment the Senior Nursing officer entered the sick bay.

'Time to check your blood pressure and temperature, Miss Warren.' She slipped the bp machine's sleeve over Caroline's arm and as she adjusted the velcro said, 'you should be fine to get dressed later. By the way, I have your suitcase in my cabin. You could be lucky, I don't think the water's got in.'

Warren and Bell exchanged glances. 'The

Aluminium clamshell case?' said Caroline, eyes wide, with disbelief.

'That's the one. It is yours?'

'Yes,' replied Warren and Bell in unison.

Skelter, Turbo, Biscuit and Lofty were shown to the small mess and plied with bacon; sausages, fried bread; eggs and beans, washed down with pints of tea.

'Well,' said Skelter, 'that beats the shit out of processed cheese and dog biscuits now, doesn't it lads?'

'Absolutely,' said Biscuit.

'No contest,' said Lofty.

Turbo, still stuffing his face with seconds, nodded vigorously.

A young rating entered mess and handed a signal message form to Skelter, who was crunching his way through a third round of toast and strawberry jam. He read it through twice to be sure he understood it before he elected to share with the others.

'Well, boys, it seems our lords and masters in Downing Street are pleased with us. So pleased that we are to get a reward.'

'Not another bloody medal,' Biscuit moaned, 'why can't they push us up a pay band?'

'Reward. I said re-ward not a-ward, you cloth-eared Jock. Two weeks leave starting today.'

'Great,' said Biscuit, 'just what I've always wanted, a two week cruise in the tropics aboard a Royal Navy warship. They're taking the piss.'

'Gentlemen,' said a voice from the doorway, 'allow me to shed some light into your dark corners. Sorry, but I couldn't help overhearing.'

The soldiers turned as one, to see Richard Bell, dressed in pyjamas, framed in the doorway. 'May I thank you all for a tremendous job. I owe you,' he corrected himself. 'We owe you our lives.'

'No worries mate,' said Turbo. 'Good to see you on your feet pal.'

'Yes,' said Skelter, 'sit down, have a brew. Steward.' The young man responded immediately.

'Coffee, black, two sugars,' said Bell.

'Another three teas too, please,' Turbo added. They could never overdo the brews.

Bell took a seat opposite Skelter. 'I've got a message from Charles Parish, first to thank you and...'

'How is he?' asked Skelter.

Bell's face betrayed his annoyance at being interrupted. He was used to having people's complete and undivided attention. However he let is pass. 'He's got some kind of bug, from the water I think, but they reckon he'll be fine in a few days. To continue, Charles has invited us all to stay at his mother's as a thank you from him. She has a business; beach bungalows, in Kilifi, up the coast from Mombasa. By way of a thank you from me I shall take care of the bar bill for the duration.'

'That's very generous,' said Skelter.

'Including Biscuit?' said Lofty. 'You may live to regret that.'

'Cheeky bastard, what about happy here? Biscuit replied playfully cuffing Turbo around his good ear. Pound for pound he drinks more than me.'

Bell smiled, 'It would be an honour, gentlemen, believe me.'

'Well lads, shall we accept this most generous offer?'

'Too fucking right we will, absolutely...'

'What about the weapons, H?' asked the ever practical Lofty.

'Good point. I'll speak to the Navy. See if there's any chance of choppering them up to Winston on the Lynx. Make sure they're all cleaned and oiled okay?'

'Will do.'

41

Monday 29th June

Lucy Ryder was sitting in one of the wicker chairs on the terrace, watching swallows sweeping the sky for insects, to feed their hungry hatchlings. Now that her big brother was safe her attention had turned to Mark. She longed for news of him, praying that wherever in the world he was he was okay and that he would come back safe to her.

Rollo walked out of the house to join her, carrying two glasses and a bottle of champagne in an ice bucket.

Lucy looked at him as if he'd flipped.

'Daddy it's eight o'clock in the morning.'

'Time to celebrate, Champagne breakfast,' he said, handing Lucy a glass and popping the cork. 'We have been invited to a party to welcome Charles back. Wednesday evening, your mother is hosting.'

'Mother?'

'I have booked us a flight to Mombasa, tomorrow.'

'Oh wow, Daddy that's wonderful,' she got to her feet and kissed him. 'If only Mark was here,' she said. 'I'm beginning to understand how Mummy felt all those times waiting for you to come home. Can't you pull some strings through your old boys' network and fetch him for me or at least find out if he's safe?' She sat down again, shoulders slumped, a slight sigh escaping her lips. 'You must think I'm really silly at my age.'

'I'm sure he's fine, darling, stop fretting.'

'Bless you, but I can't help worrying. It's awful.'

'You have got it bad, haven't you?' said Rollo grinning from ear to ear. 'If you are going to fall for a soldier you are going to have to get used to it.'

His daughter looked at him from over the top of her champagne flute. 'Why are you grinning like that? You have no idea what it's like. It's awful not knowing if he's safe, Daddy, it hurts.' She was cross with him now, but that was nothing to how cross as she was going to be in a moment.

Unable to contain himself any longer, Rollo began to chuckle and then laugh.

'Heartless bastard,' she said, getting to her feet and heading for the lawn.

'Lucy, he's fine,' Rollo called out, 'He's safe. Really he is, I promise you.'

She stopped and turned. 'It won't do, it simply won't do, it's cruel, you have no idea where he is...'

'I know precisely where he is,' Rollo interrupted.

She stopped, jaw open as if to speak, but no words came.

'Privileged information, Lucy, you know the drill. He is safe and sound aboard a Royal Navy warship. I was going to keep it as a surprise.'

'You're sure?'

'My source is one hundred percent reliable. It gets better, much better. You are not going to believe this but your brother is with him.'

Lucy almost dropped her glass. She looked bewildered. 'You mean...'

'He was involved in the rescue operation. Your new man rescued your big brother from the bad guys. How bizarre us that?'

'What?' Lucy necked the champagne in one, refilled her glass and sat down again with a bump. Inside her head was revolving like a spin dryer. 'He's not hurt?'

'Not at all.'

273

'That's wonderful, but does he know...'

'That Charles is your brother? I very much doubt it, and before you ask, no, I cannot get you aboard an operational warship of Her Majesty's Royal Navy.'

'At least he's safe. You are cruel, Daddy, stringing me along like that. You are sure he isn't hurt?'

'My source is very reliable, darling. He's fine. Sorry, sweetheart, but I wanted it to be a surprise. Would you like the good news now?' Rollo was grinning again from ear to ear..

'I thought that was the good news?'

'Oh no. This is privileged information remember, your ears only.'

'Yes, yes of course, stop teasing, Daddy.'

'You're going to need something sexy to wear at the party.'

Eyes widening, Lucy searched her father 's face for clues. 'You mean...'

Rollo raised his eyebrows and nodded, grinning like a lunatic.

'Mark will be at the party?'

'Yes, and I have it on good authority that the whole team will be. They've been granted two weeks leave.'

Lucy flung her arms around her father's neck, casting champagne to the wind. She began to cry.

Thirty-five miles northeast of the busy port of Mombasa, Kilifi creek flows into the warm waters of the Indian Ocean, where the mouth of the river is four-hundred metres wide. Two miles upstream the creek opens into a wide basin measuring three miles by three. Nestling in the greenery on the southern shore, a large bungalow built on stilts sits surrounded on three sides by several smaller versions, like a litter of cubs around a lioness. All enjoy magnificent views across the water towards the Equator, two hundred and fifty miles to the North.

Two Land Rover Defenders, one a long wheel base with a safari trailer hitched to the tow hook, were waiting beside the road as the Helicopter cut through the squally shower at the tail end of the storm to touch down in the bush on the outskirts of Kilifi. The town of forty-eight thousand souls eked out a living from fishing and tourism.

Charles insisted that Skelter sat in the front, while he and Richard Bell climbed into the back with Biscuit, Turbo and Lofty. Caroline Warren got into the front passenger seat of the other as the driver helped the two young nightclub hostesses into the back. The rain had finally stopped and the skies began to clear. Bergans and belt kit were loaded into the trailer. There was one empty space in the back. The space that should have been occupied by six foot three inches of lanky Lancastrian, leaning forward, elbows on knees, to avoid banging his bony cranium against the aluminium roof. Biscuit produced a battered hip flask from his smock. It had borne witness to many campaigns in numerous far-flung, foreign fields. He raised it in salute to the empty seat opposite This was not the first drink he had taken to a fallen comrade. He swallowed a nip and passed the flask to Turbo, who raised, swallowed and passed to Lofty who turned, raising the flask to the empty space beside him. The late afternoon sun caught the shiny stainless-steel, its fiery light ricocheting off it like a bursting star-shell.

'Don't worry, mate,' said Lofty in a quiet voice, 'we'll pay your bar bill.' He swallowed a generous measure of the G10 rum that Biscuit had cadged from the Navy. Savouring the warming glow flowing through him, a lump the size of a grenade grew in Lofty's throat as the Land Rover bucked and bounced along the rough dirt road of the Kenyan bush.

The bungalow was a shade over a mile from where the mixed bag of former hostages and their rescuers had climbed aboard the vehicles and by the time McVitie's flask had completed two full circuit, excluding the driver, they were on the final approach. Built in the late nineteen forties the buildings were neat, well maintained and looked as if they had recently swallowed up B&Q's entire stock of bright, white paint. The buildings were interconnected with well-defined sharp gravel paths, bordered by neat low rows of mixed shrubs. Standing on the verandah of the main building, a handsome looking woman in her early sixties dressed in flowing floral silk, waited to welcome them.

Natalie Ryder greeted her son with a huge hug followed by French style cheek kissing, enthusiastic and warm, not a bit like the hollow air-kissing version, hijacked by Hollywood stars and TV celebrities. Charles made the introductions and as she repeated her kissing performance with team Skelter, there was some degree of awkwardness for Biscuit and Lofty, while Turbo took it in his stride. Skelter simply bent with the breeze.

'You will have to excuse mother,' said Charles, 'I should have warned you. She's half French, you see.'

'On my mother's side,' said Natalie. 'Welcome to you all, and thank you,' she said, in a husky hint of a French accent deepened from years of smoking Gauloises. 'Thank you so much for bringing my son back to me safe.' Natalie's voice trembled a little and she took a moment to regain her composure. 'Charles, I have put Mister Bell in the guest room next to yours. Sergeant Skelter, you will be at the back next to me. We have the views over the river.' She turned to the rest of the lads. 'Asha and Jamil will show you boys to your bungalows. Get settled in, have a shower, sleep if you wish, then when you are ready come back up to the house and we will feed you. The fridges are stocked with beer so help yourselves.'

With that the two young Kenyan servants led the way out to what were obviously holiday lets for well-heeled tourists. Biscuit, Lofty and Turbo followed cheerfully, the prospect of air conditioning, warm showers and cold beer lifting their spirits ever higher.

Skelter followed his host to the back of the house and into a bedroom simply furnished with a canopied double bed, complete with mozzie net, a chest of drawers, wardrobe and a single bedside table with a small reading lamp. There was a ceiling fan and a small mirror on the wall. Bathroom's next door,' she said, you'll have to share with me. Hope that is all right, Sergeant? Charles and Mr Bell are sharing the other.'

'H, s'il vous plait Madame, je m'appelle H. Je suis honoré de partager avec cette grande dame.'

'Merci, H, merci beaucoup,' Natalie replied. 'I am impressed. Your French is superb. Where did you learn?'

'In the Army Madame...'

'Natalie, please,' she interrupted. 'They teach French in the army these days?'

'They do in the French Army. I served in the Foreign Legion when I was a younger. Three years.'

'Did you now? I can see you and I are going to get along fine, young man. I will leave you to settle in. If you would like a drink the kitchen is that way and we have beer in our fridge too, whisky or gin if you want something stronger.'

'Thank you, Natalie,'

My pleasure, H, make yourself at home. We are having dinner at seven, but don't worry if you need to sleep we can feed you when you wake.'

Once he was alone in his room, Skelter shed his clothes, showered, then towelled himself off with the huge white bath sheet that had been laid out upon the bed. He lay down and with the sound of the air conditioning humming in his ears he fell asleep.

Richard Bell left the house and made his way to the bungalow that had been allocated to his nightclub hostesses. The door was unlocked. He walked in without knocking. 'By all means enjoy the facilities while you are here girls,' he said without preamble, 'but remember you are still on my payroll. I want you to look after the boys. They risked a lot for us all, so show your appreciation ok? I don't want to hear any tales of disappointment understand?' The two girls nodded in unison. Bell turned and left.

'Bastard,' said one. The other girl put an arm around her shoulder and hugged her. 'It might not be so bad. they are nice boys I think. Maybe we help them to get very drunk yes?' Her sister responded with a weak smile and watery eyes.

Dinner was a quiet affair. The lads were subdued, the weight of Tash's loss suppressing any desire to celebrate. Delayed shock played its part also and as soon as etiquette allowed they made their excuses and headed off to their quarters. Caroline Warren seemed in a bit of a daze and Bell too was in a world of his own, reflecting upon what might have been. Natalie was the perfect host, understanding and sympathetic. By ten o'clock only she and Skelter were left. She offered him a nightcap, which he accepted, sitting out on the terrace with a large Grants and Natalie for company, serenaded by chirping cicadas and the frogs' chorus. He had little to say and she respected his silence, happy to sit and listen to the sounds of the Kenyan bush.

'If you wish to talk, H, I am a very good listener. I was married to a soldier once, many years ago.'
The Valium just wasn't cutting it and Skelter could feel his anxiety growing. He was sweating and his hands were beginning to shake ever so slightly.

Reaching forward Natalie placed her hands on his. 'Come, H, you should lie down and rest, bring the whisky bottle.' Skelter offered no resistance allowing himself to be shepherded like the lost lamb he was, drained of the will to think, exhausted by events. Natalie led him upstairs to his room and sat him on the bed. She took off his shoes and gently pushed him into the horizontal. 'You have to relax,

H. I can help you. I know how to make the tension disappear. You poor boy, you have been through so much to bring my Charles home to me. Let me do something for you.' Skelter complied robotically, his mind out in the Somali bush, searching for Tash, wanting to find him alive. He lay face up staring at the ceiling fan spinning above like the rotors of the Lynx that brought them back. He was only vaguely aware of Natalie unbuttoning his shirt. Her fingers were cool and gentle the rhythmic movement gradually easing the tension in his shoulder muscles, his eyelids heavy he began to drift away, floating gently somewhere between sleep and waking transported to safer place, a refuge from his demons. The scent of Natalie's perfume followed Skelter into his refuge. His eyes eased a fraction and through the veil of his lashes he could see her face so close he was aware of her breath upon his chest as her fingers worked their magic on the hard knotted abdomen. He watched his hand move to settle upon her shoulder as if it belonged to someone else; she turned, a soft smile upon her lips and lowered her face to his. He buried his face in her neck, as she wrapped her arms around him and held him as he let the tears come. She rocked with him stroking his hair, regretting the fact that she had been unable to give this kind of comfort to her husband all those years ago. It is with age that wisdom comes. She too shed tears.

After what seemed a very long time Skelter came up for air. He looked Natalie in the eyes still wrapped in her arms and started to apologise.

'I'm so sorr...' the rest of the sentence was smothered by Natalie's lips. Skelter responded instantly, naturally, as the remnants of pent up anger, frustration and hurt found their outlet in the oldest safety valve known to man.

42

Tuesday 30th June

Skelter woke early, alone. He lay running the previous evenings events through his head when Natalie entered with freshly brewed coffee. She was fully dressed. He was naked. She smiled.

'Good morning, H, I trust you slept well?'

'Yes, er that is...'

She laughed. 'Relax, H, last night was last night. It was good for both of us I think. It was necessary perhaps, but it was of the moment. Today is today. Let us enjoy.' She gave him a chaste kiss upon on his cheek, handed him the coffee and with a wicked glance at where the thin cotton sheet draped across his genitals she left the room humming a joyful tune Skelter did not recognise.

Natalie arranged for one of the houseboys to drive everyone, except Charles, who was still recovering from his stomach bug, into Mombasa, first thing in the morning. Caroline Warren telephoned the Hotel and arranged to collect her things, meanwhile the other two women, were in desperate need of new clothes. They had all exchanged the mismatched bits of naval uniforms by raiding Natalie's wardrobe, for shorts, T-shirts and in Caroline's case a wrap around cheesecloth skirt and shirt. The footwear problem had been solved with flip-flops from the complimentary shower room stock. The boys had their trainers, spare combats and T-shirts. Their civvy bags were still at Camp Winston. Skelter had called the Adjutant and had been promised a vehicle would be dispatched with the kit straight away.

'You will be pleased to know, Lofty, that the weapons have arrived safely at the camp, courtesy of the Navy. We can pick them up from the armoury when we finish our R and R.'

'Top man, H, Cheers.' Lofty's sniper rifle was like a favourite child to him. He was always fretting when it was out of his sight.

Natalie was looking forward to showing the other women around. It was a fine day for shopping and in a little over an hour they had travelled the thirty-five miles to Mombasa. Hardly the West End, but it was the nearest shopping centre and the only place where clothes could be bought. Skelter and his men had neither cash nor credit cards; they were yet to arrive with their kit from Winston. The women only had what they stood up in. Richard Bell had a quarter of a million US dollars in cash. He gave a wad to Caroline to get the women what they needed and he went shopping with the boys. They were totally dependent on him. He seemed to be enjoying himself. Caroline Warren was worried that the bruise on his head meant he had lost it. He was never generous with money unless he had an ulterior motive.

As the tills in Mombasa began ringing to the tune of the ransom money, Lucy and Rollo were cruising at thirty-five thousand feet over the bay of Biscay.

'You realise that your mother has no idea that you and H even know each other?'

'I know. Won't it be funny when she finds out?'

'She will be tickled pink, sweetheart.'

'Gob smacked more like. I can't wait. I'm dying to

see Mark, I haven't been this excited since you bought me my first pony.'

'Your ninth birthday. Your mother was so proud. She loved you following in her footsteps.'

'She was good wasn't she?' said Lucy threading her arm through her father's and squeezing.

'Yes, she was,' replied Rollo, his voice trailing away as he turned to gaze out of the window at the cloud field.

Natalie had booked a table for an early dinner at her favourite restaurant, a small bar away from the beaches and the tourist traps. The place was rustic and quaint. The food was superb – if you like Indian Cuisine. What soldier doesn't enjoy a good curry? Bell had a nightclub in Soho, where the two young women worked, so they could hardly escape the taste of cardamon and cumin. As for Caroline, she was happy enough being close to Richard, particularly in a social setting. She would have settled for a boiled egg.

It was a relaxed evening, with wine and beer flowing freely and while Natalie flirted with Skelter, Caroline strived to work her magic upon her boss.

'Are you married, H?' Natalie asked.

'No, but I have met someone quite recently. We've chatted a couple of times but not sure if it will go anywhere.'

'Relax, H, I was not putting myself forward as a candidate, although if I was twenty years younger...'

'I would be sorely tempted now,' Skelter replied, keeping up the pretence for the benefit of the other guests.

'Such a charmer,' Natalie said, 'such a shame too. Not for me you understand, I have a daughter, a lovely girl, but she has never found a suitable man. I am sure you and she would get along.' Natalie's bosom rose and then fell as she let out a sigh. 'The best ones are always taken.'

The two young women teased the soldiers to distraction, while they in turn tried hard to impress them. Biscuit entertained them with outrageously exaggerated tales of daring do and the girls flattered him with fake admiration of his capacity for drink, encouraging him to consume at a sustained steady rate. Lofty fell into conversation with the houseboy who would be driving them home. He was feeling sorry for him not being able to have a drink. Lofty got quietly pissed with no encouragement from anyone. Turbo drank a lot, but then he usually did. When the meal was finished Skelter rose to his feet. He banged a spoon on the table. Tapping a glass gently would not have worked, as by now everyone was well on the road to love you land. The tension of the past few days was being released in waves of white wine and chilled beer.

'Thank you,' said Skelter, 'for your attention. I would like to propose a toast to Natalie for being such a fine hostess and looking after us so well. Natalie.' 'Natalie,' the name rang around the restaurant, drawing looks from the other diners.

'Thank you all,' she said, 'I have not had such lovely company for dinner in a long time. I am having lots of fun being gloriously intoxicated. Allow me to propose a toast to you brave boys who rescued my Charles.

Bell got up next to propose thanks for his rescue, then Caroline got in on the act to toast the Navy. Biscuit toasted Bell for footing the bar bill. Everyone was well oiled when Turbo stood up.

'I want to propose one,' he said, beer in hand.

'You're supposed to stand up,' Biscuit said.

'I am stood up – Pillock.'

'Oh aye so ye are, sorry.'

'To Tash,' Turbo said, ignoring the jibe, maintaining his dignity and raising his glass.

'Tash.'

The soldiers drained their glasses. The mood changed. It was time to go.

They all climbed aboard the Land Rover, mellow and relaxed, the boys subdued, Caroline frustrated that she had made no headway with Richard, the women sleepy and grateful they had escaped without having to carry out Bell's instructions. Natalie made the most of a handsome young man's shoulder to rest her head upon. Skelter took it in his stride. Truth was he had other things on his mind, principally the loss of a man under his command. All the way back he ran drafts of the letters he would write to Tash's wife, and his mother, through his mind, trying to find the right words. He never knew Tash's dad, but then neither did Tash. The booze didn't seem to help much. What he needed was another Valium, but he had left them in the bungalow.

The civvy bags had arrived from the camp and they were waiting in the hallway when the guys arrived at Natalie's. The men collected them then tacked a zigzagged course to their quarters.

The wheels of the British Airways jet touched the runway at Mombasa airport at ten thirty PM Rollo and Lucy made their way to baggage collection and waited beside the carousel.

'Go and call your mother, Lucy, I'll get the bags. Tell her not to bother sending a car, quicker if we get a taxi.'

'Okay but I need the loo first.' Lucy trotted off in search of the facilities and a phone. Rollo gave his arms a quick stretch as he waited for the bags. By the time his daughter had returned the luggage had been located and loaded on the trolley.

'Get through all right?'

'Fine, no problem, she's waiting up for us. Apparently they've been here shopping this afternoon. Had a Curry at Jamal's for tea. She sounded squiffy.'

'She's in a good mood then?'

'I'll say.'

'Excellent.' Rollo let out a long breath. 'Right, lets get through immigration and find a Taxi.'

Natalie Parish put down the receiver and went out onto the verandah to join her guests. She settled into a comfortable cushioned, wicker armchair with a glass of wine, enjoying the moonlight reflected in the waters of the bay. Charles, Skelter, Valium at last working its way through his bloodstream, together with Bell and Caroline Warren, were also enjoying the view.

Lofty had taken to his bed while Biscuit and Turbo had retired to the girls' bungalow to put the world to rights over a crate of beer. Biscuit however, was struggling to keep up and indeed to stay awake. The reputation of the Jocks for hard drinking was taking a knock. England however, represented by corporal Turbo Thompson, 22 SAS, was more than holding its own.

'It's a myth you know,' said Turbo to the two girls.

'What's that?' they asked in unison.

'The Jocks. About them being hard drinkers.' He looked at Biscuit slumped against the bed head across from the one he now shared with the two women, who had decided that rather than face the wrath of their boss, they would entertain Turbo. He was the funniest of the three, and getting him drunk hadn't worked. He seemed immune to the effects of alcohol.

'You are a true patriot,' giggled Julie, the given name of sister one. Turbo was indeed a proud Englishman, more than that, he was a proud Yorkshireman.

'Roger that,' said Wendy, her twin.

'Bugger that,' said Julie, 'Roger me – please.' She burst into a fit of the giggles.

'Under normal circumstances it would be a pleasure, ladies,' Turbo replied. 'Right now I just need another drink.'

'Me too,' both sisters said in unison.

'I'll go,' said Julie, getting off the bed and heading for the fridge.

The three of them lay together. First the girls, cuddled together, fell asleep and finally Turbo dropped off, a half full beer bottle in his hand, one arm around the snuggled pair.

'How are you feeling now?' Skelter asked Parish, who had got a bit of colour back in his cheeks.

'A bit better thanks. You chaps did a brilliant job, you know.'

'Don't embarrass the man, Charles,' scolded Natalie. 'You'll have to forgive my son, H, he lives a sheltered life in Whitehall.'

'If you ever think of leaving the Army, H,' said Richard Bell, 'I would be delighted to have you work for me, I have a vacant position for a bodyguard. Generous package, fringe benefits,' he said with a wink, 'and excellent working conditions.'

'Thank you, I'll bear that in mind,' said Skelter.

'It's an open offer,' said Bell.

'Mister Bell is a generous employer and a fine man to work for,' interjected Caroline Warren. 'He appreciates people who are at the top of their profession and rewards them well for their work.'

'I'm sure,' Skelter replied, smiling inwardly. He had observed Caroline Warren interacting with her boss over the course of the day, particularly over dinner and he was impressed by her dogged attempts to gain Bell's attention, despite his obvious lack of interest.

The Mombasa traffic had eased considerably by the time Rollo and Lucy arrived at the taxi rank. The driver of a old cream coloured Mercedes E class pulled up smoothly and jumped out to take their bags. He held the door open for them and then put the luggage in the boot.

Lucy relaxed into the well-worn leather. 'I can't wait to see the look on Mark's face, when we walk in,' she said, 'and my dear brother, when he finds out his little sister is seeing the man who rescued him.' The Mercedes glided out from the rank and into the Mombasa evening traffic. 'Not to mention Mummy's. She'll have a fit.'

'Charles doesn't know we're coming?' Rollo sounded surprised.

'I swore Mummy to secrecy, I wanted it to be a surprise for him.'

'Didn't want him saying anything that might let the cat out of the bag with H, you mean.'

'That might have been a consideration I admit. It is so bizarre. It's fate you know. I know you keep telling me to slow down with Mark, Daddy, but I'm sure it's been written somewhere. We are meant to be. I know we are

43

Wednesday 1st July

The driver made good time from the airport to Kilifi and knew exactly where to go. No doubt he had brought tourists to Natalie's tropical hideaway many times before. The taxi pulled into the complex and up the drive, coming to a halt at the side of the main Bungalow.

'Who the hell is that, at this hour?' said Charles, swivelling in his chair towards the headlights glare. He was somewhat mellow, having consumed a couple of bottles of Claret. Bell too, was well oiled but still remained unmoved by Caroline's charm offensive. Skelter was as relaxed as a newt.

'A little surprise.' said Natalie, 'I think you will like it, Charles.'

The taxi had pulled up about four or five yards away. They watched two people get out and move to the rear to get bags from the boot. The glare from the headlights prevented anyone from identifying the couple. A tall man and a woman. What happened next would have confused the observers if they had been sober, let alone in their present state. The man paid the driver and the car swung around and drove away into the night as the passengers stepped up to the verandah.

'Dad? Lucy?' Charles, struggled to his feet.

Skelter's idle curiosity, switched to mainstream at the name Lucy. He looked, he saw, his brain rejected, refused to believe, recalculated, recognised. Rollo, Lucy and Charles locked in a group hug as Natalie turned to Skelter

'My daughter,' she said.

Skelter looked like he had taken both barrels of a sawn-off shotgun from point-blank range, a look that paled into insignificance a split second later, compared to the one on Natalie's face, as her daughter launched herself at Skelter like an RPG and locked her lips upon his, shamelessly pinning him in his chair.

'What the hell...?' Charles exclaimed.

'Steady, Charles, don't have a heart attack,' said Rollo, 'I will explain, just as soon as someone gives me a drink.'

Bell and Caroline were puzzled and amused. Lucy was still starving Skelter of oxygen. Eventually he struggled to the surface.

'Lucy? How?'

'You rescued my big brother.' Remember I told you he worked in Whitehall? this,' she said reaching out her hand to Natalie, 'is my mother.'

'Bloody hell. You're kidding me?'

'No.'

Natalie looked shocked in the way the survivor of an earthquake does. The smile of joy that replaced that expression, as the penny dropped, was a radiant joy to behold.

'This is the woman you spoke of, H, yes?'

Skelter nodded, still in shock.

'My daughter?'

'I had no idea.' Skelter had a vivid flashback to the night before, the scent of Lucy's mother's perfume, her lips in a place Lucy had yet to visit. Frozen like a deer in the headlights he shot an embarrassed, confused glance at Natalie, whose eyes seemed to grow to the size of soup plates.

Natalie hugged him and kissed him on both cheeks.

'Superb, mon fils, superb.' She stepped towards Rollo and kissed him lightly on both cheeks, 'Wine or Whisky?' she asked.

'Whisky please, Natalie.'

'Lucy?'

'Wine for me please, Mummy.'

Skelter gave Rollo a searching look, Rollo returned with the merest hint of a wink, his lips soundlessly shaping 'later.' Lucy pulled up a chair next to Skelter and took his hand in hers. Caroline Warren was struggling to keep her eyes open and Richard Bell had decided to call it a night.

'Time for bed, I think,' said Richard to Caroline, who woke up with a start.

'Sorry, Richard,' she said.

'Bedtime.'

'Now there's an offer.'

Bell ignored the remark. 'Will you excuse me, Natalie, Charles? I think I should go to bed. You will have much catching up to do.'

'But of course,' said Charles.

'Thank you for your generous hospitality, Natalie, it is much appreciated.'

'Yes, thank you,' added Caroline Warren, grasping Bell's arm to steady herself. 'Bedtime.'

Aided by Bell she made it down the verandah steps and tottered off towards her sleeping quarters.

Through the narrowed eyes of intoxication, Skelter watched them go, his mind a maelstrom of mixed emotions.

Natalie came and sat next to her daughter. 'I haven't sorted the bedding for you and your father yet. Would you mind giving me a hand?' she said, grasping Lucy's wrist and tugging it before her daughter had a chance to decline. The two women got up and walked out into the buzzing, zizzing, humming, clicking night. Croaking frogs close to the riverbank competed with a baboon coughing its alarm call somewhere in the forest.

'I had forgotten how noisy the night is out here,' said Lucy stepping over the threshold into the chalet. She sat on the bed. 'What do you want to know, mother?'

'Everything of course. How did you meet him, when?'

Lucy didn't need any prompting, the words tumbled out, falling over themselves. When she finally paused for breath, Natalie had one question.

'Does he satisfy you?'

'Mother.'

'I'm French remember? Oh you English.'

'No, Mother you are half French and I'm quarter French.'

'Don't be so so...'

'So what Mother?'

'So English.'

Lucy smiled. Her mother was not often rattled, and she was enjoying the moment.

'Do you love him?' Natalie asked.

'It's early days, but I'm lost when he's not there, I've been sick with worry, not knowing where he was or if he was okay. He only has to look at me and my insides liquidise, jelly knees – the whole thing.' There were tears in Lucy's eyes.

'What is it my child?'

'We haven't; you know done it, not yet. There hasn't been time, or opportunity.'

'There is now Cherie. Plenty of both. Make the most of it.'

This remark triggered the downpour, Lucy's tears streaming as she let go. Natalie put her arms around her daughter and whispered words of comfort. 'It is the shock, Cherie, the worry for your man, your brother, it has been too much. All will be fine now. Don't distress yourself.'

'It isn't that, Mummy, really it isn't. I'm nervous. I

know its silly at my age but...'

'You are worried about the sex?' Natalie began laughing quietly 'You poor girl, it will be fine, I promise.'

'I haven't done it for a long time and, please don't laugh, I have only had two men in my life, and briefly at that.'

'What about H? How does he feel?'

'I don't know, he was married but his wife died ten years ago. Since then he has avoided women I think.'

Natalie cradled her daughter's head in her lap, stroking her hair. 'Take it slowly,' she said. Don't rush. If he really cares for you he is probably just as scared as you are. It is harder for a man, especially one in his profession. It is a big responsibility; the pressure to do well will be huge. You will be surprised how men like him need to be led, but do it gently, you must be gentle. Demand too much too soon and you will frighten him away. Remember you are not trying to take his wife's place. Be yourself. Make him happy. Happy to be with you.'

Her mother's soothing voice and sound wisdom, aided by the gentle stroking of her hair had a calming effect upon Lucy, gradually she felt much more at ease. She was still apprehensive but a little less pessimistic.

'Thank you, Mummy, thank you so much.'

'What are mothers for my child? Now come, we had better get back to the men, before they come looking for us. All this talk of love has raked over the coals in my hearth. I had planned to put your father in with Charles but...'

'Mother!'

'It gets lonely out here at times, I am French, well, French is how I feel. It is our national sport. I do not get the opportunity to enjoy the pleasure of a man much these days.'

Lucy shook her head. She had forgotten just how much of a rebel her mother was. How she loved to shock and behave outrageously. She wished she could be a little more like her.

They found Skelter and Rollo with their heads together like a couple of conspirators. Charles had finally succumbed, mouth open catching flies, snoring gently in his chair.

'Coffee anyone?' said Natalie.

'Yes, please,' said Skelter.

'I'd love a cup,' said Rollo.

'Come, daughter let us leave the men to it. The kitchen awaits.'

The two women went off to make the brew, while the men resumed their conversation.

'I guess you do still have your finger on the pulse then?' said Skelter to Rollo, who flashed a broad grin back at him.

'It's complex, but your guess is in the target area. I still have connections with The Regiment and also with the MOD,' he paused, looking across at his sleeping son, 'and the Security Services, as I have eluded to previously. It was me who got Charles the job. Before I joined the SAS, as you know I was in the Intelligence Corps and of course I went back to it when I left The Regiment.' A wry smile crossed Skelter's face. In the distance a Jackal called out to its mate. The frog chorus ramped the volume up a notch to eleven and the moon came out as the clouds began to clear. 'Have you given any more thought to what you might do when you leave The Regiment, H? I'm not trying to push you into retirement, but it must be approaching the horizon.'

'I will be forty-four this year, but I'm sure you know that along with my blood group and shoe size.'

Rollo shrugged. 'You remember Peter and Paul from our clay pigeon shoot?'

'Colonel Catastrophe and Major Disaster? How could I forget?'

'That's them, only I know them as Peter and Paul. Not the names on their birth certificates you understand.' Skelter was smiling. 'Well as you know we run a small security business together supplying expertise and training to British and other European companies who operate overseas. Anything from providing personal protection for management, to guarding infrastructure, transport, etc. There's a job for you when you're ready to leave the army. Guaranteed.'

'Thank you, Rollo, that's good to know.' *Life is looking up,* he thought, two good offers in as many days, and both potentially lucrative.

Lucy and Natalie walked in with the coffee and joined the Party. Skelter and Rollo switched to social mode and engaged the women in small talk. When they had finished the coffee Natalie stood up.

'Time my boy was put to bed I think,' she said looking at Charles. 'He can't sleep here all night.'

'Time for us all I think,' said Rollo. 'Where am I sleeping?'

Lucy looked at her father, suppressed a smirk, took Skelter's hand and led him away, calling 'sleep tight,' over her shoulder. The giggle resurfaced after ten paces and grew in intensity.

'What is so funny?'

'Nothing, Mark, it's the wine. Come on walk me home.'

They kissed goodnight on Lucy's porch. She heeded her mother's advice. He was pretty drunk anyway so it would have been a disaster.

'Call for me in the morning to go for breakfast,' she said, it's late and I'm ever so tired.'

He needed no persuading he was dead on his feet. He would have no trouble sleeping in spite of the deafening chorus from the bush. Kissing her on her forehead he turned on his heel and plodded back to the bungalow

44

Thursday 2nd July

Skelter slept like a log, no nightmare, no sweats, just deep, sound, drunken sleep. It took him a little while to get his bearings but gradually it all came back to him; the drinking, Natalie, Lucy, Rollo's offer. He wrapped his naked body in the large white bath sheet and walked into the small neat bathroom and stepped under the shower. The shock of the cold deluge kicked him fully awake but his body slowly relaxed as the water warmed through. His head was fuzzy and full of Lucy. He remembered something about calling for her on the way to breakfast. He had no idea of the time or what time or where breakfast was, but he didn't care. He wanted to see her. It was more of a need; like the craving for the first cigarette of the day, when he had smoked. Like a piece was missing. He would not be complete until she was there to see and to touch.

He finished showering and dried himself with the towel. The luxurious feel of the soft Egyptian cotton, was heightened by the contrast with recent living conditions in the bush. He shaved, brushed his teeth and returned to his room. He reached for the Valium, opened the bottle, took one out and looked at it lying in the palm of his hand begging to be swallowed. If ever he needed one it was now, but somehow he felt that this was too important. He knew he would have to beat it some time, someday. He put the pill back in the bottle. He thought of Natalie and was amazed that he felt no guilt. She was right; there was no emotional connection just an act of mutual comfort at a time of dire need. He had the strangest feeling of being emotionally cleansed and prepared for the next step with Lucy. Natalie had been his first sexual encounter since in more than ten years. The night before Jane left to go to Bristol for Christmas shopping with her girlfriends. A night that lived in his memory like a precious pearl in the heart of an oyster. They had made love on the rug in front of the fire. It was good but he had always felt since that it should have been better, that he should have made more effort, put his whole heart and soul into it. He did not know then that it would be the last time they would make love; that the next time he would see her she would be on a stainless steel slab, grey and cold as the ashes of yesterday's fire, her slender limbs shattered by the shockwave from six pounds of Semtex travelling at four and a half miles a second.

The Bungalow was quiet. He put on lightweight linen slacks and shirt, slipped his bare feet into a pair of canvas deck shoes and ran a comb through his rather short hair. One last check in the mirror and he made his way out towards the verandah. He could hear clinking and chinking noises behind him coming from the kitchen. He checked his watch; eight forty-four. He stole down the steps and headed for Lucy's bungalow, licking his drying lips as the sound of his pulse throbbed in his ears. It occurred to him that the last time he felt this way was when he crept onto the barge. That had ended in anti climax, he crossed his fingers for a more positive outcome this time.

Rollo heard Skelter leave as he lay on his back, listening to Natalie's soft breathing, watching the rise and fall of her breasts as she lay in the crook of his arm. The smell of her intoxicated him. It had been a long time.

No such luck for Caroline Warren, the only thing she was nursing was a big fat hangover, and she was doing that all alone.

Away in the twins' bed Turbo was snoring in post alcohol contentment. The girls had met their obligation by offering their services without having to deliver. It made a refreshing change for them for which they were grateful, but unsure how to respond. It was not something they were used to but somehow it felt good. Turbo extracted comfort from their closeness, which was all he wanted. Lofty and Biscuit were still in dreamland.

Richard Bell lay awake. He had not slept well at all, despite a comfortable bed and a belly full of booze. Something was bothering him, gnawing away at the back of his brain. He had no idea what, only that whatever it was it was making him anxious and uncomfortable. The more he searched the recesses of his memory, racked his brain and ran through random thoughts and ideas, the more frustrated he became. Nothing popped up but a blank screen. He tried to convince himself that he was imagining things but it wasn't working. As if it wasn't enough he was also worried about his boat and what was happening to it.

He had never been comfortable with being unable to control events and fearful his yacht might give up her secrets. The box of serpents that would open up.

Skelter knocked upon Lucy's door. 'Come in, it's not locked.' He pushed the door open and stepped inside. The room was simply furnished with bamboo and wicker, rush mats on the floor. He didn't see her at first. The shutters were closed, it was dim. 'Good morning,' she said. The voice came from beneath the mosquito net covering the generous bed.

'Morning. Are you hungry?' Skelter asked. 'Would you like me to give you some time? To get up that is.'

'I'm fine, come and sit down,' she said, opening the net and patting the mattress beside her.

'I'll grab a drink of water and I'll be with you,' he said.

'There's a glass in the bathroom. The water in the tap is fine to drink.'

'Mouth's a bit dry,' he explained. 'Too much booze I guess.' He found the glass, ran the tap a while and then filled and drank it to the bottom. He refilled again, took another sip and walked over to the bed. Skelter did as he was bid, and sat on the edge of the mattress next to her, putting the water on the small glass topped bamboo table. The last time he had seen her in bed she was wearing cotton pyjamas, with teddy bears all over them. Not this time. This time shimmering black satin, and not too much of it. What there was clung seductively to her curves inviting investigation. He had the urge to say something but the words couldn't make it past his throat. It was Lucy who broke the awkward silence.

'I can tell you like it,' she said, sliding the tips of her fingers under the thin straps. 'I only wore it as a declaration of intent and to show you my feminine side.' She gave a little laugh, mostly with her eyes. 'There is no time limit on this offer,' she said 'No pressure, and if it helps, I'm not nervous, just scared bloody shitless.'

That did it. The ice cracked. He put his arm around her shoulder and kissed her forehead. 'You are a remarkable woman, Lucy Ryder, and I am a lucky man.'

She snuggled close, relieved that the tension had been broken. His arm felt powerful and protective, he smelled fresh and masculine, her pulse was up and she could feel her cheeks reddening.

'I know how I come across, Mark, all pushy and shameless. Flirting like a teenager. It's all a sham you know. Nerves. I don't have much experience with that sort of thing. Hardly any at all, so when...when we do...eventually. I mean we will... at some point...'

He took her chin in his left hand, tilting her head towards his. The kiss was deep, long and loving. Passion was in there, understated, reigned in, simmering below the surface. It would come. Probably some time soon, but for now it was love that was important. She responded with a warm gentleness that invaded him like a liberating army, lifting him high above himself, like an out of body experience.

When they came up for air he was trembling. Lucy's blushed cheeks were running with silent tears. Skelter was relaxed, unaided by drugs, for the first time in over a decade.

'We should go for breakfast,' said Skelter after a few minutes, 'I wouldn't want to be rude to your mother after all she's done.'

'You're right,' said Lucy, 'but could we have another five minutes? I love morning cuddles.'

'Noted in the log,' said Skelter, wrapping her in his arms, and nuzzling her neck.

45

Friday 3rd July

Breakfast was served in the garden at the rear of the bungalow, which because of its location on a narrow spit of land projecting into the bay, enjoyed views across the water to rival those from the verandah at the front. Two long rustic picnic tables with wooden benches were supplemented with half a dozen smaller round ones shaded by rush parasols. Half of these were occupied with other guests, most of who seemed to be conversing in French. A substantial heavy-duty awning made from cream canvas protected the long tables from the sun. The first was laid out with a bewildering buffet of fruit, cereals, breads and preserves. Also in evidence were fresh croissants. Two safari style urns contained coffee and tea alongside which, racks of toast were lined up for inspection. A stainless steel warmer stand held a number of containers beneath the lids of which lay bacon, mushrooms, tomatoes, fried bread, sausages, and scrambled eggs. Lofty and Biscuit were already tucking in when Skelter and Lucy appeared. Skelter helped himself to a full mashing and a mug of tea, while figure conscious Lucy settled for scrambled eggs on toast with coffee.

Natalie appeared from the kitchen to join them. She placed her coffee and croissant on the table and sat down opposite her daughter.

'Did you sleep well, my children?' she asked, looking

hard into her daughter's eyes for clues.

'Best sleep I have had in a long time, thank you,' Skelter said, lying through his teeth. They both knew that had been the previous night, after the tension of the operation had been released by Natalie's expert attentions. He felt uncomfortable, but only mildly as Natalie had clearly dismissed the incident and confined it to history.

'How about Daddy?' Lucy said, launching a counter attack.

'He still snores,' her mother countered, unfazed by the remark. 'Do you snore, H?'

'Stop it, Mummy.'

Skelter entered the spirit of the game. 'Perhaps you could tell me, Natalie? After all I slept in the room next to yours and the walls are quite thin.'

Natalie threw back her long red hair and laughed. 'You are a wicked, lovely man, Sergeant Skelter. I love you already. Lucy, do not dare to let this man slip through your fingers.'

Lucy was still blushing minutes later when Rollo joined them, carrying a cup of coffee.

'That all you're having, Daddy?' she said trying to cover her embarrassment. 'Not like you at all.'

'Some of us were up with the lark this morning, daughter. I had the full works almost two hours ago.'

'What gave you such an appetite so early?' The remark had tripped off Lucy's tongue before she could stop herself.

Her mother was about to intervene when Skelter made a flanking move. 'Beautiful place you have here Natalie,' he said. is there any chance you could spare the time to show me around?'

Smiling at him with genuine warmth she offered her services. 'As soon as you have finished your breakfast, H, I should be delighted.'

'I'm about done.' He got up from the table and offered Natalie his arm. 'Don't mind do you, Lucy, love?'

'Not at all, Mark, have fun.'

'Remember your RTI training, H,' Rollo called out after him, as arm in arm with Natalie he ventured into the unknown.

'What's RTI, Daddy?' asked Lucy.

'Resistance to interrogation,' chuckled her father. 'He's going to need it.'

Rollo spotted Richard Bell heading for the coffee. 'Will you excuse me, sweetheart?' he said, getting to his feet, 'something I need to do. Won't be long.' He walked up the steps and into the house, making straight for the stairs. When he reached the bedroom door he walked straight in without knocking, closing it firmly behind him. 'What the hell were you thinking, Charles? You were supposed to be gathering intelligence, not indulging your pathetic sordid weaknesses. God help you if you've compromised this operation, because I wont.'

Charles, still only half awake, protested. 'You don't know what it's like, the job's stressful I need to relax.'

'I'll relax you, you whining cretin. You don't know what stress is. This is the nearest thing to a field operation you have even been on and you ballsed it up. You've spent your entire career cringing behind a desk. You do realise that your friend Bell records your little games?'

Charles face lost what little colour it had. 'He wouldn't.'

'What planet are you on, boy? Wake up. Get your act together. Now, damn you.' Rollo turned his back on his stepson and left the room. He made his way back to the others and grabbed another coffee before resuming his place at the table.

Turbo turned up for breakfast accompanied by the two young women. They all looked happy, if a little tired. Charles was having a lie in, still suffering with his Gastric trouble and Caroline Warren had yet to surface. Richard

Bell went up for seconds. It was slim pickings but he managed a couple of sausages, some tomatoes and a slice of fried bread. There was plenty of cereal left and the coffee was still hot.

'Mind if I join you?' he asked Rollo.

'Be my guest.'

Bell waved his fork in the general direction of Lofty and Biscuit's table. 'These boys did a fantastic job, don't you think? You must be mightily relieved to have your boy back safe.'

Rollo nodded, studying Bell's face for any clue as to who he might be, rather than the character he was trying to portray himself as. Studying faces and interpreting body language is prep school basics for an intelligence officer. He knew a bit about Richard Bell and he hadn't found much he liked in the file.

Natalie waved her free arm in the air, while loosely hanging onto Skelter with the other. 'This belonged to my Grandfather. He bought the land when it was cheap, before the tourists came. Twenty-two acres, including two small private beaches. He was going to build a house and retire.' Skelter detected a change in tone. 'He built the house, but he never lived in it. He died from Malaria shortly after the war. I was eleven years old.'

'I am sorry,' said Skelter.

'My daughter has had an expensive education, travelled all over Europe, lived in France, the finest finishing school in Switzerland and yet somehow she has failed to benefit fully from the experience. She is not so wise in the ways of the world, H. For someone of her age she can be a little naive.'

Skelter stared out across Kilifi Creek to the deep blue water of the Goshi River Estuary. 'I have no intention of taking advantage...'

'I do not believe you do, mon fils, I wanted you to

know, that is all. She has never had much time for men. You are the first that has mattered. I worried she would not find anyone. I had resigned myself and now...' Natalie's voice faded to nothing.

'I understand. She will come to no harm from me.'

'I want only for my daughter to be happy, H, and when I see her with you, I see joy in her eyes. That makes me happy too.'

'She is lucky to have such a caring and beautiful mother.'

'Okay H, I surrender. I will stop now. The flattery is most acceptable, just the same.'

'I meant every word,' said Skelter.

'Of course you did,' agreed Natalie. 'Now you should stop while you are winning I think, yes?'

'The other night...'

'You must move on, H. It is done. It was the will of God. We have both been through so much. Think of it as therapy.'

Skelter conceded at last and for the rest of the tour walked with a lighter step as they both stuck to small talk. On the approach to the bungalow on the last leg their arms were still linked, still relaxed, but a shade closer. There was an air of understanding between them.

'Do you like Jazz, H?' Natalie said.

'Very much, you?'

'Oh yes, we have a jazz quintet playing for us tonight. They are the best band in Kenya. You will love them.'

Skelter and Lucy spent the morning at the beach and after lunch they pitched in to help with the preparations for the party, which was to be held where they had breakfasted earlier. Turbo and Biscuit got stuck in setting up the bar while Skelter and Lofty sorted out the stage for the band; a simple arrangement of wooden pallets overlaid with plywood sheets. An electrical supply box was already available mounted on a two-foot high wooden post. The caterers arrived late afternoon, the band at dusk, to an enthusiastic welcome from Natalie. Skelter watched their sound check with an air of anticipation.

Caroline Warren had only just surfaced as it began to get dark. This was first for her. She was angry with herself for letting her guard down. Making coffee in her room before languishing under the shower, gradually recovering from her excesses of the night before, Caroline struggled to understand what she was doing wrong where Richard was concerned. She was making no headway at all. *What was wrong with the man? Didn't he have a libido?*

Whether he did or he didn't a libido Bell had far more important things on his mind. He persuaded Charles to telephone to the salvage crew who had recovered his boat. They referred him to the authorities.

'They won't let me near it for now, Charles. It's a crime scene. Can you pull any strings? I mean if the press get wind of the facilities, they'll have a field day.'

Charles had a sudden flashback to his therapy session in the dungeon. 'I'll make a couple more calls,' he said, 'see if I can lean on the right people.' Charles loved every aspect of his job, including the fringe benefits it offered him. He had no intention of throwing it away without a fight. What Rollo had said about Bell recording the events was a worry though. Maybe he just said it to scare him. Whatever, Charles decided that now was not the time, nor the place to challenge Bell on the issue.

'I could throw money at the problem,' Bell suggested, 'but it might backfire, so best save that as a last resort.'

'For God's sake, Richard, the last thing we need is a

bribery allegation all over the front pages as well as a sex scandal.'

Charles spent the next hour on the telephone, calling in favours, and tightening thumbscrews. The fewer people that had access to the boat the better it would be for both of them.

'When did you get that, Daddy?' Lucy asked over Rollo's shoulder.

'Lucy! Where did you spring from? you gave me a start, I'll ring you back,' he said, ending the call and palming the Nokia.

'God, do you never stop working? I had hoped you'd left your cloak and dagger at home.'

Rollo, clearly embarrassed, grinned and with a shrug his broad shoulders added, 'I came out here to get a good signal.'

'So you wouldn't be overheard you mean.'

'Look Lucy ...'

'Don't worry, my lips are sealed, even from Mark.' After a brief pause she added. 'And Mummy. I'm guessing you will not be sharing your number so I can keep in touch.'

Rollo offered a weak grin but said nothing.

'Thought not.' Lucy turned on her heel. 'I'm off for a swim so you can carry on with your secret squirrel nonsense.' She strode away towards the house. Rollo took a good look around and satisfied he was alone he took out the Nokia and dialled. 'Sorry about that,' he said into the mouthpiece, 'what news?'

The reception was patchy and he had to ask the voice on the other end for numerous repeats as he walked around in an attempt to improve the signal. Finally he had gathered all the information available, which turned out to be disappointingly little. He hoped they would find something other than the dungeon come playroom aboard

Bell's yacht. He was pretty smart, Mister Bell. He covered his tracks well, but eventually he would trip up. They always do. Rollo was pretty sure Bell was collecting dirt on all of his contacts, to use as leverage to further his ascent of the greasy social and political pole. The ghosts in the official security services were counting on Rollo to clean up the oil before it got spilled. He had the added incentive of saving his son and thus the family from embarrassment. He would nail Bell. Nothing was more certain, it was only a matter of time.

Natalie had extended invitations to the party to all her other guests, fourteen in all, making a total of twenty-six. It was shaping up to be some bash. The bar opened at seven o'clock. Turbo finished his first beer at six minutes past, sitting at one of the round tables flanked by the two young women.

'You should not drink so fast,' said one of the women. 'You will get hiccups. He will won't he, Wendy?'

'She is correct, Turbo,' said her twin. 'You drink too much. It is not god for you.'

Turbo playfully tapped the girl's rump. 'Pack in the fucking mother act. Drinking's a serious business and someone has to do it.'

'But why you?'

'I'll tell you why ladies. I'm good at it, that's why.'

'You are so funny,' they said in unison, laughing. They felt safe around him. He was caring and courteous, and had shown no sign of wishing to take advantage of their vulnerability. He was like a little big brother. Truth was Turbo kept his condoms in his escape belt as emergency water carriers and he wasn't going to risk taking anything home he had not brought out with him. Besides he was smitten with Janice and the souvenir T-shirt he had bought in Mombasa was the only thing he planned to give her when he got home. Opposite him Lofty was sitting, sipping slowly, pacing himself. On the next table, Charles, now feeling somewhat better, was nursing a large brandy with Rollo and Richard Bell for company. They were soon joined by a radiant looking Natalie, wearing a silk trouser suit in eau-de-nil that whispered Paris whenever she moved. Holding her own in a colourful cotton print, Caroline Warren accentuated her assets with a plunging neckline. Biscuit nudged Turbo with his elbow as she entered the garden. 'Will you look at the tits on that?'

'Handful and 'alf,' was the sophisticated response. 'You know who that's for.'

'She's wasting her time,' said the two young women in unison.

'Whose working you?' Biscuit asked.

'We're twins.'

'Mister Bell's not interested,' said one.

'She's got more chance of shagging the Pope,' said the other, giggling.

'Why don't you try your luck?' Turbo suggested to Biscuit.

'I might do that, pal.' He took a long swig emptying his bottle, savouring the cold beer as it spiralled down. 'Who wants another?'

'Caroline, how are you feeling?' said Natalie, as she sat down.

'Much better, thank you, Natalie,' she answered, as Rollo and Charles zeroed in on her breasts.

'Rollo,' said Natalie with a hint of irritation, 'Get Caroline a drink would you?'

'Of course. What would you like,' he asked refocusing his eyes on her face.

'White wine please.'

Rollo headed for the bar while Natalie engaged Caroline in conversation.

The band started up with Art Pepper's 'Surf Ride.' Skelter was impressed as he stood next to stage digging the beat, glancing around the tables and out past the lights, into the darkness towards Lucy's bungalow. He had put on the new clothes he bought in Mombasa, light grey linen slacks and shirt, sock-less in navy-blue, canvas deck shoes. He was no match for Lucy. She entered wearing a long lavender one piece, full trousers and sheer top, sleeveless, in silk. She could have worn a bin liner; he would still have been stunned. Her make up was adventurous for her, particularly around the eyes but without being over the top. It gave her an air of exotic enchantment he found gently stirring. He had to restrain himself when she kissed him in greeting. 'Well,' Lucy said, addressing a her shell-shocked soldier. 'Are you going to offer me a drink or shall I fetch my own?'

'Sorry love, what would you like?'

'You know something? I don't care so long as it has alcohol. Lots of alcohol, so surprise me.' Gin and tonic was hardly a huge surprise but it came in a tall glass, ice, slice and heavy on the Gordon's. Lucy insisted on circulating, stopping to chat to Bell and Caroline Warren, before moving on to the SAS men and the twins.

Turbo, smooth as snakeskin, complemented her on her outfit. 'Very nice lass, very nice, you look gorgeous.'

'Thank you, Turbo. Perhaps you could give Mark some lessons in how to compliment a lady?'

'I might love if I thought he'd take any notice.'

This brought a huge smile to Lucy's face, 'Not a front runner in the charm stakes but I wouldn't swop him.'

The atmosphere was relaxed and easy, the alcohol flowing like the waters of Kilifi Creek, and everyone seemed to be having a good time, including the tourist guests. Well, almost everyone. Caroline Warren was still failing to make any headway with Richard. Fuelled by frustration and fortified with wine and gin she had resorted to returning flirtatious glances with Biscuit, in an attempt to get Bell's attention.

Richard Bell was preoccupied, with had a lot on his plate. He was worried about what the police might find aboard the yacht. Although it was highly unlikely given the quality of the workmanship, it was possible they might accidentally stumble upon his little spy hole and the video camera and tapes. That would cause major embarrassment and probably destroy his standing with Downing Street. His years of work towards a knighthood gone up in smoke. If they viewed the tapes hidden in the false deck he would be lucky to avoid a fatal accident arranged by the security services, probably sanctioned by Charles. Something else was nagging him too. It was Skelter. Nothing sinister, but the SAS sergeant reminded him of someone and he couldn't think who it was. He rattled through lists of celebrities, acquaintances, TV and film stars but no one fitted the profile.

As the evening wore on the music mellowed and people took to the flagstones in front of the stage and danced in time to the music. Others simply held one another up and shuffled and swayed while exploring each other's bodies in the mistaken belief that no one would notice. Plenty did. Nobody cared. Turbo danced well, with both twins who seemed to have fallen completely under his spell. Biscuit even got to dance with Caroline Warren, but she was well the worse for drink. His mind harboured ambitions that deep down, he knew, his body would not be able to fulfill even in the unlikely she would be up for it. Caroline staggered off in search of the loo.

Bell engaged Biscuit in conversation. 'How come

they call you Biscuit?' he asked.

'McVitie, name's McVitie. Like the digestives, you know? Cheers for all the free beer by the way.'

'Least I could do. You guys saved my life. Always been in the army have you?'

'Aye since I was sixteen.'

'What about your sergeant? Was he a boy soldier too?'

'Naw.' said Biscuit, Merchant Navy, when he was a kid, so I believe.'

'You don't say?'

Biscuit realised he had revealed enough already and was disinclined to say any more about anyone. Bell suddenly ran out of conversation also. With perfect timing Caroline returned and Biscuit tried to pick up where he had left off. Bell went to the bar for a drink, his head full of oscillating possibilities based on the feeling in his gut and the conversation with Biscuit. He found Charles nursing a large brandy.

'Don't suppose there's any news on the boat, Charles,' asked Bell more in hope than anything.

'Not yet, dear boy,' he lied. Tricky business, you know but don't worry I'll keep trying.'

Bell nodded. 'Do your best, eh?'

'Of course, Richard.' *You can sweat for now,* thought Parish, knowing he had solved the problem. Successfully arguing that as the crime took place in international waters and the victims were British citizens, he had negotiated a transfer to his own department's investigation branch. Palms would still need to be greased to ensure that nothing sensitive or embarrassing found aboard the yacht would be revealed, but promises had already been made. Richard Bell would only need to dig in his deep pockets and it would all go away.

Rollo wandered away from the party towards the river to

make a phone call. He struggled to get a signal at first but eventually got three bars.

'Everything in place? Good. Charles thinks he has the reins?' A self satisfied smile broke out on Rollo's face. 'Excellent let's keep it that way. You have? That is excellent. How many tapes?' A smile broke out on Rollo's face. 'Are there now? Good work. Can you get them copied and wiped?' Rollo was positively beaming now. 'Brilliant, that is a result. When can you release the boat to Charles? As soon as that. Excellent work, I owe you dinner. Great, Charles can give Bell the good news about his precious boat in his own time. Make sure everything is photographed as well. We won't get another chance like this. Send the tapes back to London through the usual channels. Any developments let me know. Everything clear? Good.' He wandered back, nodding to Lofty as he passed on the way. The SAS man was taking a walk along the shore to clear his head and to find somewhere quiet to morn the loss of a fallen comrade. Rollo surprised Natalie by asking her to dance. Rollo didn't do dancing. Not that he couldn't, his mother had spent a small fortune on lessons when he was at boarding school. He just hated dancing. The Kenyan night, the music, the drink, whatever, he had an urge to hold her in his arms. If dancing was what it took then he would dance.

The band slipped into a smooth rendition of Fly Me to the Moon, and before he knew what was happening Skelter too was dancing, well kind of, swaying, with Lucy clinging to him, almost as tight as his throat was becoming when he tried to speak. She buried her head in his neck. He closed his eyes. The world closed in. They were the only two people left on the planet

46

Friday 3rd July

Skelter couldn't remember when they left the party, only that it was late. Rain drumming on Lucy's roof together with the howling of monkeys had woken them up. It was light outside.

'Sleep well?' she asked, running her hand through the sparse hair on his chest.

'Like a log. You?'

'Same. You didn't dream,' she said, smiling.

'Actually I did,' he said. 'First time I've had a happy dream for as long as I can remember. No nightmare. All good stuff.'

'That's lovely.' She planted a kiss on his shoulder. 'What was it about?'

Skelter shrugged. 'Don't remember. Don't care. Just glad it happened and it's all down to you. I feel more content with you than I ever thought I would with a woman again.'

'You keep saying that.'

'It's true.'

'How's your head?' she asked.

'Fine, how's yours?'

Her cheeks flushed. 'Okay,' she said. 'I know I drank quite a lot and I was a bit drunk...'

'A bit?' said Skelter.

'You were just as bad. We weren't too drunk

though, were we?'

'Can't remember,' he lied.

'Like hell you can't,' she said, 'you were very attentive as I recall.' She was chuckling now.

Skelter slid his hand across her stomach.

She shivered.

'Remind me,' he whispered, his lips almost touching hers. He was astounded at how beautiful she looked; natural, last night's exotic makeup washed away. The kiss was electrifying, conducting their need through two hungry bodies, binding them with desire. Skelter let himself go, his fear of disappointing her finally dissolving.

In another room, in another bed, not far away, the eyes in the head on the pillow stared at the ceiling fan, watching the fog of history slowly lift.

A sleazy dive, in the port of Marseilles, half a lifetime away. Richard Bell, a young sailor, known then only by his nickname, Dinger, had just turned twenty-three. He was on the town with the rest of the crew of the *Torridge*, a tired, tattered, tramp steamer carrying coal from Cardiff. Seven of them, three Arabs, and a couple of Somalis, all older seasoned hands, a young steward from South Wales, named Dai Rees, and Bell. They were gathered around a heavy wooden-topped, cast iron table, smoke so thick in the dimly lit bar they could hardly make out the features of those opposite them.

Dai Rees had run away to sea at the age of fifteen, starting as a cabin boy. This was his first voyage on the *Torridge*. Bell had served aboard for two years. As the evening wore on the Arabs became raucous and argumentative. Bell took Rees under his wing and steered him out of the place and into the foggy French night. He took the lad to another dark and dingy dive, full of pimps and prostitutes, low lifes and lechers. The atmosphere was a heady mix of garlic, marijuana and cheap scent.

Rees was a little the worse for wear, trying to match Bell beer for beer. An overweight, well used old French tart, caked in makeup, sidled up to the young lad, plying her trade. Dinger Bell stepped in and sent her packing. The young lad seemed disappointed.

'Fancy a bit do you, Dai boy? Don't you worry, Dinger will take care of you. One more for the road and we'll go and find some real fun.'

Dinger went to the bar returning with a couple of large Pernods. Into one he slipped the contents of a small twist of paper, stirring the white powder with a grubby finger to help it dissolve. He rejoined Rees, and set the glass down in front of him.

'Get that down you, Dai, it'll put a man in you,' said Bell, sickly amused by the irony of his statement. Ten minutes later they hit the deserted dockside. Rees was a little unstable on his feet. Bell put a steadying arm around the boy and guided him through the dimly lit, fogbound port and into a narrow alleyway behind a cafe. Rees was reeling now. Bell helped him to lean on the handrail of a set of steps leading to a first floor workshop.

Lying awake listening to the sounds of the African night, Bell tried in vain to recall the face of the young sailor. His loins were stirred by the memory of the Welsh boy's smooth firm buttocks as he forced his way between them, pulling on the squirming steward's arms, driving himself on like a jockey in the Grand National. The exquisite rush of sexually charged adrenalin, as he rode the course with his helpless victim. The all-consuming surge of power as he cleared the last fence, the sudden, shuddering release, the slow, smooth, slide back to earth, the sweet taste of appetite satiated.

Bell remembered walking away, discarding his victim like a cigarette butt, finding another bar and drinking until that appetite too was satisfied, the vague memory of the gangplank, companionway, his bunk.

The ship had sailed on the morning tide, without young Dai Rees in the galley. Bell never saw him again, until now. Mark Skelter had shown no signs of recognising him. Why would he? After all it was twenty-five years ago and they had only met on that voyage from Cardiff. The only time they had made eye contact was in the dark and smoky atmosphere of the bar, and the lad had been shit faced. It was the eyes. There was something in Skelter's eyes. It was that, which had been nagging Bell's brain for answers, and now he felt he had them. The evidence was stacking up. Skelter had been in the Merchant Navy when he was young; he was from South Wales, like Rees. He was about the right age.

Bell wondered what he should do if Skelter were to take him up on his offer of a job, but found that the idea appealed to him. Knowledge is power they say. Savouring the thought he lapsed into dream world again, milking the memory for every last drop of satisfaction. He was confident that since Skelter had not recognised him, he was unlikely to do so in the future, so long as he was careful not to mention his connection with the sea. No one knew anything of his past except Charles. He could manage Charles. Charles was in way too deep to shoot his mouth off.

ABOUT THE AUTHOR

Stuart Pereira was born in Cardiff in 1945 just as the war in Germany was coming to an end. He trained as a Graphic Designer, and followed a career in museum exhibition design from 1965 to 2002. His short stories have won two international competitions. South Atlantic Soldier, his first novel, was published in 2012. It follows the fate of two members of the 23rd Special Air Service Regiment (TAVR) in the Falklands war of 1982. The author served for almost 12 years in 23 SAS in the 1970s and 1980s. Stuart enjoys clay pigeon shooting and plays golf very badly. Besides writing he paints vintage aircraft and wildlife. **Helter Skelter** is the first in a series of novels featuring SAS sergeant Mark Skelter. Currently working on the final edit of the second in the series **Skelter's Vengeance**, Stuart is widowed and lives in West Yorkshire.

12092875R00183

Printed in Great Britain
by Amazon.co.uk, Ltd.,
Marston Gate.